C000252465

SILENT
LITTLE
ANGELS

BOOKS BY JENNIFER CHASE

JENNIFER CHASE

SILENT LITTLE ANGELS

bookouture

Published by Bookouture in 2022

An imprint of Storyfire Ltd.
Carmelite House
50 Victoria Embankment
London EC4Y 0DZ

www.bookouture.com

Copyright © Jennifer Chase, 2022

Jennifer Chase has asserted her right to be identified as the author of this work.

All rights reserved. No part of this publication may be reproduced, stored in any retrieval system, or transmitted, in any form or by any means, electronic, mechanical, photocopying, recording or otherwise, without the prior written permission of the publishers.

ISBN: 978-1-80314-231-9
eBook ISBN: 978-1-80314-230-2

This book is a work of fiction. Names, characters, businesses, organizations, places and events other than those clearly in the public domain, are either the product of the author's imagination or are used fictitiously. Any resemblance to actual persons, living or dead, events or locales is entirely coincidental.

To Bennet—Thank you for your endless support. You will be incredibly missed.

CHAPTER ONE

TUESDAY 0930 HOURS

The luxurious dark-gray sedan crept along the rural road that led up to where Eagle Ridge Camp was nestled in the beautiful, wooded hills of Sequoia County, California. In places along the track, large pine tree branches arched downward creating makeshift tunnels. As the car climbed, the views of the rolling hills and the picturesque town of Pine Valley became even more spectacular.

William and Jane Faulkner grew increasingly uncomfortable the closer they approached the property. They watched from the car as the beautiful forestry hills turned into a heavily wooded area that was almost impassable. The attraction of the potential investment property seemed to become less valuable the closer they got to Eagle Ridge Camp.

Mr. Faulkner glanced at the real estate agent Daniel Green, who had been highly recommended, and watched him grip the steering wheel tighter as he navigated around road hazards. He turned to the backseat and observed his wife as she strummed her long, polished nails on the door handle: sour expression with a downturned mouth. It was clear that she was not happy about being dragged this far out of town. He had second thoughts too.

"We're just about there," Daniel said, forcing a smile.

"The road is... barely passable," said Mr. Faulkner. He gripped the handle of the door to steady himself.

"It's nothing that couldn't be easily cleared in a few hours with some bulldozers. It would be a cinch to clear the heavy brush—maybe remove a tree or two. The road itself is in pretty good condition, so it wouldn't be difficult to scrape and level with a good construction company. There's also another utility road that comes into the property from the other side. But..." he continued, mustering some zeal, "this road gives you the best view of the most beautiful fifty acres in the county. It's an amazing investment opportunity."

The couple stared silently out the windows—seemingly not convinced.

Daniel pushed the high-performance car up the last incline to where the land then leveled out and opened into spectacular views of stunning meadows and groupings of trees.

"Wow," Mr. Faulkner said under his breath. Finally, he could see past the overgrowth and grasp the potential. "This is amazing. And thank you for making time for us today. We're on a flight to France tomorrow."

His wife leaned forward to get a better look through the windshield. Her face softened in wonder as she gazed at the rolling countryside unfolding around them.

Daniel pulled to the left and parked. "You ready for a bit of a walk? You brought your hiking shoes, right?"

The couple nodded.

"Great," he replied and opened the car door while the couple changed their shoes.

He checked his pockets to make sure he had the keys that opened the main buildings. Filled with nervous energy, he jingled his own car keys against them as he paced in front of the car, surveying the area.

The pines arched and swayed around them in the breeze, blowing their sweet scent through the air. Daniel turned to look down the valley at the various towns he could see in the distance: pretty as a postcard. Fresh air, birds fluttering in the trees, and the warmth of the gentle rays of sun upon his face.

Mr. and Mrs. Faulkner emerged from the car and slowly closed the doors.

"How about we check out the main buildings and then have a look at the lake?" Daniel said.

"Sounds good," Mr. Faulkner said, still surveying the area. "So, how long has this camp been closed? It's been on the market, for what, almost two years?"

They began walking along a narrow trail. Before them were some large buildings, clustered around the main clearing, the gentle rolling hills visible behind them. Weeds crunched underneath their shoes as they weaved along the unkempt path.

"It closed about five years ago," said Daniel.

"I see."

"We've had several interested parties, but something always went wrong with the escrow. Investors pulled out. Money didn't get transferred. Things like that. We've even had a foreign investor wanting to turn it into a family theme park for a while now, but it's moving slowly."

As they walked around the area, Mr. Faulkner felt his enthusiasm grow. He glanced at his wife, and she, too, smiled and raised her eyebrows in growing expectation.

Daniel made an abrupt left turn on the path and began to move downward. The trees clustered closely again around them, before the huge trunks opened into another serene clearing surrounded by gently rolling hills. "This is the south end of Echo Valley, where the lake begins."

"Echo Valley?" Mrs. Faulkner asked.

"*Hello, hello,*" he called out, letting his voice resonate around them before fading away.

All three of them stood for a moment and listened. The calmness and beauty of the area was worth a moment of silence.

"C'mon. You're in for a real treat," Daniel said. He quickened his pace around two large trees. An enormous lake glistened before them, surrounded by the hills. There was not a ripple across the surface, and the reflections of the nearby trees, grasses, and the partly cloudy sky were cast back at them like a visual echo. Just to Daniel's left, a little boathouse and wharf sat at the lake's edge.

"I told you," said Daniel. "This is only *one* of many amazing views on the plot. Can you imagine taking a kayak out at sunset? Or building a dream house here? Just breathtaking." He paused and took a gentle deep breath.

The Faulkners walked over to the dock to get a closer look at the birds swooping and diving around the lake. Daniel followed silently behind them, as the weathered boards creaked gently underfoot.

A soft bumping sound could be heard from within the boathouse at the end of the jetty, and curious, Daniel took a detour to take a quick look. He pushed open the door, which hung cockeyed off its hinges. They gave way with a prickling screech. Inside was revealed a long wooden deck along with several well-worn hooks, used to secure canoes and kayaks.

Hearing the couple behind him, he called out, "Watch your footing, one of the planks is missing."

The couple followed him inside.

Mr. Faulkner looked closely at the structure. He wondered how much it would cost to build a proper boathouse. He saw Daniel looking down into the water at something dark, something that bumped against the underneath side of the deck with the lapping of the wavelets created from the mountain breeze.

"What is that?" asked Mr. Faulkner, straining to see.

Mr. Faulkner watched Daniel awkwardly kneel down to grasp the end of a piece of rope that was floating nearby. It appeared to be clean and new, totally out of place in a boathouse that had been abandoned for years. The agent pulled at it until there was a resistance.

The dark mass came closer into view with every tug of the rope. As it broke the surface, it rolled to one side and, to Mr. Faulkner's horror, they stared at a woman's face; dark eyes fixed open, skin opaque and shiny like artificial rubber. Brown hair swirled in the water around her pale cheeks, framing her face.

Daniel gasped.

"What?" said Mr. Faulkner, not believing what he was actually seeing.

"It's..." Daniel couldn't form the words. "She's..."

"What?" demanded Mrs. Faulkner before leaning in for a closer look. There was a pause before she registered the face staring back at her, screamed, and then ran from the boathouse, her hurried footsteps crashing through the valley path.

"What the hell. Is she dead...?" Mr. Faulkner whispered over Daniel's shoulder.

Daniel leaned forward. His eyes locked on the dead woman's gaze.

Mr. Faulkner had never seen a dead body before. Sucking in a breath, he watched Daniel pull at the rope once again, dragging the woman's body closer. Her torso, oversized from bloat, rolled over so her face was forced downward with one arm out to her side. The other arm was... missing. He could see that she was dressed in dark pants and a light short-sleeved shirt. Shoes missing, her feet ballooned and, cartoon-like, floated on the surface.

"Call the police," Daniel whispered to Mr. Faulkner without looking back at him.

CHAPTER TWO

TUESDAY 1030 HOURS

Detective Katie Scott hurried through the basement corridors of the tomb-like building that housed Pine Valley Sheriff's Department. The cold-case unit was located in a small section of the forensics division. The quiet hum of the air vents in the windowless basement offices always made her calm, but a few long days of court appearances had pushed her behind in searching for her next cold case to solve. Now she was done testifying, at least for a while, she was itching to focus on her next investigation.

Opening the last door on the right down a long hallway, she entered her office, a small room containing two working desks, two tall filing cabinets, a large whiteboard, and several bankers' boxes filled with files and binders of unsolved cases from the county.

Katie glanced over to where she would usually find her partner, Sean McGaven, sitting and searching police databases for answers in their last investigation. He had been recently promoted to detective, which meant he'd now be working half-time for the robbery-homicide division upstairs, and the rest of his time on cold cases with her.

From one of the shelves near her partner's desk a small brown teddy bear with a toy detective's badge pinned to its chest stared back at her. McGaven's girlfriend, Denise from the records division upstairs, had given it to him as a cute reminder of his recent promotion. Katie smiled at the sight of it, thinking about the previous cases Gav and she had worked on together and the hours they had spent trawling for clues. They didn't always agree, but in the end, they always solved the case.

Hanging her jacket up and then opening her briefcase, Katie got right to work, flipping through the files Sheriff Scott had left for her. Every month, he would select a handful of unsolved cases that needed attention. Sometimes they were twenty years old, sometimes just a few weeks, perhaps where the other team hit a dead end and there was a need to go back and retrace steps.

Katie skimmed over several files. Two were about missing women, Lisa Brando and Cecilia Gomez, both happily married mothers who were reportedly at home on the day of their disappearance, one doing laundry and the other cooking in the kitchen. They had both vanished without a trace within two months of one another and there was no connection between them.

Katie paused to study photographs of their homes. Both houses were tidy. She saw the laundry hamper at Lisa Brando's house on the coffee table with neat piles of folded laundry on one end of the couch. At Cecilia Gomez's home, the kitchen had two large pots on the stove with the burners turned to simmer.

Nothing in either home appeared to be out of place. There was no sign of a struggle. It looked, at first glance, that the women just walked out of their homes and vanished into thin air. Their cars were in the driveway, keys and purse on the counter, and all personal items still in their places.

Katie read the reports and statements, focusing not on what

she could see, but what she couldn't. Could the homes look too perfect perhaps, almost staged? Was the setting what you were supposed to see?

Intrigued, she put the files to one side to come back to later and read through another case file. This one involved the murder of a woman and child. She made notes as she read, to help her decide which case to give her attention to first.

Below that one, she glanced at the case of a man, Rick Reynolds—unemployed, occasional work as a handyman—found murdered, body dumped in nearby Bluff Park. He had been stabbed over forty times and left at the side of the parking lot. There wasn't much forensic detail in the report, and it appeared that the file wasn't complete. She would have to chase the information down.

About to close the files and move on, her eyes fixed on the name *Eagle Ridge Camp* written in the original police background check for Rick Reynolds—and her blood went cold. A long-buried memory from her past broke free and drifted to the surface. Everyone who had grown up in Pine Valley knew about Eagle Ridge Camp. It had been a fantastic place to attend as a child, whiling away long summer days making rafts and playing hide and seek amongst the trees. It was where Katie had had some of the most memorable times in her childhood—swimming, hiking, and canoeing—and she could still remember all the friends she had made, and the skills she'd learned.

But...

She also remembered something much darker from that time and place. Something that had always haunted her—one of the defining moments of her life, and the reason she had become a police officer. It was the last conversation she ever had with her best friend Jenny.

. . .

"Hi, Katie," said Jenny eagerly, revealing a mouthful of braces. She had on a pair of blue denim shorts and a white T-shirt with dark blue sneakers. Her long dark hair was loosely braided in a ponytail.

"Hi," replied Katie, beaming with joy. "Where were you? I looked for you before we went canoeing. It was so much fun. You would have loved it."

"Oh." Jenny looked down. "I was... well, I was running late and didn't really feel like it."

Katie had noticed that Jenny would disappear at times and not participate in group activities. She gave Katie excuses that she needed to call her parents and check in. They were extremely overprotective of her.

"Well, we're going again at three. You want to come?" she asked. "Please come," she insisted.

Jenny's eyes lit up and she replied, "That sounds like fun."

"Good. I'll meet you right here a little bit earlier. Okay?"

"Okay, I'll be there," Jenny answered as she smiled, clearly excited. She turned and hurried away.

But Katie never saw or talked to Jenny again. She waited for her as they'd arranged, but Jenny never showed up. Katie didn't want to be late for the canoe class, so, disappointed, she left without her friend. When Jenny didn't appear at the canoe dock or later at dinner, staff realized that she was missing from the campgrounds completely.

A search began, but as night fell it was agreed that law enforcement was needed to continue looking for the girl. There was no sign of her.

Two weeks after Katie returned home that summer, she overheard that a body had been found two counties away. It had been identified as that of Jenny Daniels—Katie's best friend.

Jenny had been lured from the camp by her own father who later murdered her and dumped her body.

Suddenly, the office phone rang with a shrill pitch, snapping Katie out of her sad memory.

Grabbing up the receiver, "Scott," she said in a croaky voice.

"There's been a homicide," stated Sheriff Scott in a matter-of-fact voice. "A woman's been found in the lake."

"Where?" She wondered why the sheriff had called her about a homicide.

"At Eagle Ridge Camp."

Those three words shot through Katie's gut as her breath caught. She felt her body temperature heat up as her arms and legs tingled. "Eagle Ridge Camp," she repeated, barely believing the coincidence.

"Copy that," he said. "We've had some trouble here."

Katie listened, eyeing the Rick Reynolds cold-case file, still trying to get her breathing under control. "Bad?" she said, hearing voices and machinery in the background.

"After we were called up here about the body, we began a preliminary search for any other victims or potential evidence on the property. It's like a jungle up here."

Katie's blood turned cold. "Has anyone been..." She couldn't make herself finish.

"Everyone is fine. But our K9 teams are currently competing in Sacramento for the police K9 trials," he said. "Hold on, Katie." She heard him firing out commands to officers and the search crew to cease before he came back to her. "They found some parts of potential explosive devices."

"I see." Katie hid her horror at the thought of explosives at a summer camp. Anyone could have stumbled upon them.

"Katie, you know there's roughly forty to fifty rural acres here."

"Yes." Chills rippled down her spine.

"We've stopped everything. Stopped searching. Stopped

moving around on the property. Everything is at a standstill. I can't let anyone proceed until we know what we're dealing with."

"What do you need?" she said, but knew what the sheriff was going to ask. Even though he was the sheriff, he was also her uncle, and wouldn't put her in any harm's way if it wasn't extremely important.

"I need you and Cisco to get up here ASAP to sweep the area for any possible explosives and traps. More than half of the property isn't accessible, but we have a perimeter, a few acres around the main buildings and cabin sections are the most important."

Katie swallowed hard. During two tours in Afghanistan as a military K9 handler, she had regularly performed searches of this nature with Cisco, her faithful German shepherd, but never since she had been a police officer. Now she was asked to search closer to home. Cisco had been there for her through some of the toughest times in her life. "What about bomb squad?"

"Negative. Bomb squad will be on permanent standby if there are more explosives found—or an actual bomb. I know you and Cisco are trained in this type of search and terrain. I want to be careful moving forward—performing due diligence up here."

Katie began running all sorts of scenarios through her mind. *Booby traps? Who was responsible? What was their intention?*

"McGaven is on his way and will be your cover officer."

She was relieved that her partner would be the one looking out for her safety. She herself would be occupied reading Cisco's alerts to clear the area. "Okay."

"Katie?"

"Yes."

"You up for this?" His voice softened to that of a caring uncle.

"Absolutely." She had some reservations about going back to

Eagle Ridge Camp after all these years. There were still dark memories associated with it, ones she hadn't resolved yet. "I'm on my way."

"See you soon."

CHAPTER THREE

TUESDAY 1145 HOURS

Katie rushed home to change out of her regular police work clothes and into more appropriate military gear—her old combat pants, heavy long-sleeved shirt, and military boots. Her adrenalin was ignited and her senses were strangely charged as she readied for whatever they were going to find at the camp. Memories from the battlefield flooded back and she pushed to keep those vivid images buried. Her mouth went dry. Her heart rate rose. It was usual for her to be nervous before any mission, but she kept her anxiety in check.

She suited Cisco up with his military vest. The dog could read her emotions well and he whined in anticipation of what was next. His amber eyes fixed on her, waiting for commands. Seeing him in his vest added to her memories, as if being in Afghanistan together was only days ago.

She switched from her patrol sedan to her personal Jeep in order to be able to navigate faster up to the camp. She wasn't sure what she would find or how overgrown the area had become. In fact, she wasn't sure of anything until she got there.

Her mind raced. Nerves tingled as she settled back against the comfortable seat and increased speed.

As she pressed the accelerator harder than she should on the rural roadway, she thought back to being in the third grade, being bussed up to the camp for part of the summer. The excitement of what to expect and all the fun of being away from home was an infectious energy among all the kids. Then her memory stuttered as she thought of her friend Jenny and what had happened to her.

Jenny, I wish I could have done something. Anything... If I'd never left your side, you would still be here today.

Her thoughts were interrupted by Cisco barking from the backseat. The eighty-pound black German shepherd with his intense, wolfish gaze grumbled and whined as he shifted his weight about. He could obviously sense the change in her energy. He looked from window to window as if he knew they were headed into something big. Dressed in his working vest, he certainly knew he was ready for action.

"Take it easy, Cisco. We're just going to make sure that the camp is safe..." she said, almost to convince herself.

The dog kept his position just behind her and watched over her shoulder as the landscape changed from the city to countryside.

She finally reached the turn for Eagle Ridge Camp. There were deep, fresh divots in the roadway, indicating that there were large vehicles already up at the camp. Bent brush and stray branches were pushed away on either side of the road. They had cleared the area for emergency vehicles. A sheriff SUV was stopped at the side of the road. A tall dark-haired deputy was standing beside it, waiting to give directions to vehicles approaching the camp.

Katie lowered her window. "Hi." She could hear the cracking of the police radio inside his vehicle.

The deputy approached.

"I'm Detective Scott," she said, noticing his nametag identifying him as Watson.

He nodded politely and pointed. "You need to keep going up to the main area that way. They're waiting for you."

"Is that the only way in?" she asked with curiosity.

"There's a back utility road that the fire department with bulldozers are clearing right now—but you need to stay on this road and go straight up."

Katie nodded. "I see. Thank you."

The deputy nodded and headed back to his SUV.

Katie drove on. She was glad that she opted for her Jeep as the final quarter mile of road was rough. Grinding the gears to gain traction, she maneuvered the last stretch into a wide, flat area like an open meadow with rolling peaks in the background. The lake wasn't far away, in between a grouping of hills at a lower elevation. It was beautiful—just as she remembered it. Except now, it was tremendously overgrown and there were police, emergency vehicles, SUVs, and trucks parked precariously around the site. She caught a glimpse of the three main buildings and surrounding cabins, which were centered in the open area that once made up the heart of the summer camp.

She parked in a space near a grove of trees.

"Cisco, stay," she ordered as she exited the Jeep and went round to open the back, keeping a view of the command center. He gave two barks to her command but waited, panting in eagerness.

The breeze had picked up some since she had left her house, stirring up the heavy scent of pine around her. The air was clean and fresh and the scenic hills a dozen varying shades of green.

As Katie turned her attention back to the cars, she saw a zone where the makeshift command center had been set up with a table and whiteboard. There were maps of the area and an aerial view of the property. She saw officers and detectives milling around in the background. There was an ambulance and forensics van parked to the right, other police vehicles to the left. She didn't see the sheriff.

Her partner, McGaven, jogged over. He was already wearing SWAT gear, including a bulletproof vest. He towered over the rest of the crew and his fair skin was already slightly sunburned.

"Hey! Glad you made it," he said, smiling like it was any other day.

"Didn't think I was going to be searching for potential bombs when I got up this morning," she said.

"That's the beauty of the job."

She chuckled. It was great seeing McGaven. She hadn't realized until then how much she had missed him the past few weeks since he'd moved to the robbery-homicide division. Glancing at her partner's short-sleeved shirt, she said, "You need to change. Trust me. Out here in this brush, you'll want protection from the sun, but also from the bugs, wasps, and possibly poison oak."

Absent-mindedly rubbing his arms, he said, "You're right. I'll be right back." He jogged over to his truck to quickly change.

"Katie," said a familiar voice behind her. She turned to see Sheriff Scott exuding his usual control and calm authority, dressed in combat boots, sporting a crew cut with graying side-burns, and a pair of dark sunglasses.

"Sheriff," she said, pulling on her bulletproof vest from the back of her Jeep and bending down to tie her own combat boots.

"Everyone has been briefed. This is your lead."

Katie nodded. A shiver went up her spine as she remembered the many dangerous sweeps of open areas, buildings, and abandoned cars she had done during her tours. She suddenly wasn't completely sure if she could force herself to do this type of search again. PTSD had ravaged her soul when she had returned, but she had worked through too much to have a setback now—but all at once, it was as if she was standing at the edge of a precipice of anxiety and panic. Pushing forward, she steadied her breath and kept her focus on the task at hand. Many people were counting on her. It was always what propelled her forward. She cared intensely about keeping people safe and it was her crutch to detach her from the harsh symptoms of PTSD.

"I'm sorry it has come down to this."

"I'm not," she said, ignoring the strange tingling filtering through her. "What about the body? Any ID?"

"Not yet. John is still documenting the scene."

"Who found her?"

"A real estate agent brought a couple up here as potential investors. We've already taken their statements and let them go."

"Wounds?"

"She had been strangled and her body dumped in the lake. But luckily, the winds had pushed her back to the docks."

"I see," she said, checking her ammunition. She looked at her uncle and his body language seemed hesitant. "What else? There's something you're not telling me."

"I don't want to burden you now."

"Well, now you have to tell me." She turned toward him, all her senses suddenly on high alert. "What else?"

"The body is missing the left arm."

"Missing? You mean the killer removed it?"

"Yes."

"That's a pretty significant signature for a killer."

"I agree."

Katie took a deep breath. Her mind was racing through possibilities and why the camp's lake could be a significant place to dump a body. If the bomb-making pieces that Sheriff Scott's team had discovered were connected to the body, then this was a major situation involving a complex killer.

She needed to see the body before it was transported back

to the morgue. Something might indicate why this particular setting, or maybe something more sinister. Was this just the beginning?

"Katie?" her uncle said. "I want you to be careful. Take it slow. You got me?"

"Of course." She kept a strong demeanor externally, but, in fact, this assignment terrified her. She could already feel a sweat break out and her hands wanting to tremble. She worried that she might not be able to keep these physical symptoms of her past trauma at bay. At the same time, she didn't want to disappoint her uncle.

Right at that moment, McGaven returned, now wearing a long-sleeved shirt. He rolled out a map of the area, and pointed to where he thought they needed to begin their sweep. "Okay, this is what we have."

The three of them huddled together as Katie examined the area. She knew it well from all her summers running wild here with her friends, as well as some of the hiking trails leading up here—but it was strange to be back so many years later as part of a police team.

"This is where the items were found," McGaven stated. "On the west side behind a cluster of cabins."

Katie remembered that she had stayed in one of those cabins.

The sheriff pointed to the southeast side of the plot. "We've blocked off six specific areas to manage the search—one to two acres each. Places that you can get to—everything else is too rural, mountain terrain, and dense with unruly scrub and trees. It would be highly unlikely for anyone to get through on foot."

Katie studied them.

"You should begin in the southwestern areas, here and here." The sheriff indicated with his index finger.

"We'll begin in block #1 and then move on to the next," she

said. The areas weren't as large as she had originally thought and they should be able to search quickly.

"Okay." The sheriff rolled up the map. "I'll be on the radio with you every step of the way."

Katie forced a smile. "Okay. I just need to secure Cisco and we'll be ready." She turned and opened the door of the Jeep. Cisco bounded out, ready for action, his head high, ears forward, and nose gently sweeping. She stroked his head and double-checked his brown-and-tan camouflage vest before snapping on a ten-foot search-length leash. "You ready, Cisco?" The dog responded with a low whine as he padded in a circle ready to work. To the sheriff, she said, "Permission to take a quick look at the body before they transport her to the morgue."

The sheriff seemed as if he was about to deny her request, but thought a moment. "Ten minutes—no more."

"Thank you," she said.

"Oh, and..." he said, "you both need to wear helmets."

"I don't think—" she began.

"No argument. That's an order," he said and left Katie and McGaven to finish getting ready.

"Now I'm going to have helmet hair for the rest of the day," he said.

Katie smiled as she checked her weapons again; both her sidearm and her ankle holster, and affixed her police radio and cell phone to her work belt. She was ready to search her childhood playground.

CHAPTER FOUR

Ten minutes later Katie stood on the small dock staring down at the dead woman's body. The victim had been removed from the water and now lay on her back—torso bloated as well as her lower extremities. The forensics supervisor, John Blackburn, was kneeling down close to the body taking photographs. He looked up when she approached.

"What do you have?" she said.

John gave a stoic smile, pausing a moment. It was rare that anyone saw his bare arms which were covered with interesting tattoos, including one that identified him as a former Navy Seal. He and Katie had an unspeakable bond and respect due to their backgrounds in the military. He stood up to face her. "Female, forties. Probably has been in the water less than twenty-four hours. ME will have a closer estimation."

Katie observed the purpling around her neck. "Strangulation?"

"Appears so."

The dark-haired woman lying before her was wearing dark pants and a short-sleeved T-shirt, which were stretched to the limit from the body's swelling. Her left arm was missing, leaving behind jagged flesh and bone. Was the killer trying to make a statement?

Katie looked around the run-down boathouse, once used to house canoes and kayaks. She remembered taking a canoe out herself from here several times. There were hooks on the wall and a place where there had once been a clipboard. Organized and bagged by the police already was a rope. It was the one thing that appeared out of place—new, just purchased recently. It didn't seem to be tied around the victim.

"Where was the rope?" she asked.

"It had been tangled in the water, caught on some rough wood underneath the decking."

"Not attached to the body?"

"Not sure, there's no evidence it was, but the body was tangled in it," he said.

"Was this the spot where the real estate agent and his clients found the body?"

"Yes." John looked at Katie closely. "What's bothering you?"

"It seems odd. A new rope not attached to the body. Was it an afterthought? Or part of the scene to make it look like she had been strangled with that rope?"

"Good questions."

Katie looked at the lake and could see a slight wind moving the surface as if there was a ghostly current at work. Her uncle's guess seemed to be correct. "She must've been dumped in the lake and floated here," she said, more to herself, and prepared to leave.

"Detective Scott," said John.

She turned to face the forensics supervisor.

"Be careful out there. Mark anything at all that needs to be documented."

Katie nodded and left.

. . .

On the southwest side of the camp, Katie, McGaven, and Cisco started their methodical sweep by a cluster of three rustic cabins nestled between a dense patch of pines. Two of them had the windows and doors boarded up, but the third was standing wide open.

Cisco's energy rose and he let out a low warning whine.

Katie leaned down to him and gave him a command to go ahead: "*Geh voraus.*" Most police and military K9s were trained to understand commands in German and English, and hand signals.

Glancing at her combat watch, she said to McGaven, "We'll work in strips going from east to west until we've covered the whole block."

"Copy that," he said.

Pushing any outside sounds from her consciousness, she focused herself on the search completely, blocking out the distant rumble of the trucks clearing the road nearby, the sound of McGaven's footsteps behind her—even the hiss of the wind through the pine trees. It was just her and Cisco now; his ears rigid, tail down, nose switching from the ground to the air, focusing on any out-of-place scents. Katie concentrated hard on his movements, muscle twitches, and head snaps, the steady rhythm of her breathing inside the helmet keeping her calm.

As the weeded, overgrown pathways became denser Katie slowly reined Cisco closer to her—about five feet—even closer still as the grass reached her knees, then her hips.

Cisco stopped to sniff a beer bottle that appeared months or years old, and then at a piece of dark fabric in the long grass. Both times, Katie turned slightly to her left and raised her arm in a fist to alert McGaven to mark it as potential evidence. It was overly cautious, so she kept vigilant for anything that possibly connected to a bomb or the makings.

They continued moving slowly through the taller wild grasses and weeds with no incidents. It soon began to feel as if they had been walking for hours. In fact, only twenty minutes had passed.

Next, they approached several stands of trees. The density of the undergrowth made for more potentially hidden traps. Katie slowed her pace, but Cisco found nothing. She began to think that they were wasting their time. All the same, she understood why her uncle wanted to clear the property.

As soon as they had finished moving carefully through the larger tree areas, Katie picked up the pace. She stopped when she heard the sudden rustle of her radio.

"How's it going?" said the sheriff through the receiver.

Katie stopped. Into the handset, she said, "Clear, except for a piece of fabric and a bottle."

"We'll meet up at the second block area," the sheriff said.

"Copy that," she replied, slightly adjusting her helmet.

They had reached an area where the dead weeds were compacted underneath their boots. She noticed that Cisco carefully padded around denser areas as if it was uncomfortable on his paws.

Finally, Katie, McGaven, and Cisco finished the first block. As Katie looked up, she saw the second area marker and the sheriff and John waiting for them.

The sheriff handed them each a bottle of cold water.

"Thank you," said Katie, barely able to contain her enthusiasm as she drank. She then shared the rest of the water with Cisco. The sun shining on her helmet was making her temperature rise, bringing back memories of the hot battlefields she had experienced. Looking at the others, she observed that tensions were high.

They moved forward to the next section.

Feeling a burst of energy from the hydration, Katie and Cisco set their trail pace in motion. McGaven was quiet behind her, but she knew that he was just giving her enough space to do her job. After a while, the scrubby terrain opened up behind the cabins and she found herself in a meadow where the ground was relatively flat, making it easier for Cisco to catch any scent.

The afternoon sun beat down on the cracked, dusty ground as they wove back and forth.

"We only have a little ways to go before we complete block #2."

Katie watched her dog closely. He didn't seem to show any signs of slowing, but it was her job to regulate his pace so he could go the distance. Soon, they approached two enormous pine trees with trunks almost as big as hundred-gallon drums. One was clearly dead, judging by its splintering branches, some already lying on the ground, and others ready to fall. She decided to take Cisco around the trees on the left walking over extra brittle weeds and dead pine needles. She felt Cisco follow her lead. She glanced behind her for a second, but before she could look back in front, there was a strange hollow sound from their footsteps as they moved forward, and her feet felt like they had walked on something spongy.

She looked back to Cisco as he sat, which meant an alert.

Looking down, she was not quick enough. A loud crack, like breaking bones, snapped beneath her, dropping her body into a pit. For a moment she felt weightless, as if she was walking on air, but her short descent ended abruptly as her body slammed into the bottom of the hole. Her head had knocked twice against the sides and a searing pain pierced her right arm.

Katie realized that she had fallen into one of the oldest types of snares. A hole disguised with debris, giving the illusion there wasn't a hole—until someone stepped onto it and fell down into the cavity. It looked to be an amateur mantrap. Luckily, it was shallow: approximately six or seven feet deep, and she could see her surroundings fairly well with the sun beaming through the trees' branches.

Cisco barked rapidly above her.

She had let go of the leash.

"Katie! Katie!" yelled McGaven. "Katie, are you okay?"

"I'm okay," she said, a bit winded. "I'm okay, except..." The intense smell hit her hard and she knew it could only mean one thing.

McGaven and Cisco leaned over the edge above her. "Except what?" he said.

"Something pierced my right arm." She winced. "And..."

"And what?"

Katie stared at a dead woman's face, eyes black, dark hair at her shoulders, patchy chunks of scalp, skin hanging from her cheeks revealing bone and teeth. She hesitated before she answered. "There's another body."

CHAPTER FIVE

"What?" said McGaven, taking his helmet off and dropping it on the ground. "Grab my hand." He reached down toward Katie.

"It's a crime scene, remember?" She tried to sit up straight but there was a shooting pain in her right arm. There were several pieces of vertical metal that caught her right side. She couldn't ascertain if it was put there on purpose or just thrown in as an afterthought.

"Make sure Cisco stays in his down position," she said. "Cisco, *platz*," she yelled up.

The dog obediently obeyed her command and lay down.

"We have to call it in," he said and pulled the radio from his belt. "Sheriff Scott, do you read? Over."

Static ensued.

"Sheriff Scott, can you hear me?" he said.

No answer, only louder static.

"There must be something blocking our signal here. Let's get back to him."

"Wait a minute," Katie said, trying to gain her focus. "We don't know if there are any more traps around here—so be careful. I've probably already caused some contamination just by falling in here, so it's best that I take a preliminary look."

"Okay. What do you want to do?"

"Let me do a survey of the hole and body, and then you can help me out. Then, we'll report back at the entrance to block #3."

McGaven hesitated, but ultimately agreed with her.

Katie shifted her body. She took off her helmet and tossed it up. "Can you take some notes?"

"Yep." He retrieved his cell phone and swiped his index finger to get a blank page for comments. "Shoot."

"Okay." Katie took a closer look. She began, "The woman's body is in a sitting position, legs bent at the knee and folded to the right side, and she appears to have her arms and hands behind her back."

"Can you see any restraints or injuries?" asked McGaven.

"No. She's wedged back against the side of the hole and I can't see." Moving closer, she said, "She's dressed in jeans and a hoodie."

"Wounds?"

"Hard to tell. Decomposition has set in." Katie could see the areas of missing skin around her face and hands, the bones now appearing opalescent as the skin curled tightly in darkened rolls.

"Toss me down some gloves," she said.

She slipped them on and carefully moved the sweatshirt away from the victim's neck area. "There are indications of strangulation. I see some snippets of purplish horizontal bruising on the remaining flesh across her neck. Her face and skull don't appear to have any blunt force trauma or other impacts that I can see." She thought about the body at the boathouse with the purple bruising around the neck and the areas of decomposition.

"Age?"

"If I had to guess, she's probably in her late thirties or forties. Dr. Dean will be able to pinpoint her age much better than I can."

Katie was about to stand up when she remembered the woman in the lake was missing her left arm. She had a suspicion, so she carefully examined the woman's limbs, noticing that she had only one sneaker. Leaning closer, she saw the woman's left foot was missing. The ankle bone protruded in an uneven pattern. Her first thought was someone had used a hacksaw—most likely post-mortem.

"Katie?"

"Her left foot is missing. There are no signs that the foot is in here. The cutting is up about an inch above the ankle bone."

She wanted to see if the dead woman's hands were intact but didn't want to disturb the soil around the body in case there was more evidence that needed to be documented and collected. The soil was packed tightly, but it was made mostly of clay and sand. She let out a sigh. Even though there wasn't definite proof, it was likely the two bodies found today were murdered by the same person, but she kept it to herself —for now.

Katie pulled her cell phone from her pocket and snapped a few photos of the body and the interior of the hole. She zeroed in on the victim's neck and missing foot.

"You ready?" McGaven said, growing impatient.

"Okay." She slowly stood up, feeling her muscles tighten. "Give me a boost." She reached up and clasped McGaven's hand and soon found herself sitting next to the hole assessing her wound. Cisco whined, pushing his nose into Katie's face, circling her to make sure she was alright.

"Did Cisco alert?" asked McGaven.

Katie nodded petting the dog. "He did, but it was too late. I had already stepped on the edge of the hole."

McGaven quickly tore one his long sleeves and made a temporary bandage. "Let's see that wound."

"It's no big deal. Maybe needs a few stitches." Katie downplayed the injury.

McGaven knelt next to her as Cisco kept eye contact on them. Her partner helped pull back the sleeve, revealing a three-inch jagged laceration. Pouring fresh water over her arm, he said, "That's going to need more than a few stiches. And you need real antiseptic so it won't get infected."

Katie grimaced as McGaven wrapped her upper arm and tightened the makeshift bandage. "That smarts."

McGaven looked at her. "Smarts? You have to have a better description than 'smarts'. Like hurts like hell. Burning like fire. Feels like someone tried to use a hot poker and sliced my arm... anything but smarts."

"Okay, it hurts like hell. Is that better?"

"Much."

McGaven helped her to her feet. "You okay to walk?"

"Of course. It's only my arm."

They began moving forward to the end of the block. They could hear voices.

"You think this body is related to the woman in the lake?" he said.

"If I had to guess at this point—yes."

"Serial killer, you think?"

"Perhaps."

"You think both of these women were reported missing? Maybe in the cold cases?"

"Maybe."

"You want this case?"

Katie stopped. Cisco kept close to her side. "What do you think?" Her eyes lit up with a slight smile on her face.

"Dumb question, I know. Of course you do."

CHAPTER SIX

A few minutes later Katie and McGaven approached the sheriff who was standing with a few others at the rendezvous area before the third search block. The group were still studying several maps of the region and figuring out where they would start bulldozing the years of overgrown weeds.

Sheriff Scott explained the rockier areas, but stopped as he saw Katie and McGaven approaching. "What happened?" He met up with them, instantly eyeing her bloodied sleeve.

Kate began explaining calmly. "Cisco alerted to an area, but I didn't catch it soon enough and fell into a manmade hole."

"You injured your right arm?"

"Yes, but it's just a cut."

The sheriff looked to McGaven.

"More like a laceration. We stopped the bleeding, but she'll need some stitches," said McGaven.

"Not a big deal. It's not an emergency."

"I want it looked at right away," ordered the sheriff.

"Wait," she said.

He turned and looked at her.

"We found a body." Her words hung in the air as the sheriff didn't immediately respond.

"Body?"

"It was in the hole that I fell in—we couldn't call it in immediately because we lost the signal right at that location. It's a woman. Here's the preliminary," she said and showed him the photos from her cell phone.

He quickly thumbed through the images.

"It's a small compact area. It would probably be best to just have John search the hole, the area around the body, and anything leading up to the trap," she said.

Sheriff Scott took a moment, glanced at the photos again, and turned back to the rest of the group. "We have another body. The area is restricted, so only two, maybe three people need to search, document, and collect the evidence."

One of the deputies said, "I'll get John." He left.

"Sir," said Katie. "I would like to finish sweeping the area."

"I don't—" began the sheriff.

"It's important. We need to clear and secure this property. That's not even including the buildings."

McGaven remained quiet but nodded in agreement with his partner.

"The afternoon is waning," he said. "You're right. We need to finish the search as soon as possible in order for us to move around freely and safely."

"Great," she said. She looked toward where she would begin block #3.

The sheriff gently touched Katie's arm. "I want that injury looked at before the end of the day. Understand?"

"Yes, sir."

Katie and Cisco moved through the rest of the property quickly. Most of it was easy to see and clear, the rest rocky and difficult to navigate, which meant that the killer would have a tough time setting up any type of trap.

After forty minutes she stopped for a rest, mostly for Cisco's sake. She let the dog drink and sit down underneath one of the massive trees. His tongue hung out as he panted. He was still bright-eyed and ready for just about anything if Katie gave the command.

Taking a gulp of water, McGaven said, "What do you think?"

"I don't know what to think yet."

"Think these are the only two bodies?"

"If this is a serial killer—there will be more. But they may have to be recovered."

"Why do you say that?" he said.

"He went to great length to put these bodies at this rural location. I don't think he really wanted them found."

McGaven glanced around him and finished the bottle of water. "What connection do the victims have with this place?"

"Maybe a better question... what connection does the killer have here?"

CHAPTER SEVEN

TUESDAY 1845 HOURS

The sun was low in the sky, leaving a speckled light that filtered through the giant pine trees. It was the end of a long day for Katie. She was exhausted, dirty, muscles aching, and her arm throbbed as a constant reminder of the body she found. All she wanted right now was a long hot bath and a good night's sleep.

Katie took off her vest after she made sure Cisco had had some water and a little bit of food. He was now snoozing soundly in the backseat—he too was exhausted. She watched him quietly breathe, his chest rising and falling.

Pouring out a portion of water, she washed her face and hands as best she could. She took some water, running it through her hair before securing her ponytail once again. It cooled her body temperature.

Leaning against the open cargo area of her Jeep, Katie watched the sun slide down in the west, making the valleys and small towns of Sequoia County darken in deeper shades of green. She remembered the last time she was at Eagle Ridge Camp, even though it had been when she was only a kid. That was when she had known that her fiancé Chad was always going to be her true love. As corny as it sounded, she knew that they would come back to one another again. She looked at her engagement ring, a simple solitary diamond, and let her memories wander.

"Hey," said Sheriff Scott, interrupting her thoughts of a much gentler time. He joined her and leaned against the SUV. "You hanging in there?" he asked, with his arms crossed in front of him.

"Quite the day, that's for sure." She studied her uncle's face, his jaw taut and his mouth pressed tightly, making his lips appear thinner than they were. It was clear he had some things to tell her. "What's up?"

"We've got a preliminary ID on the victim in the lake."

"Who is it?"

"Her name is Carolyn Sable, thirty-eight-year-old administrative assistant who lived in Pine Valley."

"And?" Katie thought a moment. "Wait, Sable... that sounds familiar."

"It should. She's been missing for two months and her case is sitting in the stack. You may have seen the file."

"Two months? Yet her body must have just been dumped recently. That doesn't make sense. Could she have been held captive? Or was she living somewhere else and just didn't tell anyone?"

"There's more," he said. "She used to be a camp counselor here."

Katie nodded slowly. It was all starting to make sense to her.

"Detectives Hamilton and Alvarez are running a list of names for camp employees and people associated with them. Plus, the usual background checks on her as well. She worked at quite a few places, it seems."

"Oh," she said. Her hopes were dashed that she wouldn't be part of the investigation.

"And they are handing everything over to McGaven."

"He's going to work the cases with the robbery-homicide

division?" she said, trying not to show her feelings. She was shocked how disappointed and dispirited she immediately felt, but she knew that there were many other cold cases that she needed to work. She was still frustrated.

"Yes, McGaven is going to work the cases... with you," he said.

"Me?" she asked, taken aback. "Isn't that going to cause a rift for Hamilton and Alvarez?" Katie had tangled with Detective Hamilton over a couple of active cases before, but they had now made their peace. She just hoped that that peace would withstand another case swiped out from under him.

"I don't think so. We're all professionals here and they even agreed you and McGaven were the best team to investigate this case. Especially with your profiling skills and crime scene evaluation abilities. The other detectives have plenty to keep them busy—it was my decision." He watched Katie's reaction closely. "I received the green light to hire another detective for one of the other divisions, so that will help ease the caseloads."

"That's great," she said.

"A few other positions in the department will also be filled —hopefully soon." He sighed. It was clear that he was frustrated with the department's budget restrictions and recent hiring freezes.

Katie remained quiet for a moment.

"I expected a little bit more enthusiasm from you. What's wrong?"

"Nothing. It's just... if both of these women were connected to the camp, then it most likely means that the killer has a more specific connection with Eagle Ridge."

The sheriff smiled.

"What?"

"You've been thinking about the case ever since you got here."

"Well..."

"Of course you have."

"Of course she has what?" chimed in McGaven, approaching them suddenly. He was drinking from a bottle of water and looking a little more rested.

The sheriff turned to McGaven. "Started working on this case in her head."

"What else would you expect?"

"Okay, okay. I get it." She smiled.

"You have any more energy to sweep the main three buildings?"

"Of course. What's up?"

"Well, I want to make sure that they are okay and that there isn't anything out of place or dangerous."

"Okay. Do we need Cisco, do you think?"

"No, I think if you can have McGaven just check it out and clear the buildings—I won't need to bring up deputies."

"Will John be doing a crime scene search of the buildings?" she asked.

"Not at this time... unless you find something of importance."

Katie nodded.

"I know you're going to document anyway," he said and smiled at her. He handed over the keys, gave a casual salute to both Katie and McGaven and left to speak with other officers.

"Will this day ever end...?" she said with some humor.

Katie checked on a very sleepy Cisco. She left him curled up in the back of the Jeep, after partially opening a window.

"According to the Sequoia County assessor's map, there are three main buildings with two outback storage areas," said McGaven studying the layout.

Katie had changed into a clean shirt and re-secured her firearms, flashlight and cell phone. She walked up to the main entrance. The memory of running with her friends to the building for dinnertime flashed before her. The large buildings were centered on the property and were the focal point of the camp.

"Katie?" he asked.

The many smiling faces of her classmates and camp friends rushed through her mind, laughing and chattering about long sunny days spent swimming in the lake or learning archery. She could almost smell the roasting of marshmallows on the summer evenings and hear the scary stories by the campfire.

"Katie?"

"Yeah, I was just remembering..." She looked to the side of the entrance and for a moment she saw her friend Jenny standing there smiling, wearing her navy-blue shorts and a white T-shirt. "Never mind."

As if reading her mind, he said, "You've been here before. I didn't come here with my class—it looks like it was a cool place. We went up to Raven Lake instead, which is up north."

The decorative rock walkway was overrun with weeds. Water runoff that must have come during storms had covered large sections with dirt. The wide wooden staircase leading up to the main building was intact. The brown building itself was peeling layers of paint. Two windows had been smashed but not completely destroyed. The porch area was empty except for piles of pine needles and dirt that had drifted into corners.

Katie remembered there were once a dozen chairs painted in bright colors and a porch swing with comfy pillows, but now it was no more than a ghost town. It had been one of her favorite gathering areas, apart from the dock. She remembered several nights sneaking out of her cabin to be with Chad as they sat by the lake talking for hours.

Jenny...

No matter how hard Katie tried, she couldn't forget her friend. Her death had been a defining moment in her life. It was an incident that resonated through her police work, and now as she stood in front of a building filled with so many memories from so many children over the years, she would never forget that fateful day when she heard that her friend was dead—and had been murdered.

She stood now at the large wooden door, which used to have creative iron decorations embellishing the corners.

As she inserted the key her uncle gave her, it initially stuck in the lock. She jiggled the key until finally it disengaged. She cautiously pushed the door open; the killer's MO, with booby traps and dismemberment of his victims, a constant presence in her mind. She peered between the cracks for any triggers. Nothing happened. The large hinges creaked with age and struggled to maintain the weight of the solid wooden door. Turning on her flashlight, she opened the door wider and swept the beam up and around the doorframe and then over the threshold. Heavy dust and cobwebs were all that was to be found.

"Look out for any sign that someone has been inside recently," said McGaven from behind her.

"Yeah, it doesn't look like anyone has been here in years. But... that seems strange. Wouldn't people viewing the property want to see inside this building?"

"You would think," he said as he scrutinized the entrance from top to bottom. "But you have to admit the condition of everything here would probably scare people away. I guess investors were only interested in the land. These buildings need to be remodeled and updated, or most likely torn down."

"I suppose," she said, directing the flashlight around the big building.

McGaven flipped the main light switches on and off—but no light. "Didn't think so, but tried just in case."

Katie turned to him and smiled.

They both searched the area, directing their flashlights back and forth. Most of the building was still intact. There were a few holes down low indicating varmint activity: rats, mice, squirrels, and even larger mammals such as chipmunks or mountain beavers.

There was only a faint smell of musty earth and rotting timber, which seemed to increase in intensity.

Katie moved forward into the meeting hall which had been used for the camp's meals and sometimes large gatherings. "This is where the kids would eat." She took several photos in a panoramic succession of the room and entryways.

McGaven looked around and noted the deer heads mounted on the wall. "I wonder how long these guys have been here?" he joked, moving with caution where there were dark corners.

Katie went into the kitchen area where most of the appliances were long gone. There were just the ventilation systems still intact. She pointed her flashlight beam at the floor—tiny scratches along with numerous rodent droppings were the only things occupying the large kitchen.

"Nothing here," she said disappointed.

"Looks like the only inhabitants have been mice..."

Katie was thorough as she opened every cabinet and storage area. Everything had been cleaned out long ago. After taking a couple of photos, she headed out of the building followed closely by McGaven, locking the door behind her.

They headed to the next building which held several small offices. Katie remembered that in her day they had housed the camp counselors, nurse, and administration.

The building itself was long in construction, with smaller windows that were also painted dark brown. It appeared to be in better condition, wearing well for being abandoned. The paint was also peeling, just as in the main meeting and eating areas, but you could see a bright blue underneath. Katie couldn't remember this building being blue.

It took her a few minutes to find the key that fitted the lock for the entrance. Once she got in, she saw an entry that led into a main area with a long hallway.

Looking to the left and then the right, she said, "I'll go this way and you go the other. We'll cover this building faster."

"I'm getting hungry," McGaven suddenly said.

Katie had to agree, she was hungry too.

Following the beam of light, she moved down the hallway. These were the rooms which had been offices for the camp counselors. Small, compact, and really a place for them to keep their supplies and notes. She counted four offices. Briefly stopping for a moment in front of each room, she noted that they were empty but there were traces of pictures and shelving units left behind on the walls.

One room caught her eye; the window was askew as if it had been opened recently. It was a sash window opening vertically instead of horizontally. Katie cautiously took two steps inside, bent forward and retrieved several pieces of coated wire and bagged them. She studied them closely as they were out of place —perhaps it was similar to the bomb-making pieces found earlier. She noticed something sharp had cut the ends. There was also something silver in the corner—it appeared to be a type of switch. She picked it up as well.

She moved to the window and could feel a breeze blowing. Running her gloved hand along the sill, she noticed some scrapes both on the bottom part and the side of the window frame.

"Odd," she muttered.

She gripped the bottom portion of the window and pulled it easily upward. The scrapes were more noticeable, and at least to her, they appeared to be recent.

"Find something?" said McGaven at the doorway.

Katie turned to face him. "Yeah, I think so. Here are some wires and what appears to be some type of switch."

He pulled a couple of plastic evidence bags from his pant pocket. "Bag them. Maybe John can run down the manufacturer."

Katie dropped the pieces into a bag. "Here," she said. "These are unusual scrapes on the window sill and frame—and they're recent."

McGaven studied them closely.

Katie took a couple of photos with her phone. Then she dialed her uncle's direct cell number.

"Katie?" he said with his usual authority. "Got something?"

"Maybe," she said. "Found some wires and something that looks like a metal switch."

"Anything else?"

"There are unusual scrapes on one of the windows which appear to be recent. The third counselor office on the western side."

"I'll get John on it."

"Okay, thanks." She returned her phone to her pocket.

"What?" said McGaven. "I've been working with you long enough to know that *look*."

Katie scanned the entire room. "Why would someone come into this particular office?"

"Maybe it's the only window that opened?"

"Maybe." She gazed out the window. In her mind, she saw Jenny, with her hair braided, leaning against the trunk of one of the large trees. She was dressed exactly as the last time Katie had seen her.

"Random? Lucky? Easier to climb into this window..." he said.

"No, I don't think so." She still watched as her friend Jenny slowly disappeared like a ghost from the past. "I wonder which office was used by Carolyn Sable?"

CHAPTER EIGHT

Katie drove up the long driveway to her yellow farmhouse, parked and cut her headlights. She sat still staring straight ahead. Her body was sore and she could barely keep her eyes open. All she wanted was sleep, but the trouble was that every time she closed her eyes, she saw the face of the woman in the pit staring back at her. It was a typical reaction for her, and soon the vividness would fade from her mind.

She glanced to the backseat where Cisco was still resting. "What a day, Cisco," she said as the dog perked up his ears.

Opening the Jeep door slowly, Katie swung her legs out and stood up. She took a moment to stretch her back and her legs, trying to ease some of the tension. Even though she ran on a regular basis, she had used her muscles in a different way today —and they were tender and stiff.

Cisco jumped out and headed to the front door. He stood for a moment and cocked his head to the right, before emitting a low guttural growl. He let out a high-pitch whine but his tail remained still indicating a mixed reaction.

Katie instantly saw Cisco's reaction. "Hey, what's up?" she

said and then she noticed a light was on in her bedroom. She didn't leave any lights on. Ever.

With renewed energy and alertness, Katie was at the dog's side. "Cisco, *platz*." She ordered the dog to lie down. She moved more cautiously and became keenly aware of any unnatural sounds.

She inserted her key, slowly turned the knob. There was no familiar buzz of the security keypad waiting for her to enter her four-digit code.

Katie stood in the middle of her living room, quickly assessing the contents. It was as she had left it that morning. Neat and tidy. Everything in place.

A prickle ran up her spine and she felt coldness wash over her. Someone had been in her home—she knew it in her gut. Slowly pulling her gun, she swiftly cleared the rooms and headed down the hallway toward her bedroom. She saw the light escaping underneath the closed door. Now she was sure someone had been inside her home. She never closed her bedroom door.

She could hear Cisco's low whine as he waited for her commands.

Katie kept her firearm directly out in front of her as she opened the door. She methodically scanned the room. She hadn't made her bed that morning and it was still unmade. Her nightstand, table, and dresser were as she had left them.

She kept moving toward the bathroom, where the door was slightly ajar.

What was going on?

Not wanting to lower her alertness, Katie inched toward her bathroom. A sudden aroma of roses hit her senses. It was strong.

She flipped the light on. On the vanity was a bouquet of red roses. Next to the vase were some beautifully wrapped spa assortments for a luxurious bath.

Katie lowered her gun—confused for a moment.
She then saw a card. It read:

My Sweet Katie,

I know you were at Eagle Ridge Camp today. And I know how difficult it must've been for you with memories of Jenny. But we had good memories together there—fishing, canoeing, and sneaking out after curfew. I hope that made it better for you. Take some time for yourself and relax tonight. I'm on twenty-four-hour shifts right now, so I will be up at the camp tomorrow helping to clear some of the heavy debris. Know that I love you and that you are loved by many.

Chad

Katie let out a breath. She stood for a moment, smiling at how thoughtful Chad was to leave this for her. How did she get so lucky?

She hurried back to her front door, called Cisco inside, and locked up behind her, realizing that Chad must've forgotten to reset the security; everything made sense. He was so thoughtful and knew the right times when Katie needed a little lift from the intensity of her job and the bad memories it left her.

After leaving a message for Chad, Katie took little time to fix herself something to eat and feed Cisco. After cleaning everything up and turning out the lights, she couldn't wait to soak in a hot tub with some scented essential oils.

Her arm began to throb with pain. She carefully unwound the makeshift bandage that McGaven had used to stop the bleeding. She cleaned the wound and put a few wound-closure strips and antiseptic on it following up with steri-strips to keep it closed. It had a discoloration to it, but it would be better tomorrow as it was healing. After it quit stinging, she slid into a hot bath.

Katie must've dozed off for a minute or two—she was suddenly jolted awake by hearing her name.

"Katie..."

Sitting up and listening, she didn't hear anything but silence. Besides, if someone had really called out her name Cisco would be barking.

Not wanting to get out of the warm bath, Katie pushed herself upward and dried off. She bandaged her arm and was back in a warm environment—which was her bed.

Usually, she would lie awake for a little bit thinking about her day, getting her case thoughts together, but the last thing she remembered was lying back against her pillow and hearing Cisco softly snoring.

Suddenly, she was walking through a dense forest following a voice saying, "Katie, Katie, don't let him get away..." And then the voice faded. She recognized the voice as Jenny's and knew that her childhood friend was trying to warn her—or give her some guidance. At least that was how Katie perceived it in her dream. She awoke suddenly with a start into the still silence of her room.

She had just faded back to sleep when the shrill ringing shook her awake again. The clock read 6:20 a.m.

Grabbing the cell phone, "Scott," she said, forcing herself to focus and completely wake up.

"We need you to get up to Eagle Ridge Camp," said her uncle. "Cabin three."

"Right now?" she managed to say.

"Now," he said.

"What about McGaven?"

"The Watch Commander is contacting him now."

Sitting up, Katie recognized the serious tone in her uncle's voice. "I'm leaving in about ten minutes and I'll see you there."

"Make it nine and half minutes."

The phone disconnected.

CHAPTER NINE

Cabin 3 kept resonating through Katie's mind as she drove once again back to Eagle Ridge Camp. It seemed familiar to her. To add to her already down mood, it was an overcast day and the gray clouds brought more gloom than necessary to the landscape. She noticed that someone had already packed down the gravel and dirt on the road which made a more stable traction for her SUV. It must've been the rural fire department with their big earth movers. She wondered if Chad was already there working.

Katie didn't know the details of what she was going to encounter yet, but she hadn't missed the tenseness in her uncle's voice. There was definitely something that he didn't want to tell her over the phone, but rather wanted her to see it firsthand.

Cabin 3...

As Katie pushed the accelerator, the Jeep lurched up the road, making Cisco stir in the backseat. It was as if he sensed there was something big coming up. At least this time, Katie had come prepared with extra clothes, plenty of water, and some good high-protein food for both her and Cisco.

She drove into the large parking area. There were fewer vehicles than the previous day, mostly police vehicles, SUVs, and the forensics unit. She found a quiet spot under a tree for Cisco and parked up. She was relieved to see that McGaven was already there because she didn't want to deal with detectives Hamilton and Alvarez by herself. It was always nice to have someone you could trust on your side—especially when she didn't know what she was walking into.

She opened her door and stepped out. The coolness of the air made her instantly shiver—quite a change in twenty-four hours. She absently rubbed her forearm; the pain was still there but now with a radiating ache up her entire arm.

Looking about, Katie listened intently. It was strangely quiet. She didn't hear any voices or car doors, or anyone moving around the vehicles. There was just the soft whisper of the breeze flowing through the tree branches.

After lowering a couple of the Jeep windows, she walked toward the cabins assuming that was where everyone was located.

Katie took the trail she remembered from almost twenty years ago, one that meandered through and around the large California pines. Shadowed areas tucked in between spots made her jumpy. She realized how many options a killer would have to lie in wait for his victims if he didn't bring them here himself.

He could've lured them under false pretenses—but why? Was that possible?

As she rounded the corner, a wave of dizziness flowed over her, making the trees appear that they were moving. She stopped to catch her breath and bent over to lower her head. After a few seconds she slowly stood up as everything came into focus again. It wasn't her usual creeping anxiety, but it still caused her to pause, a little unsettled. After a minute, she began to make her way to cabin 3 again.

As she grew closer, she heard voices. McGaven and Sheriff Scott stood at the entrance having a quiet conversation. They both turned in her direction as she approached. Neither man smiled, but nodded their greetings at her.

"Sheriff, McGaven," she said. "What's going on?" She didn't have to wait long to find out.

The approaching sound was that of metal wheels that screeched every other revolution along the leaves. It was emanating from a gurney accompanied by two technicians from the coroner's office.

Katie turned to her uncle. "Another body?"

Sheriff Scott motioned to the men, "Hold up, please." Then to Katie, "I need you to work the crime scene. McGaven will back you up with notes."

"Of course," she said. "But—"

"Dispatch received a call from an unidentified person explaining that there was a body left in cabin three. The person had disguised their voice—it could've been a woman or a man."

Katie blinked in surprise. "Is that all they said?"

"Yes. Except... deputies needed to respond right away."

"And?" she said, wondering if it was a message from the killer.

"That was it. The rest will be evident."

John from forensics emerged from the cabin dressed in a disposable hazmat jumpsuit, booties, and cap, and carrying a digital camera. Katie almost didn't recognize him. There were small spots of blood on his booties and the cuffs of his sleeves. He carried several evidence bags—both plastic and paper.

"Everything has been photographed," he said solemnly. "It's all clear for Detective Scott." He caught her eye and then moved toward the van.

Katie couldn't help but sense the despondent reactions from everyone. It had to have been bad—*really* bad. She swallowed hard, feeling a lump in her throat, and took a deep breath.

"Why is it so important that I work this scene? Is it one of our cold cases?"

"Not that I'm aware of—yet," the sheriff said, not quite giving Katie full eye contact.

"Okay." She moved forward.

McGaven caught her arm, which burned, causing her to flinch. "You need to suit up."

"Okay." Katie headed over to the forensics van where she pulled on her hazmat suit and booties.

McGaven did the same. He turned to his partner as he got into his suit. "Your arm?"

"What about it?" She glanced at her bandage and noticed that it was seeping blood again.

"It seems worse."

"It's just as sore as it was yesterday."

"Did you go to the hospital?"

Katie ignored the question.

"Did you?" he gently pushed.

She sighed. "No, I was dead tired last night and needed the rest more. If I had gone to the hospital it would have taken up a couple of hours."

"So?" he said.

"So?" she mimicked. "I needed sleep."

"When you leave here today, you need to have your arm looked at and stitched."

Katie finished preparing to enter the crime scene. "Fine." She felt so confined in her suit that it was almost claustrophobic. She'd think about her injured arm again later.

In fact, her mind was already taken up with surmising what the crime scene was all about. The first victim had been found in the lake in the dock house. The second victim had been in a booby trap hole. That meant the third victim would be...

Katie and McGaven walked back to the cabin, neither saying a word to the other. The tension of the situation was high. The two morgue attendants were patiently waiting, staring out at the thick forest that surrounded the small structure.

Senses heightened, Katie slowed her breathing and kept her wits about her as she stepped over the threshold and gave an initial overall survey. It was empty, no furniture, nothing hanging on the walls. Two large floodlights on tripods had been set up to see the space clearly. It was like daylight in the large one-roomed cabin. It made for a shocking display. Blood had been splattered on every wall, the floor, and across the ceiling. The familiar smell of death smacked her senses causing her to catch her breath. She had smelled that same smell many times before, but this time it was like a warning—a suffocating threat.

A breeze blew into the cabin, wafting the fetid air around them.

"Close the door, please," she said to McGaven and he quietly shut it. She wanted to make sure that nothing would be disturbed by the breeze. It made the smell worse, though, like being trapped in a large, uncovered grave with numerous decomposing bodies.

Katie stood firmly in place to survey the room in one three-hundred-sixty-degree turn. There were two books leaning against the farthest corner, several eight-by-ten photographs and some newspaper clippings, each in its own plastic bag lined up along the back wall. A manila envelope lay on the floor to the right, and some shiny silver objects were scattered near the books. Everything was tagged with a standing evidence number.

She wasn't quite sure how she could walk around freely with so much blood on the floor. John had put down some paper, but it didn't seem to help much. The victim, the woman, was sitting in the corner, legs straight out in front, opened in a "V" position, arms down at her sides, head drooped forward.

There was a purplish coloring underneath the skin on her hands and arms.

"Livor mortis," she said.

"How long does that usually take?"

"It starts within about a half hour of death, but the purplish coloring can take a couple of hours before it's visible." The largest patches were on her hands and lowest extremities due to gravity.

"Was she killed here?"

"Most likely. She's been here at least four or five hours, so that means that the killer, if it was the killer, called dispatch right after he killed her." She carefully looked at the victim's hands—no wedding ring or watch. Her fingernails were intact, which could mean that she didn't try to defend herself.

"I've never seen anything like this," she began. She spoke barely above a whisper.

She forced herself to look at the obvious—the body's wounds. She couldn't see at first where all the blood came from. Moving closer, Katie noted that the body couldn't have had this much blood. There must've been more splashed around. "All this blood isn't from this one victim."

"Where from, then?" asked McGaven, taking notes behind her.

"I'm not sure, but this would be enough blood to empty a human body. We'll have to consult with Dr. Dean and John to get an estimate. Maybe it looks like more than it is because of the way its spread around the area. I'm sure that John would've taken several samples from around the room."

At first it was difficult to tell if the body was partially clothed or not due to the blood. It had coagulated, as if it had an extra thickening agent. Inspecting the woman's body, Katie saw that the victim appeared to have on a T-shirt with short sleeves and to be wearing denim jeans. The silver belt buckle caught her attention. It was in the shape of an "S", or perhaps a decorative snake.

Clearing her throat, Katie said, "Female, about the same age as the other victims. Late thirties or forties. Wearing a T-shirt and jeans." She noticed the woman's long dark hair parted down the middle.

"Has anyone moved her in any way?"

"I don't think so."

Katie knelt down again and rolled the body to her left side. Two large incisions gaped from the body's waistline to lower back. The skin was jagged and the holes in the body exposed other organs and intestines. The gruesome display and the reddish blood made her appear like a Halloween prop for a haunted house.

Katie sucked in a breath in horror. "It looks like... like the killer..."

"What?"

"It looks like the killer cut out her kidneys."

CHAPTER TEN

Katie immediately summoned for John to document the incision and removal of kidneys before the body was taken away. She then waited as John assisted the morgue technicians lifting the body into a bag and zipped it up.

After they had finished she was suddenly hit with nausea and dizziness. She leaned against the back wall to steady herself. Feeling perspiration gather on her forehead as well as trickle down her spine, she thought for a moment that she might faint.

"Katie?" said McGaven. "You okay?"

"Yeah, just a little dizzy, that's all."

John turned in her direction with a concerned look upon his face. "You look a bit pale."

Feeling better, Katie stood up and moved toward some of the evidence. "I'm fine. Just didn't have enough breakfast. Once I'm done here, I'll eat something."

"Maybe you should go eat something now," suggested McGaven.

Katie forced a smile. "I'm fine. Really. I have some food in the Jeep."

McGaven didn't look convinced, but he focused on the rest of the evidence.

John helped navigate the gurney out of the cabin and onto the most direct route towards forensics. Then he closed the cabin door once again.

Once the body had gone, Katie turned to study the photos, which were images from magazines and newspapers—some from twenty years ago and others more recent. They were local newspaper clippings about the camp. Some articles were about the good years of Eagle Ridge Camp and all the positive attributes surrounding it. Then, later articles outlined the downsides: the lack of funding, falling numbers of participants. Basically, the camp had been going under for a long time and needed saving. But no one ever came and then eventually it had closed about five years ago—for good.

"Do you think these were left here?" said McGaven.

Katie looked around at the walls. "Maybe. But at least a few had been pinned up on the wall," she said. She took two of the articles and matched them to the places on the wall where pushpins had held them up.

McGaven took several photos with his cell phone. He then picked up the legal-sized manila envelope which looked new—at least the newest item in the cabin—and carefully opened it, pressing the metal fastener up releasing the flap. He shuffled through the papers and his face became troubled. His eyebrows scrunched downward and his mouth and jaw tightened.

"What's that?" she said. It looked like there were more articles inside the envelope, these ones printed on eight-and-a-half-by-eleven paper from a computer printer. All the sheets were inside protective plastic coverings as if they had once been in a binder or scrapbook.

"Articles about you, about us."

"What do you mean?" she said, taking one of the papers.

They were indeed articles about their previous cases. "What the...? Doesn't make any sense."

Suddenly, they could hear voices outside. She walked to the door and opened it. John was back and talking with the sheriff. "John?" she said.

He looked at her inquiringly.

"These plastic sheet protectors need to be dusted for prints."

"What sheet protectors?" asked the sheriff.

"There was a manila envelope with printed news articles of homicide cases from the internet. Each page is inside a plastic protector."

"Specifically what cases?" said the sheriff. His tone was now stern and steeped in authority.

"About our cases. About Katie," said McGaven at the doorway.

"It seems that whomever the killer is has been studying us and the types of cases we've worked on. Perhaps figuring out what our moves are going to be—and what we're going to do next." She paused, taking everything in and processing it. It bothered Katie because it meant that the killer was methodical and making sure that he did his homework. He didn't want to make any mistakes or leave any loose ends. It was going to be more difficult to catch him out. Now she would have to be extra careful and vigilant of her surroundings—at all times.

"Let me collect this," said John and hurried inside the cabin to take the evidence.

Katie and McGaven continued as methodically as they could as they waded through the blood mess.

"If there are more subtle clues or trace evidence, it's going to be completely contaminated from the blood," she said.

"On purpose?"

Katie nodded, frowning, as she looked around the entire area. "I believe it shows whoever did this had thought out this brutal attack thoroughly, including how he could keep potential forensic evidence to a minimum."

"What's bothering you? I can see you're disturbed by something, not just this hideous scene. Signature? MO?"

"There's a lot bothering me. We're now on the hunt for a killer that has a small amount of surgical knowledge and bomb-making experience. It could mean he works in IT, security, or possibly a hospital." She observed that the blood had seeped in between the cracks in the wood flooring and realized that they were in for an extremely difficult case. And at the moment, the killer knew more about her than she did about him.

McGaven continued to survey the corners and any areas where there wasn't an abundance of blood.

Katie walked out of the cabin feeling a bit lightheaded. She thought that she had better eat something and give Cisco a break from being cooped up in the Jeep. He would be antsy, wanting a brief walk or a few rounds of chasing the ball.

She stopped. Her limbs felt strangely weak and tingly. Her vision became blurry and her head woozy as things morphed in her vision around her. Instantly nauseated, she swallowed hard.

She thought she heard her uncle say something, but wasn't sure.

"Katie!" the sheriff yelled.

McGaven and John quickly ran out of the cabin to her aid.

Katie couldn't move as everything seemed to be getting darker and strangely distant. She didn't recognize her surroundings anymore. She tried to force herself to walk, but her legs were rubber and refused to move. She heard her name spoken several times and muddled voices all around her. She stumbled and fell to the ground.

CHAPTER ELEVEN

"Blood pressure 110 over seventy-two, steady," said the paramedic next to her. "Temperature is elevated at 102.4."

"It's okay, Katie, I'm right here with you," said a familiar voice.

Katie felt as though she was a participant in some weird, surreal time and space. When she briefly opened her eyes, everything looked like it belonged in a cartoon or a science-fiction movie. She felt incredibly hot. Then suddenly she was shivering. Struggling to open her eyes again, she saw the most beautiful face she could ever imagine—striking and handsome with sandy hair. The most incredible blue eyes she had ever seen. They were the same as the first day she met him. Chad would always be her first and only love.

"What happened...?" she barely whispered, realizing she was in an ambulance—bumping slightly. Her thoughts then went to Cisco. "Cisco..." She tried to sit up.

"Take it easy," said Chad. He gently made her lie back down. "Don't worry. The sheriff and McGaven are taking care of him."

"But..."

"You need to rest." He brushed his hand across her cheek.

Katie felt the paramedic wrap her arm.

"I don't remember anything after I walked out of the cabin."

Holding her hand, Chad said, "You really gave us all a scare. I've never seen the sheriff look like that before."

"But..." she said.

"Now, this is what you get when you don't look after a wound like that." He spoke in a caring manner rather than accusatory.

"It's not that bad," she said in a low whisper.

"Katie, that wound should have had at least ten or fifteen stitches. Now it's infected. That's why you feel so awful."

Katie let out a breath. This was the last thing she needed or wanted to happen. Now the cases were probably going to be reassigned to one of the robbery-homicide detectives. She needed to get back to work. Trying to sit up, Katie summoned all her strength to convince herself everything was fine.

"Whoa, what are you doing?" said Chad. "You are so stubborn—always have been." He chuckled, but he kept Katie from sitting up. "We're almost there."

Katie knew that ultimately it was going to be up to the doctor. Surely, they would recommend her release. After all, she wasn't a prisoner.

The paramedic had begun a saline drip and as directed gave a mild sedative to Katie.

She fought to keep her eyes open. "I'm fine, really," she said to Chad.

"Rest, Katie. Rest..."

She couldn't fight staying awake anymore—her last thoughts were the brutalized woman's body in cabin 3.

She finally succumbed to sleep.

CHAPTER TWELVE

The beeping sound was annoying, constant, and seemed to get louder with each breath. At first Katie thought that it was her alarm clock going off and that she needed to get up. Opening her eyes, she stared across the bland tan hospital room which included one emergency bed with all the hospital bling. The early morning events came crashing back to her and began to replay in her mind.

Eagle Ridge Camp...

Cabin 3...

Chad...

She was propped up in a hospital bed with the sheet tucked snugly on both sides of her body. Her arm was newly bandaged and there was a dull pain radiating from her shoulder down to her hand. She was also receiving saline solution intravenously.

Blood seeping in the cracks of the cabin floor...

Missing internal organs...

Trying to sit up, she relented and flopped back against the pillows. "Now what?" she whispered to herself. She didn't know what time it was, but she was ready to go home.

There was a glass filled with water and ice sitting on a

portable table next to the bed. She picked it up and took a sip through the partially bent straw. The cool water tasted wonderful as it ran over her tongue, which made her throat feel a lot better.

"Oh, you're awake," said the nurse as she bustled into the room. "That was quite the nasty cut you have. We had to clean it twice. And you have strong antibiotics in your drip. You should be feeling better soon." The woman was older, fifties, but moved around like a much younger woman. Her hair was short with gray streaked through the brown.

"What time is it?" asked Katie.

The nurse looked at her watch. "It's just about 7 p.m." She made notations on a clipboard.

"Seven? I need to go home."

"They said you'd be difficult," she chuckled and took Katie's blood pressure and pulse rate.

"*They?*"

"The sheriff and a nice-looking young man," she said. "Boyfriend?"

Katie assumed that the nurse was talking about Chad. "Fiancé."

"Oh, really?" She looked directly at Katie with a smile. "Congratulations. We made some allowances past regular visiting hours and they will be back soon to visit."

Katie smiled. She wanted to see them. "Where's the doctor?"

"Doing his rounds."

"Can I talk to him?"

"Of course."

"When?"

"He'll be back around 10 p.m. to do his final rounds. You can talk to him then."

Katie sighed. "I can't wait that long."

"I'm afraid you'll be with us for the night, so you have plenty of time to wait."

"Overnight?"

"I now know why you're a detective—you ask a lot of questions." The nurse made some more notes on the chart, checked Katie's drip, and headed to the door. Turning, she said, "If you need anything, use that buzzer. I'm here all night." She smiled and then left.

Katie picked up the remote with the call button. She closed her eyes and realized how tired she was—and soon fell asleep.

"Let's not disturb her," said Sheriff Scott now dressed in casual clothes—jeans and a long-sleeved denim shirt.

"I just want to sit with her for a while," said Chad as he quietly moved a chair closer to the bed.

Katie heard the familiar voices. It made her feel warm and secure listening to them. It was as if she was twelve years old again and didn't have a care in the world except for being a kid. Her life fast forwarded to the present and she quickly began to feel agitated.

Her eyes opened. "Hi," she said, forcing a smile. She noticed the worried expressions on their faces. "I'm fine."

"I'm glad," said Chad.

"I wanted to go home tonight."

"It's just a precaution," said her uncle. "They want to make sure you're responding to the antibiotic and that your temperature returns to normal."

Katie sighed. "I know. What about...?"

"Cisco," said her uncle finishing her sentence. "He's fine. McGaven and Denise are staying at your house with him."

Katie was relieved. She knew that Cisco was in good hands. Now her mind was free to wander back to the cases. "I guess I'm being taken off the Eagle Ridge cases."

Sheriff Scott walked closer to the bed and pulled up a chair. "Always thinking about the cases."

"You don't need to worry about that now," said Chad. "You need to rest."

Katie fidgeted in the bed, acutely aware that she was hooked up to a drip. She was beginning to feel better already.

"This isn't the time or place to discuss the cases now, but I will tell you that nothing has changed as yet." Her uncle squeezed her hand.

That was encouraging to hear, she thought. But she also knew that her uncle would try to keep her calm and relaxed for her own good. He was family and watched out for her.

"I promise I'll behave," she said, trying to sound upbeat. Her arm was beginning to hurt again.

Sheriff Scott stood up, leaned over and gave Katie a kiss on the forehead. "Take advantage of resting because you'll be busy when you get out of here. I'll see you tomorrow." He smiled and left the room.

Katie's attention turned to Chad. It was the first time in a long time he looked concerned. "I'm okay, really." She held his hand.

"I can't have my future wife not taking care of herself."

"I'm sorry. I underestimated the cut on my arm."

"I know, I know. When you're working, that's all you see."

Katie took another sip of water and leaned back.

"I know you're tired. Get some sleep and I'll pick you up in the morning when the doctor says it's okay."

Katie didn't want him to leave, but she knew the more she slept the faster morning would come—and the better she would feel when she had proved she was ready to tackle these cases. She smiled at him. "Okay."

Chad leaned over and gave Katie a gentle kiss. "I love you."

"I love you too," she said, not wanting him to leave.

He hesitated for a moment and then left the room.

. . .

Katie slept a few hours even though the nurse came into her room to check her vitals about every two hours. She spoke with the doctor just before 10 p.m., but didn't have any luck trying to persuade him to let her leave early.

It was dark in her room, but she could see light peeking through the cracks around the door leading to the hallway. It was quiet, too. She didn't even hear nurses talking. It was as if she were sealed inside a tomb.

The antibiotic was obviously working because she felt better, not as weak, and her arm had quit throbbing. Katie flexed her right hand and moved her arm carefully—she knew that she could go to work tomorrow. So many questions about the three crime scenes...

Were they all related?

Why were body parts missing?

Why were there news articles about her previous cold cases?

She rehashed everything she knew so far about the killer's MO and signature.

Her mind churned as though it was flipping through the pages of a book. She kept seeing each scene and the overall camp area. She knew they were all related. But why and how? The images of the gaping section in the back of the victim's body in cabin 3 and the hacked-away foot from the woman in the hole stumped her.

Katie closed her eyes just to rest them.

A light breeze flowed over her body, making her shiver.

"Katie," said a soft child-like voice.

Katie's eyes snapped open just as her door was slowly shutting.

Had someone been in her room?

Who?

She knew it wasn't the nurse.

An odd prickly feeling washed over her body. She thought it might be her fever dropping and the antibiotics taking effect.

Sitting up, Katie wanted to take a look around. A little exercise would do her some good and maybe make her sleepy. Besides, there wouldn't be many people around and no one had told her that she couldn't get up and walk.

Katie swung her legs around and realized that she'd have to roll along her drip bag that was attached to a silver pole on wheels. Dressed in a lightweight robe with slipper socks on her feet, she began to move toward her door with her pole in tow.

Opening the door, she peered out, looking left to right. No one was around. Katie stepped out into the hallway. It was slightly dimmer than during the day and there was a soft buzz emitting from the low lighting. There was no attending nurse at the station, so she decided to keep walking. She was surprised at how quickly she was breathing, much harder than usual, so she slowed her pace and rounded another corner. She figured that she would walk in a big circle and end up back at her room.

Just as she turned the corner, she saw the back of a girl walking ahead of her dressed in shorts and a white T-shirt moving fast. Her long dark hair was braided down her back.

"*Jenny?*" she whispered. Goosebumps scuttled down her arms.

Katie hurried to catch up, slowed by the pole she maneuvered, but the girl had turned the next corner and when Katie arrived she found the area deserted. She looked behind her and back in front. No little girl.

Katie waited a moment to catch her breath and to formulate what she had seen. Looking around, she saw that she was entering the rehabilitation area of the hospital. There was a door to what looked like a large supply area, but the etched wording on the glass said *Prosthetics Lab*.

She walked closer and peered inside. The lights were out

and technicians were gone, but she could see various legs, arms, feet, and hands—all different sizes, types, and shades of skin.

Katie stood a moment and stared at them. They were amazingly life-like and not like the types she had seen in the past. Technology had improved and enhanced prosthetics so they conformed better with the human body, improving the lives of those who needed them.

Katie closed her eyes for a moment, remembering all the soldiers who had lost limbs. The amazing strength and stamina they must endure to be able to function independently again was what heroes were made of. She thought of her team in the army, especially Sergeant Nick Haines, and how he had lost his leg in combat. Even after he had moved back to the area, Katie hadn't seen him as much as she should. They had shared an unshakable bond during her two tours that most wouldn't understand, and he had made Katie stronger both mentally and physically.

Now staring into the prosthetics lab, so many memories and images flooded Katie's emotions. She thought about all those soldiers and accident victims—with missing limbs.

CHAPTER THIRTEEN

THURSDAY 1015 HOURS

Chad picked up Katie the next morning to drive her home, insistent that she should take it easy and not overtax herself with work. But it didn't matter what he said. She worked the cases, with what she knew, backwards and forwards in her mind. It was all she could think about.

She hadn't slept well in the hospital because of all the interruptions from the nurse, but she still felt a lot better than she had. As they drove up her driveway, she saw her Jeep, McGaven's truck, and small white sedan that belonged to Denise.

"Wow, everyone is here," she said.

Cutting the engine, Chad looked across at her. "Of course they are. You don't realize what a scare you gave us."

Katie searched Chad's handsome face and could see that he had been shaken by the incident more than she originally thought. She was so sorry to have given everyone such a panic. "I know," she said softly, squeezing his hand.

"Stay right there." He jumped out of the SUV and ran around the front of the vehicle to open Katie's door.

"C'mon," he said.

Katie laughed. "It's just an infected cut. I can walk." She got out and before she could do anything else Chad whisked her up in his arms.

"Not when I'm here."

He easily walked with her to the front door as it swung open. McGaven and Cisco were there to greet them. It was quite the scene, Cisco barking with excitement at her return.

"Okay," she said. "Put me down."

"Practicing for the big day?" said McGaven.

"It'll be like this every day in the Ferguson household."

Katie took a moment to greet Cisco and give many pets.

Denise appeared from the kitchen. "So glad that you're home. I've made you a couple days' worth of food, so you won't have to worry about going to the grocery store. You didn't have much in the fridge."

"Oh, thank you, Denise. You didn't have to do that." She hugged her friend gratefully.

"Well, we know that your mind will be on other things and you should eat properly."

McGaven hovered at the door. "I wanted to stay after you got home, but I have to go for a briefing."

Katie moved closer to him. "About the cases?"

He nodded.

"Don't worry. I have strict instructions by the sheriff to update you on—everything. But you need to stay home today—and rest."

Katie was disappointed she wasn't allowed to go to the briefing, but she knew that she wouldn't change anyone's mind. "Okay... call me afterward. And find out if there are any preliminary reports on the autopsies or forensics..."

McGaven nodded and gave her a smile. He leaned in and gave her a peck on the cheek. "I'll be in touch."

"Thanks, Gav," she said as he left.

"Well, I need to get back to work too," said Denise.

"Thanks so much for taking care of Cisco and staying here. I love you guys."

"It was our pleasure—it's lovely staying here at the farmhouse. Now get something to eat and kick your feet up. I'll call you later." She smiled and left.

Chad sat on the couch with Cisco sitting next to him as they watched everyone leave. "We're finally alone."

Katie made herself comfortable next to Chad. "What's your schedule?"

Looking at his watch, "I'm on in two hours for my twenty-four—now that the clearing has been taken care of at Eagle Ridge Camp."

Katie snugged against him.

"You need to get some sleep," he said.

He was right. She already felt her energy dwindling and knew she had to recharge fully before going full speed on the cases. There were things that she wanted to do and it was still early.

Chad took her arm. "You need to change this bandage three times a day."

"I will. Don't worry about me."

"Too late."

"Go home. Do what you need to do before your shift." She really didn't want him to leave, but she was going to bed for a couple of hours anyway. She stood up. "C'mon, Mr. Ferguson, you have work to do."

He stood up and faced her, hugging her tight. "I don't know what I would do without you."

"You don't have to worry—at least not for a long, long time." She kissed him and held him for a moment longer.

. . .

After Chad left Katie took a hot shower, careful to keep her bandaged arm out of the water. Then she fell into bed and slept for an hour and forty-five minutes without waking once. But when she did wake, she tossed and turned, unable to get in a comfortable position as her mind ran into overtime.

Eagle Ridge Camp...

Victim 1...

Victim 2...

Victim 3...

She sat up and saw Cisco standing in the bedroom doorway staring at her. "What's up, Cisco?"

The dog wagged its tail and then took several steps and leaped on the bed.

"Aw, I missed you too, buddy."

The dog ran around in circles on the bed a couple of times before settling down next to Katie.

She looked at the clock: 3:15 p.m. She sighed, contemplating what to do. She looked at her cell phone—no calls.

Where was McGaven's call?

Katie pressed his number and waited.

"I wondered why it took you so long," he said.

"I can't sleep anymore."

"And you are dying to know what's going on?"

"Uh, yeah."

She could hear him laugh.

"Good news or bad?"

"What do you mean?" he said.

"Good or bad. Which is it?"

"Uh, good, I guess."

Katie closed her eyes with relief. She had thought that the sheriff might take her off the cases. "What does that exactly mean?"

"You decent?"

"Most of the time."

"I'll be there in ten, maybe twelve minutes."

"Okay." She felt relieved as she got out of bed.

"And Katie? I want one of those sandwiches Denise made for you."

"Done."

The phone disconnected.

CHAPTER FOURTEEN

THURSDAY 1645 HOURS

Katie had just enough time to change into sweatpants and a hoodie. She ran a brush through her hair and pulled it back in a long ponytail.

The doorbell rang.

Cisco barked, but then began to whine happily as he realized who it was waiting.

Katie hurried barefoot to the front door and opened it. McGaven stood patiently waiting and holding a banker's box.

"Hey," she said. "I think it took you longer than twelve minutes." She pushed the door wider and he walked through to the kitchen where he put the box on the bar counter.

"I didn't take into consideration having to pack up this box."

"All for me?"

"For the investigation," he corrected.

Katie took out a couple of sandwiches from the fridge and poured two glasses of iced tea. She set them down and took a seat, eyeing the contents of the box and longing to ask questions.

"Okay, first things first. How are you feeling?" McGaven said.

"I'm fine. Really."

"Hmm. I think I believe you. You look better, more rested."

Katie reached into the box to grab a file, but McGaven stopped her. "Not yet."

"What? You're killing me here." She smiled.

"Let's eat first."

"Fine."

"I'll give you the sheriff's version, okay?"

Katie took a bite of her turkey club sandwich and nodded.

McGaven had already taken two bites. "Damn, this is the best sandwich."

"I know... I think it's the cream cheese mixture with fresh herbs."

"Denise is magical." He sat back and gathered his thoughts. "Okay, we are officially working the three cases from Eagle Ridge Camp."

Yes... thought Katie.

"However, we will probably need backup. There's quite a bit of background stuff, interviewing friends and families and so forth. And there's quite a bit of work tracing the victims' last twenty-four to forty-eight hours. The sheriff stipulated this."

"And?"

"Well, here's what we know today." He opened a file folder. "I've updated our board, so we can hit the ground running tomorrow."

Katie drank her iced tea. She hadn't realized how thirsty she was. "Are there appointments set up?"

"Don't get ahead of me." He read from the paperwork. "They've officially identified one of the victims, but the other two will be forthcoming."

"And?"

"The woman that was first found floating in the lake along the dock was identified by one of her colleagues as Carolyn Sable, forty. She worked as an assistant for an investment broker, the name of the firm is..." He shuffled through the papers. "Fields, Campbell and Associates. She worked there six years."

"And her time at Eagle Ridge?"

McGaven nodded. "Yes, she was a counselor for three summers when she was going to college, making that twenty-plus years ago."

Katie thought about Carolyn Sable working as a counselor every summer in between school. "I wonder why she didn't go into a profession like teaching or something that dealt with kids?"

"Don't know. But we have plenty of people to ask, including her colleagues at work."

Katie was quiet.

"What's your first instinct?"

"I don't want to get ahead of ourselves. But we need to check the backgrounds of the other victims, when we get IDs, to find out what their connection is, if any, to Eagle Ridge Camp."

McGaven nodded in agreement.

"Was Carolyn married?"

"No. She broke up with her boyfriend about six months ago."

"Hmm."

"Hmm what?" he asked.

"We need to check the status of the boyfriend."

"The report was brief, but basically they cleared him. His name... Lenny Dickson, local mechanic with a clean record, except two speeding tickets in the last two years."

"Mechanic, speeding. I can see that." She sighed and set her glass down. "So she was found by a real estate agent and his clients two months after she was reported missing, at the place she worked summers about twenty years ago?"

"That about sums it up."

"Until the other women have been identified, we need to work on everything about Carolyn Sable."

"Agreed."

"And we have to wait for the reports from forensics and Dr. Dean." Katie felt a surge of energy. She finally felt that she had something to dig into. She grabbed a few more files.

"Okay," said McGaven, stuffing the last bite of sandwich into his mouth. "I have some more things to line up before tomorrow. This..." he patted the box, "is your homework to get you up to speed on everything we have so far. I think John emailed you photos from each crime scene as well."

"Great," she said. "Let's start at the beginning..." She was already lost in reading the reports and the missing persons report on Carolyn Sable.

"We have a meeting with Daniel Green, the real estate agent, in the morning at Red Hawk Real Estate."

"Think he's suspicious?"

"I think we'll have to wait and see," he said, smiling. He stood up ready to leave.

"Oh, one more thing."

"Yeah."

"Who owns the Eagle Ridge Camp?" she said.

"It's some kind of big conglomerate, KLM Enterprises. They are known for buying up areas to build luxury condos and entertainment venues, things like that. I'm still working on it."

"I see."

McGaven headed for the door.

"Oh, one final thing."

He turned. "Again?"

Katie smiled. "Thank you for bringing all this... and for taking care of Cisco... and, you know..."

He smiled. "Yeah, I know. See you tomorrow, Detective."

"See you in the morning—Detective," she said. It was funny getting used to McGaven's promotion from deputy to detective.

He let himself out and quietly closed the door behind him as Katie began studying and sifting through the reports.

.   .   .

"Katie..."

Katie sat up on the couch with a jolt from a sound sleep—she must've dozed off while she was reading through the reports. She thought she had heard someone call her name. It was almost completely dark in her living room, only one lamp shining. She had spread paperwork all over her coffee table and the other end of the couch—neat stacks in chronological order of when things happened.

She had learned that Carolyn Sable had distanced herself from her family years ago and that she had taken many courses at the local community college over the past ten years in finance, nursing, and information technology. She had left Eagle Ridge Camp under a mutual agreement between the two parties, but Carolyn hadn't been happy about it. Katie knew that they would need to find out anything more they could about the camp.

Eagle Ridge Camp kept gnawing at Katie—there was something that she was missing. Whenever she felt this way, she always retraced her steps and started again at the beginning. She opened her laptop, waiting for it to load her computer programs, and typed out several search words: *Eagle Ridge Camp, Pine Valley, Events, News, 20+ years ago.* She waited a moment and hundreds of pages listed in front of her. Most results were events and crime statistics in the Pine Valley area along with announcements for politicians and new business grand openings. She kept scrolling for more than ten pages until she found two old articles about an accident at Eagle Ridge Camp.

BOY LOSES HIS LEG FROM TRAGIC ACCIDENT AT EAGLE RIDGE CAMP

CHILDREN CAUGHT IN SUDDEN RAINSTORM AT EAGLE
RIDGE CAMP—BOY LOSES LEG IN TERRIBLE ACCIDENT

Katie felt a shockwave rattle through her body. She didn't
remember hearing about the accident when she was young. But
as she read through the articles she realized that she had found
an event that could have triggered what happened at Eagle
Ridge Camp and the investigation—or that was at least worth
looking into.

The name of the young boy was ten-year-old Brian Stanwick. One of the articles explained that he had aspired to
become a doctor after his mother had died from cancer when he
was only three years old. It also stated that his father, Graham
Stanwick, thirty-five, worked in construction. Brian didn't have
any siblings and the articles didn't mention any other relatives.

Katie paused. She realized that this was important information and a possible missing link in her investigations, but was
confused why the incident, or any information about Brian
Stanwick, had been buried under so many other articles. He
had lost his left leg, a kidney, and partial use of his left hand. It
had been a horrific event, but no one seemed to remember it. Or
did they want to forget it? Who knew what else had been
forgotten? She realized then that they were just scratching the
surface of the secrets of Eagle Ridge Camp.

Katie rapidly keyed up several other search sites and stared
at the photo of a young boy with a huge smile and thick hair
partially covering his eyes. "Where are you now, Brian Stanwick?" she asked herself as she scrolled through the usual areas,
but there was nothing that matched a Brian Stanwick in the
Pine Valley area for his approximate age. She expanded her
search, but could find no one to fit the parameters.

"Brian Stanwick," she said again. Her thoughts jumped to
her best friend Jenny. Many times when she was searching for

people or looking up backgrounds, especially children, her mind would remind her of Jenny years ago.

Katie tried several more searches but couldn't find anything more about where Brian Stanwick was today. This nagged at her. There had to be something to find out and she needed to talk to him.

Where are you, Brian?

Katie's eyes grew weary again. Her arm ached. It was time to change her bandages.

Cisco grumbled beside her but stayed curled up in the chair as she got up, stiff from sitting so long.

Katie turned on lights as she passed through her room to the bathroom. Carefully unwrapping her bandages, she studied the injury. Everything looked normal, no more discoloration or weeping from the wound. She put on the ointment that the hospital had prescribed for her and then wrapped new bandages.

A clunk noise came from her bedroom. Katie walked back into her room and looked around to see what could have made that sound. Everything was in its place. Walking up to her dresser, she noticed that one of her framed photographs had fallen forward and was now facing down.

Katie picked up the photo. It was a shot of her and Chad at Eagle Ridge Camp when they were nine years old. They were standing near the dock at the boathouse and each held a fishing pole. Their smiles were infectious and the happiness was clear on their faces. It was one of Katie's favorite photos and she remembered that day well. She had actually caught two more fish than Chad. She smiled, but the smile soon faded as the realization of what had happened at Eagle Ridge since that carefree day sunk in.

CHAPTER FIFTEEN

Katie hurried through the parking lot at the Pine Valley Sheriff's Department, dressed for work in her usual pantsuit, carrying the banker's box with her good arm. It felt good to get back to her work routine and she had slept well, giving her plenty of energy to move ahead.

Two uniformed officers exited the back entrance and nodded their greetings. Katie grabbed the door before it closed and then walked quickly down the hallway.

As she always did, she paused at the entrance to the forensics department for a moment and glanced up at camera lens just above her to the right before swiping her ID. The door buzzed and popped open. It was her own personal ritual to focus her mind before she went down into the basement to work.

She headed down the corridor and almost ran into John who was coming round a corner.

"Hey," he said. "How are you?"

"I'm fine. Thanks."

"You really scared the crap out of all of us."

"I know... I'm sorry, but I'm back now and fine, ready to get to work."

"Take it easy, okay?" he said, moving aside to let her pass.

"I will. Balancing the workload with three homicide crime scenes is complicated. Can't wait for some good news in forensics."

"I'm working on it. I'll let you know soon."

Katie moved on and found her office door open. McGaven was sitting at his usual station tapping at the laptop keyboard.

"Morning," she said, placing the banker's box on her desk.

"Good morning," he said. "You look rested. How do you feel?"

"I feel good. Now let's catch this killer."

"You up to it?"

"Always. But I might need some coffee along the way." She laughed.

"The sheriff gave me strict orders to make sure you don't get overtired."

"Got it."

"He wasn't kidding around. If anything happens to you I think he'd lock me up and throw away the key."

Removing the box lid and retrieving case folders, Katie looked at McGaven. "Let's make sure that doesn't happen. Did you get my email about Brian Stanwick?"

"Yes. And I'm trying to locate him or anyone related to him, but running into some brick walls," he said. "Also, I sent information upstairs to Denise about the staff at Eagle Ridge Camp. I'll have her pull up everything about the camp, especially photos, news stories, and hopefully any employment records that were missed. We'll see what shakes out."

"Great idea. Denise is great at finding things like that."

McGaven had neatly printed out what they already knew, which left room on the board for new information as it became available. The whiteboard was used for listing the victims, statements, crime scene characteristics, and signatures for the ultimate result of identifying the most likely killer. They also pinned up photographs and various crime scene discoveries.

Katie studied their wall of investigative evidence.

"Anything unusual or newsworthy that happened while they were there can go up," McGaven said.

"Like my best friend Jenny Daniels going missing."

McGaven remained quiet for a few moments. There was a silent sadness in the office that couldn't be overlooked. He finally answered slowly. "Yeah, like Jenny Daniels." He stopped typing and studied his partner. "This must be so difficult for you."

"Gav, things happen to everyone. But I have to admit being back at Eagle Ridge Camp has been like seeing ghosts. The murder of Jenny has been one of the defining moments of my life. It was one of the reasons why I became a police officer. I guess it was a way for me to help—to be a part of something important that's bigger than me."

"It didn't cross my mind that going up to the camp would be so difficult for you. I'm sorry about this."

"It's okay, really. But it's rattled some things loose that I thought I'd put to rest."

McGaven looked at his partner and patiently waited.

"It always bothered me how Jenny was taken—without anyone seeing anything. It turned out to be her own father who murdered her and dumped her body, which makes it even worse. But why didn't anyone at the camp see anything at all that day?"

"Sometimes, there are things that happen that we can't explain—and we have to live with it."

Katie nodded, knowing that McGaven was right. "Maybe working these cases will somehow help me finally put the events surrounding Jenny's case to rest."

"I hope so," he said.

Katie tried to bring her mind back to the present. "We need to do a search of anything else that happened at the camp that would be considered newsworthy."

"On it." He glanced at his watch. "But right now we need to get to Red Hawk Real Estate. You up for it?"

Katie grabbed her small notebook and jacket. "Let's go see what Daniel Green has to say."

Katie and McGaven sat in brightly colored molded plastic chairs watching the receptionist annoyingly pop her gum as she entered data from a pile of paperwork. Her blonde hair was pulled back with cute, flowered barrettes that matched her equally cute pink sweater.

The telephone buzzed. The receptionist picked up and said, "Yes? Of course, I'll send them in." She hung up. To Katie and McGaven, "You can go in now."

Katie rose and headed down a long hallway lined with windows and doors. There were well- dressed people having meetings in three of the offices. Everything was decorated in a swank, high-end style. It appeared the office spared no expense for décor and office furniture.

A tall man with dark hair exited his office when he saw them pass. "Detectives?" he said.

"Mr. Daniel Green?" said Katie.

He nodded. "Please, come in." Waiting until Katie and McGaven had entered, the agent closed the door and walked back to his desk. He awkwardly bent down to pick up a pen as if he had a bad back.

"You okay?"

"Yeah, I strained my back playing golf."

Katie paused for McGaven to do the introductions since he was taking lead on this one.

"Mr. Green, I'm Detective McGaven and this is Detective Scott. Thanks for seeing us on such short notice."

"No problem. Please have a seat."

As Katie took her seat, she glanced around the oversized office filled with a couch, coffee table, and two large free-standing bookcases decorated with a half dozen plants. On Mr. Green's desk were two piles of paperwork—one had closed escrow files and the other looked to be offers on specific properties. She could see the address 10020 Eagle Ridge, which was Eagle Ridge Camp. There were two property files that had been opted for demolition that were sitting in a separate pile, which had red labels with the word "DEMO" affixed on the front.

"We won't take up much time," began McGaven, flipping through his notes. "You were the one that found the body."

Mr. Green looked down at his desk and said, "Yes. I'm not going to forget that image anytime soon."

"According to your statement you said that you and Mr. and Mrs. Faulkner heard a noise coming from the boathouse."

"Yes. It was a strange bumping sound, so I went inside. Then I saw this thick rope, which seemed odd to me. So I leaned down to the water, pulled it, and the body floated up towards me."

Katie watched him carefully as he spoke. To her, he seemed to be a bit rehearsed; genuinely nervous, but there were very slightly exaggerated movements.

"What did you do then?" asked McGaven.

"I was stunned for a moment, then Mrs. Faulkner ran off and I asked Mr. Faulkner to call the police. It took a while for them to come up. We were anxious and wanted to leave as soon as possible."

"Had you ever showed the property before?" said Katie.

"Yes, a couple of times. But it's been a while." He keyed up a few commands on his computer and a printer buzzed across the room. Rising from his desk, he walked to the printer to retrieve the documents and handed them to McGaven.

"This list shows the dates and clients who have seen the property."

"Thank you," said McGaven.

"So it's not your listing?" said Katie.

"No. I don't have listings often. My clients rely on me finding them investment properties—whether I listed them or not. I find them the property that fits their investment needs."

"Any offers on the camp?" she asked.

"No, not yet. I thought the Faulkners would be good candidates based on their income and interests. But now, well..."

"We tried to reach out to them, but they seem to be out of the country," McGaven said. "They agreed to answer a few questions through an attorney here in California."

"Yes. They had a trip booked to France and I don't blame them for going through with it. I'm not looking forward to visiting the camp again anytime soon."

"I would assume you have some renderings or potential plans of what that property could be used for," said Katie, watching him closely as he fiddled with his hands, intertwining his fingers and releasing them.

"Normally we would. But this property hasn't generated enough interest yet for that type of expense, I'm afraid. Maybe now might be a good time to have it done."

"I see," she said. "In your experience, what would you envision?"

Leaning back, showing a more relaxed demeanor, he said, "Me personally, I think it should be developed into luxury condos with onsite stores, restaurants, and spa. Like a smaller version of Vail, Colorado."

"It's a beautiful property," she said. "Such amazing views."

"Absolutely. But it's going to take some serious vision, work, and money to turn it into something that meets those kind of expectations."

"Do you have any information about the legal owners?"

"KLM Enterprises, LLC," said McGaven, making sure that the real estate agent knew they had already done their homework.

"I don't have anything in these files. I've only been contacted by them through email." He picked up the phone and called through to reception. "Lindsey, can you copy the seller's contact information on the Eagle Ridge Camp property? The detectives will pick it up on their way out. Thanks."

"Thank you," said McGaven.

"Anything else?" said Mr. Green. He seemed suddenly rushed as he glanced at his watch.

"Not for now," said McGaven as he rose.

"Oh," said Katie. "Has there ever been anything that might be construed as a problem with the property?"

"Meaning?"

"Like someone complaining about its potential development, or an angry client or neighbor. Anything that relates to that property that you can think of?" she probed as she thought about Brian Stanwick's accident.

The real estate agent looked shocked by the question, but he quickly composed himself. "No. Not that I can think of—"

"One more question. How long have you been in real estate?"

"It's been close to ten years now."

"Are you from this area?"

"Yes. I grew up here," he said stiffly.

"Thank you for your time," she said.

Katie followed McGaven to the door. Mr. Green didn't rise from his desk or show them the way out. He didn't even look at them as they walked back down the hallway.

McGaven retrieved the papers at the front desk.

While he was doing so, Katie glanced around the foyer again. She couldn't help but feel they were being watched. She saw in her peripheral vision there were small cameras in the corners of the reception and one positioned to view down the hallway.

As soon as they reached the unmarked police sedan, McGaven turned to Katie. "Did you get the feeling that they were more interested in studying us than we were them?"

"They certainly had a lot of cameras for a real estate office. You'd think they were protecting something extremely valuable," she said.

"Information is the most valuable thing these days."

"Do you think Mr. Green is hiding something?"

"What makes you think that?" he said, studying his partner carefully.

"Think about it. He found a dead body floating in the boathouse while he was showing his clients around. That's a pretty shocking event for anyone, but he was rather calm today. Like, no big deal..." Katie scanned the parking lot wondering if there were cameras here too. "And he never asked who she was, or what we think happened to her. Most people would."

McGaven thought a moment. "You're right. It does seem strange, but everybody processes news like this differently."

"True. It could just be the company in general. Maybe they're into something illegal, but my bet is that Mr. Green is hiding something—whether personal or professional." Katie opened the passenger door and got in. "What's next?" she said with a big smile.

McGaven turned the key as the sedan roared to life. "Is that a trick question?"

"Interviews?"

"Yesterday, I tracked down Carolyn Sable's ex-boyfriend, Lenny Dickson, and he works at Harrison Auto Repair. He'll meet us tomorrow. Carolyn's boss and half the staff from Fields, Campbell and Associates are at a conference. So they'll have to wait."

"So now it's back to the scene of the crime?"

"Road trip."

CHAPTER SIXTEEN

Katie and McGaven made a quick stop back at the department to pick up Katie's Jeep. The road leading up to Eagle Ridge Camp may have been cleared and flattened, but her SUV was still more suited to the journey than McGaven's car.

Katie was quiet for most of the drive as she held the steering wheel with force, taking in the picturesque views around her as they made their way toward the camp. She never tired of the trees, which seemed to grow in size the higher the elevation. Some were clustered closely together, others grew with open spaces in between. The blue sky, devoid of clouds, accented the range of greens amid the gentle rolling hills.

The nearer they got to the camp, the tenser she became. Her fingers gripped the steering wheel, causing her sore arm to ache. Why was being near the camp making her as anxious and uncomfortable as she once had felt on the battlefield, waiting for the next attack?

She forced herself to focus on the first victim, Carolyn Sable. Where had she been for the two months she'd been missing? Had she been held hostage? Did she want to disappear by her own free will? Or had she been trying to hide and stay away from the very person who killed her?

"You okay?" said McGaven who had been watching her.

"I'm fine."

"You look really tense."

"My arm hurts a little bit. They gave me pain meds, but I opted out. I want to stay sharp."

"Are you sure that's all it is?" he said.

Katie maneuvered the SUV around a large chuckhole and they were on the last leg of the journey before they reached the camp. "No matter how hard I try, this place doesn't sit well with me."

"I can understand that."

"You see, that's just it. I have great memories here... being with my friends... and with Chad. Learning archery and canoeing. Look at it. It's a beautiful place. And the views take your breath away..."

"Archery. Should I be concerned?"

She laughed. "I loved everything about this place as a kid." She pulled the Jeep into the open area and saw a white pickup truck parked near the main entrance. "Was anyone supposed to be here?"

"Oh," said McGaven.

"Oh what?" She looked at him.

"I forgot to tell you."

"Tell me what?" she sighed. "Who *is* that?"

"A security guard."

"A security guard? Like a caretaker or something?" She turned off the engine and waited for McGaven to explain this new development.

He turned to her. "The sheriff thought it was a good idea to have someone here to watch the place. The department hasn't officially released the property, since it's still an active investigation. The watch commander was able to contact an attorney for

KLM Enterprises to let them know that it's considered an active crime scene under police jurisdiction. Sheriff Scott wanted someone with eyes up here until we release the area."

Katie shrugged. "That's a good idea."

"I think so."

"Do we have a name for someone at the law firm?" she said.

"A liaison of sorts who is working on behalf of KLM. I have the name back at the office—Charles something. Abbott. Charles Abbott."

Looking at the truck, she said, "And who is the security guard?"

"His name is Bud."

"Bud?"

"Clarence Johnson."

"That name..." she began.

"Here's the thing. He was that police officer who was shot during an armed robbery a while back—he then retired early. He's been a security guard for various equipment locations for the sheriff's department. He's staying in one of the cabins for the next two weeks or so."

"Not much here for comfort," she said.

"He's got a generator."

Katie shrugged. "Okay. Let's go say hello to Bud and let him know someone is here. Wouldn't want to get hit by friendly fire."

She quickly changed her shoes, pulled on a hoodie and made sure that she had extra magazines for her firearm.

Katie closed her Jeep up tight and followed the path toward one area of cabins, which was on the south side of the main buildings. She noticed that the path was much easier to see now that so many people had already trampled it. She saw immediately the one that Bud had holed up in. It was cabin 1 and it had now been cleared of weeds and the windows and door were open—obviously airing out the interior.

"Hello?" she called out. "Detectives Scott and McGaven."

Katie and McGaven stopped before entering the cabin. Each felt acutely aware of their surroundings.

"Hello? Bud, you around?" she called again.

"Hey, Bud," said McGaven as he slowly entered the cabin looking around. "He's not here."

Katie followed her partner inside, glancing behind her as she went.

The room had been upgraded from its grim abandoned existence to a camping-like environment. There was a foldout cot, two small tables, a folding four-foot desk, and chair. A small propane two-burner stovetop along with many packets of freeze-dried foods was neatly fixed on the corner. A dozen gallon bottles of water were neatly stacked next to it. There were two lanterns—one on each table. Two oversized duffel bags in the corner. One was unzipped revealing extra clothes.

"Cozy," she said, wondering what type of weapons he had. She saw a wire running along the floor and up the corner —disappearing.

"I like it," came a voice from the door. "Great views and plenty of fresh air. And no boss hovering around." A heavyset man dressed in casual fatigues and wearing a sidearm stood at the entry and studied them. His hair had been trimmed close, but his grayish mustache and beard were abundant.

"Detectives McGaven and Scott," said McGaven.

"Ah yes. Been following you two."

Katie thought that was a strange thing to say. She remembered the printer copies of their cases in the plastic sheet protectors in cabin 3. "Why is that?" she said.

"Why not? You two realize that you've been solving cold cases—and stopping some serial killers. Right?" He laughed.

"We're just doing our jobs," said McGaven grinning.

"Ain't that so." He walked into his cabin and reached for something beneath his thin cot mattress and retrieved a laptop computer. "I thought you might want to see this. The sheriff has been briefed with copies—you guys need it too."

Katie moved closer to Bud. Her interest had been piqued and now she was in complete investigation mode.

"I have three wildlife cameras set up. Really could use more, but I think that I set them up strategically." He inserted some type of wifi device for wireless connection. "Great thing up here is that the satellite signal is about ninety percent active. But some of the buildings must have something that interferes with reception because I can't get a signal in a few places."

"Is this just from the past two days?" said Katie, ignoring his explanation of places with signals or not.

"Yes, ma'am. That's why they wanted someone up here. This place has been considered haunted. Others say it's a place where loot has been buried from robberies. There are lots of things they say happens up here. That's why a killer's dumping ground doesn't surprise me."

Katie noticed that Bud's left hand was deeply scarred and he walked like he had an injury. She had been a teenager when his shooting had occurred but remembered her uncle talking about the incident.

Bud put up the three camera angles on a split screen and moved to saved data. "Okay, camera one is in the area where you stumbled in the trap, camera two is near the main cabin area, and camera three is where the utility road merged into this property."

Katie leaned in to see the video images.

"Okay, here's camera one."

Katie and McGaven watched the black-and-white image fast forward until a man—clean shaved, maybe thirty or forty years old—dressed in dark clothing with a hood pulled up over his head, moved around the trees and overgrown bushes near the trap as if he was looking for something. His arms moved erratically as if he was angry and it appeared that he was talking.

Katie leaned in closer and realized that the person was talking to himself. "What's he saying?" she said softly.

"Got me. We don't have audio."

Almost as soon as he appeared, he was gone again. His search had been unsuccessful.

"Any more sightings of this person?" she asked.

"No, ma'am. Timestamp is from 0315 last night. But I make sure when I make my rounds, they're around the crime scene areas and the back utility road entrance."

"Can you email this video to me?" asked McGaven.

"Sure thing. Email address?"

McGaven scribbled down his work address on a piece of paper. "Thanks."

"We're going to have a look around," said Katie. "There isn't anything else we need to be aware of—is there?"

"Nope. Everything is as you left it." He handed McGaven a key ring with several keys dangling from it. "Here you go, in case you want to go into any of the buildings."

"Thanks, Bud. I'll get these back to you before we leave."

"Oh, Detective Scott," he said. "It's a real pleasure to meet you. And I wanted to thank you for serving our country."

Katie was taken back, but she nodded her appreciation.

"It's a great honor to be working with you—even though I'm just guarding the crime scenes."

"Thanks, man," said McGaven.

Katie and McGaven left the cabin.

Once they were out of earshot of the security guard, McGaven said, "So?"

"So what?" she replied, and smiled for the first time since they had begun their shift.

"Thoughts?"

"About Bud?" she guessed.

He nodded, watching her closely as they walked down the path toward the lake.

She sighed. "My first instinct is that I don't trust him. That's not an answer—but I don't trust anyone right now around this place. That's not really any type of evidence, though."

"I see."

Katie couldn't read McGaven's thoughts by his body language. "I think it's the articles about us that were left at the third crime scene that have left me a bit unsettled."

"You don't think he's the killer?"

"No, not at this point," she said. "I just think he's a bit shifty —too eager maybe. He seems to be enamored with stories of this place—not facts—he's not acting like an ex-police officer."

"And?"

"I want to remind you that my gut isn't evidence that will hold up in court."

"It should be," he said and smiled.

"I get the distinct impression he knows more about this place than he says, but covers it with ghost stories."

CHAPTER SEVENTEEN

Eagle Lake was one of the most majestic lakes that Katie had ever seen. There was something almost magical about it. The way the current was non-existent, leaving the surface smooth as glass. Even when you went swimming or canoeing the gentle ripples multiplied in glossy rings, becoming larger until they completely dissipated. The effortless feeling you experienced when you ventured out in it.

Katie and McGaven stood at the shore watching the birds fly over and then disappear into the trees.

Breaking the moment of beauty, Katie said, "Why would the killer dump a body here?"

"Because he can. There's no one around for miles. He hoped that no one would find them."

"I'm afraid you're right."

McGaven turned toward the boathouse. "Mr. Green said they were drawn to the body by a strange bumping sound. You think that's right?"

Katie nodded. "All three of them corroborated each other's statements. But now I'm thinking: how did the body move from the outer lake area over to the boathouse dock?"

"And what about the echo?" he asked. Then, "HELLO!"

His voice echoed all around them, over and over, and then it finally quieted.

"When they heard that bumping, how did they know it was coming from the boathouse?" asked Katie.

"What else could it be?"

She walked back around and down a short trail which led to the boathouse. The large door was askew and emitted a terrible screeching noise as she opened it. Inside was a long dock leading out toward the lake. She remembered way back when you could launch your canoe or kayak from there, but now it was long abandoned.

Katie stood unmoving as she tried to get her bearings. She remembered when the body had been removed from the water and was lying on the deck showing the serrated remains of the left arm. She closed her eyes to listen.

McGaven waited several steps behind her.

Katie opened her eyes and could immediately see from the fresh scuff marks and remnants of fingerprint dusting powder where the police and forensics had pulled the body out of the water.

"I need to see underneath the dock," she said.

"I'm not getting into the water."

Katie got down on her knees, next to the edge of the decking. She didn't immediately see anything. Leaning over carefully, she gently ran her hands along underneath feeling the jagged and rough areas. "I could see how the body could get caught up here, but..."

Towering over her, McGaven said, "I'm sensing a hesitation."

"How long would it take for the body to float from anywhere in the lake area to the boathouse?" She sat back, shaking her head.

"Meaning?"

"I'm wondering if the body was put here on purpose. I know there are winds, sometimes gusty, that could move a body, but I think..."

"How long would that take?"

"It's about the same time of day as when the body was found by Mr. Green and his clients, right?"

"Yeah, about. But why would the killer drop the body right here?" he said and gestured to the dock area.

"Effect."

"I'm not following."

"Maybe the killer wanted the body here," she said.

"Why would he do this?"

Katie turned to McGaven. "Because he was watching."

CHAPTER EIGHTEEN

Katie and McGaven walked around the clusters of cabins. They were in groups of three and four all around the main buildings. Most were in desperate need of repair of the sidings, replacing of windows, and patching the roofs. They surveyed the areas where the cabins were located.

"You're still awfully quiet," said McGaven again. "Feeling okay?"

"I'm fine." She stood in front of cabin 3, scrutinizing the exterior which was in noticeably better shape than the others around it.

"Okay, what do we have? Three crime scenes. Boathouse. A booby trap. And cabin three."

"It's telling us that these three locations are important—or at least they have meaning to the killer." She paused a moment, turning slowly in three hundred sixty degrees. "The killer believes that *he's* in control—*complete* control." She paused to look more closely at the windows on cabin 3. There were the same scratch marks that they saw in the counselor's office. Retrieving her cell phone, she snapped several photos and then sent them to John.

McGaven studied them. "They do look the same as the ones in the counselor's office."

"I just sent them to John. Maybe he can compare them? Or then again, maybe they're nothing."

"What's bothering you, Katie?" he asked. His tone was serious. "You think there's going to be more bodies?"

"Yes. But... haven't you noticed that each crime scene we've seen—in order—has been more horrific than the last? First, a woman in the lake, then a woman in a booby trap, and then a woman missing internal organs. What does that mean to you?"

McGaven let out a sigh. "I see your point. How does the removing of body parts tie into the serial aspect?"

"I'm not sure—yet. But if you think about Brian Stanwick's injuries with the loss of a leg, injured wrist, and removal of a kidney..." Katie began walking toward the main building and looked around at the rest of the standing cabins.

"Let's check out the main area again, including the kitchen," he said almost as if he had read Katie's mind.

Something was bothering her about the main building, cafeteria, kitchen, and the lounge area. She couldn't pinpoint it, but she wanted to be thorough in her search. Not only did she want to reacquaint herself with the camp layout and the grounds, but she wanted to know it as well as the killer clearly did.

McGaven unlocked the main entrance double doors and they entered.

Katie stepped over the threshold first, slowing her pace. There was a smell she didn't remember from the previous visit. It was a type of commercial cleaning mixture with bleach, along with something else.

"You smell that?" said McGaven.

Katie nodded, wrinkling her nose. "Cleaning chemicals—and like, garbage."

"Yeah," he said. "I get that too." He opened the front doors wide to let some of the fresh air inside.

Katie kept her focus and followed the smell, which led to the kitchen area. She slowed her pace, not wanting to miss anything. "Someone has been here since our last visit."

"Bud?"

"I doubt that Bud would clean. He's ex-police, he knows better than that. Besides, there's no reason for him to do so."

"Still. I'm not sure..." McGaven's voice trailed off as he watched his partner.

Katie stepped into the large kitchen lacking appliances and fixtures. The yellowed linoleum was uneven and missing squares. There was an area where the floor was clean. It seemed odd. She knelt down, putting her fingers on one of the flooring tiles.

"Cleaning mixture. And it's recent."

McGaven looked around and opened some of the cupboards and closet areas. "Why?"

"Good question," she mused. Taking a step back, she studied the floor, then the walls, and finally the ceiling. There were rectangular tiles in the ceiling. Some inserts were missing, but there were about a dozen in the far corner above the clean tiles. A dark smudge smeared across one of the corners. To Katie, it appeared to be recent. She looked around. It had been swept by John during the last crime scene, but something was different since the search.

"What are you looking for?" he asked.

"Something to stand on."

Near the pantry area there was a prep table. Katie quickly dragged it over to the area under the ceiling tiles. She climbed up on the table, taking a moment to make sure it would hold her weight. It wobbled a bit.

"Here," said McGaven, stabilizing the table by gripping its sides.

Katie slowly stood up, keeping her legs wide to maintain her balance. She raised her arms up to one of the tiles. "Damn. I can't reach it."

"You don't want me on this table. I would crush it."

Katie swiftly looked at the room from corner to corner. "Over there. Bring me that broom handle."

McGaven retrieved the broken broom which was just long enough for Katie to reach the ceiling.

Katie focused her attention on the tile inserts above her. Dizziness wafted over her for a second, signaling her to take a deep breath. Gripped in her right hand, she pushed the broom handle against the tile. At first, it wouldn't budge, as if there was weight on top of it. Then she pushed the area from each corner until it began to give. Slowly at first, until... suddenly, it fell on to the table next to Katie, bringing down with it a clattering mess of body parts: an arm, a foot, and a couple heavy bloodied bags.

Katie swallowed hard keeping her nausea at bay as she stared at the mess around her.

The plastic bags were filled with internal organs, swarming with maggots and flies. The arm and foot that had hit the floor left dark red marks. They were partially decomposing, with blackened skin mixed with oozing, opaque gelatinous liquid.

McGaven was just as stunned as Katie.

"Don't move," she said, staring at the mess. "We need to try and preserve the evidence." She tried to move with great care in order to get down without touching or disturbing anything.

McGaven grabbed hold of her and gently lifted her down and away from the area.

They moved to the doorway and stared back at the cadaverous jigsaw.

CHAPTER NINETEEN

Katie, assisted by Bud, directed the CSI van to the closest parking area. McGaven met three sheriff's cruisers and directed the deputies to search the area by fanning out from the main building and reporting back on anything that looked recent or suspicious.

Katie met McGaven back at the entrance to the main building.

"Again, I didn't think that today would bring murder victims' limbs raining down on us."

"No, that definitely wasn't in my preliminary profile," she said. "The killer has been here—recently, after we'd recovered the bodies."

John approached, suited up and carrying two silver suitcases. "Hey, you guys sure know how to keep me on my toes."

"You don't have one of the techs with you?" asked McGaven.

"No. I have them working on a burglary case right now."

"Need an assistant?" asked Katie. She knew that it was the best way to see everything firsthand and to get a better understanding.

"Sure," said John, handing one of the suitcases to Katie.

"Yikes. Looking at body parts falling from the ceiling is enough for me. Don't want to see them again, thank you," said McGaven. "I'm going to check with Bud and see if his video cameras caught anything. Then I'll help the deputies search."

"Sounds good. We need to put in a request for more cameras." Looking around, she added, "We need them inside and outside all the buildings in this region. More at the entrances, or anywhere where someone could easily sneak into the area closest to the buildings."

"On it," he said and left the main building.

"Go grab some gear and protective wear from the van," said John.

"Got it," she said and performed a weak salute as she hurried to the forensics van.

After Katie returned to the kitchen, she brought John up to speed on exactly what had happened so that he could ascertain any contamination made by her and McGaven.

"Everything needs to be dusted for fingerprints," said John. "I've already contacted the medical examiner's office to have the appendages and organs properly packaged and returned to them for examination."

"And if they belong to our three victims?"

"You have any reason to believe that they won't?"

"Not sure. But the killer seems to be calling all the shots right now. I know that this room didn't have this cleaned floor or the parts tucked away in the ceiling tiles when we originally searched." Katie watched John begin his tedious search for prints. "It's as if the killer is a ghost."

"Why do you say that?"

"He seems to be able to move among us undetected."

"And how would the killer know that you would find them? You already searched this building, right?"

"Yes. But something made me want to look around again," she said.

"Good detective instincts."

"It's like our ghost is leaving a trail of breadcrumbs for us to follow." Her cell phone rang. It was her uncle, probably wanting to be briefed on the new situation. She answered. "Scott."

CHAPTER TWENTY

SATURDAY 1005 HOURS

Katie met McGaven in the Pine Valley Sheriff's Department parking lot. It was Saturday, which meant it was quiet around the administrative building. McGaven, dressed casually in jeans and a long-sleeved shirt, opened the passenger door and got in, tossing a file and a notepad on the backseat.

"Got you a large coffee," she said and handed the insulated to-go cup to him.

"Ah, you read my mind," he said sipping the hot drink. "I only had one small cup at the house."

Katie smiled as she drove out of the parking lot.

"What do you think Lenny Dickson is going to tell us about his relationship with Carolyn Sable?"

Katie shrugged. "At this point, it could be anything. If you had asked me last week, I would have said most likely nothing earth-shattering would happen on Friday."

"Well, we're going to find out today if every day will be like the day before." He reached for the file folders. "Okay, Harrison Auto Repair is the normal type of automotive place. No problems. Never had any investigations or lawsuits. Lenny Dickson has worked there for five years. His sheet is clean, never had any trouble except for the two speeding tickets."

"Was he cooperative when you called him?" she asked.

"I didn't talk to him. I spoke with the owner, Richard Harrison, and he said that Lenny would be working today."

"Didn't want him to think about what we're going to ask him?"

"I think we'll get the straight answers... or not." McGaven laughed. "Mechanics are usually hit or miss." He reread the report of everything they had for Carolyn Sable. "Go up to Third and then take a right," he said.

Katie was lost in her own thoughts, rerunning everything they had so far. It was definitely a strange set of circumstances. The profile that was slowly emerging, based on the killer's signature and modus operandi, indicated a difficult and complex motive. It was personal; there was no doubt to Katie. But did it make Brian Stanwick the killer? Was it something so personal that it deserved revenge years later? Why was the killer punishing the victims this way? Why the obsession with taking something from them, even after they were dead?

Katie took a turn into a long driveway that was steep and narrow towards a sign that said "Harrison Auto Repair."

"Have you been here before?" she asked.

"Nope. Not even on patrol. I've been down this street more times than I can count, but never had a call here."

The moderately sized auto garage was at the bottom of the road, with several parking places out front. Behind the building was unincorporated land, overgrown with trees and tall grass and surrounded by a partial chain-link fence. There were four garage doors open to the auto bays—two of them had cars, a dark sedan and a white SUV currently being worked on, hoods up. Two of the eight parking places were occupied by cars. There were several motorcycles alongside the building, including a mountain of a boneyard of auto parts.

"Charming place," muttered Katie, taking a scan of the property.

"It's a guy's place," said McGaven. "You know, a guy thing."

"I guess," she said, eying the mechanic stalls.

Katie and McGaven got out of the Jeep and headed to the service area. No one seemed to notice them. McGaven hung back to have a look around and to make sure they weren't surprised by anyone—or anything.

Katie walked slowly into the garage. She spotted a small empty office. On its window were the remnants of old advertisements of every type: from spark plugs to engine oil. The smell of mechanic's grease, tires, and motor oil filled the area.

She watched two mechanics hunched over, working on cars. One was a tall, heavyset man with a cap on backwards and the other was a slim man with cropped blond hair. She walked past the heavyset man and continued to the other mechanic. Based on his driver's license photo, this must be their man.

Katie stood behind and slightly to the left of him for a moment. He was cranking on something that she gathered had to do with replacing heavy bolts on one of the components of the engine.

"Mr. Dickson?" she asked finally.

"Yeah, who wants to know?" the man sniped, still with his back to her.

"Mr. Lenny Dickson?" she said with some sarcasm in her voice.

"Kinda busy," he said, but at least turned around toward her.

"Lenny Dickson?"

"Yeah." He looked her up and down. "You're gorgeous. A little bit skinny for my taste, though..."

Katie revealed her badge and gun. "I'm Detective Scott. I need to ask you a few questions about Carolyn Sable..."

Before Katie had finished her sentence, Lenny had thrown

down his tools and bolted from the garage like a professional sprinter.

Left without any choice, Katie took off after the man. "Stop! Police!" she yelled. She was annoyed and hoped he would stop —she hated foot pursuits.

She kept the pace as she raced around the garage building, but was surprised by how agile Lenny was as he made his way toward the dense rural area next to the auto garage. Swerving around old motorcycles, jumping over crates filled with small pieces of junk, he quickly managed to disappear into the trees.

Katie managed to keep Lenny's blue mechanic jumpsuit in her vision, which was in contrast with the greens and browns of the forest. His speed and confidence suggested to her that either he had done this before, or he'd had it all planned out in case of the need for a quick escape.

There was a well-worn path to the left of the way they were headed. Katie guessed there was a strong chance that the two paths would meet at some point, so she took a gamble and sprinted as fast as she could on to it. She could hear Lenny crushing through the brush and it appeared that her direction of travel paralleled his. She pushed her body harder, ignoring her aching arm and hoping that she wouldn't stumble and fall, wasting precious seconds.

The question kept pushing in her mind of why he would run like this. His background and police record had seemed to be clean.

Why was he running from the police?

Katie could see through the overgrown bushes glimpses of the dirty blue jumpsuit racing next to her. They were side by side. She had to cut him off otherwise he would be gone and they might not get another chance. He had his escape route and most likely would have his disappearing plans ready to go at any moment as well.

She just had moments... seconds... before she could ambush Lenny Dickson.

Three... winding around more brush.

Two... zigzagging around two large pine trees.

One... there he was...

Katie took her opportunity by making a sharp right turn, jumped a log and burst through a dead bush just as Lenny was charging by—she made a direct torso hit and took the mechanic down to the ground.

The mechanic was strong and a fighter as he slammed her onto her back. He didn't say a word, but looked as if he would beat her unconscious. Katie's arms were pinned so she mustered her strength and managed to knee him—not once but twice. He instantly stopped and fell to the side, gasping in agony.

Catching her breath, Katie pushed him face down with her knee between his shoulder blades. "Stay down!" Her arm ached and she was afraid that she had torn some of her stitches. She looked up as McGaven crashed through the last bundle of bushes breathing hard. "Took you long enough," she said.

"Yeah, well, you didn't say 'go.'"

"Give me your cuffs."

He gave her his handcuffs and she secured Lenny's wrists, pulling him up to his feet. "What's your problem?" she asked the mechanic, still breathing hard. "We just wanted to talk to you. You just couldn't handle that?" Her arm ached and her chest near her collar bone was also sore.

"I thought you were one of them," he said, still pale from the pain of being kneed in his groin.

Katie began walking back to the shop, directing him in front of her. "One of who?"

"I don't know. I never saw them."

"Did you hit your head? Because you're not making sense."

"I never saw who sent the notes. It's just..."

"What?" she said.

"They said bad things would happen if I talked to the cops. And then Carolyn disappeared and of course the cops thought I had something to do with it. Hounding me all the time."

Katie and McGaven walked Lenny back to the auto garage. "Let me get this straight," she said. "You received a note threatening you to not talk to the police?"

"Yeah, that's right."

Katie let out a sigh. "But you did talk to the police after Ms. Sable disappeared."

"And bad things happened. My motorcycle was stolen and then trashed. My garage was set on fire. And I know... I knew that someone had been following me."

"Did you file a police report?" said McGaven.

"No, genius. I wanted all this stuff to stop." He turned to Katie. "Look, I'm sorry if I hurt you, but I didn't know if you were one of them."

Katie glanced at McGaven and he nodded, knowing what she was thinking. "If I take these cuffs off, will you not run?"

"Yeah."

"Is there a private place where we can talk?"

"Yeah, the warehouse behind the garage," he said and walked ahead, taking a path between the tall weeds. There were crates and piles of cigarette butts alongside empty bottles of energy drinks and sodas. It was obviously the place where the employees took their breaks. "C'mon, this way."

They continued along the trail and then up several wooden steps held up by cement blocks. Katie bristled, thinking for a second that they could be being led into a trap. But Lenny unlocked the heavy padlock, opened the long metal doors and revealed a space which was much more organized inside than the outside. It appeared to be a large storage container.

Light spilled in from the high rectangular windows. A fan idly spun in each end keeping it comfortably cool.

Lenny walked to an area where there were several plastic chairs leaning up against the wall. He took two, unfolding them and putting them where the detectives could sit down. He pulled a metal chair from the corner and took a seat. Leaning forward, elbows on his knees, hands clasped against one another in partial fists, he said, "What do you want to know?"

Katie glanced at McGaven who stayed standing and casually looked around the warehouse while she sat down.

"First, I'm Detective Scott and that's my partner Detective McGaven."

Lenny nodded.

"You were in a relationship with Carolyn Sable?" she said.

"Yes. Two years, but we broke up more than six months ago."

"Which one of you wanted to break up?"

"She did. I wanted to work things out. Still do..." he said quietly.

Katie kept her voice even and glanced at McGaven who was surveying the area. "I'm sorry to tell you, but Carolyn Sable's body has been found at Eagle Ridge Camp."

Lenny sat up straight. "What?" he managed to say. "She's dead? When? How? And why was she at Eagle Ridge Camp?" His face clouded with grief as he fought back tears.

Katie studied the mechanic and felt his actions were honest and not played for effect. He was obviously shocked.

"This is an active investigation. I'll tell you what I can," she said.

"Okay."

"Her body was dumped in the lake at Eagle Ridge Camp. She was found Tuesday."

Lenny stood up and paced. "Why? Why would someone do that to her?"

"That's what we're trying to piece together. Can you answer some questions that might help us?"

"Anything I can."

"First, do you still have the threatening note?" She studied him closely, evaluating his body language, hands, and eye movements.

"I keep it with me." He reached into his pocket, taking out his wallet. After a moment, he carefully pulled out a folded piece of paper and handed it to Katie.

She opened it. In neat handwriting, it read: *Very bad things will happen if you talk to the cops. You will stay healthy only if you keep quiet.*

Katie used her cell phone to take a photo of it and gave it back to him. "When was the last time you saw her?"

"Uh, it was about two months ago. Before she disappeared."

"What was the reason for seeing her?"

"The same reason I always wanted to see her—to get back together with her again. I love her—loved. We met at a coffee place—The Last Cup." He tried hard to keep his composure.

Katie was familiar with the place. "Did she seem upset or frightened about anything?"

"No, not that I could tell. But she was adamant about not getting back together."

"Did she say anything to you about anything else? Think, Lenny—anything."

He shook his head as he thought about the question. "No, nothing. I'm sorry."

"Did she mention work? A friend? A neighbor? Anything?"

Lenny sat down again. "Uh, nothing. Wait... she did say that her work was going through some type of reorganization."

"Reorganization?"

"Yeah, that the partners were going to consolidate and all the assistants and secretaries were concerned, but Carolyn wasn't worried. She said her boss, Jake Fields, assured her that he couldn't get along without her."

"Was she having a relationship with her boss outside of work?"

"I... don't think so..."

"Anything she mentioned about home?"

"No, she liked living alone. She didn't mention anything—at least to me."

Katie stood up as McGaven met up with her. "Mr. Dickson, I would advise you to be careful and please call the police if anyone threatens you again."

Lenny nodded, but it wasn't clear to Katie if he would heed her advice.

"Mr. Dickson, we're not going to arrest you for your little stunt. But we may want to talk to you again. Here's my card," she said and left it on the chair.

Katie moved toward the entrance and felt the cool breeze pick up. McGaven caught up with her and waited.

"One more thing... Did you know that Ms. Sable was once a counselor at Eagle Ridge Camp?"

"Yes, I did."

"What did she say about it?"

"Not much, really. She loved working with the kids there, but she said the other counselors were sometimes a pain in the ass. There were politics she didn't like, I think that's what she said, and so she decided to move on. Besides, by then she was finishing college and wanted to get started in a new career."

"Thank you, Mr. Dickson."

"Please... please, Detective. Find her killer."

Katie nodded and hesitated before they left. She wanted to ask him more personal questions about Carolyn, but it most likely wasn't going to give her any new answers from what he had already told them.

After the detectives found their way back to the car, Katie thought about everything from the time they had arrived to leaving. She felt that Lenny Dickson wasn't the killer. But he maybe knew more than he was saying, which wasn't unusual for people close to homicide victims.

"Keys," said McGaven.

Katie tossed them to him. "Want to get behind the wheel?"

"I thought I'd give you a break."

"I'm fine," she said, knowing that her partner was worried about her. "It's going to take more than tackling a mechanic to keep me down."

They got into the car.

"How do you tackle like that? It's now the second time I've seen you do it. I've worked with guys that couldn't do it as well as you."

"I don't know," she said and shrugged her shoulders. "Gifted, I guess."

"I guess," he laughed.

"You think Lenny's telling the truth?" she asked.

"I do."

"As much as he can, I suppose."

"What do you mean?"

"I think there are some things that he's not telling us, not because he had anything to do with Carolyn Sable's death, but... there's something else going on. I think in his life—not Carolyn's."

"Something about the note?" he said looking at his cell.

"Yeah, the note doesn't fit."

"You need to check your phone," he said.

Katie retrieved her cell phone and realized she had inadvertently turned it off. "Tell me," she said as she waited for it to power up again.

"It's been a busy morning at the morgue. They have official IDs for victims two and three."

Katie looked at her phone with a text message from Dr. Dean the medical examiner:

Victim 2—Edith Crest, Victim 3—Stephanie Baxter.

"Finally, we have more to go on."

"I need more coffee if I'm going to the morgue to view more than one body."

CHAPTER TWENTY-ONE

After grabbing two strong cups of coffees to go, Katie and McGaven made their way back to the police department and to the morgue. The clues were piling up, but Katie didn't have a strong picture yet. She wanted to dig in and gather information about the other two victims. This part of the investigation was the most difficult—searching for new clues and developments where there wasn't a strong representation yet. Many theories flowed through Katie's mind, but only facts and a solid trail of evidence could lead them to the killer—or killers.

Soon she found herself standing in the main examination room of the morgue. It was larger than the other rooms and was also used for training purposes. Rows of seats were placed above the exam area so that students could view the procedures. The size and openness of the area made her feel somehow uncomfortable.

Two morgue technicians, dressed in their white uniforms along with clear facial shields, pushed the gurneys into the room. Both the bodies were covered with white sheets. The technicians left the room. Moments later, they reappeared pushing two more gurneys. One was for the third victim and the other... didn't look like there was anything on it resembling a body.

Katie was curious about the fourth gurney, but suddenly realized that it must hold the missing appendages and internal organs for review. She swallowed hard. Even seeing the bodies at Eagle Ridge Camp was horrifying, but standing in the bright fluorescent lighting, on cold tile floors, surrounded by stainless steel and the smell of the disinfectant made it even worse. Her feet felt bonded to the floor and a flood of anxious energy made it difficult to move. She could feel a slight trickle of perspiration run down the back of her neck.

She glanced at McGaven. He stood a few feet away to the side of her and it was clear that he felt the same discomfort too. His expression was grim, he was quiet, and he was fidgeting with his hands, a telltale sign that the situation bothered him. He had never taken to being in the morgue examining homicide victims, but had worked hard to conquer his discomfort.

Today Katie and McGaven both stood motionless, trying to concentrate on anything except what was under those sheets. They remained quiet as they waited for Dr. Dean to explain the findings.

Katie tuned out her immediate surroundings, distracting herself from the moment by going back through the interviews with Daniel Green and Lenny Dickson.

"Good afternoon, Detectives," said Dr. Dean as he rushed into the room. He was dressed in his usual attire which consisted of loose khaki shorts, yellow-and-pink Hawaiian shirt, and slip-on sneakers. His white overcoat was open and there were traces of blood around the sleeves and front. The chain that accompanied his reading glasses hung loosely around his neck.

"Hi, Dr. Dean," said Katie, almost not recognizing her voice which was slightly hoarse.

"I hear congratulations are in order, Detective McGaven."

He smiled and moved to the first gurney and picked up a file folder lying on the end just above the protruding feet.

"Thank you, sir," said McGaven.

"Lots to cover, I see," the doctor said.

Katie neared the first body and waited patiently. She had taken out her small notebook because she didn't want to miss or forget anything. Her first impressions were important to her, even though they would have complete autopsy reports.

"Here we have Carolyn Sable. She was immersed in water so her condition isn't the best," said Dr. Dean as he slowly unveiled the body.

Katie almost gasped out loud as she tried to stifle her reaction. Carolyn Sable's body was indeed in poor condition due to decomposition and water damage. Blackened flesh in grotesque clumps had ravaged her body, specifically her upper torso and legs. The missing left arm showed ragged torn flesh with parts of the shoulder bone present.

"Although she hadn't been in the water that long, it wasn't even twenty-four hours. I put her time of death at twelve to twenty hours before the time she was found."

"Dr. Dean, what was her cause of death?" said Katie.

"Cause of death is asphyxiation. Manner of death is homicide, but I'm sure you already knew that." The medical examiner said it so matter-of-fact that it was as if he was reciting a grocery list.

"We haven't been able to establish where she was murdered, but just the secondary crime scene in the lake," said Katie.

"I may have some promising news," he said. "Look at the strangulation marks. It wasn't done with a ligature, like the rope that was found with her. It was manual strangulation." He turned the victim's head and Katie and McGaven could see where thumbs had pressed against the front of her throat with the rest of the fingers behind.

"So the killer faced her when he strangled her," said Katie. "Did you find anything under her nails—I guess it would be under her right-hand fingernails?"

"No, nothing that would indicate that she fought. Strange, actually." He flipped through a few pages of the autopsy report. "No toxins, not much in her stomach. It appeared she had some type of salad—chicken, lettuce, and pecans—which was her last meal. Nothing unusual."

Katie studied Carolyn's neck. Just behind her ear was a strange indentation. "What's that?" She pointed.

"We weren't able to connect anything with that. Necklace, for example."

"It had to be something the killer had, like a ring."

"That's one observation, but it's too light an indentation to be able to match anything unless we had the actual object."

Katie was disappointed, but moved on to the real question. "What can you tell us about the removal of her left arm?"

"Have to say that it's not the first body I've examined that had an arm removed." He walked over to the fourth gurney and flipped back the sheet. There was a severed arm and foot with a partial calf. "I can tell you that this arm belongs to this woman," he said and gestured to Carolyn Sable's body.

"Was the arm removed post-mortem?" asked McGaven who had been quiet.

"Yes," said the medical examiner. "It was removed by someone with little, if any, experience in removing limbs."

"What type of instrument?"

"It's difficult to ascertain. There were several different marks, indicating that the killer tried to find the right cutting tool and clearly had a difficult time completing the task. I can't say with one hundred percent certainty, but it appeared that a sharp blade like that of something used to fillet fish, and then a larger blade like a hatchet was used—with chopping motions." He moved swiftly back to the body. "If you look here, the larger blade was used to break the shoulder joint that's why it looks so mutilated. It was like the killer pried the arm from the shoulder and then finished it off with a heavier cutting instrument."

Katie jotted down a few notes. She asked Dr. Dean about any foreign or microscopic evidence.

"We've done scrapings and combings, which we sent to John. He should be able to tell you more about any evidence found from that."

Dr. Dean moved to the second and third bodies. He seemed to be a little rushed, so Katie tried to quickly ask questions from the official autopsy report. She knew they had to hit the ground running if they were to find the other camp counselor before they were called to a new homicide crime scene.

Glancing at his watch, Dr. Dean said, "I'm sorry to be in such a hurry, but I have two appointments this afternoon that I don't want to be late for. I usually enjoy answering your questions, but today, I'm afraid, you'll have to be brief. A copy of the autopsy reports has been sent to you both. But of course, if you have any questions after you've read them, please feel free to contact me anytime."

"Thank you, Dr. Dean. Any time you can give us now is greatly appreciated," said Katie.

"I have to say that these autopsies were for the most part straightforward," he said.

Katie thought that strange, since the victims had all been maimed in some way.

Dr. Dean seemed to sense Katie's skepticism and elaborated. "More specifically, all three of these bodies suffered death by asphyxiation, rather than strangulation, and they are all indeed homicides." He uncovered the victim from the booby-trap hole, now identified as Edith Crest. "The same markings were made by human hands around her neck."

Katie leaned closer where she viewed the almost exact

marks around Edith Crest's neck that she'd seen on Carolyn Sable's.

Dr. Dean methodically uncovered the third victim, now identified as Stephanie Baxter. "Again, it's almost identical to the first two women."

Katie's thought was that it was unusual that the killer was comfortable using his hands to choke his victims facing the front. In her experience, most strangulations seemed to occur as a last resort or from behind.

What made this killer so comfortable facing his victims?

Did the killer know the women intimately or was it part of his signature—his fantasy?

McGaven moved to each victim and studied the marks on the necks. With little expression, he remained silent but it was clear that he was digesting all the information and trying to imagine who the killer could be.

Dr. Dean indicated the second gurney. "The second victim, Edith Crest, had several broken bones post-mortem—left ulna, clavicle, and right wrist. It's not entirely clear if they were sustained during the removal of the left foot, which was severed just above the ankle area. She had been dead no longer than forty-eight hours before you found her." He moved closer to the body's missing appendage. "Look at these ghastly wounds. As with Carolyn Sable, it's clear that the person who removed the foot had not a clue what they were doing. It's such a muddled mess of skin, ligaments, and bone fragments that the killer could have used anything that you might find in a garage."

Katie studied Edith Crest, the woman that was dropped into a pit. She couldn't help but notice that she was similar in build, age, and hair color to Carolyn Sable. There was a small tattoo of a yellow flower on her left shoulder. Looking at her wounds and missing foot, she said, "Would something found in an auto garage make these types of tearing?" She was thinking about Lenny Dickson and his access to various tools at work.

"I have to be honest. I couldn't say yes or no, but anything could have been used. And by appearances, there was most likely more than one tool, probably two or three."

Katie took everything Dr. Dean told her in. The thought of a killer using any type of tool he could get his hands on was disturbing. More importantly, how did it add to the profile? She thought that this killer had a twisted sense of fantasies or was trying to create something that only made sense to them.

The worst condition of the three victims, in Katie's opinion, was the body of Stephanie Baxter. She had the same marks around her neck, but the incisions, in what appeared to be a crisscross pattern on her back, were gaping wounds. Where the organs had been removed, areas that had been connected to the rest of her internal organs, like strands of messy vessels and stomach intestines, could be seen. The incisions were strategic and clean.

It was overwhelming to see three homicide victims on three gurneys—all missing body parts. "Both Carolyn Sable and Edith Crest are missing left appendages," she said, more for her own examination rather than waiting for an answer from the doctor. "But Stephanie Baxter had her organs removed."

"That's where the killer's skill differs," said Dr. Dean. He seemed to slow down his hurriedness and focus on the mutilation of the third found victim. "I know the victim was in terrible shape when she was found, but, once the body was cleaned up... they both had been dead for almost four to five days. And..." He showed the detectives what he meant. "It shows some skill to produce this type of incision. I would have to say, in my opinion, it reminds me of a student learning surgical procedures on cadavers."

Katie had to agree the cuts were straight and concise. The cuts weren't overkill in order to remove the organs. "The organs belong to Stephanie Baxter?"

"Yes."

"The condition of the organs?" she asked, wondering if the killer had decided to mutilate the organs after extracting them.

"They were left about ninety percent intact and don't show any signs of mutilation," he said.

Katie could only see the condition of the victim at the scene and what appeared to be more blood than what was in the victim. "What about blood? How much blood did she have left?"

"She had about two pints left," he said.

"Oh."

"The average person has between six and nine pints of blood. It depends upon the size of the person—but a good measure is that blood is approximately seven to eight percent of their bodyweight. Remember, blood can be a sticky substance and adhere to surroundings, giving the appearance of much more. You'll have to ask John if all the blood was from the victim."

"Was there anything else different about Stephanie Baxter from the others?"

"She was strangled in the same way as the first two women, but..." The medical examiner paused as if he wasn't sure if he wanted to give an opinion. "More time was taken with the extractions. As I said, it was someone who had some experience with medical skills or perhaps studied it extensively."

Dr. Dean pushed up his sleeve and looked at his watch. "I'm sorry, Detectives, but I'm going to be late for my appointment. I must rush off now. But please, once you go over the autopsy report and have any questions, don't hesitate to call me or to come in. Oh, and take your time if you need to examine the bodies for yourselves."

"Thank you, Dr. Dean. It's always quite educational," she said.

McGaven, who had been mostly quiet, nodded to the doctor as he rushed by and exited the exam room.

Katie didn't immediately leave. She wanted to see the wounds of dismemberment again and compare the amateurish tearing to the more skilled incisions.

"Gav, take a look at this," she said softly, knowing that her partner hated being in the morgue exam room more than was absolutely necessary. She approached Carolyn Sable and gently pulled back the sheet. Not looking directly at her face, she studied the remnant of her arm—skin, tendons, and what appeared to be the remaining part of the rotator cuff. Katie tried not to dwell on the victim. "Doesn't it seem as if this wound could have been done by kitchen instruments?"

"Like a butcher knife or maybe one of those meat cleavers?" said McGaven as he moved closer.

"We found these body parts up in the ceiling in the kitchen area."

"What are you thinking?"

"Is that where the killer had set up shop to remove the appendages and organs?" she said.

"Makes sense."

"Do you notice that all three victims are similar in build, age, and hair color?"

"Coincidence?"

"Maybe."

Just as Katie and McGaven were about to leave, the lights went out. Everything went black with the sound of a loud alarm droning at two-second intervals.

"What the hell?" said McGaven looking around and down the hallway.

Katie stayed in place. Her heart pounded wildly, and she tried not to think about being alone with three dead bodies. She was never going to be at ease being around them—that was just a fact about her work.

"Wait. There should be a backup generator kicking in," said Katie.

Within a couple of minutes the backup lights came on slowly and in sections. The sound of machinery buzzed as they restarted.

Several technicians hurried past. Katie stopped one of them. "What's going on? Is this routine?"

"No," the tech replied and hurried on by.

Katie was frustrated. "What do you think has happened?" she said to her partner.

"No idea. Do we run toward the excitement or quietly retreat?"

"Do the opposite of what we want to do," she said and hurried after the technicians to see what all the commotion was all about.

As Katie rounded the corner, there was a long narrow hallway leading to the maintenance area. She had never been there before, but kept moving forward followed by McGaven— at least, so she thought. Suddenly it went pitch dark again. The hall was eerily quiet. She didn't hear any more voices or see anyone.

Standing still, Katie listened. There wasn't a sound except for her heart hammering inside her chest. Her breath shortened. It was as if she couldn't move a muscle even if she wanted to. There it was again. The tingling extremities, perspiration, and a feeling of dizziness that teetered on vertigo and made her stand as still as a statue. The creeping anxious symptoms of panic and anxiety were always ready to pounce.

Where was everyone?

Where was McGaven?

"*Katie?*"

She turned in the direction of the voice. "Hello?" she said.

"*Katie?*" came the small voice again. This time, she thought it originated from where she had come from.

Katie turned and retraced her steps carefully. The darkness

wasn't inviting, but she pushed through it. She had been momentarily sidetracked.

But by what?

Did she really hear a voice calling her name?

There were voices up ahead and a flashlight beam waving back and forth. Katie could see one of the main electrical panels and two figures next to it trying to reset the circuit.

How had she gone so far when Gav was just behind her?

As she reached the area of interest, slowly the light began to return to the normal intensity. Apparently, there had been some intermittent problems with the fuses.

McGaven approached her. "Where did you go?"

"I... I... just followed the hallway," she said, trying to block the entire incident from her mind. "Let's get back to the office. We have plenty to update."

CHAPTER TWENTY-TWO

Katie sat across from McGaven while he devoured a club sandwich at Buckley's Sandwich Shack. She flipped through Carolyn Sable's missing persons report. Her boss, Jake Fields, was listed as the person who filed the police report after Carolyn didn't show up for work for two days. Unable to reach her, Mr. Fields reached out to police for a welfare check.

Katie picked at her chicken salad then put her fork down. She could still see the bodies and organs in the morgue. "So Sable's boss filed a missing persons report?"

"Does that seem strange?" said McGaven.

"Why wouldn't a friend or neighbor, or even a family member do that?" She continued skimming through reports and the steps the investigator had taken during the case. "I know it states that she is estranged from her family, but she has two friends that gave statements besides Lenny. And no one had seen her since."

McGaven watched his partner. "Maybe the boss is trying to cover for something by making himself look the most concerned."

"I'm thinking about that note that Lenny showed us."

"Think it's legit?"

"Maybe. But the wording bothers me. It sounds more like something from a movie or TV show than real life."

"It sounds like something someone would do to keep him away from her."

Katie searched for the original report. "Look here. He stated that he had spoken with Carolyn two days prior to her going missing and she had said something about wanting to take a few days off."

"Maybe she was still trying to let him down easy?"

"The big question here was where was she for all that time —over two months?" She paused and sipped her iced tea. "I want to know if there's any connection between Carolyn Sable's employment—Fields, Campbell and Associates—and where Mr. Green works at Red Hawk Real Estate."

McGaven took some notes. "On it. It's going to take some time, but I'll see what I can find out."

"And KLM Enterprises and the liaison Charles Abbott."

"Got it," he said.

"Eagle Ridge Camp is center stage in these murders and there's quite a list of players. I want to find out more about the property—any history. I'll be visiting Shane at the county building. He's amazing and has meticulously organized documents."

Shane Kendall was the county archivist.

"Oh, I see," he smiled. "It's been a while and maybe he's forgiven you by now."

"Shane and I are on speaking terms. He knows it wasn't my fault that the killer was going to demolish that historical building—with us in it. That's why I'll pay him a visit next week when he's back at work." Katie restacked the file folders. "For now, we need to go to Carolyn Sable's house."

"Isn't it empty?"

"No, it's still filled with all her stuff, according to the neighbors and Detective Alvarez. Her mortgage is paid in full." She kept reading the background information in the file.

"What's the significance?" he asked.

"Red Hawk Real Estate was listed as the selling agent for her house—three years ago."

"Don't tell me that Daniel Green was the agent."

Katie nodded. "And Daniel Green was the seller's agent."

A few minutes later, they were back in McGaven's car and driving to Carolyn Sable's house. It was farther than Katie had expected. The small cabin was near Bluff Park, a heavily wooded area with scattered homes around a small pond. Quiet and peaceful.

"Did that sign say Bluff Park?" said McGaven.

"Yes. This area is on the outskirts of the park. I suppose you can reach it from a trail." Looking around, she said, "I've never hiked this area before."

"Isn't it where the body of Rick Reynolds was found?"

"Wait. Rick Reynolds?" Her mind rewound to the cold-case files she was searching before she received the call about Eagle Ridge Camp. "I was checking out some cold cases before the Eagle Ridge Camp hit the fan. I saw the file for Rick Reynolds, but didn't research it much yet."

"Wasn't he the handyman found stabbed forty times and dumped?"

Katie thought about it for a moment. "Bluff Park. Do you remember where? And how long ago was the murder?"

"The body was found near the entrance. And it was maybe two years ago. I think I remember that there wasn't much in the way of forensics and he was some kind of recluse." McGaven used his cell phone and quickly accessed the area for Bluff Park and the hiking trails. "Hmm."

"What?"

"What's the name of the road where Carolyn Sable's house is located?"

"Alpine Lane, number 2155."

McGaven scrolled around on the map. "Here it is. There's a direct trail leading up to the main entrance to Bluff Park."

Katie turned onto Alpine Lane and slowed her speed as the packed gravel churned beneath the tires. "Let me get this straight. Rick Reynold's body was found at Bluff Park stabbed forty times and it's only what... a couple of miles from Carolyn Sable's house?"

"Isn't that a..."

"Don't say it. It's not a coincidence."

"Maybe it could..."

"Nope, I'm not buying it."

McGaven pondered the reality of it being happenstance or an accident.

"We need to pull up everything about Rick Reynolds and that crime scene. Absolutely everything. There must be some connection. Big or small. There is a link."

"On it as soon as we get back to the office."

Katie spotted the address on a cute log cutout of a bear. She pulled up into the driveway that wound around in a circle and parked.

The house was a dark wood log cabin with a second story. It was a small building with a long covered front porch. Tall wispy ferns and dense shrubs were nestled against the sides of the house and the yard was surrounded by tall pine and cypress trees. Several angel and cherub figures were placed around the porch. Their slightly eerily smiling faces would always be staring at whoever might come to visit. Two comfortable chairs with light blue cushions sat on either side of the white front door.

Katie could see two wind chimes hanging on each end of the covered porch area: one was made up of several pieces of colored glass and the other was a figural angel with stars as the chimes.

A green hose was neatly coiled next to the house. Several colored terracotta pots of all sizes were positioned in a row. What had been nice potted plants and flowers were now dead from the lack of water and care.

"Well?" she said. "It looks like nothing's been disturbed since the investigating officer was here when Carolyn Sable was first discovered missing."

"Let's see what we can find out."

They got out of the sedan and headed to the porch.

Katie paused for a moment behind McGaven. There was nothing like the fresh pine aroma mixed with the humidity of the earth and surrounding forest. She took a deep breath as a way to steady her nerves. She noticed that the constant anxiety she suffered from—a side-effect of the PTSD she had had since her time in the army—was for the time being abated. Being out in the fresh air and wilderness was helping her immensely. She still took these panic indicators on a day-by-day basis. How long they would last for wasn't known.

Turning slowly, she noticed a trail that appeared to lead away from the property and cabin. Walking toward it, Katie saw that weeds had begun to grow across its path, indicating that it hadn't been walked for a month or more.

"What's up?" asked McGaven now standing next to his partner.

"I'm not sure. Here's a trail and by what you said it leads to the main entrance and parking area of Bluff Park."

"You thinking what I'm thinking?" he said with a smile.

"I think so—as scary as that sounds. I think we should walk this trail."

"Agreed," he said, already staring ahead to where the trail led into the trees.

"Let's check out the house first."

Katie and McGaven approached the cabin. Each was intently aware of being in the middle of a heavily forested area and going into a murder victim's house. They moved toward the house with caution, staying vigilant both with sight and sound for anything or anyone that might be hiding.

Katie peered into a small window which turned out to be over the kitchen area. There were still dishes in the sink—a coffee cup and a small plate with a couple of utensils. A decorative dish towel lay neatly folded on the counter.

McGaven searched the front porch in the usual places for a hideaway key. He moved the welcome mat, inside flower pots, underneath porcelain fairy-tale creatures, when suddenly... " Got it," he said as he stood up with a single house key in his hand. "It was under the creepiest statue. Why do people like these things?"

Katie laughed. "Can't answer that."

"Could you profile the type of people who do love these things so I can stay clear of them?" McGaven inserted the key in a wobbly lock and opened the door. "Wow, not much security here. Could've probably picked the lock."

"It would make it easy for anyone to break in—you wouldn't have to be a career criminal." She reached into her pocket. "You have gloves?" she asked.

"Yep," he said, pulling his on.

Pushing the door wider, Katie entered first. "Wow," she said. The air took her breath away. It was the mix of rotting garbage and something dead.

"'Wow' isn't the right word," he said partially covering his nose. "Gross... yuck..."

Katie pulled her weapon out of instinct and experience. McGaven followed protocol as well.

The cabin was small, so it was easy to see the living room, kitchen, and small dining room as you walked into the main entrance area. A narrow staircase with a wooden banister that looked like tree branches led out of the living room and upstairs.

"Where's the smell coming from?" he said.

Katie spotted a plastic garbage can with a full load of rotting food. "There," she said and pointed. "But there's something else."

McGaven moved into each small room to officially clear it.

Katie climbed the narrow staircase, which guided her to the upstairs bedroom and bath. It was neat and tidy, but in one corner there was a birdcage and lying on the bottom of the cage was a dead bird—it was impossible to distinguish what type. It saddened Katie as she saw the poor little bird appeared to have starved to death—now only the outline of greasy-looking feathers remained.

"Up here," she yelled to McGaven.

He was at her side in seconds. Looking at the birdcage, he said, "Oh no. That's sad. Is that all there is left?"

"But we now know what the stench is."

"Who would have thought that such a small bird could stink so bad?"

Katie opened dresser drawers and looked inside a plain jewelry box. "Anything downstairs?"

"No," he said. "And it's weird, I can't find anything personal. No mail. No bills. No keys. No purse."

"Maybe she took it with her when she left?"

"All personal things? I don't think so."

It was true what McGaven had said. As Katie searched the bedroom, she couldn't find anything that could only belong to Carolyn. Everything was in place. The bed was made, clothes were either in the dresser or hanging in the closet, toiletries were in the bathroom, but where were the things unique to her?

"Hey, Gav," she said. "Does something seem off to you?"

McGaven took a look around the bedroom. "I didn't think

so at first, but the hideous garbage stink took my main focus when we first got here, but now... it seems strange."

"Everything is in place. Too perfect and too staged is the only way I can describe it."

"But missing things like a purse, keys, photographs, and junk mail."

"No address book or even a grocery list."

Katie decided to take another thorough search of Carolyn Sable's bedroom. There had to be something personal. She went through all the dresser drawers, pulling them out and feeling underneath. She pulled the linens from the bed and checked the pillow. Nothing. She looked underneath some of the knick-knacks. Nothing.

She was just about to leave the room when she decided to look underneath the bed. There was a plastic storage container tucked far back. With a little finagling, she pulled it out and lifted the lid. There was dust on top, so it hadn't been opened in quite some time and was obviously overlooked.

"What is it?" asked McGaven towering over her.

She pulled out some sweaters and a hand-knitted scarf. Some framed photographs fell out onto the floor. They were old; Katie could tell by the way the photos were processed. Most people print out or have them duplicated by an internet company; this was something that was done in a drug store. There were baby photographs and some with family group settings. "We have something here..."

She stood up and showed her partner. A dark-haired woman, obviously Carolyn Sable, and a dark-haired man, holding up a kayak vertically, were posing together with fierce smiles, partially laughing. "Look behind them," she said.

There was a wooden sign that read "Check-in" and in big letters it identified as Eagle Ridge Camp. "This was during her time at Eagle Ridge. Who's the guy?"

"Don't know—yet." She found another old photograph from

Eagle Ridge. In this photo were Carolyn Sable and three other young women. "I think we have a connection here." She quickly took a photo of the pictures with her phone.

"Are two of them the other victims?"

"Don't know, it's difficult to tell. We need to enlarge the image." She double-checked the storage box. There was nothing except winter clothes and a few small porcelain animal figurines. "Take these photos, so we can identify everyone." She walked to the closet. "I'm going to make sure that there isn't anything more hidden away. Search downstairs again, okay?"

"On it," he said and made toward the stairs.

Katie could hear her partner heavily step down the staircase. She heard him open and close drawers and closet doors.

Katie checked every clothing pocket she could find, storage areas, and the bathroom, but didn't find anything else useful. She hurried downstairs to help her partner.

"Anything?"

"Nope. Except a grocery list in the drawer next to the silverware."

Katie glanced at it. "Take it, it shows her handwriting. Just in case... That photograph was four women at the Eagle Ridge Camp."

"So."

"Well, I think we have three of them in our morgue. We need to identify and find the fourth woman in that photo as soon as possible."

CHAPTER TWENTY-THREE

After Katie and McGaven departed Carolyn Sable's cabin, they left the police sedan secured and began walking the mile-and-a-half trail to Bluff Park. As soon as they began the beginner-level to moderate hike, it was obvious that the trail wasn't one that was travelled by numerous people—or neighbors. It was as if Carolyn Sable had had her own private hiking trail.

"You actually like doing this kind of thing?" huffed McGaven.

"You know I do. Besides, Cisco is usually with me. It's how I can relax and clear my mind."

"You never clear your mind."

Katie laughed. She was reminded that she loved working with McGaven with his quick wit and astute observation. She hoped things wouldn't change because of his promotion to detective status. But she knew he was needed in the robbery-homicide division and that it would only be a matter of time before the department transferred him.

"You look deep in thought. Care to clue me in?" he said.

"Oh nothing," she said. "Look."

There was a trail marker on the side of the path that read: ¼ *mile.*

"A quarter mile to what? Hell?"

They reached the top of the trail and jogged up a dozen wooden stairs to the parking lot.

"That was fun," said McGaven.

Katie looked at her watch, ignoring McGaven's sarcastic remark. "That took us about thirteen minutes, wouldn't you say?"

"Your point?"

"My point is that it takes less than fifteen minutes to get from Carolyn Sable's house to the parking lot at Bluff Park where Rick Reynolds's body was found. Would you say anyone could see you coming up that trail?"

"Nope, not even me," he said, referring to his six-foot-six height.

"Exactly." She walked across the parking lot where there were two passenger cars parked. "Would you say that someone could use that trail, to, say, meet someone here?"

"Sure."

"And they could easily escape by taking that trail, right?"

"Again. Yes." McGaven sorted through his cell phone until he found a local article about Rick Reynolds's homicide. "Until we get back and view the cold-case file... it says in the news that his body was found near the trail entrance for the five-mile hike." He looked around.

Katie saw signs for the three main trail heads where people began their hikes. It was usually a mix of beginner and more moderate/advanced trails. "Wait," she said. There was a hiking location with a small sign that read: *Raven's Peak* and another that read: *Eagle Ridge*. "Here," she said, referring to the Raven's Peak trail head. "This was probably the approximate area. It has a bit of seclusion, but the area is still open enough for someone to find the body."

"Makes sense."

"At least for now." She walked the area, looking to see where someone had to park. "Let's just say someone came in on the hike we did. Would you say it would be easy for someone to navigate at night?"

"Sure."

"We need to verify some things. But my first instinct tells me that Rick Reynolds knew his killer and that he was supposed to meet him here. What better way than to come up a seldom used trail?"

"Because anyone who hikes here would go the beautiful scenic routes, not some shortcut to a cabin in the woods," he said.

"The force of forty stabs," she said. "That's more than just a crime. That's pure hatred, jealousy, or payback."

"Sounds more like payback, because of the overkill inflicted."

Katie stood next to McGaven. "I think you're right."

"You think the two murders are related?"

"We don't have any evidence. But my gut can't ignore the close proximity of a murder here and the home of another victim." She surveyed the area. "But..." She stopped and looked back at the trail heads.

"Don't keep me in suspense."

"Isn't the Eagle Ridge Camp about three miles from here?" She looked toward the north.

McGaven had already pulled out his cell phone and opened a map of the area. Dragging the area back and forth with his index finger, he zeroed in on the path between Bluff Park and Eagle Ridge Camp. "You're right. It's about 3.4 miles."

"Now, what's that about coincidence? We have a murder victim's house near the vicinity of a cold case, with a private trail leading from one to the other—and to top it off the Eagle Ridge Camp with three current homicides as well."

"We've got preliminary linkage."

CHAPTER TWENTY-FOUR

Katie sat perched and completely at attention on her bar stool as she watched Chad prepare their Sunday breakfast. His amazing skill to juggle several things at a time in the kitchen was legendary—at least, that's what she thought. The oven was set to warm to keep everything at the same temperature as he finished the hash browns, French toast, strips of crisp bacon, and now the scrambled eggs. The aroma was spectacular.

She had spent most of the early morning going over reports and statements. She and McGaven had lined up appointments for Monday, but there were unanswered questions that she wanted to try and solve as she sifted through files of information. But for today, she was going to conduct some internet searches, reread some of the witness statements, and study the crime scene photos. She had some preliminary information about Edith Crest and Stephanie Baxter.

Cisco sat at attention with his ears fully straight and forward. Obviously, the wondrous smells were tantalizing to him as well—namely the bacon.

"I love the smell of breakfast," said Katie taking another deep breath. She hadn't had the best night's sleep—but having

Chad in her kitchen cooking made things so much better. Although every time she closed her eyes, she saw dismembered body parts spilling down on top of her. These cases always taunted her. Consumed her. Kept her awake during odd hours of the night.

"It's my favorite meal of the day," said Chad. "It was the first thing I learned to cook at my house growing up."

"Mmm," she said. "It's like the happiest meal of the day. You always feel great after eating breakfast." She eyed her fiancé in his loose sweats and favorite rock 'n' roll T-shirt. His light hair was a bit tousled and not the usual neat fireman's haircut. She loved watching him work and the more time she spent with him, the more she loved him.

Chad made a few dramatic moves just for Katie's benefit. He flipped two pieces of French toast in the skillet as he heated the syrup. "Since I cooked, you have to clean up."

Katie laughed. "We'll just have to see about that."

"Oh wait. McGaven told me about your tackle of the mechanic yesterday. Maybe I better wash up the dishes." He grinned.

"He told you that? When?"

"Well, I didn't actually speak to him."

"What do you mean?"

"He sent a text to me."

Katie couldn't believe her partner would do that. "He didn't."

"Yep. The only thing missing was a photo, but his text was priceless." He turned to Katie. "What I don't get, you have a partner that could take down a house by himself and give a linebacker a difficult time, and you're the one tackling the bad guys..."

"Well, the mechanic wasn't really a bad guy. It was just a misunderstanding."

"Did he know that?" Chad laughed.

"Are you going to plate up or is this all just for show?" she said.

Cisco barked.

Katie and Chad sat outside in the yard at a small bistro table. The sun was shining but the air was still cool and refreshing. This had always been a favorite place for Katie; all the wonderful memories surfaced—there wasn't any shortage of great times. She had grown up in this house and couldn't imagine living anywhere else. After her parents were killed in a car accident, the house became hers. It was where she felt safe and content. It made her feel relaxed and calm—without any anxious energy or killers to chase.

Cisco barked and ran by, chasing some birds and making Katie smile. He loved to romp around the area and his black coat glistened in the sunshine as he ran to and fro. There were five acres of beautiful land with slight rolling hills and clusters of pine trees. There was always something blooming and shades of green splashed everywhere. It was an artist's perfect muse.

As if reading her mind, Chad said, "This has always been such a great place. Some of my fondest memories are of being here as a kid." He stuffed part of a piece of French toast in his mouth.

"My parents loved this house and property. They would never have moved."

"But you would."

Katie stopped eating. "What?"

"You would move, right?"

She wasn't sure what he was trying to say. Or maybe she just didn't want to hear.

Chad stared at Katie. "I'm sorry, but I thought that after we're married..."

"That I would sell this house?" Katie couldn't even imagine

it, or perhaps she just wasn't ready. Maybe she would never be ready.

"I know that you have memories here. Both good and bad. I just thought…"

"I guess I haven't given much thought to moving," she confessed. Her heart skipped a beat and she could feel the anxious feelings trying to surface through the calm of Sunday morning.

Chad took her hand. "I don't want to pressure you in any way, Katie. I just thought that we were starting our new life together as a married couple. I would sell my small house and you this farmhouse, and then we could find something that suited us both."

"I guess you're right. But I'm not ready to say goodbye to this house yet." Katie's heart would break if she walked away from this house right now. She understood what Chad was saying, but selling it had never occurred to her. Was she really ready for marriage?

"It's okay, Katie, we'll work it out. Okay?"

Katie watched Chad closely. He was irresistible when he wanted something, but he was going to have to wait. The farmhouse was a part of her past and she didn't want to say goodbye to it just yet. "Okay," she said and nodded.

CHAPTER TWENTY-FIVE

It was one of those mornings where Katie got up early, went for her usual run, and then took the long route to work. She would almost rather be somewhere far away to calm her mind than to think about what it was going to be like marrying Chad. So much thinking wore on her psyche.

She sped along the road and took the turns fast. She had lowered the front windows so she could feel the wind flow through the cabin of the Jeep. It felt good as the breeze blew past her face and through her ponytail. Whatever weighed heavy on her mind immediately seemed less stressful and more workable.

Her journey was almost over by the time she navigated back to the main road leading to the Pine Valley Sheriff's Department. She slowed and turned into the parking lot for employees, finding a place next to McGaven's truck.

How did he always beat her to the department no matter what time she arrived?

Katie smiled to herself as she grabbed her briefcase. After locking her Jeep, she hurried to the door and swiped her security pass. She thought that she would go upstairs to talk with

Denise before the day started—she knew that Denise always arrived at 6 a.m.

She opened the stairwell door and was just about to climb the stair when she heard familiar voices talking. It made her pause. Normally she wouldn't think of eavesdropping, but the words stopped her. Instinctively, she backed up almost underneath the stairwell. The low conversation ensued.

"Look, it's no secret that we're a skeleton crew in homicide and that we need another detective," said the voice that Katie thought was Detective Hamilton.

"You know that Katie and I are always available to pick up the slack," said McGaven.

"Yeah, about that. The word is that the sheriff is going to officially transfer you to robbery-homicide."

"I haven't heard anything about it," he said.

"You may be the only one that can work with Scott, but honestly, she should probably stick to those dusty old cold cases. We need you upstairs."

Katie realized Detective Hamilton still had issues with her. She had thought they had worked through their differences from a few investigations ago, but obviously he still had animosity festering. She felt her world begin to spin out of control. What would this mean to the cold-case unit?

"I don't think I like your tone or insinuations about Detective Scott," said McGaven.

"Hey, wait a minute. Don't take it the wrong way—I'm just trying to help you, give you a heads-up."

"Since I haven't heard anything about what you're talking about, I'm going to continue to work in the cold-case unit," McGaven said. "And I would suggest in the future that repeating gossip isn't a way that a detective should present themselves. You should keep your attention on the cases you're assigned. Are we clear?"

Detective Hamilton grumbled something that Katie didn't

quite hear. "Yeah, I understand perfectly."

Katie heard a door open on the landing upstairs and she took that as a cue to retreat back into the hallway and walk quickly toward the forensics division.

Once back at her desk, her mind was still reeling. Were they really going to transfer McGaven? Did that mean they would shut down the cold-case unit? Katie hated the fact that her immediate thoughts were negative. She was always trying to change that about her first response to a situation.

The door opened and McGaven walked in. "Hey, happy Monday," he said with a smile.

Katie couldn't pick up anything from him about the conversation she'd just overheard. Maybe she had nothing to worry about. Detective Hamilton was just trying to pull some type of power trip due to the fact she and McGaven had been assigned the Eagle Ridge cases. If she thought about it like that, it made sense. "Hey, yourself. And I beat you here, finally," she said turning to him as he settled at his desk. "I saw your truck here first, though."

"Yeah, I was upstairs bringing Denise her lunch she had forgotten."

That made sense to Katie, but there still was a nagging question if that was the truth or if he was keeping something from her.

Focus...

"Big day today. Lots of things to cover," he said.

Katie flipped open her notebook. "It sure is. Don't we have an appointment with Mr. Fields at Carolyn Sable's workplace?"

"Yep, later this morning." He opened his laptop which had numerous colorful Post-it notes stuck on it with reminders scribbled in his handwriting.

Katie took out her notebook and flipped through several pages. She needed to see the investigation visually and put together some sort of cohesive picture of what they had so far.

She picked up the black marker and made three large categories: *Evidence*, *Victimology*, and *Killer Profile*. Then she wrote down extra notes for *Victim 1, 2, and 3 in the margin on the left side of the board.*

Carolyn Sable, age forty, no family, worked as an administrative assistant for Jake Fields at Fields, Campbell and Associates for six years, reported missing by *Jake Fields two months ago when she didn't report to work, ex-boyfriend *Lenny Dickson broke up approximately six months ago, her rural cabin home was neat with nothing taken but nothing personal left behind. Her home is within walking distance to *Bluff Park where the body of *Rick Reynolds was found over a year ago and within three miles to the property of *Eagle Ridge Camp. She worked as a camp counselor at Eagle Ridge Camp for three years when she was at college.

Katie sighed and took a step back.

"What's up?" said McGaven.

She didn't realize that she had sighed so loudly. "Sorry. I just realized how little we really know. I've noted important points and names. It's like if I draw a line it's more like a circle— everything seems to circle back to Eagle Ridge."

She flipped through her notes. "Maybe her boss or co-workers can fill in some information about what Carolyn's mindset was like before she disappeared."

"I'm searching for more information about Rick Reynolds and Carolyn Sable. Maybe there's some connection?" he said.

"That's my girl," he said with enthusiasm. "Now, here's the big question. Killer profile?"

"Not enough information—yet."

"I know you've been thinking about this all weekend," he said turning toward his partner. "What's in your bag of tricks?" McGaven smiled.

"I don't know if I would describe criminal profiling as a bag of tricks." Katie couldn't help but laugh. "But you're right. I have been thinking about it all weekend." She tried not to think about the conversation she had with Chad regarding selling her house. "Overview. The killer is connected to Eagle Ridge Camp in some way. Until we find the possible lead, Brian Stanwick, we have to move forward with what we do have. That could mean the killer was a student that attended the camp or someone that was employed—or related to someone with a connection there."

"My vote is a kid—well, now a grown-up."

Katie nodded. "I'm not so sure, but once more information comes in it will begin to form our picture for motive and the killer." She quickly thumbed through the cold-case file for Rick Reynolds. Something nagged at her. She reread his employment history, which was spotty in places. Then she saw it. She read it twice more to make sure what she was seeing. "Did you know that Rick Reynolds was a handyman for Eagle Ridge Camp?" she asked McGaven.

"What? When?"

"Around the time that Carolyn Sable was there. It looks like for about three months."

"Wait, that's not coincidental."

"No, I know. We need to make sure Denise includes any employment records for part time or special season in her search. She needs to get everything available."

"On it," he said, already typing out a quick email to his girlfriend.

"I think the more we know, the more things are going to be exposed about that camp." She briefly thought about how she had loved attending. And then her memory always stopped on —*Jenny*.

'Yeah. What's it that they say?" he said.

"The plot thickens."

CHAPTER TWENTY-SIX

Katie and McGaven arrived fifteen minutes early to Fields, Campbell and Associates. It was a large, two-story building housing a real estate firm and an accountancy corporation in addition to the financial company they were there to interview.

Katie pulled the police sedan into the parking lot. It was attractively landscaped, with many bushes, shrubs, and flowers framing the nice flagstone walkways that led to the entrance.

"Wow, this looks like a fancy place. They must've spent a fortune on landscaping."

"And I think you need to make a high six figures to need the services here," chimed McGaven.

Katie absently straightened the blouse collar underneath her suit jacket. Now, she wished she had worn her hair twisted up instead of her usual ponytail. McGaven was right: this place would make anyone feel inadequate.

"Ready?" she said to her partner.

"Yep." McGaven opened the passenger door.

Katie got out and paused. She glanced at her watch. "We're a bit early. Maybe we should just take a look around first?"

Standing next to her, McGaven said, "For anything in particular?"

"No. Just getting a lay of the land, that's all."

"It's never that simple with you," he said and smiled.

"Sometimes it is," she said and began to walk a clockwise perimeter of the building. Katie wasn't sure exactly what she was looking for, but that had never stopped her before.

The dark paved blacktop circled around the building, then dropped down into another parking area much less used and more isolated. This lower parking lot intrigued Katie for some reason, so she walked down the hill toward it. Two four-door cars were parked and a small motorhome incongruously took up a couple of spaces in the corner.

"Curious," said McGaven.

Katie agreed. She thought it was strange—maybe it was just unusual to see a motorhome in an office parking lot.

McGaven walked around the RV roadster. It was a smaller type of house on wheels and it definitely had some miles on it. It was in desperate need of a wash. He kept his distance, but casually peered into the windows. "Nothing to see with the curtains," he said. "I'll take a quick pic of the license plate and text it to Denise. She'll have all the info back to us quickly."

Katie nodded wordlessly as her partner sent the text. As she neared the motorhome, something caught her eye. There was quite the buildup of dirt and debris around the modestly worn tires. It appeared as if the vehicle had been used recently, and had driven through some rough terrain with heavy clay dirt and small gravel.

Could it have been taken to Eagle Ridge Camp?

She didn't know anything about this type of vacation camper, but she assumed that off-roading was out of the question. Out of habit, she took a couple of photos as close as she could and then one at a longer distance which included the make and model of the vehicle.

"Let's get up there and see what Mr. Fields has to say," said McGaven.

Katie and McGaven hurried back to the entrance to the financial corporation. It took up the entire bottom floor of the building, which was bigger than they had thought when they first drove into the parking lot.

Entering the two large glass doors, they were greeted by a contemporary waiting area. It was more extravagant than most hotels. There were beautifully upholstered beige couches and two chairs with a smoky glass coffee table, which were highlighted by three towering plants.

Katie stood for a moment realizing that she was hearing the ocean. Looking at three corners of the waiting room, she spied two small speakers piping out the soothing sounds. She also noticed two security cameras, both of which moved slightly as she watched. It made her wonder if someone was sitting at a computer moving the camera around to get a better vantage of who stood in the main entrance area.

Katie and McGaven waited awkwardly, not sure if they were supposed to go down the hallway alone. They could see no receptionist, nor a reception desk in the usual sense, but it appeared that they were to sit down and wait.

Katie eyed her partner and slightly shrugged her shoulders. "Let's sit and wait, I guess." She took a seat in one of the upholstered high-back chairs and waited. For some reason, sitting still in this unknown zone made her acutely aware of her weapons. Her hip holster rubbed her side.

McGaven sat on the couch and casually scrolled through his phone. He seemed oblivious to his surroundings, but Katie knew that he was keenly aware of them, just intent on not showing it as obviously as she must be.

An older dark-haired woman with her hair pulled tightly away from her angular face appeared and forced a smile with perfect teeth. "Detectives?" she said.

Katie stood up. "Yes, I'm Detective Katie Scott and this is my partner, Detective Sean McGaven."

The woman gave a slight nod. "Mr. Fields will meet with you now. Please follow me." The woman moved effortlessly in her three-inch heels and snug suit.

Katie and McGaven followed her down a hallway, passing several offices where numerous people worked at computers. Every desk had tall stacks of paperwork. It reminded Katie of Red Hawk Real Estate, but with more employees and a higher decorating budget.

They stopped at the end of the hall. The dark wooden door there was set into the wall at an awkward angle and seemed out of kilter with the rest of the building's layout. It made Katie imagine for a second that there could be hidden rooms behind it, or that it was like the strange angles of a fairground fun house.

The woman opened the door and stood back, waiting for the detectives to enter the huge room that lay beyond.

Once Katie and McGaven stepped inside the door, it shut quietly behind them. When things were strange or unusual, Katie could look at McGaven and read his body language. She did so now and saw that he seemed to be as uneasy as she was.

What was disturbing was that the room didn't have the usual four walls: it was divided into three main areas: a cubicle for the assistant's desk, a large living-room-style sitting area, and Mr. Fields's own area, framed by floor-to-ceiling windows with a view of the scenic outdoors. The furniture all matched and was oversized in order to stay proportional to the abundant space of the room. It almost had a dizzying effect.

"Come in, Detectives," came a friendly voice.

Sitting in a huge black leather chair behind a large desk with three open laptops and multiple screens on it was a handsome man in his forties. Strong features, dark hair, intense blue eyes. Katie guessed those good looks would work in his favor when dealing with exclusive clients.

She took the lead and stepped forward, walking through the living-room area and stopping at his desk. "Mr. Jake Fields?" she said.

"Yes, of course," he said. "And you're Detective Katie Scott... and newly promoted Detective Sean McGaven, I believe."

"Yes," said Katie. She hid her surprise. Obviously, Mr. Fields had done his homework and checked up on her and McGaven before meeting with them.

"Please, have a seat, and call me Jake." He motioned to the two chairs positioned perfectly in front of him.

It was a friendly gesture, but it had a hint of an order to it. He placed his hands on the desk and gently intertwined his fingers.

"Thank you for seeing us—" Katie began.

"I assume you want to find out everything you can about Carolyn Sable," he said, interrupting Katie, keeping the interview on his terms. He spoke with authority, obviously used to being the one in charge.

"Yes. We have a few questions regarding what is now a homicide investigation. I know that you spoke initially with Detective Alvarez regarding the filing of the missing persons report."

"Yes."

"What made you file the report?" she said.

"One thing you have to understand about Ms. Sable is that she was one of the most punctual people I've ever met. She was loyal, trustworthy, and wouldn't sully her integrity for anything."

"I see."

Mr. Fields smiled and gave a low chuckle. "Detective Scott,

you have something that you want to ask me. Ask me anything, I don't have anything to hide."

"Were you having a personal relationship with Ms. Sable?" Katie kept her gaze on the man behind the enormous desk, watching him carefully. She wanted to catch every move— subtle things he did and gestures he didn't make.

"I wanted to at one time, but she politely declined."

Katie raised an eyebrow.

"I know what you're thinking, Detective."

"I don't think you do," she said. "We're trying to track Ms. Sable's last days to determine who would be the most likely suspect that would want to harm her." Katie kept the man's gaze.

Mr. Fields looked to McGaven and then back at Katie. "I see. Do you believe I'm a suspect?" He smiled, clearly seeming to enjoy the conversation, but he was still difficult to read.

"Mr. Fields, our priority is to learn everything we can about a victim. The people they encounter and the areas where they might have made themselves a potential victim. There are a number of things we're looking at. And to your question—actually, everyone is a suspect until we rule them out."

"Detective McGaven, you haven't said much."

"And?" said McGaven.

"It's one of two things. Both of you are very comfortable with one another, or you're a newbie. Which is it?"

"Mr. Fields, we would like to know more about Ms. Sable. Did she have any problems with anyone here at work?"

"Not that I'm aware of."

"I noticed that you have many cameras installed. You're keeping a watchful eye on everyone—did Ms. Sable have any problems or did anything happen out of the ordinary? Did anyone come visit her? Had her mood changed before she disappeared?" said McGaven.

"Detectives, nothing seemed any different than any other

day—except when she didn't arrive at work. We became very concerned. She didn't answer her phone. I was the one that suggested someone go out to her home."

Katie kept brief notes. "And who was that?"

"Kerry, I believe. Kerry Wilhelm—she's one of our researchers. She and Ms. Sable were friends."

"When was the last time you saw Ms. Sable?"

"When she left for the day—around 6 p.m. on that Tuesday. I never saw her again."

"Had you ever been to her home?"

"No."

"Had you ever gone anywhere together outside of business?" she asked.

"No. Except for an office party and Christmas party."

"Well, thank you for your time. We may have some further questions at a later date," Katie said as she rose to leave. McGaven followed her lead.

"Anytime, Detectives. I'll help in any way I can." He had already gone back to reading the stock exchange on one of his screens and didn't give them anymore eye contact.

"Oh, one more thing," said McGaven.

Mr. Fields looked up reluctantly. "Yes?"

"Can we see the security footage from Ms. Sable's last day?" said McGaven.

"Of course. I'll have a copy sent over to your police department ASAP." He didn't slow down his focus on his work or seemed concerned by the request.

Katie took a last glance around the office and noticed several framed photographs on the walls. She spied one of two young boys at an amusement park—it must have been taken more than thirty years previously so she knew it couldn't be Mr. Fields's children. Looking at it more closely, she thought it was likely him and most probably his brother—they resembled each other closely. Their expressions seemed mischievous, as if they were looking for trouble.

Katie and McGaven left the financial company after finding out that Kerry Wilhelm was out of the office, and they hurried out to the parking lot before they spoke. Katie had the intense suspicion that not only was the company heavy on the video cameras, but it was highly likely that there were listening devices installed at various locations as well.

As they stood next to the police sedan, Katie turned to her partner. "What do you think?"

"I think he's lying about seeing Carolyn Sable and I think he's already covered his tracks of proving that link."

"We need to find more connections with him, Carolyn Sable, and Eagle Ridge Camp," she said. Suddenly, Katie spotted a woman coming up from the parking area that lay behind the building. She was a tall blonde in a navy suit carrying a small white bag and sipping on a coffee cup.

Katie eyed McGaven and made a slight gesture to alert him to the woman.

As the woman approached she noticed the detectives, and hesitated. She appeared to be trying to decide whether or not to speak to them.

"Hello," said Katie. She made a guess. "Are you Kerry Wilhelm?"

"Yes," the woman said slowly.

"We're from the Pine Valley Sheriff's Department. We're investigating the death of Carolyn Sable."

The woman still eyed them suspiciously and then kept glancing to the building like she knew she was being watched.

"Would you have a few minutes to speak with us?" Katie asked. "Just a couple of questions."

She nodded. "Sure." Kerry Wilhelm didn't move toward the

building. Instead, she turned away from the detectives. "Let's walk. That okay?"

"Of course," said Katie. "I'm Detective Scott and this is my partner Detective McGaven."

The three of them began to head back down to the lower parking area where it was more private. Katie felt more at ease away from the prying camera lenses, and it seemed Kerry Wilhelm did too.

"I was stunned when I heard about Carolyn's death. I was called in to identify her body. I've never had to do anything like that before..." Kerry said with a slight shaky timbre to her voice. "I know you can't tell me any details, but are you getting closer to finding out who did this?"

"We're in the middle of running down leads," said Katie. "Can you tell us what your relationship was with Carolyn?"

"We were friends. I was hired a couple of weeks after her and we bonded as the newbies."

"Was she worried about anything before she disappeared? Did she appear different?"

Kerry Wilhelm took a deep breath. It was clear that was something was weighing heavy on her mind. "About a month before she disappeared, she seemed preoccupied and not her usual self. She could always power through anything, but this time she seemed scared."

"How so?"

"Jumpy. Forgetful. She looked pale as if she hadn't had sufficient sleep and wasn't feeling well. And if you knew Carolyn you would know that wasn't like her—at all. I tried to talk to her, but she reassured me that things were fine and it would work out."

"Did it have anything to do with Lenny Dickson?" asked McGaven.

"No, I don't think so. I thought so at first, but they parted on friendly terms. He tried to get back into her life, but Carolyn laughed it off. And I believed her. This new thing that was bothering her was completely different."

"Ms. Wilhelm, was Carolyn involved with Jake Fields?"

Her eyes widened in surprise. "No, not at all. She wasn't interested because she worked as his assistant. She would never do that."

"Did he want more from her?"

"I know what you're getting at, but I don't think so. I never saw anything out of the ordinary, but I didn't work next to her." She thought a moment. "There was one time at a retirement party where Carolyn told me that Jake Fields made a pass at her —but I didn't think anything of it because everyone had been drinking that night."

Katie listened and put together a mental picture of the relationship between boss and assistant. "The day that Mr. Fields asked you to drive to Carolyn's house to see if she was there— what happened?"

Kerry took a few sips of her coffee. "Mr. Fields came into my office and asked if I would go out to Carolyn's house to check on her. When I asked why, he said that she hadn't showed up for work for two days and was unreachable by phone."

"What was Mr. Fields's demeanor?"

"That's just it. He was business as usual and I didn't think there was anything wrong."

Glancing around Katie asked, "What happened when you reached Carolyn's house?"

"Nothing really. When she didn't answer the door, I knew where she kept the key and so I let myself in."

"Was there anything you saw that raised your suspicion?"

"No, nothing. Her house was just like it is normally. Neat. Organized."

"What happened then?"

"I told Mr. Fields and he said that he would take care of it. I was so worried when Carolyn didn't return my calls and then I never heard from her again... Then just last week we were told about her murder." Her eyes filled with tears and it was clear that she was being sincere.

Katie retrieved a business card and handed it to Kerry. "Here's my card if you remember anything about the last weeks before she disappeared. We don't want to keep you from work."

Taking the card, she said, "Thank you. I hope you find out who did this and they pay."

Katie and McGaven watched Kerry Wilhelm walk back through the parking lot and enter the building.

"Well?" said McGaven.

"There are a lot of things to consider," she said, looking at the motorhome. "I want to know who owns that recreational vehicle."

"Just got a text from Denise."

"And?"

"It is registered to a Mr. Jake Fields."

CHAPTER TWENTY-SEVEN

"Okay," said McGaven. "We can add to the killer's profile." He began writing on the board in neatly printed letters. "He strangles face to face with his victims. What does that tell you?"

Katie leaned against her desk reading the investigation list. "Power. Control. Not afraid of getting caught. Possibly knew his victims and that's how he was able to get so close to them."

McGaven was animated, a little more than usual, as he added Katie's observations. "Dismemberment?" He turned to look at his partner. "Hey, you okay?" he said, noticing her low energy.

"Yeah, I'm fine. Maybe a bit tired."

"You want to finish this later?"

"Nope, we're behind by my standards. We need to keep pushing forward." She read the board and there was indeed a profile emerging. "Dismemberment would be anger. Retaliation. Jealousy. Perhaps a vigilante payback of some kind." Her thoughts rambled around this type of personality and what it meant to their case. She had come to the conclusion that the killer would continue until all the people who had made him begin his rampage were gone.

"Okay. I see where you're going." He made more notes. "And perhaps someone who has had some surgical training or medical background of some sort. But why the precision on the organ removals but the violence of the limb removal? Why the difference?"

"It may not be as simple as that," she said. "We need to find a link. We'll check the names on the Eagle Ridge Camp employee list when we get it—maybe one of them had some type of medical training. It doesn't mean they were a doctor or nurse, just someone who had had some medical experience along the way."

"Got it," he said as he made a note.

"It may also have to do with who the victim is and how the killer felt about the third victim, Stephanie Baxter. Her wounds were the most gruesome. Maybe there was more of a relationship with her, or some complex history."

"I see..."

"Of course it may all be just from the killer's point of view with nothing to do at all with reality." Katie sighed. "Here we are again—so many ways to go on this case."

"Similar in appearance?"

"And they were friends. Not sure if they had kept in touch." Katie stood up. "We now have to officially compare them to the photograph found in Carolyn Sable's house. Do backgrounds on Crest and Baxter." She picked up a copy of the photograph taken at Eagle Ridge Camp of the four young women. "We need to find the fourth friend."

"Did I hear my name yet?" said Denise with her usual smile and upbeat personality. She handed McGaven a file folder.

"Hi, Denise," said Katie.

"Here's your listing for the Eagle Ridge Camp employees from payroll records—all with last known addresses and employee identification numbers. Plus details of two volunteers. There might be a few that were missing from the list because the accounting wasn't well organized after the camp closed, but hopefully you'll find what you need."

"Great. Thank you," said McGaven still smiling at her.

"Oh," said Denise. "I almost forgot. Here's a couriered package from Fields, Campbell and Associates. It came this afternoon."

"Wow, that was fast," said Katie as she took the small package. The speed at which it had been delivered made her uneasy.

"Well, I'm on my way home," Denise said to McGaven. "You working late?"

"Not too late."

She put her fingertips to her mouth, but didn't blow him a kiss. "I'll see you at home." She then quietly left.

"I've said this before, but I really like her," said Katie, smiling as she opened the package and retrieved two small disks.

"Give those here," he said, still smiling. He took the disks and read out their labels. Four areas that they both recognized from the office: reception, hallway, Mr. Fields's office, and the main area of the parking lot.

Katie remembered her initial feeling when she entered Fields's office. It was one of heavy doom and she didn't know what had caused it. It also seemed creepy the way he seemed to know all about her and McGaven. Perhaps, though, it was because he was just doing his typical background check with anyone he did business with—including the detectives that were investigating the murder of his assistant.

McGaven put the first disk into the drive. The label also had the date: the day before Carolyn Sable went missing. "Here we go," he said.

Katie squeezed in next to her partner as they waited to see the footage. It showed several people exiting their cars and walking through the parking lot to the entrance.

"There's Kerry Wilhelm," said Katie. "And that's Carolyn Sable."

They watched the two women heading to the front door of the firm.

"Strange," said Katie. "They almost act as if they don't know each other. Look, they ignore one another."

"That is weird," he said. "I thought they were good friends ever since they started there together."

Katie studied the screen and the two women. "Two reasons. One, they really don't like one another and don't know each other. Or two, they know that Mr. Fields watches these cameras and didn't want him to see the level of their friendship."

Watching Carolyn Sable walk across the parking lot wearing a dark suit and three-inch heels gave life to the body they had viewed in the morgue. She was striking with her long dark hair swaying as she walked. Her expression told another story. No smile. Her facial muscles weren't relaxed but taut, as if the real stress was about to begin.

Katie and McGaven watched the recordings of the other areas. There didn't seem to be anything out of the ordinary. People were going to and from their offices, some carrying files, while others had quick conversations in the hall before returning to their desks.

"This isn't going to show us anything," she said.

The video continued. Suddenly, one thing stood out to Katie. "I think everyone seems to be hyper-vigilant about the work cameras. They are almost like clones. Does that make sense?" She watched employees walk stiffly and glance with some hesitation at the camera.

"I was going to say robots but I like clones better," said McGaven. "No one smiles or greets the other person. Or even jokes around at break time. What the hell?"

"Did you find out who Campbell is in Fields, Campbell?"

"Not much information. Apparently, he retired more than twenty years ago and then the trail ends."

"Strange," she said. "Death certificate?"

"Strange seems to be the call of the day." He made some notes. "No death certificate, but it's like he never existed." He turned back to the laptop. "I'll make sure I watch everything. It would be easy to see something of an anomaly."

"We need to look at Mr. Jake Fields more closely. Maybe talk again to Kerry Wilhelm."

"And find out about the motorhome parked out back."

Katie opened the files for Edith Crest and Stephanie Baxter. The women had been missing for four months before their bodies were found. They had originally been straightforward missing persons cases, but then had been updated with the crime scene photos. They were killed a couple of days before their bodies were found. It bothered her that they weren't alerted sooner; they might've been able to save one of the women. Some cases weighed heavier on Katie than others, and these three women that once were counselors at Eagle Ridge Camp were among those.

As McGaven tapped the keyboard in search of more information on the list of names, Katie took the time to read about the second and third victims. She was trying to gain more information or some understanding of why and how they became victims of the killer. She pored over everything in the files, hoping to spot something that would be useful.

She picked up the photo of Edith Crest that the family had given to the police for identification. Her mother lived in Southern California and a half-sister lived in New York City. She was forty-one years old, divorced, with one child who lived with her ex-husband in Lake Tahoe, California. At the time of her death Edith had been living in the small town of Mayfield, about half an hour away from Pine Valley. As Katie looked at the photo where Edith was smiling up at the camera, an attractive dark brunette with long hair, it immediately tripped her memory back to the booby-trap hole. Katie had come face to face with that body and then once again in the morgue where the delicate flower tattooed on her shoulder still stood out in her mind. How could someone's life be snuffed out so easily? She might not have even been found if it wasn't for Katie conducting that search for possible explosives.

Had the killer not wanted her to be found?

Had the killer wanted to come back and move the body?

Katie looked again at the missing persons report filed by a neighbor who hadn't seen her in a week. The statement indicated that Edith had been unemployed and was seeking job opportunities. She had missed an interview with a software company for an IT specialist. After taking night classes for computer and information technology courses, she had wanted to get into the field of cyber-security.

Katie read through everything and nothing she saw indicated anomalies or unusual events. Edith had been a counselor at Eagle Ridge Camp for three seasons and she had only left because she was getting married and wanting to start a family. There was no indication of leaving on bad terms.

Sifting back through employment files from Eagle Ridge Camp, the only information about her job as counselor was basic, just as the others' was. There was nothing indicating any problems.

How did you get up there?

Did the killer bring you?

Katie studied the crime scene photos around the site of the hole. There were no footprints or drag marks nearby, except the footprints that were made by her, McGaven, and Cisco.

How did she get there?

The dirt from the hole had been carefully deposited in

various places to disperse it. It was obvious that the killer had taken careful and precise measures to accomplish this task. It still seemed to Katie that the killer knew the area well and was able to move around easily without being detected.

Katie still couldn't confirm if Edith Crest had been with the group that had included Brian Stanwick. Her whole theory spun on the fact that her foot had been amputated. If the theory held true and they were to assume that the victims were suffering the limb loss as Brian Stanwick had —then why wasn't her leg amputated?

Not enough time?

Was the procedure more difficult?

Katie leaned back and sighed.

"Anything?" asked McGaven.

"No. It's elusive. Nothing points to anything unusual or any interactions that might be questionable. There's no definite suggestion of where they had come into contact with the killer. At home. Another location. Or if they went up to the camp under false pretenses."

"We'll figure it out," he said.

Katie opened the file for Stephanie Baxter. She was forty-two, single, never been married, lived in Pine Valley, parents and one sibling, a brother living in Ohio. She worked at a local department store as a manager in housewares, and was known to be quiet and to keep to herself. Her photo showed her sitting at a picnic table with three other people, but she didn't seem to be engaging in the conversation. She sat with her hands in her lap, looking slightly down, while the others appeared to be laughing with each other and engaged in conversation. It must have been a work picnic or something similar, thought Katie. Again, her work had reported her missing when she hadn't shown up. Cindy Ruiz, a co-worker, had gone to the police after not finding Stephanie at home and when she hadn't answered her cell phone.

Katie still couldn't get the image out of her mind of the amount of blood and missing organs at the crime scene in cabin 3. Looking at the crime scene and morgue photos of Ms. Baxter, it was clear that the killer had taken much more time and care with the incisions for the extraction of kidneys than he had with the amputations of the limbs. The photograph of the actual kidneys portrayed them as reddish-brown bean-shaped organs approximately four and half inches long. According to Dr. Dean, they were healthy organs. They would have received blood from the paired renal arteries; then the blood would exit into the paired renal veins, which was exactly what they were supposed to do. That was why it made sense that Stephanie Baxter had lost so much blood due to the cut arteries. But the areas where the blood was then spread indicated to Katie that the killer had intentionally staged it.

Why make this crime scene more dramatic and ghoulish than the other scenes?

Was the killer escalating?

Did the killer hate Ms. Baxter more than the others?

Stephanie Baxter had worked for Eagle Ridge Camp as a counselor for four seasons. The first season was two years before the others, and the last three seasons were with Carolyn Sable and Edith Crest. The only definite linkage, so far, between the three victims was the fact that all were counselors during the same time frame at Eagle Ridge Camp, and possibly at the same time as Brian Stanwick.

Were the three of you close?

Did you witness the accident?

Is there something about the link between you we don't know?

Katie became frustrated. She had learned more about the victims individually, but nothing seemed to indicate a pattern or something out of place in their lives. She reread statements, but nothing seemed out of the ordinary. They had more people to interview if they needed to, but most of those would likely not lead to anything unusual. The statements were thorough and they had the contact information if needed. The investigation needed to forge ahead and their priority was to make sure any other employees of Eagle Ridge Camp and anyone related to Brian Stanwick's accident were safe.

At the end of the day, Katie and McGaven left the Pine Valley Sheriff's Department Administration building. They walked together out to their cars. Katie was lost in thought about the killer's motive and signature.

Her cell phone rang. "Scott," she said.

"Detective Scott, this is Bud Johnson up at Eagle Ridge," he said breathless with a strain to his voice.

"What's wrong?" she said, alerting McGaven with a wave.

"I called the sheriff's department but they can't send someone for forty-five minutes."

"Bud, what's the problem? Are you okay?"

"I'm hiding out in cabin eleven because there's someone here. He ambushed me when I was doing my rounds..." His voice faded off and Katie couldn't make out what he was saying.

"Bud?"

There was a strange buzzing sound and then the connection went dead.

"What's going on?" asked McGaven.

"Bud's in trouble. We need to get up to Eagle Ridge Camp now."

CHAPTER TWENTY-EIGHT

Katie and McGaven jumped into her Jeep. It was the best way to get to Eagle Ridge Camp in decent time, most likely before the deputies did. McGaven had checked with dispatch and found out that the call had come in ten minutes before Bud had called Katie. There were only two deputies in that region of the county on a Monday night and they were both involved in a domestic disturbance call and would be detained longer than usual.

Katie pushed her SUV as hard as she dared without over-heating the engine or taxing the transmission. It was now dark outside so she amped up her car's high beams hoping that it would be enough as they made their way up the rural road to the camp. The ride was bumpy due to the excess speed—they bounced and bobbed and weaved.

"Wasn't planning on visiting this camp again so soon," said Katie hanging tight to the steering wheel. Her focus was on Bud's safety—whether he was an active or retired cop, he was still one of them.

Bracing himself, McGaven watched the road closely. "You really didn't want to go home and watch TV, did you?"

"That actually sounds nice right now."

"Did Bud say anything else?"

"No, just that he was ambushed doing rounds and was hiding out in cabin eleven."

McGaven glanced at Katie. "Do you know where cabin eleven is?"

Chills ran up and down her arms and the back of her neck. "Yes."

"Seriously?"

"It was one of the girls' cabins—I stayed in it every year."

Jenny...

"Wait a minute. I might be slow at times, but I usually get things eventually."

"You're not giving yourself enough credit."

"So be it. But let's talk facts here."

"Okay." Katie swung the steering wheel to avoid a deep hole, causing the Jeep to skid sideways. "Let's hear it." Even though she knew what her partner was going to say—she thought about the coincidence too.

"We found background information about our cold cases in cabin three and now the caretaker security guard is hiding out in the same cabin you stayed in when you were a kid. Out of all the cabins, he's holed up there. Something doesn't seem right."

Katie didn't immediately answer, but she agreed.

"I'm calling in backup and we're going to wait for them." McGaven called dispatch and was told that the backup deputies were about twenty-five minutes out now. "Great."

"We don't need to wait. Bud can't wait since he was already attacked."

"I don't like this. We could be walking directly into a trap," said McGaven with authority. "It may not be safe for any of us. We are not equipped to deal with that area properly in the dark." He kept trying Bud's cell phone number and it went directly to voicemail.

They were almost at the main parking lot. Bud's truck was parked in its usual space, but they didn't see the security guard anywhere.

Katie's intuition kicked in at an all-time high—her skin tingled with an electric energy. She knew it was the killer toying with them and wanting the police to know that he could do whatever he wanted without anyone finding a way to stop him. This killer was in control, in his mind at least, and he was flexing his power. It was quite common with serial killers. They wanted to be special and in charge while everyone else was inept and incapable of understanding everything the way they could.

"Let's get Bud out of here for his safety. Then we can wait for deputies and do a thorough controlled search. Okay?" She was adamant and wasn't going to leave someone stranded without help.

McGaven was hesitant but obviously trusted his partner. They had been through much worse. He nodded in agreement and readied himself, checking his Glock and making sure he had a backup magazine. He hoped that he wasn't going to need it.

Katie put the Jeep in reverse and backed up, parking between two trees. It made it less noticeable, but it wouldn't give them complete cover.

She remembered she had an extra change of clothes in a duffel bag in the back, so she quickly got out and opened the back door. Without caring, she shed her work jacket and blouse and put on a sweatshirt. She pulled off her heeled work boots, and changed into a pair of hiking shoes.

"That's the fastest change I've ever seen," said McGaven quietly.

"I once changed my clothes, everything, in the back of a cab in San Francisco."

"Call *Ripley's.*"

Katie smiled, but kept her wits about her as she checked her firearms and backup magazine. "Okay." She grabbed two flashlights and gave one to McGaven.

"You ready?"

"Cabin eleven is on the north side of the main buildings. There are four cabins in between the biggest pines—you can't miss it. They're actually cabins ten through thirteen and they are set apart from the others."

"So it's the second one on the north side?"

Katie nodded. "How do you want to do this? I think we need to split up."

McGaven studied the area, remembering how they had initially searched the buildings and where cover would work to their best advantage.

He nodded. "I don't like it, but that's the best option under the circumstances."

"I'll take the path near the lake and boathouse and you take the area near the main building. We'll meet up at the four cabins."

McGaven listened. "Okay, but I want to stay in contact. Do you have your earpiece for your cell phone?"

"Yes."

"Use it and keep the line open, okay?"

"Okay," she said.

"Katie, I'm not joking around. Keep the communication open."

"Of course." She knew that McGaven was worried about her being impetuous and also the fact that she had been injured during their last search.

"Stay alert."

"Be extra cautious for booby traps," she said and gave McGaven one last look before she disappeared along the pathway toward the lake.

Katie made sure her cell phone was secured and wouldn't

fall out of her pocket. She didn't immediately switch on her flashlight. Her eyes adjusted to the darkness as she followed the trail weaving back and forth. The shadows of the trees stood high over her as if waiting to pounce at any given moment—long limbs resembling arms ready to grab her.

She stopped. Gaining her perspective, her balance, and keeping her nerves calm, Katie slowly scanned her immediate area. It was unusually quiet and there wasn't the slightest breeze. The temperature seemed to drop five degrees as she stood immersing herself in the environment.

"Everything okay?" whispered McGaven startling her.

"Ten-four," she said as she moved forward.

The soft bumping sound of the boathouse door made her turn her attention in that direction, when she turned back and concentrated on what was ahead she heard someone call her name. *"Katie..."*

It rattled her nerves and shortened her breath. She knew that voice, but there was no way that it could be who she thought it was. Katie intuitively slowed her pace. She decided to turn on her flashlight and keep it directed low and in front of her. Sweeping the area for anything that could be hazardous or someone lying in wait, she moved with purpose.

"Almost there," she whispered. Her voice sounded hollow inside her head.

"Right behind you," said McGaven.

"Right behind you," a small voiced echoed from nearby.

Katie sucked in a breath and spun a one eighty, directing the flashlight in the direction which she had come. Next to a large tree trunk, standing in the dirt, was a faint outline of a little girl wearing denim shorts and a white T-shirt.

"What? No it *can't* be..." Katie barely spoke out loud.

"Say it again," said McGaven in her earpiece.

Katie moved toward the apparition. "Jenny?" she said.

The shadowy appearance of the little girl slowly faded as

she stared directly at Katie and pointed in the direction she was heading.

"What's your status?" said McGaven. "Katie, what's going on?" His voice inflection had a distinct uneasiness.

"Almost there," she whispered as the ghostly image of her murdered childhood friend dissipated into the darkness. "Everything is fine." She shuddered even though the temperature was comfortable.

Suddenly, she snapped back into the present.

What was happening?

Was she losing her mind?

Why was Jenny picking at her subconscious?

She realized that it had to be because of the area she was in. The memories it threw up were good and bad, and those past skeletons weren't ever far away. They had stayed with her all these years.

Pushing forward, Katie could now see the cabins. They hadn't searched them the last time she and McGaven were here. The small square structures were in poor condition. Katie approached quickly, extinguished her flashlight, and waited with her back against the siding of cabin 10. She listened. No voices. No movement. She didn't hear McGaven approach.

"You here?" she barely breathed.

Silence.

She whispered again, "You close? Gav?"

Katie looked down at her cell phone. There was no signal. She had lost contact with McGaven.

Skirting the wall she moved closer to the cabin, peering into the window. It was black inside. She dared to turn her flashlight into the cabin. At first the light bounced off the window in different directions because of the crack and shined in her eyes, but once she swept the light lower she saw that the interior was vacant.

Katie looked ahead to where McGaven would be emerging

from—but he wasn't in sight. She kept moving to cabin 11. For a brief instant, memories flooded back as she remembered what it had been like staying in that same cabin with several other girls.

Jenny...

Katie kept moving cautiously along the siding until she reached the window of the cabin. Plywood boarded up the window, so she couldn't see inside. There was no other choice but to keep moving. Staying still would be more dangerous, making her a target for whoever ambushed Bud.

The door to the cabin was open a few inches. Katie stood at the entrance, listening, but there was no sound. She felt confident that the enemy wasn't there anymore.

"Bud?" she whispered at first. "You there?"

No one answered. She hated going forward with no backup and not knowing what to expect. A rustle in the trees made her jump. She knew it was only nocturnal animals, but she still felt braced for the worst.

She secured her weapon in her hand and pushed the door open. Strangely, it didn't make a sound, as if the hinges were well oiled. At first, she thought she had gone deaf. How could something so old and lacking in any maintenance for years not make a sound?

Directing the flashlight beam inside, she saw several broken pieces of furniture. There was a bunk bed frame, two legs from a desk, and broken glass from the front window.

"Bud," she said again.

Katie swung the light beam back and forth—illuminating corners where the shadows had been. There was no one there, nor any trace that anyone had been there recently except for the open door. She stepped inside a few feet and did a slow three-hundred-sixty-degree turn. Cabin 11 was empty.

Maybe Bud had been mistaken about the cabin number?

Katie looked around again, thinking she had missed something. She heard quick footsteps behind her. Before she turned fully, expecting to see McGaven, a tall medium-build person struck her hard, causing her to land on her back. Her flashlight dislodged from her hand, instantly smashing on the floor. The light was gone, leaving her in absolute darkness.

CHAPTER TWENTY-NINE

Katie lay on her back for a minute recovering from the assault and trying desperately to catch her breath. She gasped loudly as she rolled to her side and pushed her body to the far side of the cabin. The pitch blackness made her the perfect prey to whoever attacked her.

Quieting her breath, she focused intently on her surroundings, listening for any movement. Waiting. There was no light from outside. The window was securely boarded up and something blocked the door entry. She thought she could hear breathing, which meant that someone was still inside the room with her. Her skin prickled and she kept her breath shallow.

Katie slowly reached for her weapon, knowing it was some-where near her. Dragging her hand across the floor, feeling the small shards of glass against her fingertips then finally touching the barrel of her gun, she gripped it tightly. Her flashlight had shattered and was unusable.

All of a sudden, she heard McGaven's voice through the earpiece that had been dislodged and was now at her collar. She put it back in.

"Katie? Where are you? Katie?" There were still sounds of static.

Katie didn't say anything. She hoped that McGaven would reach her before her standoff was over. She wasn't going to fire her gun aimlessly into the darkness or at a shadow figure.

Keeping her eyes fixed on the partially open doorway, she saw the outline of a tall, lean figure. She guessed it was a man. What was he waiting for?

"Identify yourself," Katie said with authority as she slowly got to her feet. "Now!"

The shadow man spun and disappeared quickly.

"Stop!" she yelled and sprinted after him. Watching him disappear around the corner of the cabin, she pursued him as fast as she could. But once around the corner of the cabin, there was nothing. It was as if the figure had vanished. There was a little bit of light from the moon, but there was no one in sight. No movement of leaves.

"Katie," yelled McGaven as he rushed up to her, winded from sprinting. "You okay?" He had his gun out.

"Yeah, there was someone here but he got the slip on me. And by the way they appeared and disappeared, he knows the camp well."

"Who was it?"

"Don't know…" She still studied the pathway and surrounding areas that someone could divert. "He jumped me in cabin eleven, but waited. It was as if he…"

"What?"

"It was like he was watching me… studying me. If he wanted to kill me he could have."

"Let's get back to the parking entrance and wait for backup, then we can search the area." He readied his weapon as they began to retreat.

"He's gone. He knows this place like it's his own backyard." Katie was angry with herself at not handling the situation better. The sight of the ghostly figure of Jenny still shook her deeply.

"C'mon, let's go," he said. "I don't like standing around where there are many places to get ambushed." He directed his flashlight to clear a path back to the parking lot.

Katie hesitated, still looking to where the phantom had disappeared. She then hurried with McGaven as they made their way back to the parking lot.

"There's no sign of Bud anywhere," she said.

The detectives saw lights approaching from the road. It was easy to recognize that two police cruisers were advancing up to the camp to assist them.

Katie searched around the parking area and then went to Bud's truck. She slowed her pace. "Gav," she said. "Need your flashlight." She readied her weapon but kept it down at her side.

McGaven immediately approached and directed the flashlight into the truck. There was an outline of a slumped figure.

Katie swallowed hard, bracing for the worst.

As they neared, they recognized it was Bud. He was seated in the driver's seat with his head leaning forward. Blood was on the side of his face. His eyes were closed. His cell phone was still in his right hand, flopped to the side.

"Bud," said Katie. "Bud." As McGaven covered her, she opened the car door and immediately checked for a pulse. "He's alive."

Bud mumbled something incoherent and moved his head toward her.

"Bud? What happened?" she said.

"I was waiting for you... when... someone struck me. I was able... to... get back to my truck... but..."

"We need an ambulance," said McGaven.

"No, that will take too long. A deputy will be faster."

As McGaven briefed the dispatched deputies, Katie kept

talking to Bud. They all worked together and helped Bud into one of the patrol cars. Another deputy arrived.

They teamed up. Katie and McGaven took point and searched all the buildings on the north side and the two deputies took the south side.

Nothing. No sign of anyone. The person that Katie had encountered was long gone.

Just outside cabin 1 where Bud had been staying, there were signs of the confrontation that had taken place. Scuff marks in the dirt, broken glass from the window across the ground, and the interior of the cabin had been ransacked.

Katie sat at Bud's small desk and rewound surveillance footage from the cameras. There was nothing unusual, except for three seconds there was a dark figure skirting the range of the camera. Again, it was a tall lean figure, most likely a man, dressed in black with a hoodie pulled tightly around his head and face.

"Nothing," said Katie disappointed.

"Maybe Bud can fill in the gaps?" said McGaven.

"I don't think so. This guy was clever enough to know exactly how to stay unidentifiable." She turned around and scanned the cabin. "What a mess." Paperwork, food, and the bedding were strewn all over the floor.

One of the deputies came in and said, "Bud is reported in stable condition. Just bruises, contusions. They're keeping him overnight."

"Thank you," said Katie.

"You need us?" said the deputy.

"No, it's all done here for now," said McGaven as he walked the deputies back to their cruisers.

Katie was upset with herself. How could she have let this guy go? She left the cabin and secured the door. She felt bad that Bud had such a mess to clean up.

Jogging back to the parking lot, she saw the cruisers' tail-lights as they were heading back down to the road. McGaven leaned against the Jeep.

"Remind me next time to go home and watch TV instead," she said.

"I will, but you know you'd rather run to danger instead."

"Yeah, yeah." She got to the Jeep and opened the door to let more light disperse.

McGaven came over to her. "What am I going to do with you?" he said and gently wiped away blood from her face.

"Great," she said, trying to see her reflection in the window. "Is that going to leave a mark?"

"Let's go home. We can write up the report in the morning."

"No argument here," she said.

"You want me to drive?"

"No, I'm fine."

They both got into the Jeep.

When Katie settled herself and put her hands on the steering wheel, she felt something on the back. "What the...?" It was a small sticky note, one by two inches, with some writing on it. It said: *Until we meet again.*

"What is that?"

Katie showed McGaven.

"That bastard," he said. "He's so brazen."

"He's toying with us. He could have killed Bud or me, but he didn't. Why?"

"It's not on his time," he said.

"We need to find the fourth woman in that photo with Carolyn Sable and the others." Katie was troubled, still uneasy about what happened this evening.

McGaven sensed her concerns. "We'll find her soon and make sure she's safe."

Katie turned the key in the ignition as the SUV roared to life. "I hope it won't be too late."

CHAPTER THIRTY

Katie watched Cisco run around the backyard through the glass sliding door. He ran from side to side and then investigated some bushes. His black coat glistened in the low light outside.

She sipped some hot tea and reran everything that happened during the day and at Eagle Ridge Camp. She felt she was spinning her wheels in these investigations. Clues weren't getting them anywhere. Strange coincidences. Unusual behavior of employees at the offices of Fields, Campbell. But nothing pinpointed who killed these three women or why.

It was almost midnight and Katie would have thought she'd be extremely tired by now. In fact, it was the opposite; she had a rush of renewed energy. She kept rerunning every second that had passed when she reached cabin 11. She had more questions than answers.

Katie returned to the kitchen to pour more hot water. Her skin still felt cold and prickly as she tried to shake the uneasy feelings. There was a familiar scratch at the back door—Cisco wanted to come back inside.

She opened the slider and a black blur rushed inside. "You feel better?"

A ping noise came from her cell phone—it was McGaven sending her a text message:

You better not still be awake—get some sleep. Starting early tomorrow we'll tackle what needs to be done.

Katie smiled and appreciated the thought and assurance about their cases.

The dog circled back around from the living room and stayed by Katie's side as she cleaned up the kitchen. That was when she noticed several pieces of paper lying on the bar counter next to some magazines. They were photos of houses together with descriptions of the properties.

"What...?" she said to herself. "I can't believe that he..." She couldn't finish her sentence. Chad must've left these flyers of houses for sale for her to see. She thought they would take it slow—but he had pushed forward. They were very nice homes and there was a handwritten note on one saying there was a great yard for Cisco.

Katie put down the flyers and decided that it wasn't worth the effort right now to be upset or disappointed. Her arms and back were sore. It had been a long day—she needed to get some rest, get recharged, and hit the ground running tomorrow.

Katie climbed into bed after a hot shower and was fast asleep within minutes. She didn't toss or turn, and she didn't roll over on her side—she plunged into a deep sleep. Her breathing was steady and rhythmic, but soon turned shallow, almost stopping. She began to fight the unrest in her dream...

Katie ran through the forest of Eagle Ridge Camp. The trails repeated endlessly no matter how hard she tried to get to wher-

ever she was going. She saw the fourth counselor from the photo-
graph walking ahead of her, holding the hand of a little girl. They
walked at a leisurely pace, but Katie couldn't catch up to them.
Her frustration fueled her anger. She tried to yell in the dream,
but no voice passed her lips. A dark shadow was up ahead, big
and looming, but the woman and child seemed oblivious to it.
Katie tried harder to reach them. Things started to fade in front of
her. Just at that point, she reached out and touched the woman's
shoulder. She turned, no face, and the little girl grabbed Katie's
hand. When she looked down, she saw the face of her friend
Jenny just as she had looked the last time she had seen her.

Katie gasped and sat up in bed. She must've been holding her
breath because she was panting hard as if she had been running.
Her focus was spotty until she controlled her breath.

Cisco had jumped up on the bed and snuggled next to her.

Katie felt the warmth next to her and it helped to ease her
nightmare. The more she thought about it, the more she thought
it might be her subconscious trying to point her in the right
direction of the investigation. There were so many directions to
go—and the longer they wasted their time, the more likely that
another woman would be found dead.

Katie looked at the clock: 2:20 a.m. She swung her legs out
of bed and got up. In one of the top dresser drawers, she found
an envelope filled with photographs. Many were of her and
Chad when they were young. Some were of her parents—she
paused as she remembered where every photo had been taken.
There were two pictures of her and Jenny. She stared at them—
examining closer. She fought her critical thinking and thought
about it—was it possible that Jenny was trying to tell her something? More than likely Katie's subconscious was trying to use
someone familiar, like Jenny, as a guide in these horrible cases
that revolved around Eagle Ridge Camp.

Katie went back to bed knowing she needed to get the appropriate rest if she was going to help anyone. She fell fast asleep, but this time she didn't dream.

CHAPTER THIRTY-ONE

Katie opened her office door and McGaven was already there with piles of paper on the desk.

"Good morning," she said and put down a steaming cup of coffee for her partner.

"Slept well, I take it?" he said never averting his gaze from the computer screen. Fingertips rapidly tapping the keys with the flashing computer pages.

"Started out a bit rough, but yes, I had a great night's sleep." She put down her briefcase, jacket, and her coffee. "I'm ready for whatever today throws at us."

"Don't group me in that statement."

"Sorry, we're partners and that means you're in it too."

"Good news," said McGaven.

"That's how I like to start my day." She took her chair and rolled it close to him. "Hit me with it."

"I've been going through the list of people from Eagle Ridge Camp and their last known contact information, which is mostly outdated. But…"

"C'mon, I wouldn't have gotten out of a nice warm bed for this…" she teased and eyed the printed-out spreadsheet.

"I did find our fourth counselor. Robin Drakes, now Robin Drakes-Daniels."

"Did you talk to her?"

"No."

"What?"

"But I used the number she gave when she was a counselor, and it turns out it's her mom's place and she's still there."

"So she gave you Ms. Drakes' address?" she said.

"No, but... well sorta..."

Katie watched her partner with interest. "What do you mean?"

"Well, Mrs. Drakes said that she hadn't had contact with her daughter in almost ten years. Some kind of falling-out or something. But she gave me the last known address where she used to send letters, but never visited."

"Think she's telling the truth—not just maybe covering for her daughter for some reason?"

"Mom is telling the truth. It had to do with the guy Robin married. And she thinks that they might have gotten divorced by now. By what I could find, they are divorced." He shuffled through his paperwork.

Sipping her coffee, Katie said, "I think it's too early for this dizzying investigation."

"This is actually good."

"How so?"

"Well, think about it, if we have to dig to find out where Ms. Drakes-Daniels is, then it will make it difficult for someone else —namely the killer."

"Good point." Katie checked her phone for a text from forensics. "Nothing from John yet, so let's find Ms. Drakes." She looked at the board. "I want to add something." She got up and approached the board studying it for a moment. Then she began to write...

Profile of Killer:

Connection to Eagle Ridge Camp—employee, student, volunteer, owner, family, etc.

Knows Eagle Ridge Camp well.

Why wait so long?

Killing counselors of Eagle Ridge Camp—connection? Friend, family, student, etc.

Connection to cabins, lake, etc.

Prefers to face his victims—knows victims first and gives them some type of security. He wants them to see him, have power over them before they die.

Dismemberment—Anger. Retaliation. Power. Revenge or vengeance? Brian Stanwick?

Jealousy. Scorned?

Vigilante payback of some kind.

Planned.

Victims—kept prisoner? Why?

Methodical.

High intelligence, adaptability, staying ahead of the police, placing bodies where he wants them.

Arrogant—playing the police—wants control.

Why ambush attacks on Bud? Returning to crime scene—looking for something or information.

The office phone rang. Katie answered, "Scott." She paused. "Thank you for the call." She hung up.

McGaven waited.

"Looks like Bud's awake and wants to talk to us."

"Good news."

Katie grabbed her coat. "Let's get over there."

"Maybe he remembered who ambushed him."

Katie didn't have much hope.

"What's wrong?"

"If I couldn't see the person that got the drop on me, Bud probably didn't either."

"Maybe. But Bud is there all the time. He might've noticed other things that we haven't. Know what I mean?"

Katie nodded. She wasn't so sure, but anything Bud remembered would be helpful.

"I'll drive," he said and followed Katie out the door and down the hallway.

CHAPTER THIRTY-TWO

"Detectives Scott and McGaven to see Bud... rather Clarence Thompson," she said to the nurse seated at the station who didn't look up from her paperwork. Her dark hair was tightly pulled back in a bun.

"Room 141," the nurse said.

"Thank you," replied Katie.

The detectives walked down the hallway passing a few patients out for their walks. They turned the corner and quickly found room 141, which had a closed door.

Katie glanced at McGaven and raised her eyebrows as if to say, *Here we go.* She pushed open the door and immediately saw the security guard propped up in the hospital bed. He was receiving oxygen and there were several bandages on his face. His right arm was wrapped in heavy gauze. The bed sheet was neatly folded beneath his arms. His eyes were closed.

"Bud?" said Katie in a low tone.

The two detectives stood one on each side of his bed.

"Bud," she said again.

The security guard's eyes fluttered open and he fixed his

gaze on Katie. "Detective Scott. It's so nice to see you. We all had quite the scare last night."

Katie spotted a chair and pulled it close to the bed. McGaven remained standing and patiently kept quiet as Katie took lead.

"Bud, can you tell us what happened?"

"They already took my statement early this morning."

"Can you tell it again for us?" Katie smiled. She wanted to hear what happened from him and not from a report secondhand.

"Well," he began, "I do my rounds morning, noon, and early evening. Sometimes before bedtime. I decided yesterday to do my rounds a little early, before supper."

"Why is that?"

"I was feeling a bit tired and wanted to get my head down early. I log everything in by the day, time, duration, and anything I find or see that's out of the ordinary."

Katie patiently listened and let him tell what happened to the best of his ability.

"I checked all the cabins. I go clockwise from my cabin and then make my way around again."

"What do you check for?" asked McGaven.

"Make sure the doors are locked and the windows are the way they were the last time I checked. Looking for anything that's out of place. You know..." he said.

"What happened when you got to cabin eleven?" she said.

"Well, I saw some footprints. Human, not animal," said Bud. He grabbed his cup and drank some water. He seemed winded and needed a break. "So I looked at them, and I was about to take a photo with my cell phone. You know, to send to you."

"Of course," said Katie wishing he would get to the point.

"That's when I saw it. The cabin door was unlocked and open about two or three inches. I completely forgot about the footprints and fixated on the open door." He took a moment to catch his breath.

Katie knew well what he had seen because of what she had witnessed and experienced herself.

"For some reason, I wasn't thinking things through. Getting old, I guess. But I went inside." He paused to take another sip of water. "That's when—WHAM—something hit me. I turned and saw a man, tall, dressed in dark clothing. I couldn't make a positive ID of any kind."

"Anything you can remember at all. Build. Hair color. Age. Anything?" said Katie.

"No, ma'am. I'm sorry. And then when I tried to get up he punched me twice and I don't remember anything until I came to—then I thought the safest place to get to was my truck. Oh, and I called you guys after trying 911 and they couldn't send any deputies for almost an hour."

"It's okay," said Katie. She was disappointed because she, too, couldn't identify much of anything. "When do you get out?"

"They said maybe tomorrow if my blood pressure gets to a more acceptable level."

"Well, rest up and take care of yourself," she said and stood, ready to leave.

"Thank you, Detective."

"Call me if you remember anything else."

"Of course," he said and closed his eyes. "I'll try to remember something..." His voice faded.

Katie and McGaven left the hospital room and made their way outside and to their police vehicle.

McGaven got back behind the wheel and stared at Katie as she secured her seatbelt. "What do you think? A waste of time?"

"Yes and no."

"You sound like me—maybe I'm rubbing off on you."

"I believe his story about being ambushed, but I don't think that happened the way he told it."

"But you don't believe..."

"There's something wrong with his story about doing his rounds... I saw part of his logs and there's nothing about his observations—like footprints, open doors, or anything out of place. It was date, time, and where he checked. Just basic stuff."

"And his injuries seemed pretty extensive to get all the way back to the truck." McGaven thought a moment. "Do you think someone moved him from there to his truck?"

"It crossed my mind," she said. "What's going to happen now at the camp?"

"Meaning?" McGaven programmed an address into the GPS for 1001 Industrial Place.

"He obviously isn't fit to be a security guard there—it's proven too dangerous."

"I'm not sure. Maybe the department will have a deputy or two stationed in shifts?"

"I don't think the budget would allow for it." Katie started thinking. "Maybe someone needs to be there only at night."

McGaven turned to Katie. "No way."

"What?"

"I know exactly how you think," he said. "Maybe not *exactly*." He started the engine and backed out of the visitor's parking space.

"I was just thinking that maybe—"

"I'm going to stop you right there."

"How do you know what I was going to say?"

"Because I know that in your mind, which is brilliant most but not all of the time, is the idea that you can stay there at Eagle Ridge to crack this case and catch the killer."

"Well, maybe..."

"You want to know what your uncle would say? Huh,

Detective Scott?" He accelerated out of the parking lot and eased the sedan onto the closest freeway.

"I'm just trying to consolidate things—by getting smart. There's a woman's life at stake and maybe even more that we don't know about yet," Katie stated in a firm voice. The more she thought about it, the more it made sense—to her.

"You always think you have to do everything."

"Wait a minute, Detective. First, I don't think that, but anyway, what other alternatives are there?" She waited.

"Maybe another retired cop could fill in, or hiring a security guard, or doing a rotation from the deputy pool at the department. I don't know—something could be worked out. There are alternatives."

Katie leaned back and stared at the road through the windshield. "Let me know how that works out."

"Look," he said. "I know more than anyone that you can be impulsive—at times. But you've always been able to back it up with brains. But this time, I don't think you've thought this whole thing through."

"Firstly, there needs to be more sophisticated cameras, like the ones we're seeing in every office we've visited lately. Some safe traps need to be installed all around the buildings if anyone unauthorized gets close—like motion detectors, infrared video, and cameras. I would stay in a different place, like the commissary or stockroom, but make it look like I'm staying in my favorite cabin eleven. I wouldn't be alone. I would have you and Cisco."

"Okay, I'm wrong. You have given this some thought."

"Look, there's so much more we can do with the right planning—especially since we know that the killer seems to be visiting the camp and surrounding areas on a regular basis."

McGaven remained quiet as he drove, contemplating what his partner had said.

"I'm not talking about storming up there and putting myself

out there, but there's some reason that the killer had articles about us and the fact he didn't kill me. He stood and waited—watching me. He could've easily killed me."

"That makes me feel better and I'm sure that Sheriff Scott is going to be thrilled when you explain that to him."

"Need I remind you that I've been on the battlefield with two tours in Afghanistan. I led my team safely through bomb-infested areas. And insurgents..."

"And you and Cisco are one of the coolest teams I've ever seen."

"You know what I mean. I've been trained for this kind of stuff. We have to be smarter than this killer and stay two steps ahead."

"What do you need from me?" McGaven gritted his teeth which indicated that he was still not thrilled with the idea.

"I want you to help me convince Sheriff Scott that we need to do this."

"Oh, is that all?"

"That's all. And I'm sure that John can help with the technology..." Katie stopped explaining her plan. She wanted to let it simmer with McGaven because she couldn't do it without him or her uncle's blessing.

McGaven had driven through the industrial part of Pine Valley as they talked, and another five miles past closed industrial buildings. He pulled up next to a three-story structure that hadn't been occupied in years.

Looking around, Katie said, "Where are we?"

"Welcome to the last known address of Robin Drakes-Daniels."

CHAPTER THIRTY-THREE

"What is this place? It looks like the backdrop for a horror movie. Are you sure this is the right address?" asked Katie.

"Definitely. I knew it was somewhere like this, so we need to check it out. Robin's mom claimed that she had sent letters here. I think she was telling the truth."

"Where would the mailbox even be?" said Katie, searching the outside of the building. "There's no mailbox or mail slot that I can see."

McGaven parked on the side a short distance from the building and then opened the door. "C'mon, we're here now, so let's go take a look."

Katie was reluctant. She feared it would only be another dead end and was finding it hard to keep up her enthusiasm. She felt the killer was getting further out of reach even while they checked out these places that didn't render anything useful. Even so, her curiosity and determination forced her out of the car.

"This place could tell some stories," said McGaven trying to bring up Katie's spirits.

"And then some." Katie walked closer to the building. It

appeared to be a three-story industrial building in extreme need
of repair, which most likely had once housed a business like a
metal fabrication shop, auto mechanic garage, or something
along the lines of textiles or construction. The top floor would
have been the administrative offices. The siding was cement
with a steel-enforced structure—now dated and crumbling.
There was a long line of six large roll-up doors along the back.
Two doors led to an inside staircase.

McGaven walked around the back of the building.

Weeds had grown to immense heights as if they were in a
cornfield. Garbage had been strewn across the back for quite
some time—large bulging trash bags, old mattresses, crates,
miscellaneous pieces of broken furniture, along with faded
labels and drinking cups, and wooden pallets.

"I don't know, Gav. It doesn't look like anyone has been
here in a decade."

"What I didn't tell you..."

"What do you mean? You holding out on me?" she snapped.

"I did a quick background on the building through the
county assessor's website from my phone and it appears that
Red Hawk Real Estate seems to have sold this property twelve
years ago to KLM Enterprises, LLC."

"The same KLM that owns Eagle Ridge Camp?" said Katie
surprised. "But how can that be? Mr. Green and Red Hawk
Real Estate said that he only dealt with them through emails.
And the printouts of the contract we were given had only PO
boxes and no main contact. Tracing emails only sent us in
circles and back to dummy corporations and phony email
addresses. We need to keep digging. There has to be more information about them."

"Sounds like someone has made an extreme effort to keep
their name from being connected to the properties," he said.
"And there's no one to call to ask permission to see the interior."

Katie still studied the building. "You're right. There's no

real estate listing—it's just sitting here deteriorating. Let's get a closer look."

"You sure it's not conflicting with the breaking and entering law?"

She glanced back at the car and down the dusty street. There were no cars or sounds of anything in the distance. She felt comfortable enough to check out the building more thoroughly. "We can always claim exigent circumstances, but I don't think anyone is going to care at this point. We need to run down every lead for three homicide investigations and a potential missing person."

Katie and McGaven separated to see if there were any open doors or windows they could get a glimpse inside.

Katie tried the stairwell door and it had been sealed shut. She carefully stepped toward the roll-up doors; one of them was narrow, less than the size of a one-car garage. Dirt, debris, and weeds had built up on the bottom making it impossible to see where the pull-up handles were located.

She leaned down to make sure there wasn't something that could cut her or cause any other type of injury. Standing back up, she kicked at the dirt and eventually revealed a metal handle. Grasping it, she tried to pull it up. It squeaked and squealed from the side roll-up tracks, but would only move a couple of inches.

"C'mon," she said, straining to get the door up. Piles of bugs scattered out. "Yuck!"

"What?" said McGaven approaching quickly. "Got something?"

"Yeah, it's in serious need for pest control." Katie backed up. "I got this door to move a couple of inches, but not enough to really see anything or get inside."

"Let me try," he said and dropped to his knees, gripped the bottom of the door and heaved.

The metal scraping sent chills down Katie's spine. She

198

JENNIFER CHASE

pressed her hands over her ears in an attempt to keep the horrifying noise out. She watched McGaven push the door to about a three-foot opening, but couldn't get it to budge anymore.

"That's it," he said. "You game?"

"I guess."

"That doesn't sound so certain."

"It's just the old building and mounds of bugs."

"Wow."

"What?"

"I found something that Katie Scott is afraid of…"

"Funny. I don't like them, that's all." She bent down and entered the building without saying any more to McGaven.

McGaven followed his partner inside.

Katie stood up, furiously brushing herself off, and then studied the interior—light flowed in from the upper windows making it easy to see. It wasn't what she had expected. It was cleaner than an abandoned building and there were large crates that appeared relatively new. The floor was free of debris and there was a large natural weave rug put down in the corner.

"Not what I was expecting," he said.

"No kidding." Katie walked to where the rug was and noticed that there were some deep indentations. "Look at this," she said. "It looks like there were pieces of furniture here recently, like a couch or maybe a bed and table."

McGaven knelt down and ran his fingers over the impressions. "You're right. It looks like someone moved out recently. But how can that be? It looks like no one has been here in years. How did they get in without leaving any traces? And how did they move the furniture?"

Katie didn't respond right away. She walked around the room and on the far wall she saw metal loops. Upon closer inspection, they were some type of shackles, and she saw dark dried areas of what appeared to be blood. "Gav," she said.

He looked up from the rug and saw her at the wall. He

quickly joined her and realized what Katie knew. "It's a place where someone was kept prisoner," he said in barely a whisper.

"Could Carolyn Sable have been held here?" she said. "It would make sense, since she disappeared weeks before she was found at Eagle Ridge."

"And what about Edith Crest and Stephanie Baxter?"

"We need to call this in and get forensics out here," she said. "I want to make sure that there isn't anyone else in the building." She retrieved her gun and moved toward the stairwell.

Without wasting any time, McGaven followed suit and shadowed his partner climbing up the rickety metal staircase. Their footsteps made a ringing tone.

Katie remained alert and ready for anything. She noticed that there was a strange odor, but attributed it to the old building. It smelled like old wood, old garage material, and musty rooms. She pushed forward, clearing every area before continuing.

"Clear," she said as she directed her Glock out in front of her.

"Same," chimed McGaven.

They hurried through the area, which had boxes and an old refrigerator in the corner that was working. McGaven opened it. There were several bottles of water and three containers of yogurt. The grocery items weren't recent, but someone had been there within the last couple of weeks.

Katie continued her search and climbed the last stairs to the upper level. When she got to the top, it was a long hallway that went the length of the building with offices on both sides. Some of the doors were missing while others were shut. The upper part of the doors had opaque glass, making it difficult to see inside.

They paused, peered inside the rooms that were about fifteen feet by fifteen feet, and then the detectives worked their way to the end of the hall.

Katie relaxed, lowering her weapon to her side. "Empty. Doesn't look like anyone has been up here in a while."

"No, but someone's been here at some stage. I wonder if this is the killer's place where he held his victims?"

"We'll know for sure when John and his team get here," she said as she began calling the police department.

McGaven seemed nervous as he kept looking around.

"Crap!"

"What?"

"I can't get a signal inside here, can you?"

McGaven checked his cell phone. "Nope. Let's go back downstairs."

As they moved back down the long hallway, something shiny caught Katie's eye. She stopped and examined a wall next to one of the offices. "Look at this."

"What is that?"

"It looks like some kind of metal covering. Like they put extra metal as some type of protectant or structure support. And look here," she said and pulled some of the drywall away. "There are heavy coated and sealed wires here. That's not standard issue." She looked around. "What was this place?"

"Not sure. But I do know that software companies have reinforced walls and windows to keep anyone from peeking or picking up their signals."

"But this building?"

"If you think about it, it would be a perfect spot for a software or computer programing business."

"When we get back search for business licenses with this address," she said. "Just a hunch, but if they are as clever and covert as it appears, there's probably no record."

Two loud bangs reverberated from downstairs, startling both detectives. They raced to the staircase landing, but stopped. Smoke was rising fast from the second floor and the distinct crackling of flames roared loudly throughout the building.

"The building is on fire," said Katie with nerves rattled. Her heart pounded as she tried to keep her pulse steady. "What are we going to do?"

"Someone must've set it behind us. How?"

"There was probably some type of trigger or infrared prompt for security purposes and we tripped it when we entered." She turned and ran back down the hallway and entered one of the rooms. "I don't know why this building is burning this fast, though."

"What are you thinking?" he said.

"We can't go back downstairs or wait for the fire department to arrive. It'll be too late." She looked around the room and couldn't find anything to break the window.

McGaven aimed his weapon and fired three times, shattering the window and taking out part of the frame. The outside air entered the room and gave relief for a few minutes.

"Nice."

McGaven looked out and down. "You might not think that when you see this."

Katie looked down from three stories up. She could see smoke billowing from the cracks of the other windows in the building. The fire was bigger and more aggressive than they had realized and their time was limited. She turned to McGaven. "Not good." She leaned back against the wall in defeat.

"Maybe not," he said. "But say your thanks that someone dumped those mattresses."

"What are you saying?"

"Look, if we get up on this ledge, I think we can push off enough to make it to those mattresses."

Katie stared blankly at him.

Another explosion came from downstairs, shaking the walls. The rapidly rising smoke and heat from the flames stealthily climbed the stairs. It would be moments until they were engulfed in an inferno.

"We can do this," he insisted.

"That is crazy. The fall will kill us."

"Not if we hit the mattresses."

"We don't know if they are all mattresses or if there are bricks underneath," she said.

Smoke ballooned down the hallway.

"True. You have any other ideas?" He moved closer to the window, seeking fresh air. They began to cough. It was only a matter of about one minute, maybe two, before they would be overcome.

"Dammit! No, I don't." She secured her weapon in her holster closer to her body. She didn't have time to think about her life, Chad, or her uncle. Her focus was forward-moving and they had to get out immediately. "You'll have to hoist me up."

McGaven helped Katie up to the narrow ledge and kept her steady until she had her balance. She held to the sides of the opening, trying not to cut her hands on the jagged pieces of glass. Looking down, she estimated that she had to push out three or four feet to be able to land on the mattresses. "I don't think I can do it."

"Yes, you can. We've been through a lot together. This is a piece of cake." McGaven's eyes gave him away—he was clearly uncertain.

Katie grabbed McGaven's hand and squeezed it. She didn't say a word to her partner, but her gesture was evident. All the investigations and time they would spend together in the future now balanced on this escape.

McGaven nodded as he tried not to cough. The smoke became thicker and insistent as if looking for its victims—the raging flames became deafening. "Go, Katie! Go now!" he yelled.

Katie turned her attention back to the ground, which

seemed incredibly far away. She steadied herself, maintaining her balance and positioning her feet where she could push with some force.

"Go!" yelled McGaven again. He let go of his partner.

Katie shut her eyes and then opened them again with her target in sight. As she leaned forward and pushed with all of her strength, she became weightless and then she dropped like a stone. Not sure if she screamed or not, she kept her arms out at her sides and speared the mattresses with her legs, rolling to one side to keep from breaking any bones. She rolled farther and off the pile, landing on the ground.

Relieved that she had made it and was still alive, she looked up just at the time that her six-foot-six partner pushed his body from the window, smoke mushrooming behind him. He coasted downward with some grace and hit the far side of the mattress target, rolling immediately.

Katie scrambled to her feet and rushed to her partner on the other side of the mattress pile. McGaven was sitting up slowly with a look of discomfort on his face.

"You okay?" she said.

Another explosion ripped through the building. An earthquake-like movement made the ground rumble and the impact slammed into their bodies.

Katie ducked, covering her partner as they waited for hurling projectiles to cease.

"You okay?" she said again.

He nodded.

"You don't have any injuries?"

"I don't think so. Just a headache and my back will be killing me tomorrow."

Katie's head hurt too from inhaling the smoke, from the physical effects of the explosion, and the high adrenalin rush. She hugged her partner tight and was thankful that they were going to be okay. "C'mon, let's get farther away from this and find some fresher air," she said, helping McGaven to his feet. "Preferably upwind."

"Why am I having déjà vu?" he said in good humor, limping slightly as they made their way around the building and down the street to their car.

Katie finally got a signal on her cell phone and placed a call. "This is Detective Katie Scott, badge number 3692, we need assistance at 1001 Industrial Place. We need fire and ambulance." She waited for the dispatcher to put in the request. "Thank you." She ended the call.

Both detectives leaned against the vehicle in exhaustion.

"The evidence has been incinerated now," said McGaven.

"I know. But there's always something that we can glean from this building and I know John will be thorough. We witnessed the room and shackles firsthand. That accounts for something, right?"

"I think Robin Drakes' mom has some serious explaining to do," said McGaven.

CHAPTER THIRTY-FOUR

Katie and McGaven watched helplessly as firefighters fought and extinguished the blaze of the old industrial building. The flames had spread to the back of the property where the weeds and garbage were a perfect accelerant. Everything that would help with the investigation of the murdered victims at Eagle Ridge Camp disappeared.

Several deputy patrol cruisers arrived, followed by an ambulance and Sheriff Scott's SUV. The CSI van arrived as well and opted to park a little distance away.

Katie said, "Oh, the sheriff is here." She was determined to hold the line on the idea of staking out the camp, but now she wasn't so sure.

"Stay strong," said McGaven still giving a few coughs.

Katie remained where she stood beside her partner. She could still smell the smoke in her sinuses.

Sheriff Scott parked his police vehicle and was now approaching the detectives with his usual authority. He was dressed in his work uniform and resembled more of a general with his assertive walk and cool sunglasses. He headed right for Katie and McGaven.

"Scott, McGaven," he said and there was no friendliness about his voice.

"Yes, sir," said McGaven as he took a couple of steps toward the sheriff.

Katie nodded.

"You both okay?"

"Yes, we're fine," she said.

"Has the paramedic checked you both out?" he demanded.

"Not yet."

"There's no waiting for later," the sheriff said looking pointedly at Katie.

"We will," she said.

"Bring me up to speed."

"We received this address from the mother of one of the camp counselors. We've been trying to find her. After we got here, we entered the building and that's when we found a suspicious area where there had been furniture and someone possibly living here."

"And?" The sheriff seemed impatient.

"We saw signs of blood and there were shackles on the wall," Katie said. "We swept the rest of the building to make sure there wasn't anyone trapped. As we made our way to the third-story office area, there were two explosions and the fire erupted." Katie looked down, trying to get the images out of her mind. She was just now feeling the effects of the terror.

"I see. So you don't have any evidence, just firsthand observation and no solid proof."

Katie looked at McGaven.

"No, sir, we were in the middle of doing just that, but..." said McGaven.

"We can't use any of this based on observation, no matter how expert you both are." The sheriff turned and watched the last of the smoke waft into the air as firefighters continued to move about their duties. "I'm afraid it's out of our hands, for now."

"Why?" said Katie.

"With the explosives used and the intentionally set fire, ATF will take over from here."

"What?" she said. "But this building connects to our homicide cases."

"That's the way it is—it happens. They are going to be conducting their investigation of the fire." He turned to the detectives. "And that means you are no longer investigating this building. Stick to your cases and your leads. You have plenty to do."

Katie was going to say something, but decided remaining silent in the moment was the right thing to do.

"Get checked out right now," he said, referring to the ambulance waiting. "If they say it's okay, then get back to work."

The detectives nodded and moved toward the waiting paramedics for a brief examination.

Katie spied the sheriff talking with deputies and John. Obviously, there wasn't enough evidence left for a crime scene investigation for the sheriff's department. And now, ATF was taking over and they would have their own investigators and forensics personnel.

"What do you think?" said McGaven in a low tone on their way to the ambulance.

"Mrs. Drakes is going to answer some questions. Do you have her address with you?"

"Yep."

"Good." She looked at her partner. "You okay?" she asked.

"Locked and loaded. Jumping out of a three-story building is just my warm-up."

Two paramedics met Katie and McGaven ready to quickly examine them and take their vitals. "Detectives?"

"That's us," said McGaven still coughing a bit.

CHAPTER THIRTY-FIVE

TUESDAY 1745 HOURS

Katie was ready for some downtime as she drove into her driveway. She knew that Cisco was ready to get out and she might take him for a walk from the back of her property. She could definitely use the fresh air to clear her mind so she could see things more clearly.

It wasn't quite dark yet. Her blooming garden was fading and getting ready for fall and winter in the near future.

She retrieved her briefcase, containing copies she had made of the newest findings, and got out of her Jeep. She was wearied, but still eager to look at everything again. Being in a different place besides the office, she found that she could see things from a different perspective.

As she walked up to her door, she noticed a message taped to it.

"Chad, you are spoiling me," she said to herself. He must be up to something, but she knew that he was on twenty-four-hour shifts right now. She was glad he hadn't been called to the fire earlier, though.

She tore it from the door and realized it wasn't a note. It was a printed news article from one of her other cold cases with a photo of her coming out of the courthouse. A red marker circled her image.

Instinctively, Katie turned and surveyed her property, looked at the street to see if there was someone in a car, but there was nothing.

Cisco barked impatiently from inside.

Katie decided to do a perimeter search of her property to see if someone had been lurking around and spying. She didn't know what to expect, so she decided to leave Cisco inside the house.

She jogged down her driveway to the street looking both ways and didn't see anything that would render suspicion. Backtracking and hiking up through a wooded area, Katie made her way to the northern part of her property. Nothing appeared to be disturbed. As she made her way around her house and through the backyard gate, she noticed footprints—large man's highly treaded hiking boots, maybe size 12 or 13. The prints were headed into her backyard and then they seemed to disappear.

Who had been here and why?

It could be something as innocent as a workman or utility worker getting turned around and on the wrong property. More likely, it was the same person who left an article about her on the front door.

Katie made her way back to the front door, now keeping watch over her shoulder. Shivers shuddered through her body. She knew instinctively that she was getting closer to the killer. So close, in fact, that she could almost reach out and touch him.

Unlocking the door and deactivating the alarm, Katie quickly shut her door once again and locked it.

Cisco was happy beyond what a dog was supposed to be under the circumstances.

Katie quickly dropped her things in the living room and fed Cisco. After, she let him out, sure that no one was loitering or hiding in her backyard. She went to her laptop in a drawer in the kitchen, turned it on, and logged in to show all of her cameras. With a few keystrokes, she was able to zoom in on previous activity. At first there was nothing but the mail delivery. Then she saw a man dressed in a dark running outfit with a hood pulled close to his face. He was tall, slim, and obviously knew where her cameras were pointing.

Katie flashed back to cabin 11 and her ambush by the man who stood in the doorway with the same type of build. She quickly sent a screen grab of the man at her home to her printer.

A rapid round of barks came from the sliding door as Cisco demanded to come inside to be with his favorite person.

"C'mon in," she said as the dog zoomed around the house. "I know... we need to set up more training exercises with Sergeant Hardy and the K9 teams."

Katie began to feel better and her nerves quieted down as she made herself dinner and began sorting out the case. She used the couch, coffee table, and floor to shuffle papers around. She wanted to focus on the perspective of making Eagle Ridge Camp and Brian Stanwick as the point of origin and work suspects and evidence outward.

Changing into comfortable pajamas and heavy socks, Katie was ready to settle down and work through what they already had. She moved pieces of paper to positions that made sense—at least to her. She had the employee files of the camp, as well as printer copies of the photographs of Brian Stanwick from the newspaper, photos of the four camp counselors, and the unidentified man, and she managed to get photographs from the websites of Daniel Green from Red Hawk Real Estate and Jake Fields from Fields, Campbell and Associates. She also had a photo of Rick Reynolds from his cold-case report.

Sipping her tea, Katie felt like she was playing a matching card game, but she sorted things the way they should be at this point in the investigation. She needed to get her thinking in order with everything they had so far—she knew that they must be missing something.

Eagle Ridge Camp ===>

*Brian Stanwick—unable to locate. Serious hiking accident causing loss of leg and kidney 22 years ago

*Father, Graham Stanwick, not found under that name

*Rick Reynolds (murdered, body found 15 minutes from Carolyn Sable's house.

Employees, Volunteers ERC – accounted for except:

*Marilyn Weber, activities coordinator

Dr. Xavier Pendleton, Stanwick doctor

*Security guard, Bud, attacked at camp—his story and timeline checked out.

Red Hawk Real Estate ===>

Daniel Green, agent showed Eagle Ridge property and found body

*Carolyn Sable, had listing on her house.

Fields, Campbell and Assoc. ===>

Carolyn Sable's employment, boss Jake Fields

Owns *Industrial Building=connection with RHRE —burned up.

KLM Enterprises? ===>

Charles Abbott, liaison. No address. Faux company?

Persons of Interest ===>

*Brian Stanwick

Lenny Dickson, Carolyn Sable's ex-boyfriend

Jake Fields, financial advisor/partner for FCA

Daniel Green, real estate agent for RHRE

Kerry Wilhelm, co-worker/friend of Carolyn Sable at FCA
Robin Drakes, ex-counselor at ERC, surviving counselor
Emeline Drakes, Robin's mother
Mr. and Mrs. Faulkner, clients of Daniel Green, interested
in ERC
   *Identify unknown tall male dressed in black—at camp—
on Katie's surveillance camera

"What am I not seeing?" said Katie in frustration. She and McGaven had run backgrounds on all of these people looking for anything that might bring the investigation closer to the killer. Only three had anything resembling training in the medical industry. Jake Fields and Lenny Dickson both had tried to become firefighters early in their careers; and Daniel Green had spent one year at medical school before dropping out. But it was nothing that would require the skill of removing internal organs.

She stared at the papers wondering which of her suspects could abduct, kill, and dismember women. Everything seemed to come back to Brian Stanwick. Maybe it was something that she couldn't shake and wasn't sure why.

Cisco woke up from the chair and grumbled before closing his eyes again.

It was clear to Katie that someone was getting revenge for Brian Stanwick's permanent injuries.

But who?

And why after twenty-two years?

As Katie pored over what they knew in the investigation and what they didn't, she realized that there were some things that stood out. Carolyn Sable seemed to be in the middle of several things: Eagle Ridge Camp, Red Hawk Real Estate, and her financial firm. Were there more to these places?

Katie looked at the photos they couldn't identify and she wondered if any of her persons of interest might be in one of those photos. The one person that jumped out at her was Jake Fields. There was no doubt that he was suspicious and not telling the entire truth. And Daniel Green appeared, at least to Katie, as though he might be hiding something or know more than he was telling. Both men—one who called in a missing persons report for Carolyn Sable and the other who found her body—rose to the top of her list. She would talk with McGaven in the morning and they would move forward.

"Well, buddy, I'm exhausted," she said to Cisco who stirred slightly. She tidied her paperwork, double-checked her alarm system, and went to bed.

Katie tossed and turned during her sleep. She kept waking up and staring towards her window wondering if the unidentified man was watching her house and property. Why did she interest him? She figured it was to find out how the police investigation was proceeding and if they were getting close. If Katie had to bet, they were getting closer than they realized. She dozed back to sleep.

"Katie," came a low childlike voice. *"Katie..."*

Katie jolted awake and turned from her left side to her back. In the shadows were two children standing side by side holding hands; it was her childhood friend Jenny and what appeared to be a boy with a cast.

Katie sat up and turned on the lamp on the nightstand. Light filled her bedroom as well as the doorway. No one was there. Cisco was curled up in the corner chair and slightly stirred. The dog would have barked if someone was in the house.

Katie got out of bed. She felt her bare feet on the cold floor as she walked into the hallway. No one was there. She took a quick walk through her house checking every room and closet.

Double-checking her security. It appeared to be on and no movement had been detected either inside or outside.

She slowly went back to her bedroom, climbed into bed and turned out the light. It was 2:30 a.m. Had these cases haunted her so much that she was seeing apparitions? Had being at Eagle Ridge Camp again after all these years caused her to think of Jenny so much that she had conjured up her image?

Laying her head on the pillow, she pictured Jenny and the boy that seemed to her to be standing in the shadows of the doorway. It was as if Jenny was trying to tell her something. Katie didn't believe in ghosts, but who was she to dismiss such things?

Her mind wandered back to the moment in the hospital where she'd thought she heard a voice calling her name. Then she'd followed what she had thought was a child. Katie found the prosthetics lab then, but she would have eventually wound up there anyway, asking questions.

She saw a ghostly image of Jenny at the camp pointing to cabin 11. Now Jenny was with a young boy. Katie knew that she wasn't going insane and her PTSD had been in check. Was it her mind or subconscious trying to tell her something that she was missing?

Exasperated, Katie turned over on her side and closed her eyes, but she still saw the two children. Why the boy? She had a thought.

Katie sat straight up, tore her covers away, and leaped out of bed. She ran to the living room, turned on a lamp and retrieved her laptop from her briefcase. Waiting impatiently while it powered up, she couldn't believe that they hadn't thought about this before.

She keyed up the police database, determined to find more information.

Finding the area she was looking for, she typed in: *Brian*

Stanwick. The same result came up with *no such name* just as before.

Katie stared at the blinking cursor. She knew that there must be a birth record of Brian Stanwick, but it yielded the same results. Frustrated, she tried several other searches. Tapping her finger on the keyboard, she thought about her dream. She searched the internet for Sequoia County, California for *Brian Stanwick*, but it didn't give any results. She didn't have a middle name for him.

"Who are you, Brian Stanwick?" she whispered. It suddenly came to her. Sometimes people went by other names or middle names. Unfortunately, many databases required the entire name of the person being searched. She decided to begin with common middle names.

Katie began with *Brian James Stanwick*, then *Brian Joseph Stanwick*, then *Brian Matthew Stanwick*. No such luck. It was going to take forever to find the correct name, but she kept searching. Typing out *Brian Mark Stanwick* and then *Brian William Stanwick*. Nothing.

Katie was about to give up. She knew that McGaven and Denise were more adept and patient about these types of searches—knowing search tricks. But she tried again, *Brian John Stanwick*.

This time the computer churned out a hit and there was a notation next to his name. When she clicked on the symbol it came back that Brian John Stanwick was deceased—there was another notation below saying that he had changed his name legally to John Kendrick.

"At last," she whispered. "I can't believe we haven't found this before now." Many things surrounding the accident and death of Brian Stanwick, now John Kendrick, seemed to have been buried. Was it on purpose? Did he want to try to put his past behind him by taking a new name?

They had been chasing a ghost, but perhaps there was

someone who wanted the people surrounding Brian's accident to pay just as much as he had. Even though it had taken longer than necessary to find out anything about Brian Stanwick, there seemed to be another force at work when they were investigating at Eagle Ridge Camp.

Katie began searching through newspaper articles and police records for John Kendrick and she found many things. His name came up with drunk and disorderly and threatening someone with a gun—no jail time, just probation. His delinquency also included him being a suspect in two arsons in a two-year period, but there were additional investigator notes that according to witnesses he had an unknown partner in crime. It appeared that Kendrick's life of crime began when he was a teenager and continued until he died. His cause of death was suicide by firearm five years ago.

Katie leaned back and closed her eyes. It turned out that Brian Stanwick had a very troubled existence and then ended by taking his own life. That meant that he wasn't the killer and out for revenge. Then who was? Someone had picked up his gauntlet and decided to make people pay for what had happened to Brian "John Kendrick" Stanwick.

CHAPTER THIRTY-SIX

Katie could barely sleep with the new information that Brian Stanwick was dead. It didn't initially change everything, but it made some other things clearer—namely the killer's motive. She managed to get more information about him before McGaven arrived at the office. Her desk was covered with paperwork and printouts.

McGaven walked in. "Good morning... whoa, paper blizzard."

"I beat you to the office again."

"You want to clue me in on all this," he said as he shed his jacket and took a seat.

"Okay, first up," she said and handed him a piece of paper. "Brian Stanwick is dead."

"What?"

"Actually, he changed his name legally to John Kendrick—using his middle name."

"That's makes sense of why we couldn't easily find him. Data bases don't always cross reference unless you know what you're looking for."

Katie pulled several papers with articles and police reports on them toward her. "Unfortunately, he committed suicide about five years ago. But it shows that he had not only a troubled life, but he also decided to be involved in crime. Take a look... aggravated assault, intimidation, fighting, and was under suspicion of arson."

"Wow," he said, scanning the paperwork with a frown. "Looks like he never made peace with his injuries and handicaps, judging by the behavior listed here. And his first offense occurred when he was fifteen. Think he had a buddy in crime too?"

"It seems it was possible, but we don't have a name. I was going over all the witnesses to see if anything shakes out, but I can't find anything—yet."

"This is interesting but there's no one to ask about him."

"And..." she said, "his father, Graham Kendrick—he also changed his name—died two years ago due to a heart condition."

McGaven looked at his partner. "This is great information. It answers several questions, but how does it help the investigation? It seems we have more questions now, since our prime suspect is dead."

"I thought a lot about this last night. I think it still revolves around Brian Stanwick because of the signature and MO of the killer and the victims. Someone is avenging his death—blaming all the people who should have prevented his accident."

"But now the Stanwicks are dead. Who would care enough about Brian to kill anyone who had contact with him at the camp?"

"I don't know—yet." She sighed. "I couldn't find any information about the rest of his family, like mom, brother, sister, cousin, no one. Sad, really. He didn't have anyone to help him through this."

"I'll see what I can do," he said already keying up coordinates in the computer system.

"As I was going through everything we have right now, I noticed that both Jake Fields and Daniel Green need to be studied a bit more closely."

"Why do you think that?"

"I made a spreadsheet and it seems that Carolyn Sable is a common thread through much of it. And I felt that both men weren't completely transparent with us."

McGaven smiled broadly. "I can see some undercover work coming..."

"Well, I think we need to learn a bit more about them, but from afar."

"I like it, and we don't need prior approval."

Katie didn't want to think about her uncle giving his signature on setting up a sting operation at Eagle Ridge Camp—at least not yet.

She searched through her paperwork. "There's another thing," she said. "Rick Reynolds was murdered a little over two years ago. Whoever killed him was angry, as there were over forty stab wounds. It generally means that the person who killed him knew him well, or even intimately, to generate that type of rage. According to the ME's report, the wounds were from two, maybe three different types of knives or cutting tools. Sound familiar?"

"I see where you're going with this."

Katie grabbed her jacket and notepad, and secured her weapon and badge.

"Where are you off to?"

"I'm going to check on some things down at the county archives with Shane Kendall." She looked at her watch. "I made an appointment and hopefully the records of Eagle Ridge Camp might fill in some blanks."

"Have fun."

. . .

Katie made great time and pulled into the parking lot for the Sequoia Office Building a short time later. She parked up and quickly made her way to the building and planning department. Opening the grand doors of the old building—dated 1884 on a golden plaque—she hurried up the stairs to the second floor.

Looking around the reception area she didn't see Shane. She spoke to the woman at the counter. "Excuse me, but I'm Detective Scott from PV Sheriff's Department. I'm here to see Shane Kendall?"

"Let me call him," the woman said as she picked up the phone and dialed the three-digit extension. "Detective Scott is here to see you. Okay." She hung up the phone and turned back to Katie. "He said to come on down and that you know the way."

"Okay, thanks."

Katie moved swiftly to the back area of the department where there were old wooden stairs leading down to the basement—the entrance, as she remembered, appeared to be the door to a small utility closet or storage, when in fact it led to the underbelly of the building. It was obvious that the stairs and handrails were original to the building, not only by the style but by the smell of the old wood and intertwined wrought iron. The staircase was narrow and the steps were steep and creaky making Katie think that someone was creeping up on her. She imagined how the early county clerks must've walked these stairs carrying handwritten documents for filing.

Katie's heart beat faster the more she stepped toward the basement. The lighting was dull, and several strings of small light bulbs were the only thing that lit the way. They swung slightly as she passed by, casting strange shadows on the walls and steps. Her heart skipped a beat and then began hammering, making her head hurt. She didn't like tight places or anywhere someone could be hiding in wait. Her imagination was in overdrive making her anxiety symptoms try to scratch their way to the surface. Breathing evenly and intently focusing on something, like the staircase, helped keep the heightened sense of anxious symptoms at bay—at least for now.

Katie paused at the rickety landing. There were four more steps to the basement. The air temperature had drastically cooled and there was a hint of moisture in the air, leaving a musty smell behind. The lights must have been motion-censored on entering the area, as overhead fluorescent illumination suddenly filled the dank space, making it easy to see. She also detected some type of machinery noise she assumed was for air filtration. It didn't seem to be working efficiently now.

Katie stepped through the doors at the bottom of the stairwell into an oversized room, which took up the whole of the basement. Large filing cabinets, architecture drawers, open cubbyholes of all sizes lined the wall, mixed in with stacked bankers' boxes with perfectly printed names, letters, and numbers, two large mahogany desks, two desktop computers with large scanners, and a long backlit table for spreading out reports and drawings.

She spied Shane Kendall stooped over an architectural drawing board. He looked just as he had the last time she'd seen him, which was on the way to the hospital after the Elm Hill Mansion fiasco. Shane's thin build, dark brown shaggy hair, and his signature gold-rimmed glasses were highlighted under the bright, overhead lighting and made Katie relax.

"Shane," she said as the county archivist turned in her direction. "It's nice to see you." At first he smiled, happy to see her too, but soon the smile faded. She walked up to face him and saw the old map of Eagle Ridge Camp spread out on the board.

"You know, Detective, I could've taken a museum curator position and it would be much easier. I would actually see daylight and it would be healthier too."

Katie didn't know what to say, but obviously Shane had

something to say to her. She merely nodded and waited patiently for him to continue.

"But I love this county, I grew up here, and I wanted to work here—even if it meant being in the basement of an old musty building." He repositioned his glasses, setting his gaze on Katie. He seemed to be trying to decide whether to go ahead and say what he wanted to say. She knew that Shane was introverted and became nervous easily around people. She hastened to reassure him.

"I'm very thankful that you did, Shane. You're amazing at what you do and all of the organization and updates you've done. I wish everyone could see what I see and—"

"Wait, let me finish, otherwise I won't be able to..."

Katie became quiet.

"I really felt like I was helping the police and that made what I do seem important—more than just from a historical perspective." Shane shrugged. "But after that incident at Elm Hill Mansion, when we were trapped in a demolished building by a crazed killer. Well..."

"I'm sorry," she said. "I know that doesn't really make everything alright, but I am sorry." Katie saw the pain of rejection in his face.

"I just wanted to know why you didn't visit me in the hospital. For a while, I thought I had done something wrong, but that didn't make any sense."

"Shane, I'm so sorry that I didn't visit you. I did try, but by then you had already been released." She knew her words weren't enough, she should have made more of an effort.

"Wait, you did?"

"Yes, I did. But you see, after I got out myself, I still had to go after the killer. Then I was forced to take a little time off."

"I'm sorry," he said.

"For what?"

"Well, I did think the worst. But I knew you had an important job and I guess I was just thinking about myself."

"And I'm glad that you're okay now."

"Thanks, Detective Scott."

"Katie. Call me Katie. Okay?"

"Okay."

"Are we okay?" she said, feeling bad that he had been laboring under those negative emotions for so long.

Shane gave a shy smile. "Yeah, we're okay."

"Good."

"I've been looking at these maps of the Eagle Ridge area. Interesting."

Katie was immediately intrigued by the maps. "Interesting good or interesting bad?"

"Interesting in the fact that there seems to be some question of who the owners are and if the transfer back in 1998 was lawful."

"Really?" Katie took out her notebook and pen, ready to write down anything useful for the investigation.

"What do you already know about the ownership of Eagle Ridge?" he asked.

"The information we have currently is that KLM Enterprises, LLC, owns the property. And for whatever reason, they lost money and then the camp closed."

"Well, that's partially true." He pulled up a map from the county assessors. "This was stamped twenty-five years ago and shows that KLM was the owner even back then. It's a big investment firm that is known to buy properties that will be used for spas, vacation homes, and even theme parks."

Katie's mind began rolling. "McGaven told me. I wondered why an investment company would have a seasonal camp for kids. There's no money in it like there would be with vacation rentals."

"Exactly. That's why I began to work backwards from the

current owners." He unrolled another map that looked older by the font and the slight yellowing of the paper—the corner identified the year as 1985. "Now, look at the property lines when I lay one map over the other."

Katie studied it. The difference was immediately obvious. "There's an additional portion on the older map. Was there property that was sold?"

"I thought that might be what happened. Sometimes neighboring properties will buy sections, for whatever reason. Maybe they want more land to build more housing, or they need more room to fit a project. People do this all the time, but that's not what happened here."

Shane became almost animated as he explained. "In 1985 Charles Baron, a millionaire, which was considered a decent amount of money for the 1980s, bought the property of seventy acres."

"Seventy acres? The property is listed at fifty acres," she said.

"Nope. It was seventy acres and it's still seventy acres—never been any different except for what's written on the title and map."

"Maybe they lied for tax purposes?"

"I double-checked and that doesn't seem to be the case. Now remember, Baron bought the property only—there were no buildings, nothing, only the lake."

"What were his plans?" she asked.

"He was going to build his dream home for his family."

"It is gorgeous up there. So what happened? Why didn't he build his home?"

"Tragedy struck Charles Baron while he waited for his house to be built—the estate was in its first stages. His current house burned down, killing him and his family; wife and two children."

"That's horrible."

"So his estate, including the Eagle Ridge area, went into the dreaded probate. Interestingly, he didn't have any other family so everything was slated to go to various charities."

"What does that mean for the Eagle Ridge? It goes to the state and then auctioned?"

"That's correct. But something strange happened." He looked directly at Katie. "There was no auction. No state involvement, but a company bought it."

"You're telling me that KLM Enterprises was able to buy it?" she asked.

Shane nodded. "I called a friend of mine who deals with commercial and residential real estate and he said the only way they could legally do that was if someone related to the Baron family was involved. And there would have to be a probate judge also involved."

"Sounds like it was a strategic plan," she said. "But what's so important about that land besides the beauty of it?"

Shane remained quiet.

"Unless..." she said. "There must be something of extreme value like mineral rights."

"Good point. But this is where the trail runs cold. I couldn't find anything more."

Katie looked at the land and the boundaries. "Who is the owner of the twenty acres?"

"It shows that it's in a trust," he said pulling up another map. "It's in the John Derek Campbell trust, which is overseen by Fields, Campbell and Associates."

Katie was shocked. She remembered McGaven saying that the partner Campbell—presumably John Derek Campbell—had retired more than twenty years ago. Strange, given the fact that Jake Fields had only been working for the company eighteen years.

"Detective Scott, you seem perplexed."

Katie laughed. "That's a good way to describe it."

"I hope that I've been able to help with unanswered questions."

"Yes, you definitely have, but... it raises more questions."

"Shoot."

"Is there a name of anyone connected to the KLM Enterprises? Like a representative or an attorney?" She knew they had a contact, Charles Abbott, but they were unable to locate him.

Shane referred to his notes. "I'm sorry, Detective, there wasn't a name—at least the information I have doesn't show anyone. And I double-checked the architects that originally designed Charles Baron's estate, but they are no longer in business and there's no forwarding name. There was only PO Box 777, Pine Valley, CA—no contact details."

Katie sighed. "I'll check it out, but it could be outdated by years."

Shane smiled. "Since I've known you, Detective, you've always solved your case."

"Thanks for the vote of confidence." Kate turned to leave. "Oh, by the way, having lunch is way overdue. I'll call you when I get through this investigation. You up for it?"

"You bet," he smiled and Katie thought she detected he was blushing.

CHAPTER THIRTY-SEVEN

Katie and McGaven were on their way to speak with Mrs. Emeline Drakes, mother of Robin Drakes. They hadn't bothered to give her notice before they stopped by, as they didn't want to take the risk that Mrs. Drakes would make sure that she was somewhere else.

Katie drove today and set the GPS parameters to go to 1668 Maple Street.

"I had a difficult time getting out of bed this morning," said McGaven, rubbing his neck and the tops of his shoulders.

"At least we're alive and not in the hospital with multiple broken bones or burns."

"I thought Mrs. Drakes was telling me the truth," he said. "She seemed honest and forthright, but now it seems that she might not have been."

Katie could tell that McGaven was angry that Mrs. Drakes might've steered them into a trap. "We'll get to the bottom of it," she said as she turned down Maple Street.

"I hope so."

"I think it's that house," she said.

Mrs. Emeline Drakes lived in a small two-story tan home

with dark brown trim. There was a small front yard area that had been laid with flagstone leaving a charming walkway to invite guests.

Katie parked two houses away just for precaution and so that they didn't announce their arrival. Turning off the engine, she said, "How do you want to play this?"

"We're trying to find her daughter because she might be targeted by a killer. Well, we don't have to word it that way."

"If your hunch is true, then we need to try to get as much information from her as we can. So it's best that we are the usual sweet detectives we always are," she said smiling.

"Point taken," he said. "I think my head is still spinning from that fall. And I'll keep my anger in check. But the more I think that *maybe* Mrs. Drakes sent us to that building so that we would be harmed, the madder I feel."

"Gav," she said with tact, "it's okay to be mad. Believe me, I would love to wring some necks myself. But we have to play this cool. A woman's life may be at stake. We need to get as much information as we can."

"Thanks. Let's see what other trouble we can get into," McGaven said with sarcasm, then opened the car door and stepped out.

Katie got out of the sedan and gave the street a quick scrutiny. It was completely quiet, even though it was around quitting time for most businesses. Cars would be driving home, but this street seemed almost deserted, which told Katie that it was mostly retired people along with those who worked at home.

She shut the car door and stepped to the sidewalk next to her partner. Lots of large trees, mainly spruce and oak, adorned the front yards of most of the homes. Few yards had lawns, but most were decorated with rock, gravel, and flagstone walkways.

Katie opened the small wrought-iron gate and they walked through. Even though the curtain was closed, she saw the outline of what appeared to be a woman moving in the house.

She stepped up to a small porch with a pretty floral-patterned welcome mat and knocked on the door. There was movement from inside the home, but at first it wasn't coming toward the front door. Katie stepped back and looked at the single car garage, detached and to the back of the home.

Finally, there was the sound of a lock disengaging and the doorknob turned. With barely a crack opening, a woman said, "Yes?"

"Mrs. Emeline Drakes?" said Katie.

There was a pause. Then, "Yes." The door opened another couple of inches.

"I'm Detective Scott and this is Detective McGaven and we're from the Pine Valley Sheriff's Department."

"Did something happen?" she said.

"No, ma'am, we're just following up on a call," said McGaven staying back a few feet so that his height wouldn't seem intimidating. "Do you remember me?"

"Of course," she said, trying to hide her annoyance.

"Mrs. Drakes, may we come in for just a few minutes?" said Katie.

"Well..." she said looking back inside. "I guess so." She opened the door wider for the detectives to enter.

Katie knew why Mrs. Drakes didn't want to invite them inside her home. It was excessively cluttered. Not dirty, but there was too much packed inside the small house. Every table had stacks of magazines, DVDs, books, and various other items piled on it. The couch had more books and two large baskets of laundry. The surplus of clutter made the interior seem claustrophobic.

"Please, have a seat," said Mrs. Drakes. She quickly moved the clean laundry. After making room for the detectives, she sat down in an upholstered chair with a large crochet blanket draped over the back. She was dressed casually in tan slacks and a long-sleeved sweater. Her partially gray short hair curled around her ears. Her light green eyes seemed to watch everything in the room, including Katie and McGaven.

"Thank you for seeing us without an appointment," said Katie.

"That's alright," she said but her stiffened demeanor said otherwise.

"First, we went to the last known address for your daughter Robin and it was an old industrial building. Are you sure about the address at 1001 Industrial Place?"

"Yes," she said, not looking directly at Katie. "It's what Robin gave me and I put it in my address book. I sent her several letters and they never came back."

"When was the last time you saw your daughter?" Katie knew that the woman was covering and lying, so she would angle her questions accordingly.

"About eight or nine years. Don't know the exact date."

"If you don't mind my asking," said Katie, "what was the reason you didn't see your daughter?"

"She has her own life. No reason in particular."

"I'm sorry to hear that, Mrs. Drakes," said Katie as she casually glanced at one of the laundry baskets. She noticed that there were clothes for a younger person, thin tank tops and trendy jeans. "Do you live alone?"

"Yes. My husband died five years ago from cancer."

"I'm sorry for your loss. Do you have family visiting often?"

"No, all I have is Robin and a sister in Nebraska."

"What can you tell me about Robin working as a counselor at the Eagle Ridge Camp?"

Mrs. Drakes began to fidget with her hands. "What do you want to know? That was quite some time ago—what, fifteen, twenty years? I'm not sure. That was where Robin met her husband, Derek Daniels." She looked down. "They were only married about four years... still don't know why she kept his name even though it's double-barreled."

That struck Katie as strange the way she talked about her daughter. Katie glanced at McGaven and then back to Mrs. Drakes. "Mrs. Drakes, when was the last time you saw Robin?"

The woman looked Katie directly and her eyes narrowed. She seemed to morph into a different person. "Like I told you, we haven't talked in eight or nine years or so."

"Really?" said Katie. "Then you wouldn't mind if I take a look around?"

"Don't you need a warrant for that?" Mrs. Drakes almost spat at her.

Katie stood up and looked around the living room. "You see, Mrs. Drakes, I don't believe you're telling us the truth."

The woman stood up. "I want you out of my house."

McGaven stood up and stepped in between Katie and Mrs. Drakes.

"We are here to help Robin. We believe that she might be in danger."

She scoffed. "What kind of danger?"

"You knew all the counselors at Eagle Ridge Camp? Her friends."

"I remember them. They were the worst influence on her— she did whatever they said."

"What do you mean, worst influence?" she said.

"You know. They were always partying, making Robin do things she really didn't want to. They didn't break the law, but they were definitely... acting in inappropriate ways. I never liked them—any of them."

"Well, Mrs. Drakes, you don't have to worry about them now."

"Oh really? And why is that?"

"They are all dead. Brutally murdered," said Katie. She hated being so blunt, but she needed the woman to tell them the hard truth.

Mrs. Drakes stood speechless.

There was a distinct creaking sound above them as if someone was walking around.

"Who's here?" demanded Katie as she unholstered her weapon.

"No... no one." Her face turned ashen as if she was going to be sick.

"Anyone? Friend, neighbor?"

"No. I don't have anyone."

"Stay here with her," said Katie to McGaven as she hurried up the stairs, taking them two at a time.

Katie got to the top landing and stopped. There were three doors; she assumed it was two bedrooms and one bathroom. The sound came from above the living room, so she went to the door on her right. Slowly making her way, her footsteps were silent on the carpeting.

She stood for a moment listening. There was a slight noise as if someone was trying to be quiet. No doubt in Katie's mind that it was a person and not a cat or dog.

Putting her hand on the doorknob, she slowly turned it and found that it was unlocked. She heard Mrs. Drakes downstairs complaining about their visit to McGaven. Keeping her focus on whoever was behind the door, she pushed the door open, revealing what appeared to be a guest room. The double bed was neatly made with a light blue comforter and two floral throw pillows. A cozy reading chair in the corner and a writing desk were the only other furniture in the room. The slightly moving curtain caught Katie's eye, right next to the closet. As if someone had just passed by it.

Katie moved toward the sliding closet door still holding her gun ready. She suddenly decided to go about it another way.

Standing next to the bed, she said, "I'm Detective Scott with Pine Valley Sheriff's Department. I know you're in there. Come out."

Nothing.

She thought for a moment and it made the most sense to her. "Robin, I know it's you. Come out. You're not in any trouble."

A bump came from the closet door as it slowly slid to the side. A tall dark-haired woman wearing jeans and a hoodie emerged. "Please. No one knows I'm here." Her eyes were wide and it was clear that she was genuinely frightened.

Katie holstered her weapon. "Robin, we've been looking for you. Are you alright?"

"Yeah, but..." she barely managed to say.

"C'mon, sit down." Katie steered her to the high-back reading chair in the corner. "Wait here." Something struck Katie about Robin's appearance in the same way that the bodies in the morgue had. They seemed similar—almost like sisters.

Katie went to the door and to the top of the stairs. "Gav, it's okay. Robin and I are going to have a talk." She knew that McGaven realized too that it was probably Robin hiding upstairs. She returned to the guest room.

"Okay, Robin." Katie brought up the photograph of the four counselors at Eagle Ridge Camp. "Is this you?" She pointed to the fourth woman.

Robin looked down and nodded. "Yes."

"Who are the other women?" she asked, making sure that they were officially identified.

Robin took a moment, as if she was remembering the times they had all shared together. She pointed in order to each woman. "That's Carolyn Sable, Edith Crest, and Stephanie Baxter."

"Are you one hundred percent sure?"

"Yes," she barely whispered.

"When was the last time you saw any of them?"

"I'm not sure... maybe six months ago."

"Do you know what happened to them?"

Robin began to cry. "They're dead, aren't they?"

"Yes."

"Can you tell me about your relationship with them?" Katie tried to soften her questions, but she really wanted to shake the woman and get the answers she needed. She hadn't realized that the case was weighing so heavily on her. So she lightened her tone. "Take your time."

"Okay, I may as well tell you now." She plucked a tissue from the box on the desk. "I don't know where to begin..."

Katie took a breath and readied herself. She knew that Robin was scared—terrified. "Why don't you start at Eagle Ridge Camp."

"Oh, that was such a great time for all of us. We had plans and life was ahead for us. We loved the kids and those summers were fantastic. All of us worked three seasons, except Carolyn, I think she worked four." Her expression turned sour. "Until, that day—that day." She shook her head as if trying to rid her mind of the memory.

"Why did all of you quit?"

"It was time."

"Meaning?"

"Well, we were either going to get married or go to college. I got married. Being a camp counselor, as great as it was, wasn't forever. It was just a great time in our young lives."

"What happened the day of the accident?" Katie watched Robin carefully as she gathered her wits and answered.

"Carolyn and I were scheduled to take half the kids on a hike up along the ridge—and Stephanie and Edith were going to bring the rest of kids and meet us where we would then camp. It's the most incredible hike, the views, the nature. It was one of the highlights of the summer. We would do a camp out. It was towards the end of summer and was one of Eagle Ridge Camp's traditions." Robin choked up and her eyes filled with tears.

Katie patiently listened. "Take your time."

Catching her breath, she continued, "Well, there was a

storm forecasted that had been brewing. You know how Pine Valley Mountain weather can be, especially between summer and autumn. We decided—the counselors, supervisors and management—to go on the overnight camp anyway, not thinking it would really blow up. We really thought it would just be some mild rain."

Katie seemed to recall something about what Robin was explaining.

"Before Carolyn and I could get to the camping area, which was actually a safe place to hole up if there was a storm, it began to rain. And then the rain wouldn't cease. It got worse and worse, making the trail muddy and extremely slippery. We were at an area where it was too far to go back to the camp, so we had to forge ahead." She wiped tears from her face. Obviously, the tragedy was still embedded in her mind. "The part of the trail before the camping area was near the edge and very slippery—especially during a rainstorm. Beautiful view, but potentially dangerous."

"How many children did you have?"

"There were twenty-four. There was always one camp counselor for every ten to twelve kids."

"I see. What about volunteers like parents? Were any of them on this trip?"

"Many times there were, but this particular trip there wasn't."

"What happened?"

"As the rain continued, it slowed us down a lot. Kids were having a hard time navigating the slippery mud and the wind... and that's when, that's when one of the kids fell. It was a fifty-foot drop, then he landed on an area that jetted outwards." She began cry. "If he hadn't hit that exact area, he would have fallen all the way to the bottom..."

"What happened next?"

"We tried. I swear. We tried to save him, but even after

Stephanie and Edith joined me and Carolyn, we just couldn't reach him. Carolyn and I hiked back down to where we could call for help."

"Then what happened?"

"I'll never forget his screams from below and how it echoed around the valley. I'll never forget..."

"How does this have anything to do with the other counselors?" Katie watched Robin carefully as she answered.

"Don't you see? That boy, Brian Stanwick, lost his left leg and had permanent damage to his left wrist and arm. I think he lost a kidney too. Just like Carolyn, Edith and Stephanie. It took months, years, for him to rehabilitate to be able to function again." She stood up. "Don't you understand? It's my fault. I should have been able to keep them safe—all of them. It's all of our faults—we should have postponed the camping trip or cancelled altogether."

"Robin, Brian Stanwick is dead. He's been dead for more than five years."

"What? That can't be. Who else would want us dead for revenge of what happened that day?"

"Have there been any threats?" said Katie.

"Yes. It didn't start until about five years ago. Each of us has received threats on our phones, email, and Carolyn got a note left inside her house. Things like: *your time is up... you're going to pay... eye for an eye... there's nowhere you can hide.*"

"Did you report this to the police?"

"I think Stephanie did, but they wouldn't do anything. She told them it was Brian Stanwick, that was who we all assumed was threatening us, and why, but they said there was nothing they could do unless he did something physical." She paced back and forth. "We didn't even know where he was."

"Did Stephanie file the complaint with the sheriff's department?"

"I don't know. Someone is coming after me. I know he'll find me here at my mom's, but I don't know where else to go."

"Have you had any unusual situations? People that have maybe been following you? Anything?"

"I... I... don't know." She began to cry. "We thought it was Brian, but now... Who would do this?"

"It's okay. Come with me, we'll put you somewhere safe until we can unravel this and get to the bottom of it. Okay?"

"You will?"

"Of course," said Katie. "You're going to need to answer more questions."

"Anything. I don't know what else I can tell you."

"For starters, what is at the address 1001 Industrial Place?"

Robin froze. She stared at Katie.

"Robin, you have to be honest with me."

"I don't know. It was on one of the notes that were sent to Edith. I never went there, but I thought that Brian or whoever it is would be there. That's why I told Mom to give it to you. I thought the police might find him."

"We went there. There were explosives set and the building caught fire. There's nothing left as far as evidence is concerned."

"Oh, no. I had no idea... please believe me."

"It's okay, Robin. You wouldn't have known. Take it easy and sit down."

"He's going to find me... isn't he?"

"Not if the sheriff's department has anything to do with it. You need to pack some things and your mom needs to as well. Okay?"

"Okay," she said slowly.

"We'll get you situated somewhere tonight. We're working on this investigation and we'll soon have it wrapped up," said Katie. She knew that she and McGaven had to check some things out. "C'mon, let's go downstairs and we can get you and your mom ready."

Robin obliged readily. She was clearly still terrified.

Katie knew that she needed to talk to her uncle as soon as possible. She wasn't looking forward to it, but she had to figure out a way to get back to Eagle Ridge Camp to set a trap for the killer.

She spoke with McGaven outside Mrs. Drakes' house, updating him on the conversation she had had with Robin as they waited for deputies to come and pick up the Drakes to take them to an apartment owned by the sheriff's department. It was used for situations like this and for visiting police officers. They would have plain-clothes security around the clock.

"So what do you think now?" he said.

"We need to go back to our list of suspects and rework everything."

"I agree."

Katie pulled her cell phone out of her pocket. "Here's a text from John." She read it quickly. "Well, he has tons of stuff for us to see. But he's going to a meeting in Sacramento tomorrow and wants us to meet him at 6 a.m. in the forensics lab."

McGaven sighed. "Sounds like a plan."

"Aren't you a morning person?" she said.

"Yeah, but with these long evenings, I might be changing to a night owl."

"We need to meet with the sheriff tomorrow too."

"I know."

"And it's going to be intense if we want him to go with my plan. We have to convince him—time is ticking down..."

CHAPTER THIRTY-EIGHT

Katie pulled into her driveway and shut off the engine. She waited a moment as she rehashed everything that the day had bombarded her with—good and bad. She opened the door and expected to hear Cisco barking, but it was quiet. That was strange. More than strange, it wasn't normal.

She hurried up to her porch and still didn't hear the deep bark of Cisco. Taped to the door was a note. Quickly opening it, with relief she immediately recognized it as Chad's handwriting.

It said:

Meet me and Cisco at 1347 Monarch Street. No need to dress up. Come as you are and come with an appetite. Love you, Chad

Katie smiled for the first time today. It was so like Chad to have some surprise picnic for her, but why at that address? She went inside her house and quickly washed up. She fought the urge to call him to say she was so tired she was going to bed, but ultimately her curiosity got the better of her.

Katie climbed back into her Jeep and programed her GPS. She wasn't sure where Monarch Street was located exactly—her hunch was that it was a more rural spot. Maybe a park? Maybe one of those farm-to-table places? She was trying to guess.

It didn't take long for Katie's thinking processes to start going over Robin Drakes' revelations about Brian Stanwick's accident. But something still didn't make sense. Why would whoever the killer was wait this long to take revenge? Her mind ripped through what they had learned so far: the shackles at the industrial building, clues at Eagle Ridge Camp, the attack on Bud, her own attack, and the autopsies of frontal strangulation. Tomorrow would be telling and she was confident that John would have some amazing answers for her and McGaven.

Katie snapped back to the present as she turned down Monarch Street. It was not what she had expected. There were newer homes on five and ten-acre parcels. Suddenly, she knew what Chad had been up to. She thought they had decided to keep their housing situation in neutral for the time being.

She looked for the address 1347 and it was at the end of the road, on a site which butted up against a beautiful forest. There was no doubt all the houses were incredible: ranch-style homes with landscaped front yards. Her anger started to dissipate. She knew that Chad only wanted the best for them and these homes were fantastic. It appeared that the agent was in the process of safeguarding the homes with a gate and security guard.

Katie parked her Jeep in the driveway next to Chad's truck. She expected him to meet her but it was quiet. There were outdoor solar lights that edged along the pathway of white brick edging. The double front door reminded her of entering a large mansion. There were potted palm trees which gave a breezy vacation feel. Wow, she thought. A real estate lock box was sitting on the ground.

Stepping up to the porch, she knocked. There wasn't an answer. Feeling a bit conspicuous, she tried the door, unlocked, and entered the foyer. The house was mostly empty except for a couple of key pieces of furniture for staging. There were bar stools, a plain dining table and chairs, and a few items on the counter to give a homey vibe. Everything was fresh, new, and painted a slight gray with white cabinets and stainless appliances. She couldn't imagine cooking in such a wonderful kitchen.

There was a note on the counter that read simply:

Go to the sliding glass doors in the living room. We're outside waiting for you...

Katie couldn't help but smile. She felt the stress in her body subsiding. Chad always loved mysteries and following a treasure map when they were kids. She loved the fact that he still had this side to him even as an adult.

She followed the instructions and stepped into the large living room with a rock fireplace. For an instant, she imagined snuggling by the fire on cold evenings when there was snow on the ground.

Katie moved to the window and could see candles lining the patio and beyond. She opened the slider and stepped out. The night was cool but invigorating and she enjoyed the feel of the soft breeze on her face. It brought back a plethora of memories that she had forgotten about. Times she needed to think about because they were a part of her. Good times. Special people and family. She spent most of her time trying to figure out killers and looking at mutilated victims. This side trip, enjoying her life, was what she had so desperately needed.

She went down three steps and walked along a wooden boardwalk that passed pretty flower beds. Still following the candles, she turned the corner where she found Chad and Cisco patiently waiting for her. There was a small bistro table with two chairs, two candles, and a picnic basket.

Chad jumped up and smiled. "You made it. We were worried."

"Oh, it's so good to see you," she said, hugging him tightly.

"Hey." He stroked her hair. "Is that a new cut on your face?"

"Oh, probably. It's just been a really tough couple of days." She didn't want to go into detail about the industrial building, but he would probably find out sooner or later.

Cisco barked as if he was reminding her not to forget him.

"Cisco, I've so missed you." She petted him and hugged him. Looking back at Chad, she said, "Thank you for getting him out of the house. I worry about him getting bored and depressed."

Chad kissed her and held her close. "I thought you might be mad at me after all this."

"My first response was being mad when I figured out you were at a house for sale, but I have to admit, this is an impressive place. But the real issue—my salary isn't going to cover half of the mortgage here, not to mention the upkeep."

"Ah, that's why this is so exciting. They built this division where there would only be so many homes. You can see the incredible park and forest on the other side of this property. These are really affordable."

"Really?" Katie looked around. "Where's the pool?" She laughed, only kidding with him.

"We could put one in."

"No, I think the property should stay just like this."

"Cisco has checked out every inch and I think he gives this a paws-up," he said.

Cisco ran around the deck with renewed energy.

Katie didn't immediately respond.

"It's close to the sheriff's department and my work." He steered Katie over to the table to sit down. "Enough about the house. Are you hungry?"

"Starving."

"Fantastic. I had Chuck from the firehouse make up some yummy treats."

Chad pulled out fried chicken, potato salad, green bean salad, and sourdough French bread.

"Wow, that looks so good," she said as she realized that her stomach was grumbling for food.

As Chad filled their plates, Katie looked around. "It is really beautiful here."

"There's a hiking trail just outside the gate."

"So how did you get to do all this?" she asked.

"You remember Randy, right? From the firemen's BBQ."

"Yeah, and his wife Amber."

"Right. Amber is a real estate agent now and this is her listing. So, one thing led to another and she let me use the house for the evening to entice you."

"Entice me, huh?"

"Well, that's for later."

Katie couldn't believe how great the food tasted. She didn't know if it was because she was so hungry, or eating outdoors, or if it was just a wonderful escape.

"Wine?" he asked.

"Oh, that sounds so good, but I have a meeting in forensics at 6 a.m. tomorrow. I better pass."

"Ouch," he said pulling out a chilled bottle of mineral water.

"Yeah, double ouch."

"How's new Detective McGaven doing?"

"He's good. Every time we work on a new case I can't believe how lucky I am to have him as a partner."

"Has anything changed about him going to robbery-homicide?" Chad watched her closely.

"No. He'll still be working with me on these cases for now. But it could change—you never know with the department and the politics and budget." The thought made Katie sad. She didn't want to work with anyone else and certainly couldn't tackle some of the cases alone.

A few hours later, Chad walked Katie to her Jeep.

"Thank you for such a lovely, thoughtful evening."

"My pleasure," he said, holding her tight and kissing her passionately.

Katie could barely tear herself away from him. "I'll touch base tomorrow. Night."

"Goodnight."

Katie got behind the wheel with Cisco riding shotgun and waved to Chad as she backed out of the driveway. She watched Chad wave as she drove away.

CHAPTER THIRTY-NINE

Katie rushed into the sheriff's department building and hurried to the forensics entrance. It was still dark outside and it felt like she would perform better if she had at least two more hours of sleep. She hadn't had time to get their usual coffees because she hadn't wanted to be late.

Once inside she rushed to her office, dropping off her things and grabbing a notebook. McGaven wasn't there yet, so she went directly to John's examination room. Her day already seemed like she had been caught in a whirlwind.

The forensics exam room door was closed. Katie hesitated but then softly knocked.

"Come in," came John's voice from the other side.

Katie opened the door and was surprised to see McGaven already sipping on his morning coffee. "I hardly get here ahead of you."

"What can I say?" he said smiling.

"I got coffee for you," said John handing Katie a cup.

"Thank you." It seemed like the best cup of coffee she'd ever had. "What's all this?" she said, gesturing to the food.

"It was food left over from a meeting, so I brought it out of the fridge this morning. I thought you guys might like something to eat since it was so early."

"Don't mind if I do," said McGaven as he grabbed a meat-and-tortilla rollup.

"First of all, Katie, I ran some light sources on the note that was attached to your front door. Nothing. They must've been wearing gloves. I have a dental stone impression of the footprints, but if there's nothing to compare it to...?"

"Thanks, John," said Katie. "I knew it would be a long shot, but I wanted to make sure we had everything possible for when we catch him. I don't want any more victims."

John continued, "As far as the industrial building fire goes, ATF have their forensic examiners handling it. I'm trying to see if I can get a copy of the preliminary report from someone I know. Glad you guys are okay."

"Yeah, Katie and I just roll with it," said McGaven.

They all laughed, but all of them were intimately aware of the circumstances and how it could have turned out a lot worse.

Katie looked around the room and saw there were three different stations for examinations. "You've had a lot to contend with." She couldn't help but notice that John was dressed casually in jeans, T-shirt, and his work boots. There was a pair of slacks, white shirt, and casual tie hanging on a hook behind the door. She assumed it was for his meeting.

"Just wanted to let you know that Jake Fields's motorhome didn't offer any evidence—after the search warrant was executed by Detective Hamilton, it was a bust. The interior appeared to have been wiped down fairly well. Nothing inside was personal —I examined it very carefully. It's just an empty shell. Sorry that there's nothing more."

Katie was disappointed, but it didn't mean that Jake Fields wasn't still a suspect. "Thanks, John. That was a rush request because we didn't want to give Jake a heads-up, but it looks like we were too late if there was any evidence."

"I'm still working on the soil in the tires and wheel wells."

"Okay," she said.

John cleared his throat. "Okay, I figure the best way to start is at the beginning. Let's have a look at the bomb fragments that were taken out from the camp." He moved to the area where he had separated them into categories. "There really wasn't much to examine, but what we do have really consists of someone not being an expert. I think with what we found, it was more about the scare or fear and not about taking a life or maiming."

Katie noticed that there were fragments that looked like plastic, wires, and some smudges on clear plastic.

"What remained after the small explosion was similar to what you would find with a pipe bomb—think of a small portion of one of those."

Katie and McGaven moved closer to the bomb pieces.

"It's my professional opinion that this was designed to scare rather than kill. And the person who assembled it was a novice. Maybe even got their information from the internet." He moved to one of the computers with a large screen. He clicked on an icon and several sequential photographs appeared. "This is the area where it detonated. See the burn marks here?" He gestured to the computer screen. "It was made to be mostly self-contained and not explode outward." He went to a photo of a simplistic drawing of where the bomb was set and when it would detonate.

Katie studied the picture carefully. She recognized exactly where the area was. "How would they know that someone would be going through that area?"

John clicked on more photos. "See how the weeds and bushes are trampled and cleared away—giving it a recognizable path to walk."

"So the killer was guiding us..." said Katie softly.

"Sort of." He picked up the pieces of plastic. "We have some plastic, which is typical polyvinyl chloride—PVC—which is easy to mold into different shapes and can take temperatures over 140 degrees. It's used primarily instead of metal piping in construction, like plumbing, and various types of building—commercial and industrial."

"And you can buy it at any hardware or superstore," said McGaven.

"We're just getting started." He clicked through more photos. "The wires didn't seem to coincide with anything. I believe it was something that the perpetrator might have dropped or even left behind on purpose."

"That's interesting," said Katie as she made notes.

"And of course there's a remnant of black powder—but interestingly there were no trace pieces of blasting caps so that's why it leads me to believe that it was more for show."

Katie remained quiet. She was thinking about why the killer chose to proceed this way—and then she remembered how he had just stood there in Eagle Ridge, watching her instead of adding her to his list of victims.

McGaven said, "That's an interesting signature move, isn't it?"

"It could be. Now I'm going to go in order of crime scenes."

Katie nodded. She was still thinking about why the killer would have set up only one place to have a bomb detonate like that.

John rolled his chair over to another large computer station. He expertly clicked up files with the name: *C. Sable.* "This is the crime scene of the first victim found. She was immersed in the water." He waited while Katie and McGaven studied the photos. "I'll send you files of all these photos."

That image was forefront in her mind. She remembered how the body looked after it was just pulled from the water.

"I assume you've already talked to Dr. Dean?"

"Yes."

"So you know that the left arm was removed post-mortem."

"Yes, and he said that it was a mess and difficult to tell what type of knife or cutting device was used. He said it was a combination."

"I have to agree with him," said John. "There's really no way of pinpointing the exact implements used. It was like a mélange of cutting instruments."

"And there's no way of telling if the killer was simply inept or doing it on purpose," she said.

John smiled. "That's your department."

"What about the rope?" asked McGaven, stuffing part of a doughnut into his mouth and washing it down with coffee.

John led them to another exam table where the rope had been studied and tested for foreign matters. "This is a twisted sisal rope, quarter-inch thick. An interesting choice; most ropes I see are not all natural like this one, which are fibers from the Agave sisalana plant. There are no chemicals, oils, or other processes used. The most common ropes I see are made of polyester and have a high tenacity and a resistance to stretch and UV light."

"Doesn't sisal shed quite a bit? I've had carpets made from this," she said.

"That's correct; you'll see why it's important when I get to the victims."

That gave Katie some hope. "So I take it this rope is new."

"Yes, we're talking just-bought-at-the-store brand new."

"Was there anything found embedded in between the fibers?" asked McGaven. He was completely engrossed with the forensic examination.

Katie was just about to ask the same question and remained hopeful.

"We did photographs with different light sources and filters to try and pick up anything that shouldn't be there, but there were only minute traces of blood which were too small and diluted to test any further. It was most likely the victim's blood

—but still no solid proof, just speculation. There was no foreign trace evidence of any kind."

Katie felt her enthusiasm diminish. Yet again they were left with nothing that would help catapult the investigation forward —or connect them to any particular suspect.

"However, you're going to love this. Those same individual fibers consistent with the sisal rope were found on the second and third victims' clothing."

"You're saying that fibers from the rope found with Carolyn Sable's body were found on both Edith Crest and Stephanie Baxter?" she asked.

"Yep."

"Well, that just means they were all in contact with the rope at some point," said McGaven.

"Or that the killer transferred it to them—Locard's Exchange Principle. Where the perpetrator comes to a crime scene and leaves something of evidence and then leaves with something from the scene." Katie thought about it and wondered if there was more evidence of fiber from that rope around in the buildings at Eagle Lake Camp.

John watched Katie as she began to piece things together.

"Wait, I have a favor," she said suddenly. "There's a cold case of a guy named Rick Reynolds from about two years ago. He was found out at Bluff Park with multiple stab wounds. Could you find out if he possibly had any of those fibers found on his clothes? And if they are consistent with the ones on the women at Eagle Ridge Camp."

"Of course," he said, jotting down the name before continuing.

"We performed an in-depth search and testing of the scrapings from the bodies, fingernails, and from their clothes and weren't able to find anything that didn't belong to them."

"You're losing my confidence again, John," said Katie in a jokey tone. "We need more."

John brought up more photographs with graphs. It first appeared to be more plastic pieces. "Take a look at this," he said.

Katie leaned in to see the small plastic pieces that had been taken from the office in the main building. "That doesn't seem like the ordinary kind of plastic."

"It's not. It's a common type of polymer called poly-oxymethylene, which is a much harder type used for specialty items. It usually has a coating of polyvinyl chloride." He leaned back. "You want to know what polyoxymethylene is used for?"

"My best guess would be automotive or maybe engineering or electronics?" said McGaven.

Katie nodded in agreement.

"You're right. It can be used for things such as gear wheels, fasteners, ball bearings, gun parts, and items like that. But something interesting came to my attention because of the combination of the plastic and polymers. It is often used in the manufacture of prosthetic limbs."

"Bingo," said McGaven.

"So the plastic pieces I found by the window of the counselor's office at Eagle Ridge are fragments from a prosthetic limb?" Katie's mind went into warp speed with the killer being someone with a prosthetic limb—like Brian Stanwick, but he had been dead for five years.

"It would seem. There are no other explanations. Now, your real problem is..."

"We don't know when those fragments were left there," she said. "It could have been a week before we found it or a year."

John looked at the detectives. "That's all I have right now and it should be in your incoming email. I need to get ready for this meeting."

"Thank you, John. You've given us more to work with," said Katie. "Oh, I have to ask you something."

"Shoot."

"Gav and I are working on something that will entail

surveillance at Eagle Ridge Camp—a much more sophisticated set-up than what's there now. As part of that, we may need help with making it appear that I'm staying in cabin eleven, but not."

"I think I know where you're going with this. When would you need help by?"

"Well, I have to meet with the sheriff and it's going to be a tough sell, but I wanted to know if you could help us, or have the time, if we get a green light."

"Absolutely. Check back with me when you know."

CHAPTER FORTY

Katie raced back to the office, which was only down the hallway and to the right. She had renewed energy and wanted to get to work. For things to move forward quickly, she knew that they had to split up to cover more investigative territory.

McGaven burst through the door and made his way to his work station. "We have a lot of things to cover."

"We do," she said as she organized her notes and began adding to the murder board.

McGaven looked at his text messages. "Looks like Robin Drakes and her mother are settling in and cooperating."

"Oh, that's good. We need to keep them safe."

"I've managed to track down most of the previous employees and volunteers at Eagle Ridge Camp," he said. "Most are in other states. It's difficult to get in contact with quite a few of them, but they didn't seem to have any connection with the hike and Brian's accident."

"And?"

"I'm tracking down the remaining individuals from the list, the general manager—Janice Shipman; activities coordinator—Marilyn Weber; and maintenance technician—Sid Wells. All of them are in nearby areas according to their last known addresses."

"Sending a deputy to their houses? We want everyone safe," she said.

"On it. I will brief the local police department on the situation."

"It's got me thinking... when I was in the hospital I took a walk in the middle of the night."

"That sounds like the prologue to a horror film."

"Seriously, I couldn't sleep so I took a walk around the hospital. I ended up in the rehabilitation unit and where the prosthetics area is located—there are serial numbers identifying each piece. Brian Stanwick had lost a limb, so wouldn't he have had an identifying number? We might be able to find out more information about him."

"Katie, you're a genius."

"Why thank you, Detective McGaven." Katie smiled. "I think the prosthetic link might have viable information."

"You got it."

Katie hesitated. She wasn't sure if she wanted to broach this next subject with McGaven, but it felt like something had to be said. "Hey, Gav."

McGaven immediately stopped typing when he heard her tone. "What's up?"

"Let's just say a little birdie told me something."

"Like what?" His full attention was on his partner.

"Are you considering joining the robbery-homicide division?" Her words hung in the air as she waited for an answer. As soon as she said it out loud, she regretted it.

"I'm not going to lie. They've approached me about that and I've enjoyed some of what I've been doing, but nothing is like working cases with you." He paused as if trying to get his words in order. "Katie, I don't think you realize how amazing you are, and how incredibly difficult these cases have been. Sometimes I think, there's no way we can catch the killer—but we *always* do. I've pushed myself to work these cases, but I wouldn't want to work cases with anyone else but you."

Katie was a bit stunned.

"I know that the department has been going through some changes, namely reassignments, but unless I'm ordered to do so, I want to stay with the cold-case unit."

Katie didn't immediately look McGaven in the eye, but she valued what he had to say and the sincerity behind his words. "Thanks, Gav. I appreciate your honesty."

"You're so silly," he said in an upbeat tone.

"What do you mean?"

"Like working with those guys upstairs would be better than working with you. Those guys are totally boring and predictable."

"Yeah, and maybe safer to be around."

"Every day I drive to work I know that I'm going to be doing something different and even exciting. That's what I love about this kind of police work—and *working with you*," he emphasized.

Taking in a breath, Katie said, "Okay. Well, we've certainly got a few things in the fire."

"Yep."

Katie stood up and added to the killer's profile on the whiteboard:

Carefully planned attacks/twenty years?

Make the people pay that were there during the accident /eye for an eye.

*Who would want to avenge Brian Stanwick's accident and suicide?

*Could it be one intended murder and the others are to cover it up and throw us off?

McGaven's phone rang. "Detective McGaven," he said, listening to the caller. "Fantastic. Give it to me." He scribbled down some information. "Thanks, babe," he said and hung up.

"I hope that was Denise," said Katie smiling.

"She is so amazing how she can dig things up." He read from his notes. "She managed to find the doctor through newspaper articles. Dr. Xavier Pendleton, who worked at Pine Valley Memorial Hospital—and wait for it—he was the surgeon who operated on Brian Stanwick."

"That's great," she said. "Let's go." She got up and grabbed her jacket.

"Well, wait a minute."

Katie sat down. "Oh no. He's dead, isn't he?"

"Well, not exactly."

"What does that mean?"

"He's retired and lives over in the eastern area of Pine Valley. But he's suffering from the early stages of dementia."

"How bad?"

"Don't know, but he still lives in the same house and not in a retirement home. Maybe he'll remember something that could help us?"

Katie stood up. "Let's go."

CHAPTER FORTY-ONE

Katie drove with purpose, breaking the speed limit when she could. Her nerves were tense. She had been fighting a wave of anxious, creeping feelings that desperately wanted to come to the surface. Keeping her focus was the only thing she could do. There was so much to cover in this investigation and she knew that McGaven wanted to get back to his searches at the office. This trail was like disjointed pieces of a huge puzzle with so much detail still to find to fill in the blanks.

"Good news," said McGaven as he ended a cell phone call. "Looks like Janice Shipman, who was the general manager at Eagle Ridge Camp, has been found safe and alive. She told the deputy that she could go to Arizona and stay with a sister for a while, but would check in."

"We have her contact info?"

"Yep. And she'll let the local law enforcement know if there are any problems."

"Okay, that's good. Let's follow up." Katie took a couple of breaths and tried to relax her shoulders. "Is it up here?"

"Go past the stop sign and then make a left on Fern Street. It's... 143 Fern Street."

Katie turned down the street and was surprised how run-down the small houses were as they drove past. "Wow, this reminds me of an area that time forgot."

"It hasn't always been like this," said McGaven. "I've patrolled here before. The community had been trying to clean it up, but it seems as though that attempt failed."

Katie was shocked at how dilapidated the area had become. She suddenly remembered the beautiful new community of homes that she had visited recently with Chad and felt deeply saddened. It seemed that housing policy was about always building more and just forgetting the rest.

She pulled up in front of a small house that wasn't in as bad condition as some of the others on the street. The weeds were overgrown, but the house itself appeared to be in good shape. It was dark green with white trim, and obviously once had beautiful landscaping.

"I hope that Dr. Pendleton is home," she said.

"Let's find out."

Both detectives got out of the sedan and walked to the front door. There was no fencing or gate to enter, but there was a slight trail through the weeds that had been traversed by visitors or delivery men recently. A tiger-patterned cat jetted out from behind a patch of overgrown foliage and ran past Katie. She stepped up to the dirty white front door and knocked.

They waited and didn't hear any movement from inside.

"I guess he's not home," she said. "Maybe he's at the store or a medical appointment?" She looked at mail slot in the door and there was a faint stencil marking that read: *Pendleton*. "We're at the right place." She knocked on the door again—this time louder.

There was a bumping sound and then a strange sliding noise.

"What is that?" she said.

"Don't know," said McGaven who was suddenly hypersensitive and ran his fingers over his gun holster.

The door unlocked and opened slightly. There was no one there. A voice said, "Give me a minute, please." More scraping noises.

Katie leaned closer to the door. "Dr. Xavier Pendleton?"

The person on the other side of the door laughed.

Katie looked questioningly at McGaven as they patiently waited, glancing once or twice behind them.

The door opened. An elderly man appeared, wearing a navy sweater, jogging pants, and sneakers, and pushing a walker. His hair was sparse, skin wrinkled by sun exposure, but his spirit seemed high. He smiled with almost sparkly eyes. "You know, no one has called me Dr. Pendleton in a very long time."

"I'm Detective Scott and this is Detective McGaven. May we come in and talk to you for a few minutes?"

The man had clear, direct eyes as he gave the detectives a once-over, checking out their badges. "What's it about?"

"It's about a patient you had—Brian Stanwick—about twenty years ago."

The doctor's eyes lit up as he seemed to remember. "The amputation," he said flatly. Shaking his head, he added, "That was a tough one, such a young boy. And such a tragic accident." He moved back so that Katie and McGaven could enter.

"Thank you," said Katie and she walked into the living room, relieved that he remembered the case.

McGaven nodded.

"Please, have a seat and make yourselves comfortable. Would you like some coffee? I just made a pot."

Katie approached and said, "Please, I can get the coffee."

The doctor nodded and moved to the living room with McGaven. The interior of the house was neat and organized—no clutter, and things were put away out of sight. The furniture was old, but it had been expensive and was wearing well. There were a couple dozen framed photographs of family lined up along the top of a small piano. Along two of the walls were oil paintings of various seascapes and landscapes.

Katie found three coffee cups and poured the steaming fresh brew. Noticing several prescription bottles on the counter with notecards indicating when to take them, she glanced at the labels. There were taped pieces of paper on cabinets and the refrigerator to remind him of all sorts of things like when to eat, what day it was, and how to run the dishwasher.

She felt her heartstrings pulled. There was something about him that made her miss her parents and she wished she had been from a large family. It was just her and her uncle, Sheriff Scott, which sometimes made her feel lonely and disconnected.

Katie returned to the living room carrying a tray with the coffee cups, sugar, and a little cream pourer with milk. "I wasn't sure how you like your coffee," she said setting down the tray.

"I've always taken my coffee black," the doctor said.

"Me too."

"Tell me, what do two Pine Valley detectives want to know about an amputation patient from twenty years ago?"

"We are doing some research and wanted to know more about his case," said Katie. Even though she wanted to tell the doctor more, she had to be careful what type of information she offered. It was still an open case, after all.

"I don't know if you understand anything about amputa- tion, but it's used as only the last resort when all other proce- dures fail or if the condition of the limb in question is extremely damaged. By the time Brian Stanwick arrived, many hours had passed since his fall. They had rescue people sent up to the camp and unfortunately it took a while. The poor boy had lost quite a bit of blood too and was extremely dehydrated." The doctor cleared his throat and took a moment.

"Are you alright?" asked Katie.

"Oh yes. It amazes me the way I'm still kicking."

"What about Brian's parents?"

"I don't remember anyone except his father—or it might have been an uncle. I'm not sure which, thinking back. I remember he was a tall, stern-looking man, who never said a word as I explained to him that his son was going to lose his leg." He paused as if remembering that conversation like it was yesterday. "I was able to save the boy's wrist, but there was permanent damage, giving him only partial usage. I had to remove a kidney as well." He shook his head.

"How long did it take for him to recover?" asked McGaven.

"Initially?"

"Yes."

"I don't remember the exact timeframe, but in general, a patient can go home in about a week to two weeks. Children usually heal faster than adults."

"I see. Would you have any idea what happened to the boy after he left the hospital?"

"No, I don't have any idea." He paused. "You have to understand. There is a fair amount of healing before a person can be fitted with a prosthetic. After leaving the hospital, there are psychological considerations and then another month or more before they are ready for their new limb. And after that, there is time to learn how to use it, continued therapy, and still ongoing psychological support."

"For a ten-year-old boy, I can't imagine how difficult it must've been," she said.

"Detective Scott, so many times, we as a society merely walk past people with a disability and don't think twice." He picked up his coffee cup with slightly shaking hands and took a long sip, seemingly lost in his thoughts. "Please forgive me if I seem aloof or distant at times—it's my condition."

"That's quite alright," she said.

Katie and McGaven were quiet. Katie thought about the lab at the hospital and all of the various prosthetics.

"I can see you're troubled," Dr. Pendleton said to Katie as he watched her. "There's something else that you're not telling me. Perhaps you're not allowed, but know that whatever you say will go no further than this room."

Katie glanced at McGaven who gave a slight nod. "We are investigating those murders up at Eagle Ridge Camp."

"Ah, I figured it had to do with the camp if you were looking into Brian Stanwick's accident. It's been too long for any type of court case regarding the incident."

"Yes."

"I didn't know about any murders, though. I stay away from news and I'm not one for the internet. I think you'll live longer without indulging in either."

Katie smiled. She felt an unusual closeness to Dr. Xavier Pendleton—there was something familiar about him.

The doctor raised his eyebrows crinkling his forehead wrinkles. "Did I offer you coffee?" He looked at the three coffee cups. "Oh, of course I did." He paused for a moment. "You don't have to say anything to me, but I would guess that the victims' conditions have something to do with prosthetics."

"Each victim was missing a limb or internal organ."

"I see. And you're doing your due diligence?"

Katie shifted in her seat. "We think they may be possibly linked to Brian Stanwick so we're trying to get as much information as we can about him. Or someone that was related to him."

Dr. Pendleton looked toward his built-in bookcase, which was filled with books. "I used to keep records of articles pertaining to my patients. There were quite a few amazing people that I operated on over my career."

"May we see them?" asked Katie.

"Of course. See those light blue binders on the bottom shelf?"

Katie rose and went to the bookshelf. She spotted the blue binders that had neatly typed spines with dates. Finding one labeled with dates covering approximately twenty years ago, she pulled it from the shelf.

Katie went back into the living room and handed the binder to Dr. Pendleton.

"I haven't seen this in a while. My late wife used to put these together for me from newspaper clippings and such." He flipped through the neatly pressed articles under plastic until he came to the one in question. "Here it is," he said and handed it back to Katie.

BOY LOSES HIS LEG FROM TRAGIC ACCIDENT AT EAGLE RIDGE CAMP

Katie skimmed the article, which was like the ones she had read, and didn't have much information except about the fall itself and the rescue. It didn't mention a name of a parent or uncle. It was the information she had already found, but from a different news source. It didn't say anything about a sibling—or more precisely, a brother. She flipped the page and there was a short follow-up article about Brian Stanwick when he was released from the hospital, but still, nothing about a parent's name. There was a photograph, grainy, but it showed a boy being pushed in a wheelchair by a tall man with a baseball cap. He was looking downward, so it was difficult to identify him. In the background, a young boy, about the same age of Brian Stanwick, was also exiting the hospital. It was unclear if he was part of the family or not. She used her cell phone to take a picture of each article.

Katie gave the book to McGaven.

"Something?" said the doctor.

"I don't know, but there's a photo of his dad and then there's a young boy in the background. Do you remember a brother about his age?"

Dr. Pendleton thought a moment. "I don't think I ever saw anyone else. Sometimes I get people mixed up and I don't remember someone from today."

"Thank you so much, Dr. Pendleton, for the coffee and giving us a moment of your time." Katie rose and gathered hers and McGaven's coffee cups.

McGaven took a photograph of the article.

Katie rinsed the coffee cups and put them in the dishwasher. She noticed the prescription bottles with identifying numbers.

As she returned to the living room, she asked, "Is there a way we can find out who has a particular prosthetic limb?"

"Well," the doctor said, "there are NPI numbers, which means National Provider Identifier."

"Would that have the name and contact information of the recipient?"

"Of course."

"Who would we need to talk to about that?" said McGaven.

"Let me see," he said as he thought a moment. It was clear that he had some trouble remembering names or events. "Oh yes, the prosthetist is Candace... Candace Peterson at Pine Valley General. I believe she's probably still there. If not, someone would be able to answer your questions."

"Thank you."

Dr. Pendleton rose slowly and took hold of his walker. He followed the detectives to the front door. "It was nice visiting with you, Detectives. I hope you get your killer." He grabbed Katie's hand and squeezed it. "I hope that I helped in your investigation."

"Yes, you've helped us more than you know."

Katie and McGaven left.

As the detectives returned to the car, Katie said, "I think we need to have patrol in this area drive by Dr. Pendleton's house on a regular basis."

"Think he might be in danger?" said McGaven.

"I'm not sure, but he was connected with Brian Stanwick and did remove his leg. He could be blamed for not saving the leg instead of amputation. We need patrol to be stationed here if we can."

"On it," said McGaven as he dialed his cell phone and talked with the patrol sergeant.

As McGaven conducted his call, Katie took a step back and scanned the neighborhood. She noticed that two of the houses appeared to be abandoned and would make a good place to hole up or view Dr. Pendleton's house. It wasn't completely clear to Katie, just an instinct, but something seemed to be amiss in the neighborhood. She had the prickly feeling that they were being watched.

Was Dr. Pendleton in imminent danger?

"Okay," said McGaven. "He's on the schedule of deputies patrolling the area. I told them he makes good coffee too." He watched Katie. "Katie? Something wrong?"

She took a moment before she answered. "No. Just one of those gut feelings, I guess. Did you see that car when we arrived?" A dark green four-door sedan was parked across from the homes—on the side of the street where there was a large empty rural property. There was no license plate on the front of the car, and the rear wasn't visible.

"I'm not sure," he said. "But I don't think there was any car parked on the street."

He took her cue and looked around the neighborhood. "Those two houses look like no one's lived there in a while."

"I thought the same thing," she said. "But they have a vantage on Dr. Pendleton's house."

"Someone could use the house to hide or conduct surveillance, I suppose."

Katie took a few steps toward the houses and stopped. They were both painted a dark green with tan trim—in serious need of maintenance and new paint. She saw a garbage bag on the front porch on one of the houses, but there were "no trespassing" signs and two of the windows were boarded up. She strained her eyes to see if there were any video cameras, but she didn't see any. Her thoughts turned to the Eagle Ridge Camp and the cameras Bud had positioned.

McGaven used his phone to search the county assessor's office to find out if the houses had legitimate owners and weren't bank foreclosures. Through a few minutes of searching, he found out. "Both of those houses are bank-owned. No one should be living there before they're auctioned off."

Katie took a few more steps and saw a curtain move in one of the front windows. She unsnapped her holster, but didn't immediately pull her weapon. "We need to check it out," she said in a whisper, turning to McGaven.

Moving closer to his partner, he said, "How do you want to play this?"

Thinking quickly, Katie thought they should appear as if they were leaving. "Let's go." She went to their sedan and got in —McGaven followed. He didn't say anything, but realized what Katie was doing.

Katie turned the engine over and put the car into drive. She slowly drove out the way they had entered, turned the corner and then parked out of view from the house in question.

The detectives got out.

"I'll go around from the back," McGaven said.

"I've got the front," said Katie as she made her way to the house.

She knew that she had seen the curtain move before, as if someone was watching them. This time, managing to get close and stay along the left side of the house, she took a moment to listen. There should be movement. Maybe the person thought they had left? Maybe they went back to what they were doing?

Katie's foot sank slightly into the ground. She looked down and saw the hose spigot was dripping water. Wouldn't they have turned off the water?

She moved toward the front of the house, staying close to the siding. Passing the first boarded-up front window, she kept moving. Once she stepped onto the porch, it creaked loudly. There was a noise inside the house like someone crashing into furniture and running. She pulled her Glock and readied it.

Katie took a few steps backward and then toward the front door, slamming it with a hard kick—only making it crack. She repeated her kick and this time the door burst open. Quickly inside, she cleared the first room. She yelled, "Police, come out now!" She knew that the person inside wouldn't comply, but she made her presence known in case McGaven came crashing in not knowing where she was in the house.

There was a crash and a door slammed out the back. Katie raced through the house, ready for anything. Once in the backyard, the person seemed to have vanished. She wasn't sure if they had jumped the partially dilapidated fence or circled back around.

McGaven came into view with his gun drawn.

Katie raised her arms, indicating she didn't know where they went.

There was the sound of a car starting and screeching off down the road.

Katie and McGaven ran around the house in time to see the car blow through a stop sign and disappear to the left.

"We lost them!" said Katie.

CHAPTER FORTY-TWO

After Katie and McGaven lost their potential suspect, they called in the disturbance and three deputy cruisers arrived shortly.

McGaven briefed the deputies about the events, as well as on the potential safety of Dr. Pendleton amidst their pending investigation of the murders at Eagle Ridge Camp.

Inside the house again and donning plastic gloves, Katie did a preliminary search. In the front living room and kitchen area there were two folding chairs, a small table, and bags from fast-food joints together with empty soda cans. She ascertained by the placement and the food consumed that there had only been one person watching through the front windows of the house. There was also a small pair of binoculars, two torn pieces of paper, and a partially eaten piece of red licorice.

She examined the floor, but couldn't see anything unusual. There was just a tattered shag carpet and a dirty linoleum floor. There were deep scuffs and grime, but nothing looked recent. She walked through the house and none of the other rooms looked used. Finally, at the back door, she saw some wet areas around the door casing, most likely caused from dripping from the rain.

McGaven joined her. "What do you think?"

"It's unclear if it's related to our cases, or even Dr. Pendleton, but I think we should have John dust for prints."

"Okay, I'll get him out here," he said and moved back through the house and out the front door to speak with deputies and coordinate CSI.

Katie looked around one more time as she ran the new information through her mind. She hurried back to Dr. Pendleton's house and spoke briefly with him. He agreed that he would go to his granddaughter's house in Monterey, California until the investigation was over.

Katie drove to Pine Valley Memorial Hospital. McGaven had double-checked to see if there was still a Candace Peterson working in prosthetics—which there was. She had been there for almost thirty years.

"I wonder if Ms. Peterson will be able to give us any useful information," said McGaven.

"I don't think there is client confidentiality for prosthetics—especially since it's for a homicide investigation." Katie pressed the accelerator harder, wanting to get the hospital.

She turned into the hospital parking lot once again. Her stomach churned. She remembered her recent overnight stay, which still gave her an uncomfortable feeling. Her arm still had a twinge of pain every once in a while; otherwise, it was healing nicely. She wasn't certain if the feelings came from her anxiety, or if they were just from being in a place that made her uncomfortable. She pushed her feelings aside and focused on finding out more information about Brian Stanwick.

Katie and McGaven entered the main administrative entrance of the hospital. "I know where to go," she said and took the elevator to the second floor. She then hurried down the hall-way, passing the area where she had been admitted. She was now taking almost the same walk as she had that night.

"Wow, it's like a maze with all the new upgrades and the new wing," said McGaven.

"I thought so too when I was walking around here last week." She looked up ahead and saw the rehabilitation unit. "There," she said. It was the same entrance to the prosthetics area. This time the lights were on and there were several people moving around.

McGaven opened the door followed by Katie. The area was laid out like a laboratory with several smaller rooms that Katie assumed were areas for fittings.

A young woman with blonde hair and a ponytail approached the detectives. "May I help you?"

"Yes, I spoke with a Candace Peterson earlier," said McGaven.

"Oh, yes of course," she replied. "Are you the Pine Valley detectives?"

"Yes."

"Wait here and I'll let her know you're waiting. I think she's finishing up with a patient." The woman left and disappeared into another part of the building.

Katie and McGaven patiently waited, scanning the area where there were technicians working on various types of pros-thetics: legs, arms, feet, and hands. It saddened Katie to think so many people needed these artificial limbs due to accidents, illness, and being in the military. She thought of Sergeant Nick Haines, her army sergeant, who had lost a leg and had been forced to retire early.

There was a distant buzzing noise. Katie saw an older woman coming towards them: striking, long white hair twisted up in a bun, wearing jeans and a bright yellow sweatshirt and navigating an electric wheelchair. It caught Katie by surprise.

"Hello," said the woman.

"Candace Peterson?" said Katie.

"Yes, that's me."

"I'm Detective Katie Scott and this is my partner Detective McGaven."

"It's nice to meet you both," she said. "And it's nice to put a face with a voice," she said to McGaven.

"Do you have some time to speak with us?"

"Of course. Anything I can do to help in your investigation." She turned her wheelchair. "Follow me." She led them through the manufacturing area and past some exam rooms until they were at an office. "Here we are with some privacy."

Candace Peterson's office was large with two desks—one work area with a computer, printer, and scanner. The other area was a large desk with two chairs that was obviously for meeting with patients. The office was roomy enough to accommodate a wheelchair and patients who were on crutches.

Katie noticed immediately in the corner lying on a pet bed was a beautiful golden retriever. The dog immediately rose and greeted Katie.

"What a beauty you are," Katie said.

"That's Ginger. She's the mascot around here and my full-time assistance dog. She sure seems to be taken with you."

"That's because Detective Scott is a veteran, former army K9 handler," said McGaven grinning from ear to ear, showing how proud he was of his partner.

"Oh, my goodness. Thank you so much for your service to this country," Ms. Peterson said.

Katie smiled. "That's very kind of you to say." She was always a bit uneasy and humbled when people commented on her army tours.

"Please have a seat."

Katie and McGaven sat down across from her.

"I understand that Dr. Pendleton referred you to me

regarding a previous patient. He's such a wonderful man and was an amazing surgeon until his health began to fail. Once his mind wasn't working as it should he was forced to retire. Miss him around here."

"We're investigating several cases," said Katie. "There has been a connection with Eagle Ridge Camp. And we think it's possible that the accident of Brian Stanwick has some bearing on the cases."

A screensaver on the computer screen at the other desk showed a gallery of landscape photos scrolling through slowly. Katie recognized them as some areas around Pine Valley. She assumed that Ms. Peterson was an avid photographer.

"I see. I remember the case well. We have such a fraction of children in need of a prosthetic, so it's easy to remember him. It was that terrible fall from Eagle Ridge." She picked up a file folder and opened it.

"Yes," said Katie.

"All our cases are completely computerized and have been for about fifteen years. Now, this one," she said, shuffling through the paperwork, "is the file of Brian John Stanwick and it was before we automated everything."

Katie wanted to see the paperwork, but waited patiently for the older woman to scan the file.

"Oh yes," Ms. Peterson said eventually. "I remember now, we're talking twenty-two years ago. But this case was one you didn't forget."

"That's what Dr. Pendleton said too," said Katie.

"It says that the operation was long—more than normal. And Dr. Pendleton did everything he could to save the limbs. The boy lost his left leg about mid-thigh, had one of his kidneys removed, and there was some extensive damage to his left hand. It says that his left hand was about seventy percent repaired."

"What does that mean?" asked McGaven.

"It means that it's useable, but with dexterity problems.

Sometimes physical therapy helps, but in his case it didn't. I remember working with the boy. He had such a terrible time with everything. Half of the time he didn't want to cooperate... and the file says he was also in therapy."

"How long?"

"It looks like the last entry for physical therapy was about a year and four months after the accident."

"Is that usual in a case like this?" asked McGaven.

"There's a wide timeframe because everyone is different and the extent of the amputation is also different." She looked at the detectives. "But in my opinion, it wasn't long enough. There aren't any more visits—at least here at this facility."

"I understand that prosthetics have a serial number. How does that work?" she asked.

"Well, it's actually an NPI number and that puts it into a database for the healthcare provider information. So the information would be what we have in our files."

Katie decided to carefully word her next questions—which were crucial in the investigation. "What was his contact information?" She knew it was a longshot after twenty-two years but they had to follow every lead if they wanted to find out who would avenge his death.

"Let's see now," Ms. Peterson said. "His last known address was 1377 Spruce, Pine Valley, and his guardian was Mr. Graham Stanwick."

Katie wrote down the information in her small notebook. "Would you have any idea what happened to the boy after he quit coming here for therapy?"

"No, I'm sorry I don't. And I don't remember hearing about anything. Patients are free to go elsewhere."

"Is there anyone else listed in the file? A sibling? Mother?" she asked.

"No. Oh, except for someone to call in case of an emergency. Like a backup phone number."

Katie and McGaven waited in anticipation.

"Richard John Reynolds."

"Rick Reynolds?" said Katie barely able to breathe.

"I suppose he went by that name, but I never met him or recall ever seeing him," Ms. Peterson said. "That's all the information I have for you. I cannot give you any specific medical information—at least not without a written consent from Brian Stanwick or a family member."

After Katie and McGaven thanked Candace Peterson for her time, they quickly left the hospital. Katie couldn't believe that they'd found a link between the cold-case homicide of Rick Reynolds at Bluff Park, only a short hike from Carolyn Sable's house, and Brian Stanwick.

"I bet I know what you're thinking..." said McGaven as he looked across at his partner.

"After all this time... you should be able to read my mind." She smiled and travelled onto the freeway heading back to the sheriff's department.

"So we have a connection between Brian Stanwick and Rick Reynolds. What are the odds?"

"Really high, I would say. But they're both dead."

"Eagle Ridge Camp, Brian Stanwick, the counselors from the camp, and now Rick Reynolds. More pieces to the puzzle, but how and why are they connected?"

"I don't know. But I have to file reports now to the sheriff. I'm behind and he's not going to be pleased. He needs to know what we've found out so far."

McGaven's phone rang. "Detective McGaven." He listened for a few minutes and wrote down a phone number. "Thanks." He ended the call.

"Anything?"

"They've found Sid Wells, who was the maintenance tech

at Eagle Ridge, and he's relocated to Houston, Texas according to his ex-girlfriend."

"Make sure to talk to him personally and let him know that he needs to stay safe. If he feels threatened in any way he needs to contact the local police immediately," she said.

"On it. And I'll see if he has any information about the camp in general."

Katie nodded. As they approached the Pine Valley Sheriff's Department, her mind was already on how everyone connected to the camp and to each other.

"And by my calculation, almost all are accounted for from the working list at Eagle Ridge Camp except Marilyn Weber."

"I tried contacting her several times, but there was no response. She works independently now as an accountant from home."

"Maybe she's out of town," she said.

"We need to find her."

CHAPTER FORTY-THREE

Katie and McGaven sat in their favorite burger place. It had outdoor seating, which was where they often frequented as a good place to unwind and talk about cases without being overheard.

"This is incredible information," said McGaven. Katie had finally had the chance to catch him up on what she had learned from Shane at the county archives.

"I know, but I'm not sure how it all fits. Someone is not who they say they are."

McGaven nodded. "But I think you're right. We need to find out more about Jake Fields and track down the PO box."

"Absolutely," she said as she took another healthy bite of burger.

"I know what you're going to say," he said, dipping one of Katie's fries into catsup.

"Oh really?"

"Once we've found Marilyn Weber, we need to tail Jake Fields and find out who he really is and what he's up to."

"Yep."

"Surveillance."

"Your favorite," she said. She became quiet then, picking at her food and thinking about how Brian Stanwick fit into everything.

"Okay, what's up?" McGaven asked, watching his partner. "I can't read your mind this time."

"The killer might not be taking lives for revenge."

"Then for what?"

"I don't know, but what is it we always do with cold cases?" She smiled and pushed her plate of leftover fries toward her partner.

"Start at the beginning."

She nodded.

"Revisit the crime scene."

"And in this case it's Brian Stanwick's accident scene."

McGaven's cell phone chimed and he read the text. "Uh-oh."

"What?"

"We've found Marilyn Weber. Sheriff's department received a panic call from her. That someone was trying to kill her."

"Where?"

"The call came in from her residence and then disconnected. It's near that new strip mall under construction."

"We're only five minutes out," she said.

Katie stood up and dropped some cash on the table to cover their meals. "Tell dispatch that we're on our way. We're most likely closer than patrol."

They hurried out of the restaurant.

McGaven drove, since he knew the area well.

Katie watched the road as her partner took the turns fast but with expertise. "Marilyn Weber worked as the activities coordinator at Eagle Ridge Camp."

"Yes. That would make her vulnerable to the killer if he was choosing people who he felt were responsible for Brian's accident."

Katie thought about that. If Marilyn was the one who coordinated the overnight hike that would make her a prime target.

"Possible. But now she needs our help. We're looking for 323 Pine Trail."

McGaven took another turn as they headed toward the area.

Katie kept her wits and watched for the street.

They turned onto Pine Trail. It was a quiet area with small modest homes. There was a large truck with an open trailer full of gardening equipment blocking the road. They were using the residential area as backup access to the small shopping center under construction. They must've been installing landscape.

McGaven leaned on the horn. "Get out of the way!" he yelled to a couple of workers drinking coffee while walking across the road to get into their vehicle. They seemed to be leaving for a lunch break. Finally, they drove off.

"I think I see the house," she said. "There—323." She pointed. "The tan house." A small one-story light beige house from circa 1940s sat in a tidy front yard amid an abundance of flower pots. The white stepping stones formed a path to the front door.

McGaven pulled up in front and they were both out of the sedan the instant it stopped. He radioed to dispatch to inform them that he and Katie were at the location.

Looking around she said, "I don't see any vehicles. Shouldn't there be a deputy stationed here?" Katie readied her weapon just in case.

"Not unless she wasn't home or was away somewhere. The deputy would be dismissed by the watch commander," he said.

They went to the front door and knocked. The bottom of the door had black scuffs from a shoe and some chipping near the doorknob. Both damaged areas looked recent. Even though the door appeared intact and locked, it gave the impression that someone had tried to force it open.

"Ms. Weber, it's the police," said Katie knocking again.

No answer.

McGaven tried the door, but it was locked.

They listened, but it was quiet. There was no movement inside.

Katie moved toward the side of the house. "Around back."

The gate was open as they rushed through to the backyard. The surroundings in the small outdoor area were similar to the front—filled with colorful pots and a small iron table with two chairs. Immediately they went to the back door which was lying open. The partners assumed protocol and prepared to enter.

"Marilyn Weber?" called Katie. "Are you here?" She entered the residence, keeping her weapon directed out in front of her. "It's the police. We're here to help you."

McGaven covered his partner and then entered the home himself.

Inside, the interior resembled that of a small cabin. The furnishings were eclectic, with bright pillows and colorful prints on the wall. A small couch with one high-back chair was in the living room. A small kitchen table had been pushed in a strange position and both chairs were lying on their side, meaning there had been some type of scuffle.

"Ms. Weber."

Katie eyed the chairs and the broken plate and glass on the floor. She made a motion to McGaven to check the bedroom while she cleared everything else.

It took less than a minute to clear the home of Marilyn Weber. She was nowhere to be found, but her cell phone was on the floor.

There were several photos on the fireplace mantel of smiling people inside silver frames. The same woman with short blonde hair and a stockier build appeared in several of them. This must be Marilyn. Katie studied a picture of what could be family members at a restaurant. She studied Marilyn's bright smiling face and thought that her appearance was very out of step with the four counselors at Eagle Ridge Camp. It seemed that it didn't matter after all what she looked like, the killer was targeting anyone who was there when Brian Stanwick fell.

"Clear," said McGaven returning to the main living area.

"She's not here and she doesn't have her phone." Katie's deep concern was that the killer had abducted Marilyn.

Both detectives walked out the back and returned to the front yard as two Pine Valley Sheriff's Department cruisers pulled up.

McGaven greeted them and gave an update.

As her partner spoke with deputies, Katie looked around the neighborhood. The back door was open as well as the gate, which meant either that Ms. Weber had fled and run away—or that the killer had taken her by force. Katie kept looking and saw the neighbor's gate was also open.

"Gav, I'm going to check something out at the neighbor's house. I'll be right back," she said.

He hesitated, then nodded to her and turned back to the deputies.

Katie walked to the neighbor's open gate and peered into the backyard. Empty. It was bigger and more spacious than Marilyn's yard. Walking cautiously through the area, Katie noticed that there was another gate on the other side that led to the alley backing onto the lot of the new strip mall under construction. The gate was closed, but Katie guardedly approached and opened it. Nothing unusual. There was a narrow gravel alleyway that ran alongside the homes, just wide enough for a vehicle.

Looking closer, Katie saw fresh divots in the gravel. There were curious clumps left behind, which looked again as if there must have been a scuffle. She inspected the alley in both directions, but she couldn't be certain if there had been a car or truck driven through recently. If Marilyn had had someone trying to break into her house, it seemed likely she would have tried to flee in any way she could, and she would probably have known about this gate.

Katie walked back to the neighbor's gate and stopped, turning around again. Something told her to keep searching. It was either her experience or the exigent circumstances of the case, but she kept moving down the alley.

The small strip mall was in construction disarray. Piles of lumber, glass fixtures and display pieces, as well as interior and exterior doors were haphazardly placed around. There was chain-link fencing as a way of minimally protecting the supplies. Whether it was budget or permit issues, there were no construction trucks at the location. And it seemed that the landscapers were gone too. The small strip mall had a total of seven storefront buildings waiting for completion.

The sound of heavy plastic moving in the breeze caught Katie's attention. At one side of the building, a heavy tarp moved over a doorway.

Katie pulled her cell phone and directly dialed McGaven. It went to voicemail, so she sent a text: *Meet me at strip mall.* She returned her cell phone in her pocket.

Moving forward, Katie took a quick inventory of what was around her and looked for some type of vehicle that might have passed through the alley. She didn't find anything, but kept progressing until she reached the heavy plastic. There were tears in the material vertically, which seemed strange. Katie peeled back the plastic and peered inside. The smell of sawdust and other new construction materials hit her senses. She hesitated. Not wanting to make her presence known, she moved quietly.

A soft whimper came from the furthest area of the store building behind large storage containers.

Katie stopped. Her senses were on overload. She knew there was something wrong or unnatural inside the building and she wasn't going to move until she knew what was in there with her. Her perspiration chilled her back and goosebumps prickled her arms. Even though it was daytime, the interior was darkened due to the windows covered with plastic and wood. She remained grounded, unable to move and hoping that McGaven would burst through the plastic at any moment.

Suddenly, she thought she heard movement, so she inched her way toward the sound. She had to weave in and out and around equipment and supplies until she reached an area for small offices.

"Marilyn?" she whispered.

There was a sound of someone inhaling—sucking in a breath.

Katie kept moving and stopped when she sensed someone near. Straining to see in the dim lighting, she saw the tip of a running shoe. She quickly moved in and revealed a blonde woman hiding behind a wooden door—it was Marilyn.

"Marilyn?" Katie said.

The shaken women nodded tears ran down her face.

"It's okay. I'm Detective Scott. You're safe. Come with me."

The woman screamed.

Katie turned and saw a tall thin figure wearing a dark hoodie dart by. The unknown assailant pushed over some interior wooden doors.

"That's him!" the woman yelled.

"Stay here," Katie ordered and ran after the fleeing perpetrator.

Once in the daylight, Katie ran in the obvious direction toward the parking lot, but there was no one there. She ran to each side of the building, not wanting to venture too far away from Marilyn. Whoever was inside the building, they were gone.

Katie retraced her steps to Marilyn and had to coax her out from her hiding place.

McGaven met them in the parking lot. "What happened?"

"That man," said Marilyn. "He tried to get into my house as I called 911, and then chased me here. I hid but I could hear him searching for me."

"Did you get a good look at him?" asked McGaven.

"No," she whimpered. "I couldn't see his face."

Katie was disappointed, but relieved that this wasn't the killer's fourth victim.

McGaven pulled Katie aside. "Why would the killer take such chances in coming here?"

"We tried to contact you. Were you out of town?" asked Katie.

"Yes, I was visiting family in Arizona and Idaho. I just came back last night. What's going on?"

"Okay, we're going to get you to a safe place, and then we can explain. But everything is going to be fine."

Katie and McGaven took her back to her home where she quickly packed a bag. A deputy then took her to a safe apartment where she would be protected until she made other arrangements. One of the deputies would take her statement.

McGaven followed Katie to the car. "Do you think it was the killer?"

"Absolutely. I didn't see his face, but I saw his build, his movements, and the fact he had an escape route indicating that he knows the area. It was just like the figure that ambushed me.

We need to step up the safety of everyone connected with Eagle Ridge Camp."

"He retreated because the odds were he would be caught—or identified."

Katie looked around the neighborhood. "He's not done hunting down his victims yet. He's just getting started."

CHAPTER FORTY-FOUR

"This car smells funny," Katie said wrinkling her nose and looking around at the seats.

"Denise transports homeless dogs to rescues and foster people," said McGaven. "She tries to clean the interior, but sometimes the cleaners smell funky too."

"I didn't know Denise did that. She's an amazing woman. I didn't think it was possible to like her even more."

"This car was the only one I could think of that wouldn't stand out in a crowd. I know it's small too," said McGaven as he hunched a bit in the compact vehicle.

"I said I could drive."

"No, it's okay. That seat is just as bad."

"Maybe you could recline," she said smiling.

"Oh, that wouldn't look funny."

"How is Denise getting home?"

"She's taking my truck."

McGaven drove the compact white car into the parking lot of Fields, Campbell and Associates. He zipped through and turned around easily and headed back out. There was an available space on the street with a perfect view of anyone coming or going from the parking lot. He cut the engine and retrieved his notes. "He has three cars registered with the DMV: blue Mercedes, silver Range Rover, and, of course, the lovely motorhome."

"Great spot," she said glancing around.

"Do you think that Jake Fields is the kind of guy who leaves work at 5 p.m.?"

"If I was a betting person—I would place a bet that he would leave between 5 and 6 p.m."

McGaven stared at his partner as she kept her eyes glued to the parking lot entrance. "We have his home address."

"I'm still betting that he's going to be here."

"I wish Cisco was here," said McGaven. "We could use him to track this guy."

"I don't know if he would like the smell of all those rescue dogs in here." Katie thought about it. "You're right—we might be able to use him. We'll see what happens to this guy tonight."

"Look," he said. "It's the blue Mercedes."

"And that's Jake Fields driving." Katie readied herself as McGaven eased out from the parking spot, slipping in a car length behind Jake.

"Wow, this guy really sticks to the speed limit. Who does that?" he said.

"He's probably on his cell phone."

The Mercedes turned down several side streets and then sat waiting to make a left-hand turn. The detectives patiently waited their turn. There was only one car between them. Jake pulled out and then merged onto the freeway where he maintained a speed within ten miles of the limit. He drove in the slow lane, but didn't take any exits for four miles.

"Where is he headed?" said Katie. "There's not much out here as far as residences go—only commercial units. And not many of those at that."

"There are commercial properties for sale. It's nearing the dump."

"Maybe he's looking at some properties for investments for his clients?" she said.

"Wouldn't that be something for Daniel Green from Red Hawk Real Estate?"

"Maybe that's how they are connected?" Katie sighed. "I wish it was that easy. We're getting ahead of ourselves again."

McGaven slowed their speed as the traffic became less busy. He continued to follow at a greater distance, copying Jake as he took the exit going towards the recycling and utilities plants.

"What's this guy doing there after hours?"

They followed as Jake drove into the parking lot of the utility company. He continued through a gate and disappeared.

"What do you want to do? We're going to lose him."

"Put your cell phone on to walkie-talkie mode and let me out here," she said.

McGaven stopped the car. "Stay in contact and don't do anything. We're here to observe. Got it?" he strongly stated.

"Got it," she said and jumped out, not turning back toward McGaven. She put her earpiece in so that she could hear him.

Katie kept close to the parked cars, trying to act casually, and then bypassed one of the buildings. People were still exiting the office buildings and walking towards their cars—some were already gone. Employees appeared to be caught up in their own conversations with each other as they strolled across the lot, and no one paid any attention to Katie's presence.

There weren't any identifying names on the buildings— only capital letters followed by two-digit numbers. She hurried to find Jake and the Mercedes.

Glancing up and searching for video cameras affixed to the outside of buildings, she was able to keep out of view. There were far fewer cameras than she thought there would be at a facility like this—and that worked in her favor.

Katie made sure her badge and gun weren't immediately visible as she walked through an open gate. On her right were several small mobile-home-sized offices and on the left a road that led to the actual utilities. She saw that Jake's car was parked near a fence. He was the only one parked there, which could mean that he visited on a regular basis.

"You inside?" said McGaven.

"Not yet."

"Do you have eyes on the subject?"

"Negative."

Suddenly she heard voices talking—escalating into an argument. She couldn't quite hear what they were saying. She made sure that there wasn't anyone else around before moving forward.

"I hear Jake in a heated conversation."

"Keep out of sight."

"Ten-four."

Katie dared to move closer to where the men were talking. She knew it was Jake and one other male. She didn't recognize the other man. She saw a big electrical box as high as the first floor of a building and some other miscellaneous pieces of large utility equipment of wires, switches, and levers. Some of the components had been removed and replaced with new wiring. She took her opportunity and sprinted toward the components that acted as her cover. Peering out from behind the boxes she saw Jake facing a man and deep in conversation. He seemed relaxed, but from the back the unknown person seemed to be agitated. She strained to listen to their conversation.

"I don't care what you say. The cops know something and I think they're closing in," said the unknown man.

"You're getting paranoid. They're on a wild-goose chase," said Jake.

"Oh yeah, how did they find the industrial building?"

"Who cares? It's gone. There was no evidence to find. You set it up brilliantly—the fire wiped everything out."

"What about the camp?"

"What about it?"

"The female detective. She's different, she's smart."

"Not smart enough."

"They are still sniffing around. What if...?"

"What if *what*? Do yourself a favor. Go home. Relax. Everything is under control."

The other man was clearly fuming by the way he was clenching his fists.

Jake changed his demeanor. All at once he seemed more intense and impatient. He suddenly grabbed the man by the throat, pushing him backward against the side of a building. "I'm telling you. Go home. I'll let you know what's next when it's time." He released the man just as suddenly as he'd grabbed him.

"What... what if they go back to the camp?" the man asked, rubbing his throat but making no move to retaliate.

"So what? We'll take care of them. Remember, accidents are a good thing." He smiled in a sinister manner and walked away back toward where he had parked.

Katie strained to see the other man, but he didn't turn around for her to identify him or get a good look. He moved on and entered one of the buildings.

"Jake is on the move," said McGaven into Katie's ear.

"I'm going after the other man," she replied.

"Katie!"

"Just to see if I can identify him."

"We can lose Jake if you take too long," he said.

Katie hurried toward the building that the unidentified man had disappeared into. The loud machinery inside made it difficult to hear anything else. She moved cautiously, but hurried. Large piping ran both horizontally as well as vertically. There were power controls every so often. Katie continued to go deeper into the building, but still saw no one. Where had the man gone?

"Katie, we've got to go," McGaven said into her earpiece.

She moved further and then doubled back without seeing anyone. It was clear that she wasn't going to find him in the next few minutes, so she was forced to retreat.

"On my way," she said and hurried back to the parking lot just as McGaven pulled up in Denise's small car.

"Hey, what took you so long?" teased Katie as she shut the door and strapped in.

"Looks like our guy is going somewhere else now," said McGaven.

Katie updated McGaven on everything she'd seen and heard as they cautiously followed Jake in his Mercedes.

"How would you physically describe him?" asked McGaven.

"Tall, at least six feet, lean, dark hair, common haircut and resembled the person that attacked me at the camp. Age: I would say thirty-five to forty maybe..." Katie thought about the man and how angry he had seemed. "He fidgeted, clenched his fists a lot, but one thing is for sure, he was submissive to Jake Fields."

"That's not much to go on."

"I know, but I got the feeling that he's usually one of those quiet types. Something had pushed him to let Jake know that he was unhappy."

"Would you recognize him if you saw him?"

"I don't know for sure. But his voice, I would recognize that if I heard it again," she said.

They followed Jake to a few more places that didn't turn up anything unusual or criminal. Finally, they decided to return to the sheriff's department where McGaven dropped Katie at her Jeep.

"Tomorrow's another day," said McGaven.

"Don't worry about our updated report to the sheriff. I'll get that emailed to him along with a reminder of our request."

"Thanks, partner." He smiled and drove away, heading home.

Katie returned to the office to complete an updated report for the sheriff. She hoped that he saw the Eagle Ridge Camp cases the same way that she did.

CHAPTER FORTY-FIVE

Katie opened her office door to find McGaven gathering paperwork and tidying up. She set down the two coffees and her briefcase.

"Better not get too comfortable," he said.

"What's up?" Katie saw that her partner was anxious, which wasn't characteristic of him.

"Just got a message from the sheriff."

"I didn't. And?"

"We've been ordered to the briefing room at 0900."

Katie glanced at her watch. "Did he say why?" She knew why, but felt the impulse to ask anyway. As if it would change anything already set in motion.

McGaven stopped what he was doing and grabbed his coffee. "Thanks. I'm going to need this."

She waited patiently for her partner to take several gulps of coffee.

"The message I received was for you and me to meet him in the briefing room."

"Why the briefing room?" she said. "That's only when there are other people involved."

"I think you've just answered your own question."

Katie felt slightly lightheaded and an inkling of defeat. Her uncle was putting together a task force for Eagle Ridge Camp—she knew it in her gut. That wasn't the way she'd wanted it to go. With how crazy everything had been in the last two weeks, she hadn't had a chance to catch up with her uncle or assess which way he was leaning on the proposal of her and McGaven setting a trap at Eagle Ridge Camp. She now envisioned all of their hard work being handed over to some kind of special task force, or worse yet, the detectives in the robbery-homicide division.

"Katie? You okay?" asked McGaven. He stopped what he was doing and turned his office chair to face her. "Are you going to be okay? No matter how this turns out?"

Katie turned her attention to the murder board, which needed some updates, but she read each word and name thoroughly. "I think we should be continuing this investigation," she said carefully. "And no, I'm not going to be okay."

"I agree."

"Why is it human nature to always think of the most negative outcome when faced with unknown territories?" She turned away from the board and sat down.

"You're the profiler. You tell me."

"We're so close—I can feel it. Like I said in the diner, I want to go back to the very beginning. To the exact location where Brian Stanwick fell. Everything else is an offshoot from that incident. *Everything*."

At 0859 hours, Katie and McGaven stood at the closed briefing door. She looked to her partner for much-needed support on what she wanted to propose for Eagle Ridge Camp. McGaven gave her a nod and a slight smile—it was clear where he stood on the situation. She hesitated before opening the door.

Katie heard low voices from inside, which meant that whoever was in there with the sheriff had already been discussing the situation before they arrived. Not a good indication. She straightened her suit jacket, took a deep breath, and turning the doorknob entered the room.

As they walked in she realized to her surprise that the desks had been arranged in a semicircle on one side, with two more desks facing the semicircle. Sheriff Scott was at his rightful place in the middle. On his left were Undersheriff Dorothy Sullivan and John from forensics. On his right were Detectives Alvarez and Hamilton.

Katie concentrated on making it to one of the facing desks and took a seat as McGaven followed suit. She knew it was worse than she had first thought—no one said a word as they eyed her and McGaven taking their seats. She thought she detected a slight smirk from Detective Hamilton, but John remained stoic and difficult to read.

It was oddly surreal. She felt as though she was up against the parole board for permission to do her job and everything was at their discretion. There was nothing she could do, but sit, present their ideas about the cases and Eagle Ridge Camp, and then listen to the verdict.

The only sound was the shuffling of paperwork.

"Good morning. I see that everyone is here," Sheriff Scott began. He was dressed in a business suit instead of his department gear. The attire usually meant he had meetings for the rest of the day. He appeared his usual strong authoritative self. "The reason I've called all of you here today is to discuss the Eagle Ridge Camp case. This has been an investigation that has been unprecedented."

Unprecedented...

Katie forced herself to remain calm, but that description usually meant that the investigation was too big for a pair of detectives.

"I've been kept up to date from the beginning, which has been hugely complex. Everyone here has been briefed and is up to speed. Detective Scott and Detective McGaven have handled these cases with the utmost professionalism and dogged investigation that it deserves. We have Robin Drakes and her mother, and Marilyn Weber, in protective custody, as best as the sheriff's department can offer. It appears that the killer is systematically killing anyone who has any connection with Brian Stanwick, who we now know died five years ago by suicide." He turned a couple of pages and continued. "This killer poses an extreme threat to the public. I have been made aware of a carefully planned detail that would intentionally draw out the killer." He turned to his undersheriff, Dorothy.

"Sheriff Scott and I have discussed this proposition thoroughly," she said. Her blonde hair pulled back made her appear more like a mean school teacher. Her eyes settled directly on Katie.

Thoroughly...

"Detective Scott, what are your plans once the camp is secured and set up with additional security cameras?"

"I planned on staying at the camp. It would be me, Detective McGaven, and my K9 Cisco."

"And why do you think that the killer will even show himself?"

"The killer has shown that he often revisits the camp cabins and surrounding areas. I believe from his behavior and the nature of his crime scenes that he will absolutely make his presence known, like he did when he attacked the security guard." Katie felt that she wasn't explaining it well.

"I see. But it seems that the killer also wishes to target you— based on the articles you found in cabin three about your previous cases, and when he ambushed you in cabin eleven."

"Sheriff Scott, permission to speak without restrictions," said Katie standing up. She could feel McGaven's stare and knew that he backed her decision. The room appeared to shrink around her, but Katie ignored it. Her drive and ambition to catch this twisted monster before he killed again was stronger than her anxiety.

"Of course. Please proceed, Detective. We're all interested in what you have to say," said the sheriff. Katie thought she caught a hint of favor in his eyes. He knew Katie better than anyone in the room.

"Well, as you all know, this killer has been killing mercilessly, taunting us and not backing down. He's not going to deviate or stop until his fantasy is completed. There are a number of suspects, but it's not yet clear how everything connects. It could take weeks or months to track and conduct surveillance for each person." Katie paused and looked at everyone in front of her. She saw that they were all listening, but knew that her uncle and John were the ones that were truly on her side. "We don't have that kind of time..." She gestured to McGaven as well. "We believe that we need to be proactive in order to draw out the killer. He's arrogant, driven, and his misaligned perception is clear. I believe he won't allow anyone to stop, or even pause, his prime intention. He won't stop until he's finished what he started. We cannot afford to wait for another life to be taken."

"And you believe that you can stop him with this operation?" said the undersheriff.

"I *believe* that we can stop him based on our investigative work, knowing the players, studying the evidence, and by getting ahead of him and changing the rules of his game at Eagle Ridge Camp. He can and will make a mistake and that's when we can arrest him on his own turf."

Katie's words hung in the air. She spoke with conviction and truth. There was no room for pleading or guesswork—it was the evidence and experience that would convince her boss and peers to let this operation go forward.

"I know that my experience hasn't been as long as some would like. Many still consider me a rookie detective, but I think that my solve rates speak loudly," said Katie.

Detective Hamilton leaned over to Detective Alvarez and whispered something in his ear to which he nodded. John nodded too, showing his support. Her uncle contemplated what Katie had said and he had the best poker face—it was hard for her to tell which way he was leaning.

Katie sat back down. There was nothing more to say. They had heard everything from her and they had already read the update reports of the investigation as well as the outline of the proposed plan. This was the final leg of the journey to find out what came next—negative or positive.

Sheriff Scott turned to his panel. "Does anyone have any questions for the detectives?"

Detective Hamilton spoke up. "I read the initial report for the plan at Eagle Ridge Camp. How do you propose to set everything up without potentially alerting the killer?"

Katie glanced at McGaven and he let her explain. "We've divided it into three phases. The first phase would be updating the technical equipment. No big trucks. No groups. No vehicles with identifying titles. It would be done by John and us. It will appear to onlookers that we are spinning our wheels and updating the technology as a last-ditch effort."

"How long would it take?" asked Hamilton.

"I can answer that," said John. "We have everything we need. I've pulled together what we have in the forensics department, and have been given several video cameras, recorders, and infrared video by a company to use as a favor in return for a review of their performance. They are small, some almost undetectable. I can install them with the help of Detectives Scott and McGaven in a few hours—maybe longer in the rural areas away from the buildings and cabins."

Detective Hamilton seemed impressed. "How are the other

two phases going to be implemented? Are you going to stay in a cabin? Wouldn't that put you at risk?"

All eyes were on Katie. "That's where the second phase comes into play. I will stage cabin eleven so it seems that I'm staying there, but in fact, I will be safely tucked in another area with the technology at my disposal. And finally, we want to make it appear that we are unprepared for prying eyes and that we're grasping at straws. The killer has made contact with me once, with the note left on my front door—I have no doubt he'll do it again. The killer has done his homework; he's prepared and determined to complete his mission. But this time we're prepared too."

The panel talked among themselves in quiet hushed whispers. Katie couldn't really hear what they were saying, but had the impression that they had voted already before she and McGaven walked into the room. Now it at least appeared that they were discussing it. Katie wasn't sure if they were supposed to leave or not.

"Detective Scott and Detective McGaven, I have made my decision. It wasn't an easy one to make due to the type of operation you are proposing," said the sheriff.

That didn't sound encouraging...

"My first priority is the safety of everyone involved as well as the witnesses under our watch. This is an unorthodox mission, which is usually better suited for FBI or special state investigators. However, this is where we are right now. Time is not on our side and something needs to be done to move forward."

Katie could barely move. Her breathing was shallow, and she didn't think that she had blinked in over a minute. There was a thick tension in the room. Some things were in her favor, but her gut told her that there were other things at play—such as politics, which was the weight that kept the balance at the department.

Jenny...

For some reason, her friend Jenny popped into her mind. It was strange to Katie that whenever situations got stressful, or when something important was on the line, her thoughts settled on Jenny. Eagle Ridge Camp was stirring up all of these memories and emotions—probably not that surprising as Jenny's death had been a defining moment in her life.

"This hasn't been a unanimous vote, but I've made my decision based on everything combined, including the opinions of others," stated the sheriff. He looked directly at Katie and McGaven. "It is my decision and the decision of the Pine Valley Sheriff's Department that Detective Katie Scott and Detective Sean McGaven are granted approval for their operation at Eagle Ridge Camp. But—and I stipulate—if it is necessary to retreat, or to add more officers, then you must adhere to that order. Understood?"

Katie let out a sigh of relief. "Thank you, Sheriff. And all of you." She stood.

"I don't have to tell you that I need updates from you every step of the way. And if anything could jeopardize anyone's safety in the operation, you cease immediately. Have I made myself clear?"

Katie and McGaven nodded and stated almost in unison, "Yes, sir."

CHAPTER FORTY-SIX

Katie and McGaven returned to their office in the forensics division. They stayed quiet for a few moments as they seated themselves at their desks, obviously letting everything sink in.

"Did that really just happen?" she said.

McGaven made a positive whistling sound. "It sure did."

"I could barely breathe in there. What do you think was up with Hamilton and Alvarez?"

"Not sure, but I think that something else was originally going to happen. But your speech was fantastic and tipped this operation in our favor," he said.

There was a knock at the door.

"Come in," said McGaven.

John poked his head inside. "Hey! Congrats on the mission. Now it's time for the real work... What do you two need from me right away?"

"Are you sure this isn't putting your workload behind?" said Katie.

"You're asking me now?" he laughed. "I've talked with my techs and they all know what to do. If something really huge came up, I would have to return. But everything else looks good to go."

"I want to go to the place where Brian Stanwick fell and take a look around the area," she said. "I know it's been over twenty years, but I want to see it for myself. Who's up for it?" Katie looked at McGaven and then John. "Well?"

"I think that's something for you, John," said McGaven.

"He needs to update all those camera units," she said.

"How long is the walk?" asked John.

"It's up along the Eagle Ridge itself. I'd say it will take about an hour or hour and a half."

"Sure, I can do it. It would be better to do the installations late into the evening, when visibility is poorer for an outsider to observe," he said.

"Thanks," said McGaven. "Not really up for the walk myself."

John looked at his watch. "Caravan up to Eagle Ridge Camp?"

"No, I want to make sure things are very low-key. I don't want it to look like we're planning something yet. Just get up there when you can."

"Okay, I'll head up in about an hour."

"Sounds good. All three of us need to be in contact," she said. "I need to pick up some things—and Cisco, of course. We won't be staying overnight until tomorrow. Hopefully, we can wrap this up before the end of the weekend." She had a second thought. "Oh, John, make sure you have something for self-defense."

"Never go anywhere without them," he said and winked.

John left the office.

After he had closed the door, McGaven said, "You really think the killer is going make an appearance?"

"You're not doubting me now, are you? Yes, he'll definitely make an appearance. I just hope that we'll be ready."

"I have a question."

"Shoot," she said.

"Since things are a bit precarious with Jake Fields and the unidentified man he was talking to... I wonder if maybe it might be a good idea to somehow let him know that we've found some evidence and are close to solving Carolyn Sable's murder."

"I see where you're going with this."

"Just a thought."

Katie's phone chimed with a new text from John:

Update: no fingerprint matches from the house on Spruce.

Katie slouched her shoulders in disappointment.

"What?"

"No matches from the fingerprints taken at the house next to Dr. Pendleton's house on Spruce Street."

"That's okay. We're slowly working our way through things."

Katie began to gather her belongings. "I'll be on my cell phone."

McGaven stared at his computer. "Wait, I just received a file with the original articles about Brian Stanwick's accident from Denise." He quickly skimmed the articles. "Looks like it's everything we saw at the doctor's house." He looked closer at the photo of Brian being pushed in a wheelchair by his father as they exited the hospital and there was a boy following a few feet behind him. "Still can't see clearly the boy behind him. What do you think?" he said.

Katie took a moment to securitize the photo. "It's just too blurry. The photographer was focusing on the subject of Brian in the wheelchair." Katie thought more about it. "Maybe it was his cousin or a best friend."

"Or it could be just some kid coming out of the hospital."

"You're right. There is no credit to the people in the photo except Brian and his dad." She grabbed her things. "See you later."

McGaven kept trying to enlarge the photo, only making the blurriness worse.

CHAPTER FORTY-SEVEN

The forest stood at attention against its amazing backdrop with some of the biggest specimens of Jeffrey, ponderosa, sugar, and white pine trees. The density and height of the breathtaking Californian trees looked like a painter's rendering on an amazing canvas. The fresh forest aroma was intoxicating and there was no mistaking the clean air of the higher elevation. The sun was low in the sky, but the warmth it still gave contrasted against the cooler air. The high vantage of placid Eagle Lake was serene and photo-worthy.

Cisco padded along the trail, stopping every once in a while to smell a bush or the remnant scents of something that flew or scurried in the forest. His black fur glistened in the sun, his tail, held low, was relaxed, but his ears were perked, always waiting for something.

Katie hiked and stared ahead as John led the way at a brisk pace; he seemed to know the trail well or had an instinct of where they were going. The path was easy to follow even though it wasn't used on a regular basis.

Katie was slightly winded due to the altitude but enjoying the brief outing was what she needed. She as well as John carried a light backpack with warmer clothing, water, and power bars. They didn't chat. Each was lost in thought. Katie thought constantly about the cases, wondering if she really could entice the killer to come into their camp.

As soon as the trail leveled off, Katie noticed there were larger clearings where you could camp or take a break. The soil was mixed with clay and rock, which made for good footing even if it rained. She wondered how Brian Stanwick had slipped and fallen from the edge. Why were the children so close to the edge? It was true that there was a storm that day, double-checked by McGaven, and the ground could've become slippery, but from what Katie was seeing now it didn't make sense. There was something more.

John turned and said, "Hey, let's take a break."

"Sounds good," she said. Cisco ran up to them once he heard their voices.

There were several large rocks and two of them were the perfect substitute for a chair. Cisco jumped up on one of them and sat obediently.

"Did you teach him that?" said John.

Laughing, Katie said, "No, that wasn't a part of obedience class." She put her backpack down and took a seat. It was peaceful and calming. Something that Katie hadn't experienced in a while. She had felt the stress of the case beginning to take its toll on her body in the last few days—leaving an opening for her PTSD symptoms to re-emerge and overwhelm her whole being again.

"From the articles in the news, I think this is close to the area where the accident happened," he said.

Katie looked around, studying the area. "I think you're right, but..."

John took a drink of his water. "But what?" He studied her closely and sat down next to her.

"Based on the reports and testimony from one of the counselors, they made it seem that this area was treacherous and close to the edge. That doesn't make sense because why would you bring a group of ten-year-olds to a place that was dangerous?"

"I see your point."

"And even in twenty years, this place wouldn't change much, right?"

Cisco barked, wanting a treat.

Katie dug into her backpack and retrieved some his favorite chicken snacks. She tossed them into the air where he caught them with expertise.

"Correct. The only thing that could change the natural erosion would be ongoing torrential rain or if the trees were eradicated by fire or forestry."

Katie thought for a moment about how and why Brian Stanwick fell. She got up from her seat and walked toward the edge. Looking down, she could see jagged areas where rocks were prominent. It was plausible that he had slipped and then landed on one of those areas below. She leaned down and took a handful of soil in her hand and then let it slip away. Dizziness suddenly waved over Katie as the land below seemed to morph in and out in her vision. She put her hand to her forehead and steadied herself.

"You okay, Katie?" said John.

Katie instinctively took some steps backward away from the edge of the mountainside. Her head pounded and she had difficulty catching her breath.

"Katie." John was at her side and steadied her by guiding her back to the rock seat. "I think the altitude is giving you trouble. Just sit there and breathe slowly. Relax." He gave her some water.

Cisco sensed Katie's distress and was immediately at her side.

After a few tense moments, Katie began to feel better. "I've lived here my whole life and I've never felt this way before on a hike or going to a higher elevation."

"Have you ever had the kind of cases you've had recently?"

"I know where you're going with this... but..."

"I'm not a doctor, but... you should probably take some time off after this case." He sat down on the rock next to her.

The breeze kicked up in intensity and then simmered down again, almost as if it were in agreement with John's sentiment.

"You sound like Chad."

"Chad's a very smart man," he said and smiled. "Tell me about Brian Stanwick."

"What do you mean?"

"Something's obviously bothering you, so, you know, tell me everything you know about him that's not in the newspaper. You seem to be drawn to the accident location—and it's obvious that Eagle Ridge Camp is the center to your investigation."

Katie surprised to hear John suggest this. There had indeed been something bothering her about the accident the whole time, and she hadn't been able to shed any light on it. "Yes. Truthfully it *has* been bothering me."

"Didn't you come here yourself as a kid?"

"Yes."

"Did you ever hike this trail?"

"No. Actually, I was more interested in archery and canoeing, so I stayed down by the cabins for campouts."

"Look at where we are," he said gesturing to the landscape setting and beautiful views. "Take this time and brainstorm. No one is going to hear you besides me and some birds—oh, and Cisco, of course. But we aren't going to tell anyone."

"I know what you're doing. You want me to concentrate on something specific, so I don't go into a panic."

"Maybe."

"Okay." Katie stood up and paced back and forth for a bit. This usually helped her to relax, allowing ideas to come more easily. "Firstly—this has been such a tragedy all the way around. Brian Stanwick's accident, then his death via suicide later as a young adult. There's no one to talk to about him. His father died. His emergency contact, family friend Rick Reynolds, was murdered. And I don't know who the other boy in the photo was."

"Those are facts. Tell me about him, who he was, what happened that day."

Katie knew that John wanted her to give a profile, but she didn't have enough information.

"Get inside his head. Start with this camp. What was it like for him when he arrived here?"

"Okay," she said and remembered what it was like when she had arrived the first time at Eagle Ridge Camp. "Excited to be at a camp, I guess, and wondering what to expect. Away from home, maybe for the first time—maybe escaping problems at home. Wanting to learn new things. Meeting new people—hoping the others liked you."

"Okay, you're warming up."

Katie actually felt calmer and more focused. "First night jitters. Sleeping away from home. Making a new friend or two. Spending time with them through the duration of your stay. Excelling in swimming, or archery, or art." She reminisced, remembering her time at camp with Jenny. It was a memory that would last a lifetime. "Feeling connected, safe. Couldn't wait to share experiences when you got back home. But..." She hesitated.

"Go on."

"But maybe you find out something about someone in charge, like your counselor or the maintenance person. It puts a damper on things and you become distrustful." Katie began to theorize. "You're taken on a hiking trip and it wasn't a good time. You're scared. A storm comes. Something scares the kids and you end up falling—thankfully not dying. But your life has been altered forever. Who do you trust now? Will you actually ever trust anyone again?"

John and Cisco both appeared to be listening to Katie and waiting for her to continue.

"When you're ten, who do you trust more, your dad or your best friend?"

John nodded.

"Maybe Brian Stanwick had a close friend at camp that saw firsthand what he went through. Would that push you to kill everyone who had something to do with the events that led up to the accident? Because you know that these experiences caused him to take his own life?"

"Maybe his friend wasn't as good and stable as he thought. Maybe the friend didn't have a close family or any other friends —so Brian Stanwick was it."

"That's a bit of a reach, don't you think? It doesn't get me any closer to the killer." She sat back down on the rock.

"I wouldn't dismiss it so quickly. You've finally taken a look from the boy's possible perspective."

"Maybe the friend could be one of the adults. Maybe it wasn't one of the kids?" Katie sighed. She took another look around but this time it didn't open up any new revelations. She glanced at her watch. "Maybe we should head back now. It should take about thirty minutes."

They hiked back down to the main area, taking only a little more than twenty minutes before Katie saw the cabins again.

"Katie, I just realized that I left a box back at the office that has some of the wireless cameras in it," he said.

"Do you have to get them today? Can't you just install what you have?"

"I better go back and get them now. Then I can just about finish the hook-ups today and not draw any unnecessary attention by taking another day to do it. But I'll wait for McGaven to arrive first—I don't want to leave you alone."

Katie agreed, and called McGaven.

"Detective McGaven," he answered.

"Hey, Gav, are you on your way? John has to go pick up some more cameras."

"Yep, ETA in about half an hour."

"Okay, see you then." Katie ended the call.

After reassuring himself that she would be okay for thirty minutes, John said his goodbyes and left in his SUV.

"Okay, Cisco, let's go eat a late lunch and wait for Gav." She walked to the commissary building where the security guard had placed a picnic table to eat meals in the main area. Cisco happily followed.

Katie put her backpack on the table and retrieved a turkey-and-Swiss sandwich of which she gave half to Cisco. She felt one hundred percent better as she enjoyed her sandwich.

Cisco let out a low guttural growl.

Katie didn't immediately dismiss him and tell him no. She knew that he had sensed something wrong.

She got up slowly, listening for anything that was out of the ordinary. Moving toward the back of the commissary and toward the kitchen, Katie kept her wits about her and put her mind on full alert. She whispered an order to Cisco in German: "*Fuss!*" This would keep him to heel and at her side. She didn't want him to charge into something that could potentially be dangerous, like a bear.

"Hello?" she said, thinking that someone could have arrived she didn't know about. They had all been directed to park their cars in a different area, one that had originally been used by the maintenance and garbage crews. "Hello?" she said again, loud enough for most to hear.

Katie felt Cisco at her left thigh. He was tense and alert and the fur that ran along his spine bristled. She knew that her dog could sense or detect things that she couldn't. Their bond was undeniable and she trusted his instinct in most cases more than her own.

Everything was quiet as she moved forward into the large kitchen. Nothing. It was empty and just as they had left it previously after finding the body parts above the ceiling tiles.

Katie cleared the area and moved back into the commissary. She noticed a side door that was open and she knew for sure that it had been closed and locked before she and John hiked up to the ridge.

Turning toward Cisco, she said softly, "*Platz*," to put him on a down so that she knew where he was and that he was safe.

Katie pointed her weapon out front and slowly moved outside the door. She directed her gun in front of her when she looked to the left and then the right. All was clear. She walked a bit further, but there was nothing. Cisco must have picked up a scent of an animal—it could have been anything.

Just as she was about to re-enter the door to the commissary, she heard Cisco's growl and low bark.

Katie turned around. Standing in front of her with hands down at his sides and staring directly at her was Jake Fields. "We have to talk," he said.

CHAPTER FORTY-EIGHT

Slowly, Jake raised his arms with his hands and fingers spread wide to show he was unarmed. He was dressed casually in khaki pants, long-sleeved shirt and a windbreaker. He wore hiking shoes that looked like he had bought them just before coming to the camp.

"You sure have a weird way of requesting a meeting," said Katie, not taking her eyes off him.

"This was the best way to talk to you alone, away from prying eyes."

"Where did you come from?" asked Katie. She was on edge, thinking that he had backup and she would get ambushed.

"You mean, where did I walk in from? I parked at the back entrance where the utility road is... actually, I got lost."

"How did you know that I was here?"

"Detective... really? It's not that difficult. I followed you— just like you followed me."

"What do you want? To confess?" She held her ground, her Glock still trained on him. "I can help you with that." She couldn't recall anyone following her, but then as soon as she had turned on the main road heading to Eagle Ridge Camp it would have been easy to figure out where she was headed.

"Confess?" he laughed. "I figured you were trying to make a case around me after searching my motorhome, so I want to set the record straight."

"That you killed your assistant." She kept her voice and gun steady.

"What?" He looked shocked. His dark eyes no longer held the hard stare that would be so effective in board meetings. Instead, they were now wide with surprise. "Kill Carolyn? *Never*. I may be guilty of a few things—well, many things—but I would never kill her. Or anyone, for that matter." He started to lower his arms. "I'm not a killer."

"Keep 'em up!"

"Okay—they're up. Look, I didn't want to go to the police department—for obvious reasons. But I didn't want you to come back to my office either. This is the perfect place. It's quiet and it's just us."

Katie wasn't so sure. It was so odd that he was here, right where she was expecting the killer to show. But she couldn't now shake her first instinct that he was indeed telling the truth. Her investigation was crumbling around her. If Jake Fields wasn't the killer, were there possibly two killers? She knew that he was a shrewd businessman and that would make crafty manipulation and lying second nature. "What do you want to say?"

"I know you were following me yesterday and I'm not sure what you heard, but I haven't been on the up and up with my clients or dealings."

"So?" she said, losing patience.

"I. Did. Not. Kill. Anyone." He took a couple of steps forward. "I'm telling you the truth. I didn't kill Carolyn or anyone else in your investigation." He took another step.

"Stay where you are!"

Jake stopped.

Katie wasn't sure if he was angling for some type of move. She pulled her cell phone and pressed the speed dial for McGaven.

He answered. "Okay, what kind of snacks do you want?"

"We have a situation." She kept her intense gaze on Jake.

"Talk to me," he said as his voice turned serious.

"Cisco and I found Jake Fields loitering here."

"Keep him there. Stay safe... I'll be right up there with reinforcements."

Katie put her cell phone back into her pocket, still live for McGaven to hear.

"Look, I don't want to talk to anyone else. I want to talk to you," he said with his voice rising an octave as he became strangely fidgety. He moved to one side.

"Stay there, Jake," she said.

"I'm not going to go down for something I didn't do." He swung his arms in a strange fashion. "I loved her. I didn't kill her. Please..."

"Take it easy."

"No, I can't..."

"Jake, listen to me. Just relax. Let's talk." Katie could see that Jake was now unraveling faster than she could talk him down.

"I know what you're doing. Don't you think I know what you're doing?" He began sweating profusely and pacing.

Katie couldn't ascertain if he was off some medication or having a nervous breakdown.

"You might as well kill me. But I'm telling you right now, I didn't hurt anyone."

Katie could hear Cisco barely able to contain his position with low whimpers and grumbles. The dog had inched his way in an army crawl motion to get to the doorway—closer to Katie.

"Why won't you believe me?" he pleaded. "I came to you."

"Jake, take a breath and slow down..." She didn't want to hurt him. It was obvious that he needed assistance.

"NO!" The financial advisor lunged forward at Katie, slamming her back against the side of the building.

He pushed her hard, but Katie maintained her upright position. She yelled, "No, Cisco, stay!" She didn't want the dog attacking him. It was obvious that Jake was unstable and Katie didn't know yet if he had something lethal on him that could hurt or kill Cisco.

Jake turned and sprinted into the forest.

Taking a second to regain her composure, Katie ran after him. The sunlight was waning and the light fluttered through the branches casting a weird pattern across the ground, almost like an outdoor strobe light. She tried to keep Jake in sight, but his speed was unparalleled, like the devil was chasing him.

The path zigzagged until she could barely make out Jake's outline. He reached his silver Range Rover, got in, then redlined the engine. Light sand and gravel sputtered and then a growing dust cloud plumed into the air.

Katie knew she couldn't catch him, so she turned and ran as fast as she could to get back to the parking area they had created for the weekend operation. "Gav!" she said.

She had called for Cisco at the commissary building and the canine easily caught up to her. She flung the door open to her Jeep, Cisco jumped inside, and she was behind the wheel speeding down the road in seconds.

She took the short road to meet up with Jake's Range Rover. It was a more powerful vehicle than hers but she had superior knowledge of the roads.

"Gav!"

"Heard everything. Backup is on its way," he said.

"Jake Fields is driving on the utility road heading west. He's in a silver Range Rover."

"Ten-four."

"I'm following him so that he won't turn around. He'll be surrounded."

"Stay safe."

"Ten-four," she said and tossed the cell phone on the passenger's seat.

The light was now dwindling and she was forced to slow her speed to navigate the dusty road behind the larger SUV. The utility road was much more unstable. She secured her seatbelt tighter.

"Cisco, *platz*," she said, making him get down on the floor behind her. The dog immediately took his position, so he wouldn't be tossed around inside the vehicle and risk injury.

There was a narrow area of the road barely wide enough for a car to pass. Katie slammed on the brakes and skidded to a stop. She could see a flicker of silver in front of her—which meant she was catching up.

She thought she heard sirens, but it was probably wishful thinking. But up ahead there were bright lights flashing the usual red and blue.

They were here...

Relief filled Katie as she renewed her pursuit at a safer speed. They were going to catch Jake Fields and he was going to have to answer questions. She couldn't stop seeing his desperate face, pleading that he didn't kill Carolyn Sable, and his ensuing erratic behavior.

Was he telling the truth...?

If he didn't kill Carolyn Sable and the rest, who did?

Katie steered around two back-to-back turns, forced into making almost a figure-eight maneuver. The Jeep was still looping down the treacherous and rocky incline of the utility road before its junction with the main road into town. As she turned to her left, she caught a glimpse of silver far down the hill. She slammed on her brakes, turning her steering wheel to the right until the Jeep completely stopped with its back end spun out. She flung open her car door and ran to the edge.

Jake Fields's Range Rover had careered down the rocky ravine and was now upside-down. The wheels were still spinning. She caught a whiff of the distinctive smell of gasoline and burning brakes.

McGaven's truck roared up to where she stood, followed by three sheriff deputy cruisers. Her partner must have leaped from his truck which was still idling behind him.

"What happened?" she asked.

"I don't know. I came around the corner to this."

"Okay," he said to the deputies. "Call this in to get fire and rescue." He began to climb down.

"No! It's not safe," said Katie as she watched her partner begin the rocky descent.

"He may be still alive. We need him in the investigation. To get to the truth."

Truth...

"I'm going with you," she said.

McGaven pushed her away. "No, you're not."

"I am, and I'm not prepared to argue about it."

Another deputy joined them and all three made their way as quickly as possible down the ravine.

The passenger door of the large SUV was wide open. McGaven was the first to get to Jake. He slowly backed up and shook his head. "He's dead."

"No," she said. There were too many unanswered questions.

Katie glanced inside the crushed cab of the SUV. The window was pushed inside and part of the engine department was in the front seat. It was clear that Jake had been crushed upon impact. His chest and face were bloody masses. It was difficult to tell that it was the same man who had pleaded with her only minutes ago.

"C'mon, let's get out of here now!" yelled McGaven.

Katie caught the heavy smell of gasoline, making her cough. She ran with McGaven and the deputy and they climbed and clawed their way to the top of the ravine.

"Get back! Everyone back! Now!" yelled McGaven to the rest of the deputies.

Not waiting for another order, everyone ran.

Katie yelled, "Cisco!" and the dog exited the Jeep from the driver's slightly open door, joining the group.

Katie felt the impact of the explosion even before she felt the heat or the ringing in her ears. Like a punch to the gut, she went down, covering Cisco even as McGaven protected her and the dog.

After a few minutes, her ears still ringing, Katie moved her body and ran her hands over the German shepherd.

"You okay?" said McGaven in a hoarse voice.

Katie nodded.

McGaven checked on the deputies. Thankfully, no one was injured.

Katie sat down on the dusty ground with Cisco, catching her breath and desperately trying to make sense of everything.

As one of the deputies put in a call to dispatch, McGaven returned to his partner. He helped her up. "You sure you're okay?" He touched her face, wiping away dirt and pine needles.

"Yeah, Cisco and I are fine," she said.

"You could've been killed if we didn't arrive in time."

"We all survived and we're all going home tonight. That's all that counts."

CHAPTER FORTY-NINE

Katie tried to relax in her living room with a glass of wine. After today's events, the investigation was upside-down, just like Jake Fields's SUV had been in the gully. It wasn't certain if Jake Fields was the killer or even if he'd had anything to do with the murders at this point.

McGaven and John sat on the couch in her living room working on their second beers. They had followed Katie back to her house. They wanted to make sure she was safe and secure at her home.

"I'm sure that both of you have somewhere you need to be and not babysitting me. I have Cisco," she said. "And remember, I was in the army." Katie turned on another lamp.

"She always says that," said McGaven to John.

"It's a good point," said John.

"You don't ever leave one of your teammates alone with killers on the loose."

"Don't you mean you never leave anyone behind?" she said.

"That too." McGaven laughed.

Katie looked at her co-workers. They looked tired and worn-out. McGaven's clothes were dirty and his sleeve was torn.

There was a hint of gasoline smell—she wasn't sure if it was her or him.

She realized at that moment that they were her family. She was always worrying that the only family she had was her uncle, but these two people that were in her living room always had her back. That was family in her view.

"What's the matter?" asked John studying Katie. "You look worried."

"No. Well, maybe. I've been thinking about Jake and his behavior before the crash." She sipped her wine as she petted a snoozing Cisco. "From everything that I've seen from him, I just don't imagine he had what it would take to commit those murders, remove limbs and organs. It just doesn't fit. Something is amiss."

"I would have to agree," said McGaven. "In his office, he acted like he was in charge of everything. Smoke and mirrors for his clients."

"We need to go forward. If we get nothing out of this weekend, then we have to go back to our murder board and dig some more." Katie realized that she sounded matter-of-fact, but inside she was a bit unsure. She didn't want to make a mistake where someone on her team would get hurt.

"I've been thinking..." she said.

"She says this a lot too," said McGaven grinning from ear to ear.

"Today, John made me look at everything from Brian Stanwick's perspective. And the more I think about it, the more I see another suspect coming to light."

McGaven leaned forward. "What do you mean? And exactly who is it?"

"I don't know—yet."

. . .

Katie had finally gently persuaded McGaven and John that she would be fine alone with Cisco and the security alarm activated. They didn't put up much of a fight as they were growing wearier by the minute themselves. Eventually, they agreed to go home and get a good night's sleep.

Once alone, Katie jotted down a few notes, trying not to think about what would happen tomorrow. She had to move forward as if everything was still on schedule.

She pulled a few things from her briefcase, including a copy of the property map that Shane had sent along with a current map from Red Hawk Real Estate. She laid them out on the coffee table. The current recorded map showed all the buildings and how they related to the entrances and exits. She traced the routes that she and McGaven had taken when they first searched the area.

The killer had to know every aspect of the camp in its overgrown and dilapidated condition. She didn't see Jake as having been that person.

Cisco twitched his paws and whined in a low tone in his sleep.

Could the person she was searching for have lived there undetected? Plotting? Planning? For the perfect kills of revenge? His own revenge? Or on Brian's behalf?

Katie knew that everyone on the list of employees and volunteers had now been accounted for and had had it verified that they were where they said they were.

Was there someone they had missed? Was someone not who they said they were?

"What am I missing?" she whispered, looking at the map and trying to make connections.

Katie counted the cabins, main areas, offices, and outward buildings, then put a number next to each one, rating the condition. Many of the cabins were in terrible shape and two were practically falling in on themselves. The outer buildings were used for storage and utilities and in decent shape. There was a small twenty-by-twenty structure that had once been a refrigerated freezer, used to store food when the camp was in full operation and feeding kids and employees three meals a day.

If someone knew the camp as well as she thought they did, based on how the killer had ambushed her and then escaped so easily—it was as if it was his playground. He knew when and where to run and hide—and when to kill.

CHAPTER FIFTY

Katie's cell phone buzzed and rattled on her nightstand, announcing an incoming call. She sleepily grabbed for it. "Hello?" she said with a raspy voice.

"The operation at Eagle Ridge Camp still has a green light," said Sheriff Scott. "I see no reason to pull out now. The investigation is still the same—even with the new complication."

"What?"

"Do I need to repeat it?"

"No. Thank you." Katie sat straight up in bed, rubbing her eyes and glancing at the clock.

"I will stipulate again. The safety of my officers and forensics supervisor are the department's top priority. I do make myself clear?"

"I understand."

"Katie," he said with more of his usual inflection. "Be careful."

Katie had packed her Jeep with some personal things like bedding, a framed photograph, and an old laptop that would indicate she was staying in cabin 11. She had an alternative bag of things for her hidden surveillance spot, including her working laptop. She had two coolers with food and drinks that would last for a couple of days.

She put Cisco in the backseat as she made her rounds on her property, making sure that her security was intact and operating properly. Once she was confident that everything was fine, she drove to the All-Day Diner to meet up with McGaven and John. They were going to formulate a plan that would be the least invasive and wouldn't attract unnecessary attention.

Pulling into the parking lot, Katie saw both McGaven's truck and the Suburban that John only used on fishing and camping trips. She found a parking spot and cracked a couple windows for Cisco.

"Be a good boy, I'll be back in a little bit," she said to the dog. Cisco watched her walk away and enter the diner.

Katie stepped inside the restaurant and immediately saw McGaven and John sitting in a corner booth waiting for her while enjoying their morning coffee. They noticed her and smiled as she approached the booth.

"You haven't ordered yet?" she said.

"We were waiting for you," said McGaven.

"I'm starving." The waitress brought her a cup of steaming coffee. "Thank you."

"Is everything still a go?" asked John.

"Yes, the sheriff called me. He said he didn't need to remind me that safety is a top priority." Taking a moment to enjoy the hot drink, she said, "I keep running through my mind what Jake Fields said and how insistent he was about not killing Carolyn Sable, or any of the other victims. I've seen many criminals say they're not guilty—and of course, often they still are. But he was different. It was almost as if he was reaching out for help."

"Or wanting to confess his sins—no matter what they were," said McGaven.

"Have you heard anything about the crash investigation?" she said.

"They haven't finished yet, but nothing seemed to indicate foul play. It looks as if he took the turn too fast and veered off the road. It happens," said John.

"I suppose."

The waitress came back and took their orders.

Once the server left, Katie leaned in and spoke with a softer tone. "I don't think Jake was the killer." Her words hung in the air as John and McGaven contemplated what she had said. "He doesn't seem to have the constitution or motive to commit these crimes."

"But he does seem the type to be involved in fraud, maybe even bribery and corruption," said McGaven.

"It's what you can prove that counts, but I agree with you."

"So where does this leave the case?" asked John.

"Right where we're currently at... drawing out a killer before he takes another victim," she said.

Their food arrived and they ate mostly in silence. There was no mistaking how intense and potentially dangerous the operation could be for them.

After some light conversation, John readied to leave. "I'm going up to sweep the place for any bugs or devices before I install the cameras. See you later," he said.

"Stay alert," said McGaven.

"And safe," said Katie.

John put down some cash for his meal and left.

Katie was nervous, but in an excited way, not knowing what to expect. Her stomach was tight and she concentrated on her breath to ease the anxious energy. Anything that would take her mind from the killer, even for a moment, helped.

She put some pieces of ham and egg from her omelet into a napkin.

"For Cisco?" he said.

"Yep."

"Go on ahead. I'll be up right after you. "

Katie pulled some cash from her wallet.

"Nope. It's on me."

"Well, okay. Thanks, Gav."

"We're parking in that cleared area that's out of sight, right?"

"Yes, I think John made it a bit more camouflaged." Katie rose from the table.

"Hey," he said.

Katie turned to her partner.

"We're going to get him."

CHAPTER FIFTY-ONE

Katie drove to Eagle Ridge Camp rerunning all facets and characteristics about the cases, and about Jake Fields's behavior. He presented himself completely different than the in-control man they'd met at his office. He reacted like he was scared of something or someone. But who or what?

The traffic before the cutoff to the road leading up the mountain was more crowded than normal—making Katie take side streets to weave around the congestion. The weather had turned overcast and cold. No rain was predicted, but it was still going to be cold and damp at the camp, making their job that much more challenging.

Katie knew that she wouldn't be catching much sleep and conserved her energy as much as she could. She and McGaven had already talked about taking turns at guard duty so the other could get a couple of hours of shut-eye.

Dark low clouds seemed to extinguish any ray of sunshine and made it feel like driving at nighttime. Katie's automatic headlights switched on and she felt the air turn colder. Glad that she had packed extra blankets, she shivered at the chill. She was surprised that McGaven hadn't caught up with her as she glanced periodically in the rearview mirror.

Before she reached the top of the road and drove through the open parking lot, which now had been trampled by numerous vehicles, she saw some sunlight peeking through the ominous clouds.

Katie parked as far as she could so that she could unload her things to cabin 11. She didn't see John's vehicle, but knew he was around somewhere doing his job. He was more than capable if something happened to go awry.

She stepped out of her Jeep. Out of habit, she paused, listening and scanning the area. It was quiet and relatively serene. Even though the day was mostly dreary, the birds were still flying around from tree to tree.

Grabbing a box and letting Cisco out, Katie headed for the cabin. She couldn't stop remembering what a wonderful place this had been when she was young, so many fond memories except...

Jenny...

But her juvenile attachment for Eagle Ridge Camp had turned unpleasant. Her arm suddenly ached even though her wound was healing nicely, and she felt a headache rising to the surface of her mind. The tenseness she felt about the grounds and what had transpired there made her jumpy and overly alert. The camp seemed to be giving her a warning—stay away.

As she kept to the path with Cisco keeping in sync, she came to cabin 11 and opened the door. It was as she had last seen it. Nothing had been moved. No fresh footprints around the entry. No ominous notes.

Katie shook off her irrational creepy vibe and went to work. She wanted to get everything in place before it turned dark. After making three short trips to the cabin, she made it appear that this was where she was going to stay. She rolled out blankets on the cot with a pillow, draped an older jacket over the camping stool, and left her phony laptop on the desk. She even put one of Cisco's doggie beds in the corner.

As Katie and Cisco left the cabin, she was startled by the loud sound of a machine starting up. She laughed to herself, realizing that it was a generator. Following the noise, Katie found John attaching some lines to the utility shack.

"Hey, can you do that quietly?" she joked.

"Hi. Just wanted to make sure that the generator would work for the outbuildings and the kitchen as backup. I have electricity running to the kitchen area and I brought a small fridge. It should be cold soon."

"Great. Better than an ice chest." Katie watched him expertly roll up cable and attach it to the small building.

"I tried to get some of the other electricity connected. Whoever designed this place wasn't very organized. It's a bit haphazard. I called the utility company and they said it was turned on here, but I can't seem to get things working except for a few cabins and the main areas with the counselor offices."

"Is this the utility building with all the electrical panels?" They had never investigated the building, mostly because it looked like it would cave in on itself any second. She looked inside.

"Check it out. It's not nearly as bad as it looks."

The door was so crooked that it didn't want to move, but she managed to make an opening wide enough to squeeze through. Inside, it was much cleaner than she imagined. Strange. There were rectangular electrical boxes on the wall with breaker switches. She studied them closer, running her fingers over the old levers, finding them clean and smooth. Looking around the area, it didn't appear that anyone had been in there recently besides John. The floor was dusty and the two larger wooden boxes used for storage were cracked from time. There was an old CB radio.

"Wow," she said as she picked up the handset.

"You done in here?" said John leaning in through the narrow doorway.

"Yeah," she said and exited. "Cisco," she called. The jet-black dog came running, staying within six feet of her.

"He must detect so many scents here."

"I'm sure," she said scratching behind his ears.

"I've organized everything. I did a sweep and found two old cameras, but nothing nefarious. I will attach the new cameras and text you and McGaven the locations along with how to run the backup here."

"Sounds great."

"See you later."

Katie watched John disappear as he rounded a corner leading to a section of cabins. She spent the rest of the time securing everything and checking to make sure nothing had changed.

It wasn't much for Cisco, but he seemed to enjoy it. Katie had wanted to see if the dog alerted to anything or acted strangely around the area. She knew that her K9 partner wouldn't let her down.

After everything was done, she was still waiting for McGaven. He seemed to be running late. Katie hadn't seen John around in a while either. She wondered if he had run into any problems.

Putting her earpiece in, she called McGaven.

He answered almost immediately, "I'm just about there. Miss me?"

"Of course."

"Where are you?"

Katie and Cisco just walked into the commissary and sat down at the picnic table. "Commissary."

"See you in five."

Katie still didn't know where she would be watching from

tonight or where she would be to get some sleep when McGaven was doing the rounds.

Cisco trotted up to her and dropped a blue ball at her feet.

"Where did you find that?" She threw the ball across the mess hall a few times and Cisco bounded after it.

Something caught her attention. It was McGaven, who was now wearing casual clothes instead of his suit, approaching from the area they had agreed upon. He entered smiling.

"Hey, partner." He leaned down and picked up the ball and threw it for Cisco. "That's disgusting," he said, referring to the slobbery ball. His cell phone rang. "Detective McGaven. Yes. What? Are you kidding me?" He listened a bit longer. "Yes, I understand. Thanks. Keep us posted."

Katie felt her stomach drop. "What is it?"

"Robin Drakes is missing."

"How? I mean, did she just leave and not come back? Who's been watching her?" Katie stood up and paced. "This is exactly what I didn't want to happen." She felt her adrenalin rise along with her usual anxiety symptoms.

"Her mom said she went out for a quick walk. They said she had been going stir crazy."

"I knew something like this could happen. How long has she been missing?"

"She went out around noon."

"That's several hours ago. Anything could have happened to her."

"Detective Hamilton said they are on it and will get to the bottom of it. He'll call us to give an update."

"You're sure?" she said sarcastically.

"He will. He knows that we're here, not to mention that he has to update the sheriff with anything pertaining to these cases."

"You're right." The more she thought about it the more anxious she felt. "Maybe we missed our window and all this is for nothing." It made her sick that the planning might have been too late.

"Let's just keep on track. We don't know for sure if anything has happened to her."

Katie nodded. Her suspicions were that the killer might have already taken her. Robin Drakes could be being held hostage right now—or worse. In her mind, Katie thought the investigation was going too slowly. "Let's just hope she's not already dead."

CHAPTER FIFTY-TWO

The sun had set almost an hour ago, casting fiery orange and red strips through the heavy cloud cover. Eagle Ridge Camp turned silent and the darkness seemed to envelop the area. Daytime brought the entire landscape into view with the mountains, lake, and acres of trees. Now the camp felt suddenly claustrophobic, the dark trees closing in faster on them.

Katie was uneasy as she waited for McGaven's cell phone to ring with some news about Robin Drakes. To her dismay, there was nothing.

"Okay, looks like everything is in place," said John. "It took a little bit longer than expected, but it's done." He slung a backpack over his shoulder. "Katie, you want to see your lair?"

"My lair?" She laughed.

"Actually, you'll be taking guard duty shifts? Right?"

"Yep," said McGaven.

Katie and McGaven followed John through the commissary, through the kitchen, and to the back stockroom area. It was quite large, with two big walk-in pantries.

"Have a look," he said.

Katie looked at both doors.

"The one on the right."

She opened the door and there was a room about twelve feet by ten feet. There was a camping cot with an inflatable mattress with two neatly folded blankets and a pillow. On the table there was a laptop, which was showing the camera angles on the screen.

"You can tab and you'll get the next screen. If anything moves or there's something out of the ordinary—basically: bigger than a skunk, it will alert you."

Katie nodded, then looked up, noticing a vent that pumped in air or heat.

"I've made sure the duct is clean and so you'll get fresh outdoor air. It might be a bit cold tonight, but it should be comfortable for a few hours of sleep at a time."

"It's like a nice version of a prison cell," said McGaven in good humor. "I'm not sure the cot is long enough for me."

"You'll just have to rough it," John said. "You both have the map layout on the laptop and your phones—and I've sent a link to the security cameras too. You can see it on your phone as well."

Katie hit the tab key on the laptop and brought up several more views of the camp.

"Well, I guess I'm out of here," said John. "Don't forget the sheriff's department is on high alert, knowing that two Pine Valley officers are in operation and it could be dangerous. There will be several cruisers on their way up here if there's any type of problem."

"Okay," said Katie. "I guess we're all set." She tried to sound upbeat but she was worried about Robin Drakes and nervous about the unknown factors of the camp.

"Thanks, bud," said McGaven.

John smiled at them and then left.

"Let's get some snacks before I take first watch," said McGaven.

Cisco's ears perked up when he heard "snacks".

Katie followed him to the commissary and chatted about unimportant things before the two-hour guard shifts started. "Looks like it's going to be a long night."

"I'm up first," he said and left.

CHAPTER FIFTY-THREE

SATURDAY 2230 HOURS

Katie grew weary watching the laptop as McGaven went on his rounds checking buildings and possible entrance and exit locations. Her eyes were tired so she decided to stretch out on the cot and rest, but within five minutes she was fast asleep. Her breathing became slow and even. Once her body relaxed, arms at her sides, and her hands open, she slept.

She was suddenly jolted awake again to the sound of the computer alarm. At first, she was a bit disoriented. Cisco whined and circled around the small room. An hour and half had passed.

Sitting up, Katie looked at the computer screen. It appeared that one of the cameras near the section of cabins, including cabin 11, had been tripped. She studied it, but there was nothing.

"Gav," she said into her small microphone for her cell phone's walkie-talkie mode. She waited. "Gav," she said again. A strange noise interrupted her connection. It sounded like someone working on a telephone landline, but she knew that wasn't the case—the phones were jammed. "Gav?"

She quickly got to her feet and slipped on her jacket after

checking her gun. Something was wrong. It could just be equipment-oriented, but she wasn't taking the chance that it was something else.

Cisco whined and clearly wanted to go with her. "No, Cisco. You need to stay here." She suddenly realized she had misplaced her flashlights. One must still be in cabin 11 and the other she must have left back on the picnic table. With everything happening, she had overlooked the simple task of making sure she had a flashlight handy.

Katie quietly shut the door and entered the kitchen with her weapon ready. The low backup lighting that was working before John left was now out—leaving the place dark except for small glimpses of light from the moon piercing through the moving cloud cover.

She crept along slowly in stealth mode, hoping that she would hear McGaven's voice. Now her phone was quiet, as if it had turned off. Glancing at the cell phone screen, there were no signal bars.

Moving slowly, she allowed for her eyes to adjust to the darkness. From back in her cubbyhole room, she could hear Cisco scratching at the door. She couldn't let him out without knowing what was going on and what dangers were ahead. Her focus was on the job and the operation. She didn't want to worry about Cisco's safety too.

The commissary was also dark, but Katie could make out the outlines of cupboards and the picnic table where she, McGaven, and John had sat together only hours ago. There was no flashlight. She knew that she had left it there. Prickling anticipation crept up her spine and her breathing accelerated. Pins and needles rose up her arms.

She continued to move forward, keeping an expert eye on anything that moved. Shadows played tricks on her, creating many dark corners and places for someone to hide. She quietly opened the door leading outside. She stood on the threshold and looked from left to right, and back to the left, listening intently for anything unnatural. The temperature had dropped more than ten degrees since she had fallen asleep. She could feel the cool air penetrate her jeans and chill her neck. Her hands had become very cold.

Deciding to take the familiar path to the first group of cabins, she made every step purposeful, hoping that she would see McGaven. The only objective she could think of was tracing McGaven's route. She didn't know why the lights and cameras were all out. She hoped it was just some kind of hiccup in the electricity power or generator.

It was painfully quiet. There were no sounds of the creatures that dwelled in the nighttime. The breeze from earlier was nonexistent. Her face and ears felt like ice, but her intense focus penetrated the darkness.

As she approached the cabins, she noticed that there was a dim light flickering through the cracks around a window. To Katie's disbelief, it was cabin 11. She took a moment and stopped, turning slowly three hundred sixty degrees, making sure that she wasn't going to be ambushed—again. She considered that it might be McGaven and he had found a lantern. Cabin 11 was the only one that had a desk. Maybe he was figuring something out? Or maybe he was waiting for her?

Katie eased her way closer to the cabin. The door was closed. Light escaping through the gaps around the window and door gave the outside some illumination. It wasn't much, but it gave her some comfort.

Taking one last look around her, she put her hand on the doorknob. It was loose under her grip and unlocked. She briefly reconsidered entering the cabin, but taking a steady breath, she opened the door pushing her gun out in front of her. She didn't know what to expect.

The small battery-operated lantern sat on the desk and flickered from the dwindling batteries inside. But that wasn't what made Katie stop in her tracks. There was a metal chair in the middle of the room and a woman securely tied to it, her hands behind her, and her back facing Katie. The dark-haired woman's head slumped forward—her body rested unmoving.

Katie could barely breathe as she inched forward without saying a word. She swept her gun back and forth in the room and back at the entrance. Still moving at a steady pace, she stepped in front of the woman, pulled the blindfold off her and gasped. It was Robin Drakes.

CHAPTER FIFTY-FOUR

SATURDAY 2345 HOURS

"Robin," said Katie in a low voice. "Robin, can you hear me?"

Katie knelt down and gently pressed her index and middle fingers to the woman's carotid artery on the side of her neck to detect a pulse. There was a steady heartbeat. "Robin," she said again.

The woman stirred and emitted a low groan as she slowly became conscious. There was a cut above her eyebrow. She lifted her head and stared at Katie, blinking in surprise. "Help me," she whispered. "Please."

Katie holstered her gun and immediately began untying the woman. "It's okay, Robin, you're going to be safe." It took several minutes, but Katie was able to get the woman's hands free.

"How did..." said Robin, clearly groggy from some type of drug or blow to the head.

"Can you tell me what happened?"

"I... don't know... I took a walk... and..." Her speech was slurred. "My head hurts." Her eyes opened wider. "Please hurry... he's coming back..."

"Who Robin? Who's coming back?" said Katie needing to know.

"I don't know who it is... he grabbed me from behind."

"How long ago did he leave you?" Katie kept glancing at the door.

"I don't know. I'm sorry." Her eyes were glazed and her face pale.

Katie finally got the last rope untied and freed Robin.

"C'mon," said Katie.

"Where are we going? He's going to get us... he... he killed my friends." Robin began to cry as her body shook.

As much as it sickened Katie thinking about everything the killer did, she needed to find McGaven, keep Robin safe, and to leave Eagle Ridge Camp immediately. Before they left the cabin, Katie put out the lantern, leaving a blanket of darkness.

Katie guided Robin out and down the path past the other cabins. She hesitated at each cabin, making sure that no one was in the shadows waiting for them. They were going to keep going until she could find McGaven.

Robin slowed after a few minutes and appeared breathless. "I'm sorry, but I just can't seem to catch my breath."

"We have to keep going," Katie said in a whisper.

Robin swallowed hard and nodded.

Katie had an idea that if McGaven knew that their cell phones were jammed and the electricity wasn't working, he would most likely go to the utility shed.

Katie grabbed Robin's arm and guided her to the shed. It was off the usual pathway, dark, and difficult to see their way.

As they approached, Katie slowed and could see an outline of a tall figure. For an instant, dread filled her body, but she looked closer as the person moved—it was McGaven.

"Gav," said Katie in a forced whisper.

He turned so she could see his face. He appeared relieved

and stressed at the same time. "Katie! I'm so glad you're okay." He looked to Robin. "Robin Drakes?"

"The killer had her tied up in cabin eleven, knowing that I would find her." She moved closer to the shed. "We need to hide her."

"I was trying to get the generator started, but no luck. It's been sabotaged."

"Did you see anything or anyone?" asked Katie.

"No. Nothing. Not until the lights went out and my phone beeped telling me the signal was lost." He looked at his cell phone again. "I had been checking in with the deputies. If they try to contact me and can't get through—they'll be on their way."

"How often do you check in?"

"Every two hours."

Katie looked at the shed. "Wait. Would a CB radio work?"

McGaven thought about it. "As long as there is some type of antenna and something where it can get power."

"Like a battery—a car battery? I saw various batteries in the back of the shed."

"Yeah, that would work."

Katie devised a plan. They couldn't stay out in the open. "See if you can get the radio to work. Robin should stay here with you."

"What are you going to do?" he said.

"I'm going to circle back to the commissary and get Cisco. I need to find a place in a higher elevation to see if I can observe anything around the camp—or find the killer." She grabbed a flashlight and made sure it worked.

"Wait," said Robin. "We should all stay together."

"Maybe she's right. You have no backup," said McGaven.

"There's no other choice and you know it," she said. "If I get in trouble I'll alert you."

"How?"

"I'll fire a gunshot."

"The killer will know where you're at."

Katie understood that, but there wasn't anything else she could do without their cell phones or any electricity. "I know. But maybe the electricity will be back on by then." She knew it was highly unlikely. "Hopefully I'll have the element of surprise. Both of you get out of the open area and stay safe." She gave McGaven a last reassuring look before she turned and disappeared into the darkness.

CHAPTER FIFTY-FIVE

Katie weaved around the paths and cabins on her way back to the commissary, making sure that nothing looked out of place and she wasn't being tracked. It seemed oddly familiar to her, reminiscent of her army days trying to stay safe and away from the enemy. The entire time she was running, she kept trying to figure out the identity of the killer, and why he would bring Robin back to the camp if he knew there would be two cops here. It didn't make sense.

Once inside the commissary, she paused. Her hammering heartbeat was the only thing she heard and felt. Even though it was cold outside, she was hot. Perspiration ran down the sides of her face and her back as if she had been running in the middle of a sweltering summer.

She moved quietly with the reflexes of a cat as she made her way back to her cupboard closet. Opening the door, she was greeted by a very happy Cisco.

"I didn't forget about you," she said petting him furiously.

She knew that time was passing only too quickly, and that now the burden of finding the killer pushed down on her. As fast as her heart was beating, thoughts and ideas were running through her head. She pulled out a box she had packed. Inside was what she called her safety box. There was Cisco's training vest, which she immediately put on him. The covering would keep him warm as they got to higher ground. There was a knife hidden in a Velcro pocket.

Katie sorted climbing clips, ropes, high tensile wire, combat knife, extra loaded magazines, and a lightweight bulletproof vest.

She hurried as she put on her vest then secured her extra loaded magazines, her cell phone, climbing clips, small binoculars, and the wire. She pulled her hair back into a tight ponytail. The rope she coiled around her shoulder and then around her waist, securing it. She double-checked her gun and holster as well as double-tied her combat boots.

The sounds and smells of the battlefield accosted her mind as she readied herself now for her own personal battle. Her hands shook with anticipation, but her mission was well-defined and planned. The PTSD symptoms were pushing their way to the surface, causing her vision to dizzy and her limbs to weaken.

"No," she said, willing her growing panic to leave.

Cisco's energy was soaring as if he too knew that something big was going to happen. Katie put him in watch/guard mode, which meant that he would passive alert her if someone or something approached. That would be essential during the search and while she waited for McGaven to get a message out from the CB radio. She prayed for perseverance and for luck to stay on their side.

She opened a bottle of water and drank nearly twelve ounces before giving the rest to Cisco. She was going to need the hydration and energy. At the bottom of the box, she had remembered to put a pair of black climbing gloves, which she quickly pulled on. Making sure everything was secure on her body as well as Cisco's, she was finally ready to find the killer.

She stood up and opened the storage door with Cisco at her side.

Taking only a minute, she closed her eyes and visualized where she would run as her pulse lowered and steadied. She remembered that when she passed the last cabin in the grouping of buildings that held cabin 11 she had seen an old wooden ladder lying horizontally on the ground. That's where they were headed.

Katie and Cisco were ready—on high alert.

CHAPTER FIFTY-SIX

Katie's footsteps were almost silent and Cisco's paw pads made no noise as they hurried through the area around the cabins. The dog's dark coat and camouflage training vest made him almost disappear next to some of the grouping of trees—except for his glowing yellow eyes shining in the darkness.

The air temperature continued to slowly drop a few degrees before Katie saw the building up ahead and made some adjustments to her surroundings and security checks. The particular cabin was at one of the highest levels in the camp, slightly out from the trees, which meant she could see virtually everything in the brighter light.

Now she would remain silent with only hand signals to Cisco. It had been a while since she had done this type of training, but the dog was ready. Katie put Cisco on a down. Now he wouldn't move until she gave him the silent command to release his position.

With her weapon ready, she made sure the areas around the cabins were secure without anyone lying in wait. Shadows played tricks on her eyes, but she stormed through them anyway and came back to the side of the cabin.

The old wooden ladder looked decrepit, with mold snaking along the footholds, but it seemed to be intact and strong enough to hold her weight as well as Cisco's. Katie quickly put the ladder up against the cabin wall. After checking a few of the steps, she guided Cisco upward. His four legs worked in unison to find a hold upon the rungs, and she had him down immediately once on the roof. She then moved up, making sure her feet were firmly secure on each foothold before climbing to the next.

Once on the roof, she pulled up the ladder and laid it down quietly. Katie dropped into an army crawl position, giving Cisco the command to drop and scoot along on his belly to keep out of sight. They moved to the corner where she could gain a vantage of about eighty percent of the area. She retrieved the binoculars with infrared mode and did a sweep of the area, including the utility shed. McGaven wasn't in sight; she hoped he was having luck connecting the radio inside the small building.

* * *

McGaven was in fact working to find a battery that still had some energy left. He had found wires and the handset seemed to be intact. He kept glancing at Robin; she wouldn't stay still and kept pacing and peering out the crack in the door.

"Try to calm down, Robin. We're going to get out of here."

"You don't understand... he's out there... he's coming back."

"Not if we have anything to say about it."

McGaven finally found an old car battery that had some juice left. Within a few minutes he was able to get the radio to intermittently go on and off. He was relieved. It's almost working, he thought to himself.

* * *

As she waited in the darkness, Katie ran through the whole course of the investigation for what seemed like the thousandth time. The more she thought about what had transpired, the faster the details seemed to spin through her mind like an accelerated card file.

Memories of Katie's time at the camp.

Jenny.

Brian Stanwick.

Carolyn Sable's body found at the dock. Found by Daniel Green with clients.

Searching for booby traps—finding Edith Crest's body.

Body in cabin 3.

Injury—hospital.

Prosthetics.

Lenny Dickson.

KLM Enterprises.

Red Hawk Real Estate.

Daniel Green.

Security guard Bud.

Jake Fields.

Rick Reynolds.

Dr. Pendleton.

Boy in the photo.

Katie wondered again if the boy in the photo had been a friend of Brian Stanwick's, not a relative. She remembered the tiny pieces of plastic found on the window sill in the counselor's office. She was sure that this case revolved around Brian Stanwick and his terrible accident at Eagle Ridge Camp. But had they even got the killer on their radar yet?

Katie knew they were close. She could sense that she almost had the killer in her sights. It had to be someone in their investigation. Things had possibly pointed to Jake Fields, but he had then taken himself irrevocably out of the equation. He was guilty of something—but not of the murders. But who then was? What was Katie missing?

* * *

McGaven was still working on the connection. "Just about got it," he said under his breath. "We're going to get out of here."

Robin had continued to be restless and twitchy, but McGaven had just dismissed it as a stress reaction from her experiences and the knowledge of the fact there was a killer who wanted her dead.

She walked back and forth and then fixated on McGaven. Suddenly, lunging forward, she grabbed his gun. He fought back, pushing the woman away from him just as the gun went off.

* * *

The gunshot rang out and echoed around the camp. Katie turned her attention to the utility shed just as McGaven and Robin burst out the door. Her partner tried to get hold of the gun. Katie couldn't see exactly what was happening, but what was Robin doing?

Remaining as calm as she could, Katie took aim, looking through the sights of her gun. She watched as Robin pointed it at McGaven, moving it with strange jerky actions. Katie couldn't quite hear what she was saying, but it didn't matter.

Katie narrowed her vision just as Robin pointed the gun at McGaven, then, she squeezed the trigger. Her shot was true and Robin was immediately knocked to the ground. Katie watched helplessly as McGaven got control of his gun once more. Katie hadn't gone for the kill shot, but had wounded the woman enough to take her out of the scenario. McGaven could handle the situation now.

Katie got up from the rooftop and made her way to the edge, lowering the ladder again. She turned and told Cisco to stay—she wanted him safe until reinforcements arrived. The dog obeyed despite clearly wanting to come with her. She hurried down, feet hitting each rung, and then ran to the utility shed.

"Gav," she said, winded. "Gav, you okay?"

Robin was leaning up against one of the utility boxes used to cover the plumbing. She had a look of pure hatred on her face as she held her injured shoulder.

"Great shot," McGaven said.

"What happened?"

"I was putting together the radio and the next thing she attacked me and went for my gun. I've never lost my gun yet, nor would I ever relinquish it."

Katie looked at Robin. "What were you doing?" she said to the woman. She could see that Robin's wound wasn't life-threatening from the minor amount of bleeding.

Robin sneered at her and looked away.

"I think we found the killer," McGaven said as he took a plastic cable tie from his pocket. "You're not going to do anything like that again." He restrained her. She grimaced in pain but didn't say a word.

Katie went over things in her mind and she whispered to McGaven, "No, something doesn't feel right." Robin Drakes couldn't be the killer—she couldn't have tied herself up in the chair. Walking up to the woman she asked, "Who are you really?"

"You know who I am."

"So you're the one who murdered all your friends?"

Robin shrugged. "I hated those bitches. It wasn't a secret."

"Answer my question."

"Yeah, sure, I murdered all of them. They deserved it. I thought they were my friends, but they were hypocrites and liars. I knew someday, somehow, I would make them pay. So I waited for the perfect opportunity."

"And it was you that climbed in the window of the counselor offices?" said Katie. "And vandalized the kitchen to throw off the cops?"

"You like it?" Robin spat out.

"Tell me, why did you kill Carolyn?"

"She thought she was so special. She was the worst."

"What do you mean?"

"She acted like the leader, but she neglected the children that day when Brian fell. She ruined that boy's life."

"And that's why you killed her?"

"Duh."

"Why did you kill Rick Reynolds?"

"Who?"

"Rick Reynolds."

"Because he had to die."

"So you just happen to like dismembering people?"

Robin looked the other direction, avoiding Katie's eyes.

The crackle of the radio suddenly interrupted their talk. Katie pushed Robin toward the building and dragged her inside. McGaven was still on the radio trying to find the correct channel.

"Anything?" Katie said.

"Not yet, but I think I can get someone to call dispatch for us." He looked at his partner. "Did you get anything out of her?"

"Not really. There's no way she did all of this. Not on her own."

"Yes, I did!"

"Then we should get out of here," said McGaven. "The operation has definitely been compromised."

"Okay," she said. "We need to go now."

"We are."

"No, I mean we need to leave right this second. My gut is telling me that this is all a set-up. We need to get out immediately and reorganize. Hopefully we'll run into the deputies sooner rather than later."

"I've almost got through this..."

Katie didn't want to split up but she needed to get a few things and Cisco. "Okay. I'll be right back."

"No. We all go together," he said.

"Okay." She looked at Robin. The look on her face was still one of boiling-over hatred. "Hurry."

Within a few minutes, Katie was relieved to hear McGaven talking to someone over the radio. She wanted to leave right away.

"C'mon," he said as he helped Robin to her feet.

Katie took point and gave every shadow a second look as they moved quickly toward the commissary, but she needed to get Cisco first.

"Katie."

Katie stopped. "Did you hear that?"

"No, what?" he said.

"Never mind." She slowed her pace. She remembered seeing the outline of her friend Jenny and the little boy. Who was that boy? Who was the boy in the newspaper photo?

McGaven was having trouble guiding Robin. She slowed them down as if she wanted to stop them altogether.

Katie couldn't quit going over what they knew about the investigation—the killer knew how to navigate around the camp. She had the feeling that the killer was here when they were searching. She kept thinking about the connection with prosthetics. Remembering everyone they interviewed, none of whom had a prosthetic. *Jake Fields. Lenny Dickson. Rick Reynolds. Bud.* But...

There was a loud thud.

Katie turned round. Suddenly, she didn't see McGaven or

Robin. Her heart hammered and she instantly felt queasy. "Gav?" she asked. She slowly started walking back the way she'd come. There was no sign of her partner or Robin. "Gav!"

As she turned the corner, she saw a tall figure standing in the darkness. She instantly recognized the shape and height. It was the man that had watched her from the doorway in cabin 11, the same figure who'd been inside the strip mall. She directed the gun at him. "Show me your hands."

The figure walked slowly towards her with a slight sway.

"Stop right there! Show me your hands."

"Detective Scott. You need to drop your weapon or your partner dies," said the phantom shadow.

Katie looked to her left and saw McGaven lying on his side on the ground. "Gav," she gasped. To the figure, she pointed her gun. "I will shoot you if you don't show me your hands. Now!"

"I don't think so."

She thought she recognized the voice. Where? Katie took a step forward and felt the electricity of a Taser rattle her body. She couldn't fight it—as the excruciating pain hit her she fell, relinquishing both her strength and her gun. Katie blacked out.

CHAPTER FIFTY-SEVEN

Katie couldn't open her eyes, but she felt her body being dragged along the ground. Every rock and unevenness she felt batter against her back and legs. Gav? Her mind went immediately to him. She tried to speak but was unable due to her weakened condition from the Taser.

She heard two voices, that of a man and a woman. The words seemed to be garbled and floated around. She felt a floor beneath her, and knew that they were inside one of the buildings. It was one of the cabins.

Something moved on her left side, pushing against her left elbow. Gently pushing twice. She realized that it was a person. It had to be McGaven. Relief washed over her that he was alive, and she nudged him back. Her mind was racing with thoughts about the investigation bombarding her at once, faces and facts flying through—some erratic and others that she pondered for more than a second. She knew that the killer was someone they had already talked to...

Her mind swirled with the investigation fast-forwarding through interviews. It occurred to Katie that the only person she had seen walk strangely or with some peculiarity was Daniel

Green. He had given them a cover story that he had strained his back playing golf. Suddenly, she realized that he was about the right age of the boy in the photo. He had grown up here. He hadn't seemed to be shocked by finding a dead body and hadn't asked the usual questions about who it was and how they died. And he had handled Carolyn Sable's real estate transaction for her house. Could it be Daniel Green? Would he really systematically kill all the people who were around when Brian Stanwick had his accidental fall?

So many things filed through Katie's mind. She felt off balance but Daniel Green seemed suddenly to be a person of interest—rushing to the top of her list. But why would he want to see Carolyn Sable's body? He must have known that he would be the one that would find her.

Katie managed to open her eyes. She realized she was staring at the ceiling of one of the cabins. Not just any cabin—cabin 11. She sat up with a jolt just like that she had received from the Taser. Instinctively she reached for her gun—it was gone. She looked around and saw McGaven lying next to her.

"Gav," she said. "Gav." He stirred slightly. She noticed that he had a nasty wound on his head, obviously he had been struck with something. "Don't move."

Katie stood up and stopped for a moment until the merry-go-round dizziness stopped. Everything looked the same, even in the darkness. The walls morphed into one another and she fought hard to dispel the vertigo rush. It finally ceased. She rushed the door and pushed as hard as she could until it burst open.

"Not so fast, Detective," said the man standing outside.

He walked closer to her, slightly dragging his left foot. Finally, he stood in the light holding her own gun directed at her. "You don't seem surprised?"

"Mr. Daniel Green. The great avenger of Brian Stanwick. I bet that was your idea," she said with some dramatic flair. She knew that if the killer liked to talk about his kills, and they usually did, she could try and buy some time until backup eventually arrived.

He smiled. "I knew from the moment I met you, you were going to be trouble."

"For doing my job?"

"Normally I would be appreciative, but in this case..."

"When where you planning to stop?" she said, keeping eye contact with him.

"Until they ALL paid."

"By my count, they have."

"Oh, Detective. You didn't know? You're not as smart as you think you are."

Katie watched him as she stared at the barrel of her own gun. "What more is there to know?"

"You see, Brian and I were friends, best friends. He couldn't live with what had happened to him. Counselors, psychologists, doctors: no one could reach him—not even his best friend. He even supported me when I wanted to be a doctor. As you probably figured out—I'm not the kind of person with a bedside manner. I prefer to maim than to heal. But then Brian killed himself. That was the end he wished for and the one thing he ever got that he really actually wanted."

She watched his posture, calculating if she could rush him—but the risk was too high. "We can't control what people do or don't do." She knew as she said it that that would be a trigger for him.

"Are you serious?" he said, raising his voice.

Got him...

"You know about Brian from the articles in the papers, right?" he asked.

Katie didn't respond.

"But what you don't know is that I fell too that day," he said and gestured to his leg. "But for whatever reason, they didn't think I was important enough to report," he scoffed. "Just as well, my injury was nothing compared to Brian's."

Katie retraced the list of students from Eagle Ridge Camp documents, but there was no Daniel Green. "You had a different name, of course."

"I was born Nathanael Davies, but that person doesn't exist anymore and no one cared about me or my injuries—I was sent to another hospital for initial treatment forty miles away. They never reported it so the camp wouldn't have more bad press. There was no excuse for what happened to us! They ruined two lives in seconds with their lack of care. It was all totally avoidable! I waited years, but after Brian killed himself, that's when I began planning... tracking... researching... getting close to the right people." He laughed. "It was so easy."

"So what? Carolyn Sable didn't reciprocate your affections? Was it as simple as that?" She tried to catch him off guard. "You were angrier at her the most. Is that why you made sure you had clients with you when you *supposedly* found her body just by chance? Where's Robin now? You've used her too."

He stopped talking. His arms stiffened and he gripped the gun harder. It was clear he was done with his monologue. "Move!" he said, forcing her back inside cabin 11.

Katie tried to get back out, but somehow Daniel secured the door, trapping her and McGaven inside.

"Hey," said a weak McGaven from behind her.

"Gav, you okay?" said Katie, rushing to her partner's side. "Can you move?"

"I think so." He sat up, wavering a bit. The bleeding had stopped on the side of his head.

"Take it easy. We're going to get out of here."

"I heard everything. Did you know it was Daniel Green?" He used the wall for support as he stood up slowly.

"It had been bothering me with Robin. And then I started

putting together prosthetics and who might the boy in the photo be... and well, I eventually got my answer."

"How are we going to get out of here?" he said.

Katie checked the window and door. They were sealed solidly shut. Even in the darkness, she could see where something was coating the wall. "Gav."

"Yeah."

"We have a serious problem."

"No kidding."

"No, remember those weird sealed and coated lines in the walls at the industrial building?"

"Don't remind me."

"Well, we have the same problem here. This cabin is going to burst into flames—I'm sure that the other buildings are too. We need to get out now. Now, McGaven!"

She began looking around for something to pry the wood from the window or the opening for the door. There was a flimsy desk, cot, and chair. She picked up the chair and smashed it against the wall several times until she had two solid metal poles. She handed one to McGaven.

"Now we're talkin'," he said.

Both of them began trying to pry anything open, but all their efforts accomplished nothing.

Katie felt physically weak, but her adrenalin was running high. She looked up and remembered that there had been a kind of sunroof on the ceiling, now boarded up. "Hey, Gav—come here." She stepped up on the cot but couldn't reach the ceiling. She let out a grunt. "A little help here?"

McGaven carefully stepped onto the cot, not sure if it would hold his weight. Once up there, he began working on the ceiling. Slowly the chair leg chipped away at the covering until most of it came down.

Katie couldn't do anything but wait. She paced as she

watched her partner try to open up a space in the roof. Then she remembered... "*Cisco...*"

"What?"

"I left Cisco on the roof two cabins away. I didn't know what I was walking into so I left him up there to wait... if anything happens because I left him..." She held back tears trying to keep her focus. Suddenly the sound of nearing gunfire and long-distance rockets flooded into her mind—the stress she was experiencing pushing her right back to the horrors of the battlefield.

"Nothing is going to happen to Cisco. Not on my watch," McGaven said as the last of the window crumbled and dropped to the floor. The space he had smashed and pried open was barely wide enough to squeeze through.

A strange sound rumbled. Katie thought it was an earthquake, but there was a different pitch and feel to it. "That sound," she said. "That sound is like..."

"The sound of the industrial building going up," McGaven finished her thought. "Get up here and I'll hoist you on the roof. Hurry!"

Crackling sounds ran up the walls. It sounded like runaway electrical wiring, but she knew it was the fire trap that had been set by Daniel Green, just like the one at the industrial building.

Katie stepped up and McGaven hoisted her through the gap. She grabbed the rim of the opening and crawled onto the roof. She could see flames and smell the smoke from the nearby buildings. All she could think of was Cisco.

No... Cisco...

Looking down, she saw McGaven struggling and then managing to hoist himself onto the roof.

The sound of the fire below them in cabin 11 became intense. The heat was almost unbearable and the smoke unavoidable. Her hot skin felt strangely dry and as if it would burst into flames itself. Everything around them looked like a layer of smoke-filled fabric had covered the forest.

"Go!" yelled McGaven.

Katie looked down and saw a wooden structure built to cover pipes. She lowered herself on the edge of the roof and dropped down onto the makeshift wooden box. Once on the ground, relief filled her. She looked up and saw McGaven following her example.

"Go!" he yelled.

Katie ran, trying to cover her nose and mouth, but she was soon disoriented by the gathering smoke and her dwindling strength. She turned around, unsure of her direction. Again, her mind reverted to the horror of the battlefield after gunfire battles. The smoke was now so heavy it was easy to get confused and lose your sense of direction. She looked down, seeing the familiar path under her feet.

"Katie..."

Katie stopped even with all of the chaos around her. She thought she heard her name called, but the sounds of the fire overrode anything she could possibly hear. She thought she might be lost again, but in amidst the smoke she saw the faint outline of Jenny, standing near one of the biggest trees and helping Katie realize where she was. Everything that happened to Jenny suddenly plunged down on Katie as she saw her friend's image exactly the way she had last seen her.

Eagle Ridge Camp.

Jenny's father abducting her.

Jenny murdered and her body dumped.

The camp had been the resource for him to carry out his intent. She wasn't going to let Daniel Green follow in the footsteps of another monster.

Katie ran toward the apparition with more strength and determination, but the image soon faded and she knew at last it was her imagination and the subconscious memory of the layout of the Eagle Ridge camp. She sprinted with everything she had toward the cabin on which she'd left Cisco. It was smoking already and the sounds of thunderous crackling and sizzling of the walls had begun. Looking up, she made out the outline of Cisco.

Once the dog saw her, he began barking furiously running back and forth.

Katie looked around and couldn't find the ladder. She didn't know how she was going to get the dog down. Flames had reached the roof. The orange flickering light and flame tentacles were getting close to Cisco.

Cisco...

Katie saw movement in her peripheral vision. Daniel Green stood six feet away, poised with a gun, and taking aim at Cisco.

"No!"

Cisco kept up his loud incessant barking, staying dangerously close to the edge of the roof.

Without hesitation, Katie charged Daniel. He swung the gun toward her as she slammed into him. Using her fists and feet, she began beating him on the ground with every ounce of strength and rage she could muster.

Daniel Green stopped moving.

Katie's vision blurred, her chest felt heavy as she got to her feet. Everything had a surreal dizzying effect around her. The smoke changed how things were supposed to look. She turned and looked up at Cisco.

Daniel ran up behind her, took hold of her and wrapped his hands around her neck. Katie felt the extreme pressure being applied and began to pass out.

In a black blur, dropping like a tactical war bomb, Cisco landed on Daniel, taking hold of his shoulders and neck and flinging him to the ground. Katie was thrown down too as the dog mauled Daniel. He screamed in agony and his shrieks echoed strangely through the inferno. He had dropped the gun, leaving it for Katie to retrieve.

"*Aus!*" she yelled for Cisco to release his bite on Daniel. "*Aus!*"

Cisco stopped biting and slowly released his jaw. The dog trotted over to Katie and stood at her left side with blood dripping from his mouth.

"Stay on the ground," she yelled at Daniel. Her voice was barely audible.

McGaven approached, limping and moving slowly. "You okay?" he said.

"Cuff him," she said.

McGaven tied Daniel Green's hands with a plastic zip tie he had in his pocket.

Katie dropped to her knees to check out Cisco. He appeared not to be hurt, but he had taken a long jump and some of his fur was singed.

"Is he okay?" yelled McGaven coughing.

"Yeah. Quick, let's get out of here."

"Where's Robin?"

"I don't know—I didn't see her after I was knocked out."

The fires were now in full force, raging their way across the entire camp, jumping to a couple of trees, but mostly skipping from one old wooden building to the next.

McGaven directed Daniel Green toward the roadway as flashing lights were visible as they approached through the heavy smoke. He pushed Daniel face down on the ground.

Katie and Cisco met up with him there.

They moved away from the smoke as best as they could and sat down. Exhausted. Coughing. They couldn't move another inch.

McGaven leaned against Katie as they watched emergency vehicles arrive and park precariously around the area.

"Can I go home now?" he said.

Katie hugged him tight as Cisco squeezed between them. "Yeah, we're going home."

"I need a vacation."

"I think the sheriff won't have a problem with that," she said.

Deputies ran over to them. "Ambulance and fire are on the way," they said to McGaven and Katie. Two of the deputies took Daniel Green and placed him the back of a police cruiser.

Katie hugged her partner tightly.

"It's over," said McGaven.

Katie nodded. "It's over."

CHAPTER FIFTY-EIGHT

TWO AND HALF WEEKS LATER...

The clear morning made a picture-perfect day for a special visit. It had been long overdue, but now it was time to put one of the things from the past to rest. The vivid blue sky, absent of any clouds, made a scenic backdrop to the birds flying overhead, while the mild breeze swished through the trees.

Katie stood at the grave of Jenny Daniels, her best friend from childhood. There was a sweet angel statue watching over her that Katie thought was appropriate and beautiful. She remembered the fun Jenny and she had had together, talking about what they wanted to do when they were older—staying up late on sleepovers, playing games, and enjoying the summers together. Everything had seemed so simple then.

The horror of the day she had found out her friend was murdered would never completely go away, but healing was the first step. Katie hadn't been to Jenny's grave since she was a girl. The intense grief had been something she'd carried with her all that time.

"Jenny, I miss you," said Katie now. "I know that you were watching over me at Eagle Ridge Camp. I'll never forget you. May you rest in peace, my sweet friend."

She bowed her head and said a prayer, taking a few minutes to feel the peace overwhelm her and slowly letting go the emotional burden she had been carrying too long. It was time. When Katie opened her eyes, she saw someone standing next to one of the trees a short distance away. It was the shadowy figure of a little girl dressed in denim shorts, a white T-shirt, and sneakers. She paused a moment and smiled.

Katie turned her attention in the other direction as Cisco ran up to Katie, followed by Chad making his way toward her.

He kissed her, pulling her close. "Everything okay?"

Katie glanced up at the tree where the image of Jenny had been standing. She was gone. There was only the wind wafting through the branches as a subtle reminder. "Yes, everything's fine."

The new ranch-style house at the end of the housing development looked beautiful on a bright sunny day. The Spanish-style influence made it seem like a single hacienda with a combination of rock and flagstone construction, blooming pink bougainvillea already climbing up the side walls. A for-sale sign had "Open House" attached to it.

Chad and Katie parked on the street and sat in the car staring at the house.

"I heard that they found a woman's body at Eagle Ridge Camp in one of the cabins after they put out the fires," he said.

"She's been identified as Robin Drakes and had a gunshot wound to the head before perishing in the fire—Daniel Green's accomplice. He used her as a ruse. He knew he needed someone to help him out with the camp counselors. She was the only one who agreed to help him with his revenge plan because of her animosity toward the others. And now," she sighed, "there's going to be legal ramifications for Eagle Ridge Camp and the extra acreage. It wasn't completely clear how Jake managed the property scheme and everything it entails. It'll probably be in litigation for years."

"The camp is completely gone now. Not one building remains. It seems strange to think about the fact it's not there anymore."

"It was time to build something new. Memories are fine, but we can't live in the past." She looked at the house with a beautiful entrance and nice cobblestone driveway, but her heart still felt heavy.

"You want to go inside and check it out again?" said Chad.

"Sure," she said.

"There are many houses we can look at any time. No hurry. I want you to be ready." He kissed her gently.

"It's okay," she said smiling. "I want to see it. And we can look forward to viewing others too." Katie had been coming to terms with the fact that she could have to move on from her parents' farmhouse. It had been their dream house, not hers. They would have wanted her to find her own dream house with Chad—and make new memories there.

Cisco popped his big head and perfectly pointed ears between them. He panted slightly as he stared out at the house in anticipation.

"I think Cisco wants to check out the backyard," she said.

"Let's go."

Chad opened the car door for Katie and Cisco. They walked up the driveway together as the real estate agent came out to greet the couple while they made introductions. Cisco ran circles around the group as they entered the house.

A LETTER FROM JENNIFER

I want to say a huge thank you for choosing to read *Silent Little Angels*. If you did enjoy it, and want to keep up to date with all my latest releases, just sign up at the following link. Your email address will never be shared and you can unsubscribe at any time.

www.bookouture.com/jennifer-chase

This has continued to be a special project and series for me. Forensics, K9 training and criminal profiling has been something that I've studied considerably and to be able to incorporate into crime fiction novel has been an amazing experience for me. I have wanted to write this series for a while and it has been a truly thrilling experience to bring it to life.

One of my favorite activities, outside of writing, has been dog training. I'm a dog lover, if you couldn't tell by reading this book, and I loved creating a supporting canine character Cisco for my police detective. I hope you enjoyed it as well.

I hope you loved *Silent Little Angels,* and if you did I would be very grateful if you could write a review. I'd love to hear what you think, and it makes such a difference helping new readers to discover one of my books for the first time.

Thank you,

Jennifer Chase

KEEP IN TOUCH WITH JENNIFER

www.authorjenniferchase.com

 facebook.com/AuthorJenniferChase

twitter.com/JChaseNovelist

ACKNOWLEDGMENTS

I want to thank my husband Mark for his steadfast support and for being my rock even when I had self-doubt. It's not always easy living with a writer and you've made it look easy.

A very special thank you goes out to all my law enforcement, police detectives, deputies, police K9, forensic, and first-responder friends—there's too many to list. Your friendships have meant the world to me. It has opened a whole new writing world filled with inspiration. I wouldn't be able to bring my crime fiction stories to life if it wasn't for all of you. Thank you for your service and dedication to keep the rest of us safe.

Writing this series continues to be a truly amazing experience. I would like to thank my publisher Bookouture for the opportunity, and the fantastic staff for continuing to help me to bring this book and the entire Detective Katie Scott series to life. Thank you Kim, Sarah, and Noelle for your relentless promotion for us authors. A very special thank you to my editor Jessie Botterill and her editorial team—your incredible support and insight has helped me to work harder to write more endless adventures for Detective Katie Scott.

Printed in Great Britain
by Amazon

86305467R00215